Buffy
THE VAMPIRE SLAYER

1

More Buffy is coming!

Buffy the Vampire Slayer 2

Buffy the Vampire Slayer 3

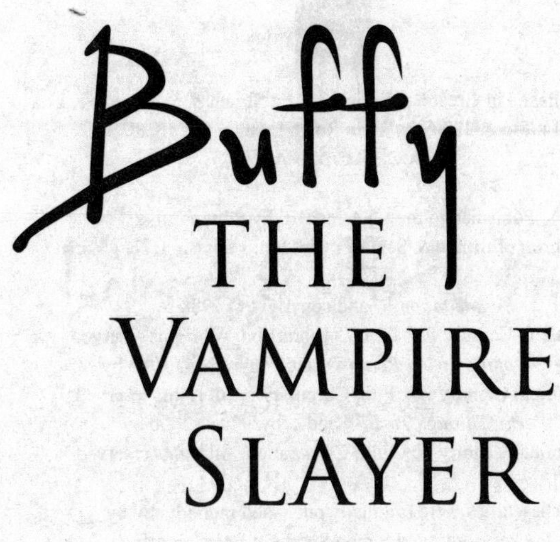

Buffy the Vampire Slayer 1

Coyote Moon

JOHN VORNHOLT

Night of the Living Rerun

ARTHUR BYRON COVER

Portal Through Time

ALICE HENDERSON

Based on the hit TV series created by Joss Whedon

SIMON & SCHUSTER

First published in Great Britain in 2010 by Simon & Schuster UK Ltd,
1st Floor, 222 Gray's Inn Road, London WC1X 8HB
A CBS COMPANY

Published in the USA in 2010 by Simon Pulse,
an imprint of Simon & Schuster Children's Division, New York.

These titles were originally published individually by
Pocket Books and Simon Spotlight Entertainment.

A CIP catalogue record for this book is
available from the British Library

ISBN 978-0-85707-060-9

10 9 8 7 6 5 4 3 2 1

Printed in the UK by CPI Cox & Wyman, Reading RG1 8EX

Born into a legendary role, Buffy the Vampire Slayer carries the burden of humanity on her shoulders. Her true identity is known only to her watcher, Giles, her best friends Willow, Xander, and Cordelia, and the mysteriously good-hearted vampire Angel. Living in Sunnydale, California, above the Hellmouth, she is a high school student by day and a demon's worst adversary by night. These are her stories.

Table of Contents

Coyote Moon

To my researchers,
Nancy, Sarah,
and Eric Vornholt,
and Lee Whiteside

CHAPTER ONE

The night wind brought a howl that was sharp and high-pitched, like a baby crying. Only it wasn't a human baby. Buffy Summers paused to listen as she stepped out of the Bronze, Sunnydale's coolest club. Of course, it was Sunnydale's *only* club, and they let everybody in—but it was still cool, somehow.

The door opened again, and Xander, her friend, stepped into the dark alley, bumping into her with his gangly body. "Hey, Buffy, this is a doorway, not a parking lot."

"Sorry," she said. "Do you hear that?"

Xander frowned as he listened to the rock music thumping through the walls. "Do you think the band finally hit the right chord?"

"No way," Buffy answered. "It was something else, like a howl."

The door opened again, and Willow stepped out and bumped into them. "Are we pretending to be the Three Stooges?" she asked.

"No," Xander answered. "That's when we all try to go through the door at the same time. This is where we stand in the alley and listen to . . . What are we listening to?"

Buffy shook her mane of honey-blond hair. "I don't know, just some weird sound—like a howl."

"Are you sure it wasn't the lead singer?" Willow asked.

Buffy sighed. "Okay, so tonight wasn't Lollapalooza at the Bronze. Have you got a better idea where to go?"

"We could go home and sleep?" Willow said hopefully.

"There's plenty of time to sleep once school starts again," Xander scoffed. "Biology, English literature, study hall in the library—what could be more restful? But for right now, we've got to *party*!"

"He's right," Buffy insisted. "The break's almost over, and it's our duty as teenagers to have as much fun as possible before school starts."

Willow looked wistful. "I think school's more fun than vacation."

"That's why we hang with you," Xander said. "You're really bizarre."

Buffy started walking down the service road that cut between the warehouses around the Bronze. "During those

desperate times when there's no party a
two guys who never let you down—Ben an
just put in a supply of cookie dough ice cream.'

"My favorite!" Xander exclaimed.

With Buffy the Vampire Slayer leading the way, the t
friends wandered from the bad part of town, across the tracks, onto a well-lit suburban street. Buffy had to admit that things had been a bit boring lately—what with no school plus no vampires to slay—but she wasn't going to complain. Vampire vacation was even better than school vacation.

"Listen," Willow said excitedly. "I just heard there's a carnival opening this weekend in the vacant lot on Main Street, where the drive-in movie used to be!"

"What kind of carnival?" Xander asked.

"You know," Willow said, "a cheap, tawdry affair with creaky rides and hokey fun houses."

"Cool!" Xander exclaimed. "Just the thing we need to end the break."

"And blow all the money we made from babysitting," Buffy added.

Enthused about the coming weekend, the three teenagers walked more quickly past the grassy lawns and sedate houses. Except for the way it looked, there was nothing sedate about the town of Sunnydale. It was perched on the Hellmouth, a very special place where the forces of darkness converged and attracted monsters from all over the world. *Real* monsters.

ey walked under a streetlamp, Buffy turned and saw mudge under Xander's lip. She licked her finger and started to wipe it off. "Hold still, Xander, there's chocolate milk shake on your lip."

He smiled sheepishly and pushed her hand away. "Uh, that's my new mustache and goatee. I've got that whole Johnny Depp thing going."

Willow grinned but quickly covered her mouth. "Oh, it's very dashing."

Xander beamed proudly. "Do you think so?"

"If you want a mustache," Buffy said, "I think you'd better grow the hair in your nose longer."

"That stinks," Xander complained, slouching ahead of the girls. "I'll probably shave it off, but you could let me enjoy it until school starts, okay?"

"Okay," Buffy said with amusement. "Don't wig out."

Willow frowned puzzledly at her. "Why do men want to grow hair on their faces?"

"They're primitive," Buffy said with a shrug. "Deep down, under all that deodorant and aftershave, most of them would like to sleep in a cave and pick bugs out of their hairy hides."

"But Xander is more refined," Willow said with a hopeful lilt to her voice. "He wouldn't really grow a bunch of facial hair, would he? I'm scared of things that are *too* hairy."

Buffy twitched as the fine hairs on the back of her neck stood on end—they must not have liked Willow's remark. She also felt a slight cramp, reminding her of the next full moon.

But she couldn't think about that now, because the hairs on her neck continued their edgy dance.

She knew they were in grave danger. *But from where? From what?* Instinctively she slowed her pace and went into a crouch.

Suddenly a pack of wild animals burst from one of the side yards and loped to a stop in front of Xander. With a startled howl, the mustachioed hero sprang backward and scurried toward Buffy. While her friends fell in line behind the Slayer, the pack completed a lazy circle around them. Their actions reminded Buffy of a pack of hyenas she had once encountered at the zoo, but they looked more like dogs.

Then the Slayer realized what the predators were—*coyotes*.

She had seen coyotes often in the hills around Los Angeles, where she used to live, while horseback riding in Griffith Park or walking near Dodger Stadium. But that was always from a distance—she had never seen a pack of coyotes at close quarters, and it was a startling experience.

Numbering about fifteen, they were a scrawny, scruffy bunch, with mangy coats and darting eyes. Their tongues hung languidly over long jaws and jagged teeth, and they panted as if they had run a long distance. In their wary eyes, Buffy saw mischief and intelligence. She knew she should stay on her guard, but it was hard to be afraid of them when they looked so much like dogs. *Well, maybe dogs that need a bath and a trim. And a decent mud pack*, she thought.

None of them would meet her gaze except for one—an old

gray coyote with rheumy yellow eyes. It stopped and stared at her with a wisdom that seemed to be ancient.

To cover his initial fright, Xander swaggered toward the scrawny predators. "Hey, man, it's just coyotes. Shoo! Go away!"

Some of the scruffy beasts did back away a few steps, but others bared their long canine teeth.

"Xander, leave them alone," Buffy ordered, still in her fighting stance. "Don't start any trouble."

"Oh, come on, they're just coyotes. You're new here, but we see them all the time."

"Duh," Buffy said testily. "I saw coyotes in Los Angeles all the time too. This bunch *looks* normal, but there's something wiggins about them."

Even Willow scoffed at her fear. "He's right, Buffy. It's unusual to see them this close, but coyotes come down from the hills this time of year, looking for water."

As if on some silent command, the pack of coyotes whirled gracefully on their haunches and loped away. Their joyous, high-pitched yips sounded like a bunch of marauding bandits in an old John Wayne movie. Within seconds, most of them had disappeared around a corner.

"See, they're chicken!" Xander claimed, proudly puffing out his chest. He shouted after the coyotes, "Yeah, go on! Get out of here!"

The old coyote with the weird eyes stopped at the corner to look back at Buffy, and she felt the cramps, the chills, the heaves, and just about every other warning sign her body was capable of producing. The animal didn't look annoyed—just curious. Finally it dashed off after its buds, and their eerie yipping continued to pierce the night for many minutes.

"They're on the hunt," Willow said cheerfully. "I did a report on coyotes in zoology, so I know about their habits."

"Don't you think there's something way bizarre about them?" Buffy asked. "Apart from the fact that coyotes are bizarre anyway."

"No," Willow answered thoughtfully. "But coyotes *are* strange. Did you know, you can train bears, tigers, elephants, and just about every other creature on earth—but not coyotes. In the wild or in captivity, coyotes do their own thing. Native Americans have all kinds of tales about them."

"They're just dumb dogs," Xander said, grinning at Buffy. He put his arm protectively around her shoulders. "Don't worry, Buff. If you're scared of those big bow-wows, I'll protect you."

She shook off his gangly arm. "That's real Hercules of you, but as long as they stay away from us, we'll have no problem."

"Xander is right," Willow said reassuringly. "We see them around here a lot. Even though coyotes live all over the West, often near urban areas, it's very rare for them to attack humans."

"I'll remember that." Buffy gave her wispy friend a smile. She didn't want to get mad at Xander and Willow; after all, it wasn't often they got to act more macho than the Slayer. Maybe it was just a pack of especially bold coyotes, new in town, razzing the locals. Still, she couldn't get the aged eyes of that grizzled coyote out of her mind.

With her heightened senses, Buffy could still hear the coyotes as they continued their romp through Sunnydale's quiet streets. Their depraved yowls sounded like a combination of tomcats, wolves, and two-year-old toddlers. Buffy was glad when the awful yelps faded into the starlit distance.

"The children of the night," Xander said in his best Bela Lugosi imitation. "What beautiful music they make."

"You know, he always gave me the creeps," Buffy said, "because I don't think he knew what he was saying. He, like, learned it phonetically. And why did he walk around with his cape in front of his mouth? Did he have bad breath? All the vampires I know like to have their fangs hanging out, primed and ready."

"I'm going to pass on ice cream," Willow said with a yawn. "It's time to go home—to dream of returning to school and ending this pointless existence."

"It's called *va-ca-tion*," Xander insisted. "The absence of work, the natural state of being, the purpose of life."

"It's boring," Willow said. "But maybe it will pick up this weekend."

"Maybe it will," Buffy agreed, taking a last took around the quiet suburban neighborhood.

• • •

Buffy never slept well or deeply anymore, and it didn't take much to jolt her out of bed like a rocket. Still dressed in a clinging sleeveless shirt, she rolled out of bed onto her bare feet and listened to the disturbing sounds coming through her bedroom window. The warm night air brought demented yapping that was unmistakable—the coyotes were on the hunt! They were nearby, coming closer.

She knew instinctively that it was the same pack of coyotes they had met earlier that night. Although it was now close to four o'clock in the morning, they weren't done terrorizing the neighborhood yet. Truthfully, Buffy relished an opportunity to observe the pack without those skeptics, Xander and Willow, slowing her down. She had never seen coyotes that bold, and she wanted to keep an eye on them.

Rising like a wave, the eerie yapping passed over her house like an aural ghost. Buffy pulled on a pair of jeans and her tennis shoes, crawled out the window, and scurried down the roof. By the time she jumped to the ground, all she got was a glimpse of the pack as they charged brazenly down the middle of the street. In the lead was a swift blond canine, clutching something white in its mouth.

In a frenzy of demented yapping, the others chased it down an alley and were gone a second later. Although she doubted whether she could catch them, Buffy was about to try when she heard a frenzied shout. She turned to see a middle-aged woman in a nightgown bearing down on her.

"Stop them! Stop them!" the woman screamed. "My baby!"

"Your baby!" Buffy said with a gasp. Had they really snatched a baby?

Panting for breath, the distraught woman rushed up to Buffy and grabbed her arm. "They took my Tiger!"

The teenager blinked at her. "Okay, did they take a baby or a tiger? Or was it a baby tiger?"

"Oh, no, my precious *Tiger*!" the woman shrieked. "He's a little pug-nosed chow."

"Oh, a dog," Buffy said, trying not to look relieved. It was terrible that the coyotes had snatched the woman's dog, but that was better than a baby. She remembered similar tragedies in Los Angeles; that's what happened when coyotes went hunting in the suburbs.

"They took him right out of my backyard!" the woman said in a quavering voice. "He was old and infirm, and he couldn't fight back. We have to *save* him!"

Buffy held her hands and tried to be comforting. "I'm sorry, but I don't see how we're going to save Tiger. He was probably dead within seconds of them grabbing him. Besides, there's no way we could catch them."

The distraught woman buried her face in her hands and began to weep, and Buffy glanced around, amazed that nobody else had come out to witness this dramatic scene. Even now, the yelps of the coyotes sounded distant, as if they had only been a passing nightmare.

There wasn't much for Buffy to do but walk her home. "Where do you live?" she asked.

"Can't we do *anything*?" her neighbor blubbered.

"Well, sure, we'll report them to Animal Control, or the dog catcher, or whoever handles stuff like this." Buffy mustered a hopeful smile.

"They won't do anything," the woman grumbled. "Tiger is gone, all thanks to those damn coyotes! It must be Coyote Moon that brought them here. Curse them!"

"Coyote Moon?" Buffy asked warily.

The woman stared grimly down the deserted street, which looked so peaceful that it was hard to imagine it had just been the scene of a grisly hunt and kill. "Coyote Moon comes in August," she intoned, "when it gets hot. It rises red, and it brings the coyotes. That's what my grandmother always said."

"Grandmothers are usually right about that stuff," Buffy remarked lamely, thinking of Grandma Summers playing bridge in Clearwater, Florida.

The woman began to weep uncontrollably, and the Slayer guided her to the sidewalk. "Just point the way home."

She only lived half a block away, yet it took about ten minutes to walk her home. Buffy listened sympathetically to lighthearted tales about Tiger's exploits. He was a much-beloved little dog, and he had lived a full, spoiled life. Talking seemed to make the woman feel better, and she thanked Buffy profusely.

The teen made sure that her neighbor was safely entrenched behind locked doors before she left her. Although the woman was safe, Tiger was still gone, and nothing would erase the savagery of that attack.

As Buffy walked home, the warm wind again brought the eerie sound of coyotes yipping and yowling. She hoped the pack would move on to some other town or go back to the wilderness, but she wasn't counting on it. Unfortunately, when nasty critters got a taste of Sunnydale, they usually made themselves right at home.

CHAPTER TWO

For the next two days, there was no further sign of the coyotes, so Buffy started to relax and fell back into the lazy rhythms of summer. Sleeping in late, waking after her mother had gone to work, eating chocolate brownies for breakfast—it was a life she could get used to.

Buffy had Giles's home telephone number, and she thought about calling him to report the coyotes—but he would probably just scoff at her too. Thinking about it now, it did seem lame to be afraid of a few wacked-out coyotes, even if they did snack on dog-kabobs. Once school started, Giles would be back in his beloved library, and then she could ask him about coyotes and Coyote Moon. Until then, it was her duty as a teenager to enjoy the long, hot nights.

The coyotes were gone, but signs started popping up around town advertising the carnival. By the time Friday night rolled around, the Bronze was empty, and every self-respecting teen was eating cotton candy and pitching quarters into fishbowls.

"Cool!" Xander exclaimed as they crested the hill and got their first look at the whirling neon lights of the Ferris wheel, the Octopus ride, the Tilt-a-Whirl, and other stomach-churning delights. Overnight a vacant lot had been turned into a gaudy wonderland, swarming with young people. The tawdry sights and sounds drew them like moths to a patio bug light. Surfer music blasted from crackling speakers, promising the endless summer they were all dreaming about.

Well, all of us but Willow, Buffy thought.

Even from a distance, Buffy could smell the greasy french fries and sugary apples. She heard a jumble of sounds: calliope music from the merry-go-round, screaming girls on the roller coaster, barkers working the crowd, and gasoline generators keeping the lights burning. Buffy knew she should run in the other direction, because all of this was designed to separate her from her hard-earned cash—but her feet began moving of their own will. Transfixed by the throbbing neon lights, Buffy shuffled down the hill toward the carnival.

"Isn't this fun?" Xander asked with a grin.

"Lots of fun," Willow agreed. "I'm just trying to decide whether to have my corn dog first, then throw up—or whether to throw up first, then eat the corn dog. The second way makes more sense, but the corn dog doesn't taste as good."

"That's our Willow, always being practical," Xander said with amusement.

Buffy pulled her eyes reluctantly from the dazzling sights. "Why does it have to be either/or? Why can't you just ignore the rides that make you hurl?"

"They *all* make me hurl," Willow answered. "And I always get talked into going on them anyway."

Xander put his arm around her slender shoulders. "Hey, Willow, to make it easy on you, we'll start with the fun house. We'll work up to the rocket ship thing where you're strapped inside a cage, spinning around. If you're brave enough, maybe *I'll* even buy you a corn dog."

Willow looked plaintively at Buffy. "See what I mean? The only time Xander ever buys me anything is to get me to go on the rides with him." She sighed. "But it works."

"I'm going to be sensible," Buffy vowed. "No upchuck express for me."

"But the roller coaster is calling your name," Xander said with a twinkle in his eye.

"Okay," Buffy admitted. "How did you know I liked roller coasters?"

"Because you're Danger Girl!" he proclaimed.

"That's Vacation Girl," Buffy reminded him.

They walked under banners and lights stuck high on slender wooden poles. Xander pointed toward a weathered metallic skeleton that stood three stories high and was the size of a large barn. The roller coaster didn't look safe to stand under, let alone ride on. As a string of cars rose slowly up the first hill, the tracks clacked ominously, like a busted jackhammer.

"That's a rickety-looking roller coaster," Xander said with a worried grimace. "You know, it's the kind that moans and shakes a lot when you go around the corners."

His theory was verified by the terrified screams that rent the air as the coaster took its first and deepest plunge. Then it whipped noisily around a sharp corner, eliciting more anguished shrieks. Buffy gave Xander a look of dread, which she managed to hold for a few seconds before they both grinned.

"No, I wouldn't like that at all," Buffy said.

"We'll do it first," Xander agreed. "And Willow can hold our food and our stuffed animals."

"No, no," Willow said stalwartly. "It's corn dog express, full speed ahead!"

The three friends were laughing as they entered the giddy realm of the carnival. *It is its own shimmering town,* Buffy thought, *with all the features of a real town.* There was food and drink, none of it even remotely healthy. The music was a jarring combination of surfer records, heavy metal, and gooey kids' songs. There was entertainment, but not even the cleverest boy could win the stupid games, unless he discovered the magic of a first date on a hot summer's night. Then a lucky girl might take home a gigantic stuffed animal.

As they wandered down the midway, Buffy found herself

watching the people more than the attractions. The carnival was packed with teens in muscle shirts and halter tops, hanging all over one another. *Raging hormone time,* Buffy thought. At moments like this, she really regretted being terminally single.

It was bad enough that Willow and Xander knew about her Slayer secret and insisted on helping and/or meddling, as the case may be. A boyfriend would never fit in with her student-by-day, Slayer-by-night lifestyle. As she had discovered, even trying to have a simple date with a guy was way too complicated.

Buffy was afraid to ask Giles what became of Slayers when they got older. She was certain they ended up as old maids and spinsters, or dead. Probably dead.

Still, it would be nice to bump into Angel at a place like this, Buffy thought. She quickly squelched that thought. *Bad Buffy, bad!* Angel was a good vampire, cursed to have a soul and feelings, which made him even weirder than she was. It was better not to think about boys at all, but that was difficult when so many were on display under the sizzling neon.

If the teens from the town looked hot, so did the carnies who ran the rides and games. Buffy was surprised to see that so many of them looked young and buff, not like the grizzled dudes she remembered as a kid. Oh, they were kind of scruffy and dangerous-looking, as if they needed a shave and a new tattoo, but that was part of their charm. So was the leer in their eyes and the promise of fun in their voices.

"A free shot for the woman with the great legs," said a

muscular young carny, spinning a basketball on his fingertip. He had a deep tan and about four days' growth of beard; his insouciant smile stopped her cold. Buffy knew that the hoop behind him was a lot smaller than regulation, and a stop to talk to the carny would likely cost her two or three dollars.

"Later," she said, meaning it.

She had to shove Willow out of the way, because she had also stopped to gape at the carny. "Uh, maybe we should play some games," Willow suggested innocently.

"Okay, Miss Money Management—we discussed it," Xander said impatiently. "Ride tickets first, then food, then, if we have any money left over, games."

"For once, he's right," Buffy replied.

"Hello, nurse!" Xander exclaimed as he veered toward a pretty young woman in cutoff shorts and a skimpy top. She smiled like a gypsy as she beckoned him to her booth, which was already crowded with guys. After exchanging worried glances, Buffy and Willow trailed along to see what the scam was all about.

The beautiful dark-haired girl was only the bait. The main attraction was a seedy clown in a dunking machine. With a rainbow wig, streaked makeup, and old clothes, he didn't look like much of a clown; but he was sitting on a wooden plank perched over a big tank of water. The sign said that it cost two dollars to throw five balls at the disklike target, in the hope of dumping the clown into the water. He looked awfully dry to Buffy.

The clown also had a microphone hanging over his head,

and he wasn't afraid to use it. "I've never seen so many beautiful women in one place," he grumbled in a voice that boomed across the midway. "So where did you babes get these *ugly guys*? Man, the dog pound must be empty!"

One clean-cut young man stepped up to the dark-haired girl and declared, "I'll knock him in."

"Two dollars, farm boy," she said in a teasing voice.

"Oh, now we got a local hero!" the clown crowed. "Let's see if you're *man* enough to knock me into the drink. Maybe you can win a kiss from Rose!"

The girl pouted and posed, showing off a rose tattoo on the top of her cleavage, and Xander drooled along with the rest of the guys. Rose collected two dollars from the dazed boy and handed him five old softballs. Buffy and Willow exchanged a sigh. Didn't boys ever learn?

The clown sneered. "What a *wimp*! I bet he can't even *get* it to the target! Go on, wimp, take your best shot!"

Huffing and puffing, the boy wound up and threw. He was wide, but he threw hard and with authority.

"My *grandmother* throws better than that!" the clown roared into his microphone. "But I think the peewee league has found a new pitcher!"

In angry succession, the boy hurled four more balls, each one farther away from the target than the one before.

"Come on," Rose said with a purr. "You want to try again?"

"No," the boy muttered, completely embarrassed. "I'm outta here."

Although a lot of people were watching the proceedings, not that many were digging into their pockets for two dollars. The failure of the last contestant had scared some of them away.

"What is this town?" the clown asked. "Sunny Jail?" The kids laughed at the takeoff on the town's name of Sunnydale, and the professional heckler continued. "I don't want to say people are stupid here, but the biggest decision after high school is whether to marry your cousin or your sister."

Laughter and groans came in equal measure, and some of the guys were thinking about parting with their money. Rose turned to Xander and batted her eyelashes. "How about you, big boy? Have *you* got what it takes?"

The teenager turned to mush and nearly melted under the stage, but Rose's dark eyes held him up. When he didn't move fast enough for his wallet, the clown on the platform sneered. "Hey, kid, is that a mustache or a third armpit?"

Buffy had to laugh at that one, and Xander looked at her accusingly. Now there was no hesitation as he reached for his wallet and took out two dollars. He didn't like clowns much, anyway.

"Clown. Water. Prepare to meet," he vowed, and the crowd cheered.

"Money management!" Willow shouted to no avail.

Xander took careful aim at the disklike target, but it was hardly any bigger than one of the softballs—and it was forty feet away. It would require a perfect throw to soak the obnoxious clown, and Xander would never be confused with a great athlete. His first pitch missed by six feet.

"Omigosh, did he kill anybody?" the clown asked, to much laughter.

"You can do it," Rose said encouragingly.

"Yeah, you can do it!" Willow shouted, not to be outdone.

Xander reached back and threw hard, coming within two feet.

"Visualize it!" Buffy shouted.

"You visualize this," the clown said, staring directly at Buffy. "You and me on a little date, at a fancy French restaurant. We'll order some truffles and some fine wine—I'll get you some soda pop."

She gave him what she hoped was a disgusted look, but his words were having the desired effect on Xander. Looking so angry that he couldn't even see the target, he threw two straight misses. He only had one ball left.

The clown mocked him. "Maybe it would help if we got you a Seeing Eye dog!"

That was it for Buffy. She walked up to Xander and held out her hand. "Time for a relief pitcher."

He looked at her with a mixture of anger and frustration, but relief soon spread across his face. She could see his mind working: *Buffy has perfect coordination, and Buffy could hit that target with any weapon known to mankind. Let Buffy throw the ball.*

"I'm giving her my last ball," Xander said to Rose. He

said it apologetically, as if he was sorry that her clown was about to bite it.

"Oh, he's the *supreme* wimp!" the clown hooted. "By all means, give your *girlfriend* the last ball. I'll make it even easier for the little lady. Rose, give her an extra ball from me, too."

"No thanks," Buffy said, hefting the spongy softball. "I'll only need one."

"Awfully confident, aren't you?" Rose sneered.

This was called showing off, Buffy thought, and she shouldn't be doing it. She could imagine the horrified look on Giles's face if he knew what she was up to. *But a Slayer has to do what a Slayer has to do.* At least she was going to make an awful lot of people in the crowd very happy.

The clown was saying something else insulting, but she tuned him out in order to concentrate. Unlike Xander, she *did* visualize the ball leaving her hand on a perfect trajectory and striking the target dead-center. She saw it trip the lever that held up the plank, and she saw the plank drop. She didn't have to visualize the obnoxious clown falling into the water, because she was about to see that for real.

Whirling nonchalantly, Buffy threw the softball on a line with hardly any arc. It struck the target with a reassuring *clang*, and the plank dropped with a loud *clack!* She relished the startled look on the clown's face as he plunged into the water with a gushing splash. The crowd went wild, applauding and cheering, and the clown waved from the tank, as if he was taking the bows.

"Nice throw," Rose said, looking suspiciously at Buffy.

"Beginner's luck," the Slayer replied with a cute giggle. She grabbed Xander and tried to pull him away from the carny, but he was still fixated on Rose.

"Hey," Xander said sheepishly, "don't I get a kiss? It was *my* ball, even though she threw it."

Rose leaned over dramatically and whispered to him. "Come back in half an hour, and I'll take my break."

Xander gaped at her, then looked around, as if she had to be speaking to somebody else. Buffy rolled her eyes at how helpless he was around this vamp. That was *vamp* in the old-fashioned sense, because she didn't sense anything undead about the girl. In fact, she seemed to be very lively. Buffy didn't think that Rose was a proper playmate for Xander, although she doubted he would agree.

Ignoring the hound-dog look on his face, Buffy used all her strength to drag Xander away from the exotic carny. Willow cut off his escape route to the rear.

"Money management," Willow insisted.

"Creaky rides! Screaming girls! Whiplash!" Buffy reminded him. "All rides guaranteed to leave your stomach outside your body!"

"Take me wherever you want," Xander said blissfully. He checked his watch. "But you have exactly thirty minutes."

Willow shot a worried look at Buffy, who shrugged helplessly. With the vibes in the air tonight, they would be lucky if it was only Xander who got carried away. Buffy had to admit that Rose was quite an attraction—wild cheerleaders probably couldn't stop Xander from keeping his date.

They rode the roller coaster, and the girls screeched as they roared up and down the rickety peaks. Xander, meanwhile, kept looking at his watch. They rode the Ferris wheel, and Xander worried that they would be stuck at the top for too long. He couldn't even enjoy the fantastic view of the carnival, shimmering like an island of light in the vast dreariness of Sunnydale.

When they got off the Ferris wheel, Buffy noticed a grizzled old carny with oil stains on his face and hands. He stood beside the groaning machinery and slapped a wrench against his palm, watching them walk away. Buffy felt a disturbing sense of déjà vu, as if she had seen him before, looking at her that same way.

At least there went the theory that all the carnies were young and gorgeous. *He* looked like the carnies she remembered from her childhood—gnarly and creepy.

They still had plenty of ride tickets left, but Xander led the way as they drifted back toward the hucksters.

"Free practice shot!" one shouted.

"Everybody's a winner!" another called.

Xander stumbled along, transfixed by the lights, the noise, the games, and the girls. Buffy tried not to be angry with him.

"Hey, Xander, keep it under control. Don't be too eager," she warned. "She said half an hour, not ten minutes."

"Yes, you're better off to keep her waiting," Willow

suggested, not sounding very convincing. "And it may only be a fifteen-minute break."

"Fifteen minutes with Rose," Xander said dreamily. "I'll take it."

"I wonder how many guys she's said that to?" Buffy asked.

"Neither one of you is gonna spoil this night," Xander vowed. He checked his watch again, then held it to his ear to make sure it was running, which was dumb, because it was a digital watch.

"Hey, beautiful! Break my heart!" a masculine voice called.

Buffy whirled around to see a tanned blond hunk with sleeves rolled up over brawny muscles. He was the most handsome carny yet, and he was standing in a dart booth, surrounded by posters of hot rods, puppies, TV actors, and bikini babes.

The hunk pointed to a pink heart-shaped balloon on the corkboard behind him. "Look how big my heart is. I bet you could break it without half trying."

"Like I'm sure that hasn't happened," she admitted. The heart-shaped balloon was surrounded by smaller balloons and lots of white space. He seemed to be giving away the posters, but she didn't need any more posters in her bedroom. Still, Buffy's feet propelled her toward the booth, and Willow was right beside her.

"Two lovely ladies—it's my lucky night." The carny smiled, revealing hidden dimples in the stubble of his blond beard. A merry twinkle in his blue eyes said he knew his game was a rip-off, but that made it even more fun. He held out three darts to Buffy. "Break it, and anything I have is yours."

Buffy noticed a tattoo on his brawny forearm, but it was so faded that she couldn't tell what it was. She wondered whether the carny was older than he looked.

"Let me try," Willow insisted, cutting in between them. She fixed the carny with her best femme fatale expression, but it was hardly fatal. Nevertheless, the carny was happy to play along, and he flirted brazenly with Willow.

"No rush, little lady, we've got all night. My name is Lonnie."

"Pleased to meet you," she answered cheerfully. "I'm Willow, and this Buffy." When Willow glanced back to see what Xander was doing, Buffy finally realized what was going on—Willow was trying to get Xander's attention by flirting with this hunk. Of course, Xander was too busy looking at his watch to care what either one of them was doing.

"What are the rules?" Willow asked.

Reluctantly, Lonnie pulled his eyes away from Buffy to his paying customer. "You give me two dollars, and I give you three really sharp darts. You get three chances to win. Break my heart or break any balloon, and you take your choice of anything I've got."

Willow giggled, and Lonnie motioned around at the posters, most of which were worth about a dollar. "None of them are as pretty as you," he told Willow, who rolled her eyes but giggled in spite of herself.

Not a bad deal, Buffy thought. *Spend two dollars trying to win a prize worth half that.* Most people didn't win, of course, but even if you lost, you still got Lonnie's charming company.

Taking a deep breath as if she were about to run a marathon, Willow hefted the first dart and let it fly. It hit the board, but just barely—near the bottom, far from any balloon. Willow smiled gamely and tried again. This time, her weakly thrown dart hit a balloon and bounced off, without breaking it.

"Hey!" she said in protest. "Are those trick balloons?"

Again Lonnie had to tear his eyes away from Buffy. "They're just regular balloons. Listen, if you miss your last one, I'll give you one more, on the house."

"That's very decent of you," Willow said, sounding pleased. She threw her third dart, and it landed perfectly—in the white space between two balloons.

With a charming smile, Lonnie handed her another dart. "Don't tell my boss," he said.

Willow looked concerned. "Will you get in trouble?"

Lonnie laughed, and it was a warm, decadent sound. "I was *born* in trouble. Go ahead and throw."

Willow took careful aim and threw the last dart; it sailed over the board and stuck in the canvas at the back of the booth.

Lonnie immediately turned his full attention to Buffy. "Your turn to break my heart."

"No thanks," Buffy said, knowing full well she could

clean him out of his crummy posters. "I've reached my tacky wall-hangings quota. Maybe later."

"Speaking of later," Lonnie said, leaning intimately toward her, "meet me back here in half an hour, when I take my break."

"Give *me* a break." Buffy groaned. "Are all of you trained with the same come-on line?"

"Huh?" Lonnie asked.

Willow broke in with nervous laughter. "Don't listen to her, Lonnie. What were you saying about taking a break?"

But he wasn't through with Buffy yet. "Are you shutting me down?" he asked incredulously.

"Guess it doesn't happen too often," Buffy replied, getting ticked. "About as often as somebody wins a prize around here."

"Hey, it's your loss," Lonnie said. His blue eyes weren't so merry anymore.

Buffy started to drag her friend away from the booth, but Lonnie produced three more darts. "Not so fast. I like you, Willow. I want to give you another chance. Have a free play!"

Willow's eyes widened with excitement, and she yanked her arm away from Buffy. Never taking her eyes off the handsome carny, she said, "Buffy, you should be nice to Lonnie—he's giving me a free play."

"Yeah," Buffy muttered. "Why don't you stick around for his break? I hear it'll be in half an hour."

Buffy turned to look for Xander, but all she saw was

the back of his shirt disappearing into the crowd. He was headed in the direction of the dunking machine, and Buffy didn't think she could catch him. Probably a master vampire couldn't stop him.

Willow smiled coyly as she took the darts from Lonnie. The handsome carny shot a glance at Buffy, then put his arm around the slender girl's shoulders. "Let me show you a technique that never fails."

Buffy groaned and started to stalk away, disgusted with her friends. After a few angry strides, she realized that she was really disgusted with herself. Why should Willow and Xander be deprived of a little fun, just because *she* felt deprived? It wasn't their fault that she was a Slayer and couldn't have a normal boyfriend. It wasn't their fault that on a night ripe with romance, she was all alone. Even around a bunch of people, Buffy always felt alone.

In every generation, there is a Slayer. Not a bunch of them, just *one*. She was the freak—even the people who worked this seedy carnival were normal compared to her.

Buffy stepped out of the circle of neon light and found herself on the outskirts of the carnival. She could still hear the blaring music and smell the greasy food, but she wasn't part of it anymore. From outside, she could see the weather-beaten trailers, dirty tents, snaking wires, and chugging generators that kept the fake city alive.

With her senses finally cleared, she had time to think. There *was* something wiggins about most of the carnies being young and gorgeous. She would deny ever thinking it, but gorgeous people hitting on Xander and Willow was also off the wall. Maybe she was just being paranoid, but it was never far from Buffy's mind that this unlikely town was located on the Hellmouth. Nasty types were just naturally drawn here.

While she had a few minutes by herself, Buffy decided to look around. It was dark behind the trailers and tents, but she didn't need much light to see.

She wasn't looking for anything in particular—just looking. Ever since Buffy was a little girl, she had been the type of person who peeked inside people's medicine chests when she visited their bathrooms. She was naturally curious, and maybe that was all part of who—and what—she was. For a Slayer, it was either be nosy or be dead.

Ripe smells of rotting fruit and putrid meat twisted her head around, and she saw a row of garbage cans in the shadows behind the fun house. Looking through people's trash was not something Buffy enjoyed doing, but it was the next best thing when there wasn't a medicine chest handy. Breathing through her mouth, she walked gingerly toward the dump.

The trash cans were filled to overflowing, and there was garbage all over the ground as well. Since the carnival had just opened that night, most of this stuff had to belong to the carnival workers themselves, Buffy thought. With the toe of her boot, she kicked through old food wrappers, eggshells, greasy paper towels, rotten fruit, and the usual refuse of society.

The carnies' garbage was disgusting but nothing special, and she was about to explore elsewhere when something shiny caught her eye. Buffy kicked a gooey rag off the object and bent down to see a curled strap of red leather with shiny silver studs and a silver buckle. She turned it over and saw metal tags hanging from it.

It's a dog collar.

With a feeling of dread expanding in her stomach like a wad of cotton candy, Buffy picked up the dog collar and read the tags. One tag was a dog license, and the other had a name inscribed on it. The name was Tiger.

Licking her dry lips, Buffy remembered a few nights back, when the pack of coyotes had snatched a dog named Tiger off her street. How come the poor dog's collar had ended up here?

A twig snapped, and Buffy jumped to her feet and whirled around. The grizzled old carny from the Ferris wheel now stood about ten feet away from her, staring at her with pale, rheumy eyes. Again she was sure that she had seen those eyes before somewhere. More troubling was the fact that he had sneaked awfully close to her before she heard him, which wasn't typical. She also didn't like the way he was slapping his heavy wrench against his grimy palm.

"What are you looking for?" he demanded.

Buffy held Tiger's collar behind her back and stuffed it into her belt. His eyes were so familiar. But from where?

Buffy gasped as she finally remembered where she had seen the man's eyes before.

But that is impossible!

"Who are you?" he snarled. His pale eyes flashed with anger, and he lifted the wrench as he strode toward her.

CHAPTER THREE

Buffy leaped away from the creepy carny, but she didn't assume her fighting stance. She still wanted to look helpless, if possible. She checked out escape routes from the rear of the carnival, and she saw cars parked nearby.

"Listen," she said. "I didn't mean to cause trouble. Actually, I . . . I was feeling a little gross from all the rides, and I was looking for a good place to heave. Is this okay? Can I heave right here?"

The old carny stopped in his tracks. Even the baddest dude didn't want somebody to hurl all over him. Buffy stared at the man, certain that she had to be mistaken about him. Could he really be the old coyote she had seen on the street a few nights ago? He was staring at her just as that coyote had stared at her, and his eyes were eerily similar.

But that meant he was a *werecoyote*, if there was such a thing. Well, Buffy decided, if there were werecoyotes, sooner or later they would end up in Sunnydale.

He took another step toward her, and she began to gag and bent over. "Look out!" she warned.

The old carny quickly backed away. "This is not a good place for you to be. Try the Porta Potties at the end of the midway."

"Porta Potties," she said gratefully. "What a good idea." She staggered back toward the gaudy lights and manic music. "Thanks a lot, Mister . . . uh—"

"Hopscotch. The name is Hopscotch."

"I'll remember that," she said truthfully. If she was right about Hopscotch—that he could turn himself into a coyote—then maybe some of the other carnies were also in the pack. Come to think of it, the carnies acted like a pack, working together to run the rides, games, and food stands. She had to find Xander and Willow before they got too hung up on Rose and Lonnie!

Buffy ran first to the dunking machine, but there was now a pretty redheaded girl collecting money and handing out softballs. Rose was gone, and Xander was nowhere in sight—so they were probably together, taking the fabled break. The last thing Buffy wanted to do was attract even more attention by asking a lot of questions, so she dashed off to Lonnie's dart booth.

The blond hunk was also missing, and so was Willow.

Feeling worried and slightly jealous, Buffy wandered down the midway, looking for her friends. They had been such fools—they hadn't even arranged for a place to meet in case they got split up. And, boy, had they gotten split up.

After a few minutes of roaming through the swirling lights, pounding music, and laughing teens, Buffy began to relax. Once again, the carnival seemed like nothing but harmless fun on a hot summer's night. How could she think those cute carnies were werecoyotes? It was a ridiculous leap of faith, even for Buffy.

For the moment, she decided, she would keep quiet about her suspicions. More than likely, Xander and Willow would be disappointed by their exotic dates, and life would get back to what passed for normal.

Buffy spotted Cordelia and a few other acquaintances from school. They didn't have dates either, which made her feel better, and she briefly crashed their group. Cordelia was her usual snotty self, but it felt good not to be alone. Buffy kept her eyes open for Xander and Willow.

She finally spotted them both, walking happily together and acting as if *they* were on a date. *If only Xander would wake up and smell the garlic,* Buffy thought. He couldn't do any better than Willow, who idolized him. Buffy fantasized that they had been stood up by Rose and Lonnie and had discovered each other on this romantic night.

She slipped away from Cordelia and her friends and headed them off. "Hey, guys, what's happening?"

Xander grinned as if he was the coyote who ate the dog. "We had a great time."

"You two?" Buffy asked hopefully.

"Yeah," Xander answered with a worldly chuckle. "Me and Rose. I got my *kiss*."

"I had a great time with Lonnie, too," Willow insisted. "But he had to go back to work."

"How tragic," Buffy said sarcastically.

"But we're going to double-date tomorrow," Willow said.

"You *what*!" Buffy exclaimed. "The *four* of you?"

"It's just a lunch date," Willow replied, "before the carnival opens. They're going to give us a behind-the-scenes tour."

"Maybe you could tag along, like a fifth wheel." Xander glanced at Willow. "We wouldn't mind, would we?"

"Not at all," she answered cheerfully.

"Thanks, but I have to trim my toenails," Buffy muttered. "Willow, could I talk to you for a second?"

"Sure." She smiled innocently at Xander, then allowed Buffy to drag her behind a lemonade stand.

"I know that Xander has no sense when it comes to women," the Slayer whispered, "but what's *your* excuse?"

"Lonnie was a perfect gentleman," Willow answered, sounding surprised and a little disappointed. "If I can double-date with Rose and Xander, I can keep my eye on Xander."

"Okay, that makes sense," Buffy said with relief. "But these aren't choirboys running this place. I want you to be real careful."

Willow frowned and put her hands on her narrow hips. "It's only a date, Buffy. Do I tell *you* to be careful when you go out on a date?"

"You could," Buffy said, "*if* I ever went out on a date."

"But when you hang out with Angel, he's a lot more dangerous than these people."

"That's debatable." Buffy took a few deep breaths, knowing that her suspicions would sound crazy to Willow and Xander, even though they had seen a lot of crazy things since meeting her. She had to have more proof than a dog collar in the trash.

Xander poked his head around the corner of the stand, and he was smirking. "Are you ladies discussing *me*? I'm very popular with the ladies tonight."

Buffy rolled her eyes and bit her tongue. "Xander, I just want you to be way on guard around these people, that's all."

"Ah, jealousy—it's not pretty, even on you, Buffy," he said smugly.

"No, just a use of brain cells." Buffy sighed, knowing it was pointless to reason with Xander about women. "Listen, your new friends went back to work, so now we can go back to the original agenda—having fun. Are you ready to ride some more rides and eat some food with no nutritional value? I'm getting hungry!"

Xander looked sheepishly at the ground. "I, um . . . I spent the rest of my money on games."

"Me too," Willow admitted.

Buffy tried not to laugh in their faces. “Okay, my treat. But if any more carnies make goo-goo eyes at you, you just keep on walking.”

“I’m content with Rose,” Xander said blissfully.

“This is so touching, I’m gonna hurl,” Buffy muttered. “Come on, I smell corn dogs.”

They went to the front of the lemonade stand and were reading the menu, when Buffy felt eyes on the back of her neck. She turned to see the old carny, Hopscotch, standing across the midway, watching her. She had a feeling he would be watching her for the rest of the night, and whenever she returned to the carnival.

Well, Buffy decided, the next time he and his friends ventured into the streets of Sunnydale, she would be watching *them.*

Much later that Friday night, when Buffy heard the coyotes howl, she was ready. She rolled out of bed fully dressed, wearing binoculars around her neck and her best running shoes. She bounded out the window while the cries of the pack were still fresh on the wind.

I knew *they would be going out tonight,* she thought with satisfaction.

After leaping to the ground, Buffy hid behind a tree in her yard. The night sky was full of clouds, but a translucent glow high in the heavens revealed the hiding place of a bright moon. With all the moonlight, she had no problem finding the pack of scruffy canines romping down the street, sniffing about. They didn't seem to be on the scent of any prey—yet.

Although they acted as if they owned the streets, word of their last visit must have gotten out. Buffy heard muffled barking, but it sounded as if all the neighborhood dogs were safely ensconced behind locked doors.

As the coyotes loped farther down the street, Buffy lifted the binoculars to watch them from a distance—she didn't want to get any closer than necessary. The suburban street looked deserted, except for her, the coyotes, and ghostly wisps of fog.

The mist was thickest in the low-lying dips in the road, where it was almost impossible to see the coyotes. She hoped the fog wouldn't get any worse, or her binoculars would be useless.

Buffy didn't move from her hiding place until the coyotes loping in the rear were almost out of sight. She dashed down the street, moving from tree to tree and house to house for cover. This was an older suburb with lots of big oaks and sycamores, and she was able to keep hidden. She knew that the wind might carry her scent and alert the coyotes to her presence, but she had no control over that. Luckily, they were running against the wind, looking for the scent of prey, and she was downwind of them.

For several blocks, she kept the coyotes in view with her binoculars, until one of them gave an excited howl and dashed off. The others gave chase like greyhounds at a dog race, and their yipping was frenzied and excited. *They must have found something to hunt!* Buffy put her head down and ran as fast as she could to catch up with them.

As she cautiously rounded the corner of a house, the Slayer saw the pack of coyotes at the end of the block, huddled under a tree. Some of them ran frantically in circles, while others sprang up and down. Most of them sat and stared forlornly into the high branches.

Beyond the coyotes was a black open space with spooky tendrils of fog drifting through marble tombstones. A chill wind blew from the old cemetery and made Buffy shiver. Since coming to Sunnydale, she had often encountered vampires in the crumbling mausoleums of this place. In fact, it was practically a vampire retirement home.

Staying in the shadows so as not to be seen, Buffy lifted her binoculars to her eyes. She tried to forget her memories of the cemetery in order to concentrate on her mission. *What do the coyotes find so interesting in that tree?*

By watching their eyes and where they were jumping, she pinpointed something large and tawny-colored, trying to crawl to the uppermost branches. One of those thin branches snapped, and the poor thing plummeted toward the slavering jaws below. The coyotes went nuts, yapping and leaping in a frenzy, but their prey managed to get a grasp at the last second and swing itself to safety. It gave a pitiful yowl for help.

The coyotes had treed a cat! Not content with dog-kabobs, they were going after kitty-kabobs!

Buffy knew she couldn't stand idly by and let them munch

on a kitty after playing football with it for a while. She had to intervene, but then she would lose her opportunity to observe them unseen. At the moment, they were acting disgustingly like regular coyotes—as if nothing could be more exciting than treeing a cat. If she were logical, she would forget all about her crazy theory and go home to bed. After all, coyotes had to eat too.

Fortunately, Buffy had never given in to logic. She had to save the kitty, but how? In a melee, she wasn't sure she could fight the whole pack of coyotes at once. Three or four she could handle, but not fifteen or twenty. But if she waited too long trying to think of a plan, the kitty might be toast.

Suddenly, the scene brightened as if somebody had turned on a giant streetlamp. Buffy looked up to see the clouds parting overhead, and an almost-full moon gleamed in the heavens like a beacon. The yipping of the coyotes stopped, and they all looked at once at the moon, ignoring the cat. They held so still, it was as if the moon were a glow-in-the-dark satellite dish and they were receiving signals.

Buffy hugged the side of the house, hoping not to be spotted by their sharp eyes. She needn't have worried, because the pack turned in unison and bolted in the opposite direction—toward the cemetery. With high leaps, they cleared the wrought-iron fence and vanished amidst the lonely tombstones and tendrils of fog.

There seemed little point in staying hidden—unless the pack stopped, she would never catch them. Buffy jogged down the sidewalk directly under the tree where the frightened cat had taken refuge. She looked up and saw the feline clinging to a branch like a stone gargoyle.

"You're down to eight lives now," she whispered. "Go on home."

At once, the cat leaped to the ground and scurried across the street and under a house. Buffy nodded with relief and continued her run toward the cemetery. With an effortless leap, she cleared the spear tips of the iron fence and landed on the soft earth of a large grave. She rolled onto the grass, jumped to her feet, and brushed herself off.

It was an old cemetery, and they packed them in, except for the mausoleums and monuments in the well-to-do section toward the middle. Despite the bright moon, it seemed darker here. The cemetery was in a vast hollow, so the fog was thicker, and there were no streetlamps or house lights to spoil the darkness.

Buffy put the binoculars to her eyes, not expecting to find the coyotes unless by some miracle they stopped. If they were using the cemetery only as a shortcut to get somewhere else, she had probably already lost them.

Patiently she scanned the landscape of gnarly trees and creepy tombstones for any trace of movement. Buffy also listened for their cries, but she could hear nothing expect the wind rustling ominously through the trees. Somewhere a gate clacked open and shut in the wind, lending an eerie rhythm to the sounds of the cemetery.

I should've brought some backup. A nice stake or two . . . just in case. Squelching her fear, Buffy kept the binoculars glued to her eyes. She finally spotted a four-legged figure cutting through a patch of fog. It raced across the ground, then leaped to the top of a mausoleum. Fog obscured her vision, but at least she had a direction in which to head. Of course, the animal was headed toward the well-to-do section with all the fancy mausoleums and monuments.

Going back into stealth mode, Buffy padded quietly from one tombstone to another, using the fog for cover. She kept her eyes open for other denizens of the cemetery, but they seemed to be minding their own business. Like the rest of the town, they wanted nothing to do with this weird pack of coyotes. Buffy was the only one foolish enough to chase them around in the dead of night—through a cemetery.

She saw several more fleeting figures, and they seemed to be gathering around a tall white tombstone. It looked like the spire of the Washington Monument, only it had a marble ball on the top. When Buffy looked through the binoculars, she saw that the ball was actually the moon, complete with craters.

Thanks to a hill and a copse of trees between her and the grave, Buffy couldn't see more than two or three coyotes at a time. They seemed to be running around in circles, yet they weren't barking and yipping as if they had cornered some unfortunate prey.

Buffy knew she had to sneak closer to see what they were

doing. Her usual style was to walk right into danger, make a few clever quips to loosen everyone up, then kick butt. She wasn't used to creeping about on her delicate knees, but this was intelligence gathering. It had to be done. Coyotes were known for being unpredictable and weird, so before she could go to Giles with her suspicions about *these* coyotes, she had better be sure.

The Slayer scrambled forward through the tall, damp grass, resting behind tombstones and tree trunks. She kept moving until she reached the top of the hill, where she finally had a decent view of the crazed coyotes. Buffy got down on her belly between two tree trunks and crawled to the edge of the mossy hill.

She was no expert on coyotes, but this bunch seemed to be acting strangely. They were running in a counterclockwise circle around the spire and the old grave, which was covered with withered flowers. But that wasn't the strangest thing they were doing.

Every few seconds, one of the coyotes would leap out of the frenzied race and attack the grave. Whimpering pathetically, the coyote would dig a shallow hole, tossing the withered flowers in every direction. Just as suddenly, the coyote would stop digging and rejoin the race, and another one would take its place.

If the whole pack really started digging, they could unearth the coffin in a few minutes, Buffy thought. It didn't seem as if they were really trying to dig up the grave—they were only *pretending.* But why? She watched this strange ceremony, getting more puzzled by the second. *What in blazing underpants are they doing?*

Pretend or not, coyotes digging up a grave was still enough to give her a major case of the willies. Buffy made a mental note to come back in the daytime and see who was buried under the moon spire. It must have been somebody who was important or rich, because that massive headstone didn't come cheap.

Mixed in with the panting and running sounds, Buffy heard a low growl. It sounded way too close and too loud—in fact, it almost whispered in her ear. She heard long jaws clack together, and she knew a beast was right behind her, ready to attack. Buffy whirled around and lifted her hand to ward off the attack, but it didn't come—at least not at that instant.

Through the mist she saw the old coyote with the yellow eyes, standing about ten feet away. It drew back its slobbering lips, showing her rows of jagged teeth. The hair on its neck stood like a bad punk haircut.

Hopscotch! Buffy thought grimly. If she wasn't sure before, she was sure now. She started inching away, wondering how far she could run before the scruffy coyote could pounce on her back or sink its teeth into her leg.

The wise old hunter was too crafty to take her on all by itself. It lifted its snout and howled in a chilling tone that sounded like Mom calling the kids to dinner. When it was answered by excited yipping, Buffy bounded to her feet and looked for an escape route.

There was none. In every direction, all she saw were wild-eyed, snarling coyotes charging toward her!

CHAPTER FOUR

As the coyotes vaulted toward her, howling like the possessed, Buffy crouched in the graveyard. She saw a shadow move on her right, and she spun her left foot just in time to catch Hopscotch before it could reach her throat. She kicked the old coyote a dozen feet into the bushes, then leaped skyward as two more coyotes crashed under her feet.

Landing on top of the dazed beasts, the Slayer pounded their jaws shut with flying fists. She looked around—still more were coming from every direction. They were all slashing teeth and smelly hair!

Buffy did a cartwheel, kicking two of the coyotes in their toothy chops, and she twirled like a hula hoop down the hill—

straight into the mysterious grave. She crashed in a heap on top of the wilted flowers, and the coyotes howled with indignation. Their anguished cries brought her quickly back to her senses, and she staggered to her feet. With no other options and coyotes bearing down on her, Buffy started to run.

Two feet weren't as good as four, and the pack of predators was closing in fast, snapping at her heels and calves. In desperation, Buffy leaped ten feet into the air and landed on top of one of the old mausoleums. She weaved back and forth, trying to get her footing on the slippery marble roof—it was raked at an angle like the roof on a real house.

Coyotes could jump too, and several of them came hurtling toward her. Buffy lashed out with her fists at the beasts, but they were wiry and quick—and hard to hit. She didn't dare use her feet, because she didn't want to lose her balance and tumble off her perch. Since she couldn't land a full punch, she hit the coyotes just hard enough to knock them off course and send them spiraling to the ground.

When they started leaping at her from all four sides at once, Buffy was forced to whirl around and kick with her feet. Twice she nearly fell into their deadly jaws, but she caught her balance at the last moment. The excitement of the hunt drove them into a frenzy, and they yipped and yapped as if Buffy were a cat caught in a tree.

From a distance, it's entertaining to watch this behavior, but when you're the prey, it's no fun at all!

With her lightning reflexes, Buffy was able to defend the

roof of the mausoleum, but she never got a moment's rest from the enraged canines. Buffy quickly realized that a persistent attack would wear her down. There were enough attackers that some could take breathers, while she had to fight desperately every second. Her coordination and strength couldn't hold out forever!

From her precarious perch, Buffy spotted another mausoleum two hundred feet away; she knew it well, and hated it. Inside that dreaded mausoleum was a secret passageway, which led underground to a vampire lair. *Who knows what's waiting there?*

With her feet slipping off the cold marble and her arms getting heavy from smashing at teeth and snouts, Buffy knew she had to do something fast. She dropped into a crouch, sprang forward, and leaped as far as she could off the roof of the mausoleum.

She cleared the first ring of coyotes and landed next to one that was taking a rest. Instinctively, she grabbed the surprised canine by its bushy tail, swung it around, and threw it into the others. That slowed their pursuit by a second or two, which was all she wanted.

Running all out, Buffy tore through the cemetery with a pack of Cujos nipping at her heels. She could see her goal, the old mausoleum, shimmering in the fog. But would she make it?

Sensing that she might escape, the coyotes made frantic leaps and landed on her back. Buffy stumbled and nearly went down under their wiry limbs and sharp claws, but she tossed them off like an ugly coat and ducked inside the tomb.

Fighting back half a dozen snarling coyotes, Buffy leaned against the heavy marble door. Only the Slayer's extraordinary strength saved her as she succeeded in slamming the door shut.

Gasping for breath, she slumped against the cold marble and gazed at her gloomy surroundings. An old crypt, peeling walls, mountains of dust and debris—it looked just like her room. For all her cleverness, she had locked herself in a place that was practically a vampire's rec room.

However, Buffy wasn't about to go outside. Deprived of their sport, the coyotes yapped and yowled in protest, and she could still feel them pressing against the door. There was only one way out, and she had to go *down* before she could go *up*.

Buffy moved reluctantly away from the door, afraid they would discover that she wasn't holding it shut. Overcoming her fear, she ran toward the secret passageway and ducked inside. There came a crash as the marble door collapsed to the floor, and coyotes poured through a cloud of ancient dust.

In the dim light, she saw the lead coyotes skid to a stop and back off, whimpering. They sensed something wrong with this place, and she couldn't blame them. Nevertheless, others behind them were trying to push their way in—the thrill of the hunt was more powerful than a few pangs of fear!

Buffy couldn't see any point in standing around watching, because every second counted. She dropped into a crouch and scurried down the dank tunnel, trying not to brush against the slimy, smelly mold that coated the walls. If she met a vampire down here, she had no ammo—not so much as a toothpick! If a vampire met her tonight, it was his good luck, because she was through fighting for one night.

Occasionally, Buffy stopped to listen and glance down the tunnel behind her. As far as she could tell, the coyotes were not pursuing her. Nevertheless, she didn't want to hang around to see if they changed their minds—she just kept plowing ahead.

Her superb vision and unfailing sense of direction led her to a metal utility ladder, and she began to climb. After pushing off a heavy manhole cover, Buffy emerged in the middle of a power plant, surrounded by electrical wires and towering transformers. *That's all right—they're better than the coyotes.*

She looked down at her clothes and saw that her jacket, jeans, and T-shirt were ripped and stained, but somehow the binoculars still hung around her neck. Amazingly enough, she had been saved by the vampires' tunnels. The undead had wisely kept out of the way tonight, and the coyotes had recognized their stench in the mausoleum. She had to think about all of this—and tell Giles.

Nursing sore muscles and numerous scratches and bruises, Buffy climbed slowly over the fence and shuffled home through the deserted streets.

The Slayer jumped out of bed and stared bleary-eyed at her alarm clock. After she realized that it was after ten o'clock, she cursed herself for sleeping in. Of course, she had stayed up late last night and had spent the wee hours of the morning dodging a pack of coyotes through a vampire playground, but that was no excuse.

Wearily, she recalled that it was Saturday, and the first thing she had to do was see Giles. She grabbed her clothes.

Stumbling downstairs to the kitchen, Buffy found a note from her mom saying she was off playing golf. *Golf? They must put something in the water of this place that warps people's minds,* Buffy thought. *Mom has never played golf in Los Angeles—that is Dad's job.*

Well, her mom's absence was a blessing, because Buffy didn't care to explain why the clothes she was stuffing into a garbage bag were all ripped up. The only person she wanted to talk to was Giles.

When she called the librarian's private number, he didn't answer. *Where could he be?* she thought angrily. *Giles doesn't have a life.* She thought about how school was starting in a week or so, and she wondered if the high school could be open for staff preparation and student enrollment. It was worth a try. Even if the school was closed, she could sneak into the library and try to find books about coyotes . . . and werecoyotes. *Didn't Willow say she'd done a report on coyotes?* Then the library was the place to start.

When Buffy got to school, she was relieved to see several cars in the parking lot. For sure, they weren't students showing up early. Walking quickly past the windows so as not to be seen, Buffy slipped in a side door and dashed to the library. As soon as she pushed open the unlocked door, she knew the Watcher was in attendance. The place had a musty smell that was like Giles's personal cologne.

She found him behind his stacks, bent over a pile of magazines. "Hello, Buffy," he said cheerfully. "What brings you to school before absolutely necessary? Not studying, I'm sure."

"Believe it or not, that sounds better than the real reason," the Slayer said glumly, "but I'm here on official business."

The handsome Englishman gazed over the top of his glasses. "Do you mean the undead?"

"No, I mean the unbathed and untrimmed. I'm talking about coyotes."

Giles smiled and picked up a catalog of computer furniture. "Coyotes are very common in this area. I've enjoyed hearing their cries the last few nights."

"Well, I haven't," Buffy snapped, "because I've been out there on the street, part of their dog fest." She held out a forearm that had a nice grid of scratch marks on it.

"Oh, my!" Giles said with concern. "Have you had these wounds treated?"

"Later. I expect to get a lot more of them before I'm done."

"Why fight coyotes?" Giles asked in astonishment. "They're usually not a danger to humans."

Buffy rolled her eyes and began to pace. "Before I go into the gory details, is it possible for there to be *werecoyotes*?"

"Certainly," Giles answered. "The phenomenon of humans

turning into animals has been reported in the folklore of every culture on earth. In Africa, there are werecrocodiles; in the South Pacific, weresharks. Werewolves are simply the best known in this country because of our European influence. I believe there are tales of werecoyotes in Native American folklore."

"Can you look it up?" Buffy asked worriedly.

Giles moved stiffly up the stairs and into the stacks of rare books that were kept at the back of the library. He seldom allowed anyone to go into the "Reference Only" section unless he accompanied them. With a troubled frown, Buffy slowly followed him.

Hesitantly, Giles asked, "What makes you think these coyotes you battled were, in reality, human?"

"The way they *looked* at me. Bad breath. Lazy attitude. And a pierced nose," Buffy answered. "And the wiggin' out they were doing in the cemetery. That's our next stop."

"It is?" Giles asked warily. He stopped at a shelf of old books at the back of the room, perused the titles, and pulled out four dusty volumes.

"Why would someone want to be a coyote?" Buffy asked.

Giles frowned thoughtfully. "In this modern age, it would be foolish to be a werewolf. Wolves are too rare, except in the wilderness of places like Alaska and Siberia. But if you were a coyote, you could roam all of the western United States, much of Mexico and Canada, and live close to people. No one would think it odd to see you on the street. After all, coyotes usually don't attack humans."

"Well, these do," Buffy muttered.

Giles opened a book, flipped a few pages, and pointed to a passage. "'Coyote is a popular character in Native American literature and mythology. He's the hero of many tales, and he's usually depicted as a trickster. He's a cunning, curious figure with a penchant for the ladies. Coyote has been known to exchange his skin with that of a man in order to bed the man's wife.'"

The proper librarian raised an eyebrow at this improper suggestion, then went on, "'In one story, Coyote was given the job of guarding the moon, but he used his lofty position to spy on humans and learn their secrets. Coyote is often associated with the moon.'"

"No kidding," Buffy muttered. "*Were*coyotes we're talking about, not *storybook* coyotes."

Giles leveled her with a gaze. "You do know that coyotes are famous for their odd ways. I don't know what you saw them doing, but it could be a natural behavior."

"Giles, remember your job description," Buffy said with frustration. "I decide what's wiggins, and you decide what it is."

"Uh, yes, I see," the librarian said, adjusting his glasses and gazing deeper into his tome. Buffy hated putting the Watcher in his place, but Giles had to trust her gut instinct on this.

"You can laugh at me later, if I'm wrong," she promised.

"I've learned not to laugh at you," Giles said testily. He flipped a few more pages.

After a few minutes of reading, he reported, "I can't find anything about werecoyotes in particular, but there's plenty in here about skinwalkers. You might recall, a skinwalker is a type of sorcerer in Native American tradition. A skinwalker can turn himself into an animal by wearing its skin and performing a secret ceremony. Skinwalkers often live in groups away from other people, and they are considered dangerous and to be avoided."

Buffy shuddered. "That sounds like them, all right. Then I should look for coyote skins."

"I believe that shooting and skinning coyotes is illegal," Giles replied. "Are you ever going to tell me what happened to you?"

"Yes, while you drive me over to the cemetery. First, one more question. Do you know what a Coyote Moon is?"

"I presume it's a phase of the moon and not some new restaurant."

"Moon phase, not burrito phase."

Giles set down his stack of Native American books and searched out a new volume. After a moment of study, he said, "Yes, it's here—a rare phase of the moon. I'm sure you know what a Blue Moon is."

Buffy nodded confidently. "Sure, a song they play on the oldies channel."

The librarian winced. "No, it's the second full moon of the month. Of course, most months don't have two full moons, so a Blue Moon is relatively unusual."

He located a passage in his book and began to read: "'*Coyote Moon* is a folk term used in the southwestern United States for a rare phase of the moon. A Coyote Moon is a Blue Moon which rises red on the ninth lunar month in August. The appearance of a Coyote Moon is often associated with trickery and magic.'"

"And all that other wiggins stuff about coyotes," Buffy added.

Giles squinted thoughtfully. "This is late August—the right time of year for a Coyote Moon. I haven't gotten out much, but I think it's nearly a full moon."

"It is, believe me."

"I should run some calculations and see if a Coyote Moon is coming tonight or tomorrow."

"Later," Buffy replied. "That was just something I heard—it might not be related. Right now, we've got to go to the cemetery and see whose grave was getting the coyote treatment. Then warn Willow and Xander."

Giles snapped his book shut. "You don't have any proof at all about these so-called werecoyotes, do you?"

"Nope," she admitted. "If I saw one of them pull on a ratty old coyote skin and morph into a wild animal, I would tell you."

"All right," Giles said, tapping the pockets of his sweater-vest. "Let me find my car keys and get a notebook, and we'll be on our way."

• • •

Willow studied Lonnie's chiseled features, blond stubble of beard, and blue eyes, and she thought: *It's probably hard to take a bath when you're living in a vacant lot.* Perhaps that explained the earthy odor emanating from his person. A lot of girls wouldn't mind it—and Willow wasn't exactly gagging—but she did like her dates to be a bit more well groomed than Lonnie.

She liked them like Xander. Well, normally she liked Xander's style, but he had also affected the scruffy carnival look—greasy jeans, a stained T-shirt, and that mustache thing under his lip. *The third armpit,* she thought with a chuckle. Lonnie, Xander, and Rose turned to look at her.

"Something funny?" Rose asked with a sneer.

"No," Willow answered, stirring her soda with her straw. "I'm just having fun."

"Good," Lonnie said with an easy smile.

The four of them were sitting outside at a table and chairs by a corn dog and lemonade stand. Because the carnival wasn't open yet and the rides weren't running, the only people milling around were the carnies and their invited guests. Several kids from town had apparently stuck up friendships with the carnies—Willow saw about half a dozen of them.

It would be great to hang out with Lonnie and Xander at the closed carnival, Willow thought, *if only I can get rid of Rose*. For some reason, the sexy dark-haired girl didn't seem to like Willow very much. Or maybe she was just a naturally obnoxious person, like Cordelia.

"Where's your other friend?" Rose asked.

"My other friend?" Willow smiled. "Oh, you mean Buffy. I almost expected her to be here."

"And crash our date?" Xander muttered. "I hope not. Buffy doesn't date very much."

"Why?" Lonnie asked.

Willow shot Xander a warning look, and he shrugged. "She's sort of like . . . like a nun."

"She didn't dress like a nun," Lonnie said with a grin.

"She's a junior nun," Xander answered.

Rose shook her head. "Nun or no nun, that was a great throw she made last night, the one that sank Eddie. She should be pitching in the big leagues."

"She's more the cheerleader type," Willow remarked.

"Why are we talking about *her*?" Xander asked, grabbing Rose's hand and gazing into her dark, vivid eyes. "There's only one girl in the whole world for me—my Rose of San Antonio."

Now Willow began to gag, but she kept her cool. "What are we going to do next?" she asked brightly.

"Let me see," Lonnie said, tapping his chiseled chin. "We showed you the office, the light panel, the motors, the trailers, the generators, and the trucks. And the air compressor."

"I'll never forget the air compressor," Willow said, trying to sound enthusiastic.

"Would you like to see where we sleep?" Rose asked.

Xander nodded as if his head was on a spring, but he tried to stay cool. "Yeah, yeah! That would be great!"

"Where you sleep?" Willow repeated uncertainly. "Don't you sleep . . . right here?"

Lonnie gave her a dimpled smile. "Well, not right here in the dirt. We each have our own trailer, although some of us have roommates. Rose and I have seniority, so we don't have roommates. Do we, Rose?"

"Not unless we want them," she said with a sly smile. The carny jumped up from the table and pulled Xander up with her. "Enough talk, let's party."

Xander grinned stupidly, as if he had been hit on the head by a baseball bat. Like a farmer leading a lamb to the slaughter, Rose dragged the poor boy away from the table. "See you later!" she called back.

Willow leaped up. "Wait a minute! Aren't we going with them?"

"Why?" Lonnie asked, rising to his feet and towering over her. He touched her cheek with his callused hand and angled her face toward his. "There's only so much you can do on a double date, before you have to make it a single date."

Reluctantly, Willow pulled away from him. "But I . . . I haven't seen the *fun house* yet! Yes, I always dreamed of being inside a fun house . . . when there was nobody else there."

She turned and looked for Xander and Rose, but they were gone. In a panic, she feared that Xander might be gone forever. How could she, or even Buffy, compete with a girl who had tattoos?

"Okay," Lonnie said. "Let's make your dreams come true."

Wrapping his brawny arm around her slender waist, he led Willow toward the fun house at the end of the midway. It loomed ahead of them—a metal facade with a painted mural depicting lovely scenes of murder, mayhem, and decapitation. Scantily clad women ran screaming from gooey, bloody monsters.

This was actually *not* the kind of place that Willow had always dreamed of exploring when it was closed, but she had to back up her lie.

When they got closer to the fun house, she noticed that the entrance was shut and locked with a padlock. "It's locked!" she said cheerfully. "We can't get in."

"Not to worry." With a smile, Lonnie pulled a hefty ring of keys off the belt buckle of his jeans. "I work here, remember?"

He strode toward the fun house in his dusty cowboy boots and climbed the stairs to the entrance, while Willow stood and mentally wrung her hands. She wondered if she should try to escape, but it took only an instant for Lonnie to unlock the padlock.

If I run now, she reasoned, *that will leave Xander alone and unprotected. Well, not exactly alone* . . .

Lonnie pushed the door of the fun house open and motioned toward the darkness. "After you, sweetheart."

CHAPTER FIVE

Although the sun was shining brightly, Buffy and Giles walked slowly through the cemetery. They could see their destination in the distance, a white spire that towered over the other tombstones and mausoleums. They moved cautiously, not because of vampires or coyotes but because of the police. Two squad cars sat in the parking lot, and Buffy was sure the police were investigating the grave she had visited last night.

Even before they saw the cops, Buffy heard the disembodied voices droning on their radios. She nearly turned back, preferring to wait until after they had left, but she kept walking.

It wasn't that Buffy feared the police, it was just that they were in her way. Most of the time, they didn't believe her when she told them the truth. Of course, if they ever did believe her, they would probably lock her up for sticking wooden stakes in dead people who were still walking around. When it came to the supernatural, the police were extremely dense.

She was relieved to see just two uniformed officers standing near the spire and the molested grave. Withered flowers were strewn all over the grave site and the surrounding lawn. The cops weren't in heavy investigational mode, with yellow tape blocking off the site and techies crawling all over one another. They were just checking things out.

"I presume that is the grave," Giles whispered. "Should we go down while the police are there?"

"Might as well," Buffy answered. "I want to find out who called them."

The pert Slayer strode ahead of the cautious Watcher, and the two police officers turned to observe her. She strode up to the grave, which was covered with fresh holes that looked as if they had been dug by dogs looking for bones.

"Please stay away, miss," one of the officers warned. "Crime scene."

"Okay." Before Buffy stepped back, she took a long look at the letters carved into the massive tombstone. The largest letters spelled a strange name—Spurs Hardaway—and there were Wild West sheriff's stars beside his name, as if he was some sort of lawman.

"What happened?" she asked dumbly.

"That's what we're trying to find out," the younger of the two cops answered, giving her a friendly smile.

"It's none of your business," the gray-haired older cop grumbled. "Why don't you just run along?"

Buffy glanced at Giles, who was hiding a smile. He knew she hated it when people were condescending toward her.

"Okay," Buffy said. "I'll go away. But I know exactly who did it."

As she strode away, the two cops staggered up the hill after her. "Wait a minute, miss! You know about this?" the younger one asked.

"I have a theory," she said teasingly. "You must have some clues. Who called you?"

"The groundskeeper," the older cop answered. "He found the grave all messed up and called us. There's always trouble in this cemetery—I'd like to pave it over."

"Me too," Buffy muttered.

The cop gave her a quizzical look, then gazed at the grave. "It doesn't look like regular vandalism—more like wild animals were rooting around. So why don't you tell us what *you* know?"

"I think those coyotes did it," Buffy said angrily. "I live nearby, and I've seen a big pack of them running around the cemetery the last few nights."

The young cop snapped his fingers and turned to his partner. "That's got to be it, Joe. We've had a lot of calls about coyotes all this week. You know, it's the dry season, and they come down from the hills looking for water."

Joe nodded sagely. "Yes, I believe we've cracked this case, with the little lady's help. Now we can turn it over to Animal Control."

"If we only knew *why* they tore up the grave," the young cop grumbled.

"Why do I eat doughnuts? Why is the best wrestling on pay-per-view? You don't need a why with coyotes," his partner scoffed. "They're just plain weird."

Buffy peered innocently at the grave again, and Giles edged closer too. "Is this guy anyone important?" she asked. "Who is Spurs Hardaway?"

The young cop grinned. "Only Joe here is old enough to answer that one."

The old cop scowled. "How quickly they forget. Spurs Hardaway used to be a big Wild West star toward the end of the last century. I mean, he was as big as Buffalo Bill Cody and Annie Oakley. He had a combination Wild West and magic show, which toured all over the world."

"So how come he's buried here?" Buffy asked with amazement. "In Sunnydale?"

The cop shrugged. "I don't know the whole story. I only know he settled here after he retired from showbiz. He was already old when he died—shot to death, he was."

"Exactly one hundred years ago," Giles said, looking at the dates on the tombstone.

"Yes, that would be about right," the cop agreed.

"It was a big deal back then, this celebrity getting murdered in our little town."

The young cop looked back at the mauled grave.

"Maybe the flowers on this grave had been freshly watered, and they were only trying to get a drink."

"More than likely," the older cop agreed.

Hardly likely, Buffy thought. She turned to Giles. "I think we can go now."

"Absolutely!" he said, his eyes gleaming with excitement. Now that he had a ton of things to research, the librarian was happy.

"Thanks for your help!" the younger cop called as they walked away.

"Anytime!" Buffy answered, marveling that the police had actually believed her about something. Instead of being reassuring, this only made her doubt her own theory. What if they really were just coyotes acting like . . . coyotes?

"Buffy, I apologize," Giles said when they got out of earshot of the police. "This case is sufficiently unusual to make me think we should investigate it. After all, anybody who settles down in Sunnydale—near the Hellmouth—is automatically suspicious. First, I'll research Spurs Hardaway, then I'll do more work on skinwalkers and Coyote Moon. I wonder if I should ask Willow to help me."

"Willow!" Buffy's eyes lit up with terror. "Oh my gosh, I left them alone with those major creeps!"

"What creeps?" Giles asked in alarm.

Buffy jogged ahead of him toward the car. "First, drive me to the carnival, then you can do your research. Come on! There's no telling what nasty stuff is happening to Xander and Willow."

"Oh, dear!" Giles muttered, running to catch up.

In the dark stillness of the fun house, Willow melted into Lonnie's strong arms. She lifted her chin so that their lips could meet, and it was instant polarity—the current flowed from his lips to hers and back through their bodies, molding them together.

I didn't want this to happen, she told herself, *but it's not too bad.* As he kissed her tenderly, she began to lose her regrets. She hadn't been kissed like this since . . . well, never!

What about Xander? the loyal part of her brain reminded her. *Who?* answered the rest of her brain and most of her body.

His kisses moved from Willow's lips down to her neck, and his blond hair brushed against her nose. Suddenly her senses were filled with the earthy smell of Lonnie's hair, and she pulled back a bit in surprise.

But Lonnie's kisses on her neck grew more insistent, and she worried—not that he was a vampire but that he would give her a hickey! As Willow squirmed to get away from him, grimy strings hanging from the ceiling brushed against her face, and she almost screamed.

I'm in a deserted fun house, she told herself, *with a guy who thinks I'm a carnival ride!*

What would Buffy do?

She decided not to knee Lonnie in the groin, but she did pry his lips from her neck and push him firmly away. "Please, Lonnie, no!" she insisted. "I need a break."

He gave her a hurt look. "Hey, honey, you wanted to come in here—when it was dark and deserted, and we were all alone. Remember?"

She nodded breathlessly. "I did, and it was all I expected—very dark, very all alone. Now I'm ready to leave."

With his skilled hands, he gently brushed the hair off her face. "What's your rush? Rose and Xander will be busy for a while."

If he was trying to get her to stay, that was the wrong thing to say. She fought off his hands as she stumbled deeper into the spooky fun house. When her foot brushed against a metal plate, a scream sounded and a hideous creature popped out of a barrel.

"Aaagh!" Willow screeched, frightened out of her wits until she realized that the monster was just another thrill in the fun house.

Lonnie's arms were all around her again, trying to be comforting. "What's the matter, Willow? What's your hang-up?"

"We're just going too fast, that's all," she answered, trying not to whine or whimper. "I mean, I just met you last night."

"And tomorrow night, I could be gone," he said glumly.

"That's the way it is in show business. We don't have much time."

"We'll have to *make* time," she insisted, pushing him away. "You know, like have a few more dates."

"That's great," Lonnie said with a derisive laugh. "I'm working every night, and you want to go out on *dates*."

"I'm sorry, that's just the way I am. Sort of proper."

Lonnie nodded, and he was once again calm and reasonable. "Okay, Willow, we'll play by your rules. Let's get to know each other first."

She smiled with relief. "That would be nice."

"You've got to come by the carnival every free moment—like tonight after it closes."

"Tonight?" she asked with a gulp.

"After midnight."

Willow tried to sound brave. "Okay, tonight after midnight."

"It'll be our second date," Lonnie said, holding her hands. "We'll get to know each other so well, I'll be like your high school sweetheart."

"Oh, yeah," Willow said with a nervous laugh. *"Him!"*

"And I'll work as hard as I can to make sure the carnival stays in Sunnydale for as long as possible. Maybe a month." He gave her a tender kiss on the cheek, like a true gentleman. "I suppose I should go out there and do some work. Want to watch me oil the Octopus?"

"Sure," Willow answered with false enthusiasm. "Let's oil that sucker."

Lonnie isn't a monster, Willow thought, *just a handsome guy who is used to getting his way with girls.* Deep down, he seemed to respect her, and he genuinely wanted to see her again. Maybe it was unusual to have a date at midnight, but that was the soonest they could get together. At least the summer was no longer boring.

Feeling a new tenderness toward Lonnie, Willow let him hold her hand and guide her through the dark fun house.

Xander stood outside a small, beat-up trailer, listening to thudding and clunking noises as Rose cleaned up her living quarters. For some reason, she wouldn't just let him come in; she had to put things away first. In a way, this was reassuring, because it made her seem more like a regular girl. Nothing else was regular about her.

Rose was worldly, had a great body, and was a terrific kisser. Xander tried not to wonder what she was doing with someone like *him.* There was always the possibility that she thought Buffy was his girlfriend, and since she didn't like Buffy, she was trying to hurt her by stealing her boyfriend. Xander was not going to say or do anything to dissuade her from this notion. If it would help, he would say he was *married* to Buffy.

Even Willow had found a summer romance at the carnival. It was truly a magical place, although it looked better at night under the twirling neon than during the harsh light of day. In the sunlight, the trailer, rides, and booths looked old and grungy, as if they had been touring for centuries.

Xander put these grim thoughts out of his mind and concentrated on happy thoughts. *Maybe the carnival will stay forever, or maybe I can find a way to stay with the carnival—and Rose—forever.*

Suddenly, the door of the trailer creaked open, and Rose stood there, wearing a Japanese silk robe and not much else. His gaze traveled up her tanned, well-shaped legs to the giant dragon splashed across her chest, and he gulped.

"Come in," the dark-haired seductress said.

In his rush, Xander stumbled as he entered an old one-room camper that was even stranger than he could have imagined. There were prints and paintings on every inch of the walls, shelves full of strange animal figurines, a big wooden sea chest, a tiny bed, and what looked like a torture chamber in the corner. Or maybe it was an ancient dentist's chair. Whatever it was, the corroded needles and tubes didn't look very inviting.

On top of this, the smoke of heavily scented incense floated around Rose's cramped quarters. Xander tried not to cough, but finally he could hold it no longer—he burst out with a large hack.

"Poor boy," Rose said with amusement. "Can't stand a little smoke? The incense will clear your senses."

"My senses have never been clearer!" Xander croaked. Now he knew where Rose got her husky voice. He lurched forward through the smoke and banged his foot on the big sea chest. "Ow!" he groaned. "What's in this thing, an anchor?"

When he touched the dark wood and brass fittings, Rose bolted to her feet with fire in her eyes. “Don’t touch that chest!”

“Sorry,” Xander said, backing up and bumping into a shelf of pewter dragons, bears, and wolves. He knocked several of them onto the floor with a clatter.

“Sorry,” he said again, even more sheepishly. He reached down to pick up the figurines.

“Just leave them,” Rose ordered with exasperation. She sank onto her tiny mattress, which was built more for her petite frame than Xander’s.

“Come sit over here, it’s safer.”

When she patted the edge of her bed, Xander was there like a guided missile. “Nice bed,” he gushed. “I mean, nice place! Nice *everything*!”

“It’s home,” she said with a shrug. “The towns change around us, but my lair stays the same.”

“Your lair,” Xander echoed with a laugh. He looked around with amazement. “It is almost like a cave.”

“Isn’t it, though.”

“How long have you been doing this?” Xander asked. He quickly added, “I mean, traveling with the carnival.”

“A long time.” She squeezed his shoulders as if he were a side of beef. “I’m older than I look.”

He gave a high-pitched giggle at her tickling fingers, then tried to compose himself. “Well, you look great, no matter how old you are.”

"Take your shirt off," she ordered.

"Shirt. Okay!" Xander said enthusiastically. He fumbled with the buttons, couldn't get them open, and ended up ripping the shirt off his own back. Then he grinned stupidly at her. "I never did like that shirt."

"You're so funny," she said, studying his naked back and shoulders. "Now, where do you want your tattoo?"

Xander blinked at her. "Tattoo?" From the corner of his eye, he again noticed the archaic tubes and needles on the contraption in the corner. *Uh-oh.*

"I want to brand you, you know," she said with a wink. "Show everyone that you're *mine*."

"Uh, what kind of tattoo am I going to get?" Xander asked, trying to stall for time.

"A rose, of course."

"Of course!" He laughed nervously. "I've seen your rose tattoo. I suppose you have more than that?"

"Oh, many. Would you like to see them?"

"Yes," Xander rasped, trying not to drool.

She teasingly touched his nose with a lacquered red fingernail. "I bet you would. But you can't see most of them until you get to know me better. Here's a little one you can see."

Rose lifted the hem of her silky robe and showed him a tattoo of a scorpion high on her hip. Her tan went all the way up, and she didn't appear to be wearing any underwear.

"Nice," Xander breathed. The incense and Rose were both doing a job on him—his senses were on overload.

As he reached to touch the scorpion, she dropped the hem of her robe and pointed to her ankle, where there was a tiny blue star. "I love that little star," she said. "And you should see my moon."

"And . . . and where is that?"

"Where a moon ought to be." Rose winked at him, stood, and crossed to the tattoo machine in the corner. "You didn't tell me where you wanted your tattoo."

"Uh, well—" Xander gulped and rose uneasily to his feet. "You know, I really hadn't thought too much about getting a tattoo—until now. I think I should study them, look at some books, and think about all the possible places you could put one."

He grinned. "Maybe if I saw more of *your* tattoos, that would inspire me."

Rose sauntered back to him and wrapped her arms around his neck. She pulled him tantalizingly close to her. "You're a smart boy, aren't you? You're not going to give something for nothing. You *will* belong to Rose, whether you wear her brand or not."

"That's okay with me," Xander said heavily, his lips almost touching hers.

"The carnival closes at midnight," she whispered. "Come back and meet me, and you'll see the stars, the moon . . . and everything else."

"Midnight," he muttered as his lips eagerly found hers.

Xander tried to control himself, but he kissed like a man

in a vacuum chamber, gasping for air. He wanted to consume her, to drink her, to *breathe* her! Nothing was ever so wonderful as her embrace, especially when she pressed her body against his and ran her fingernails through his hair. Just when he thought he could stand no more, the door banged open.

Both of them jumped with surprise, and they turned to see an ominous figure standing in the doorway, silhouetted in bright sunlight. Xander was reminded of old westerns, when the hero strides into a saloon to clean out the bad guys.

"Buffy!" he gasped. "What are you doing here?"

She ignored him and strode right up to Rose. "Okay, Thorny, turn him loose."

"He's mine now," Rose declared. She dropped her hands and balled them into fists.

Xander quickly grabbed her hands and tried to put them back on his neck. "No, no, don't turn me loose! Hold on to me. I might get away!"

But the mood was broken, as Buffy and Rose glared laser beams at each other. *Gosh,* Xander thought, *things could be worse. They're both beautiful, and they're fighting over me!*

"That's all right, ladies, there's plenty enough to go around," he assured them. *But, Buffy, why don't you split now—I'm on a date,* he tried to tell her with his eyes.

The Slayer never took her eyes off Rose. "Xander, there's something I've got to tell you about these people. Can you wait outside?"

"*You* wait outside!" Rose snapped, pushing Buffy toward

the door. When the Slayer dropped into her fighting stance, Xander feared that Rose would get a mouthful of feet.

"Oh, are you going to do some kung fu on me?" the carny asked with a laugh. "I think you watch too much TV."

"Don't get into a fight with her!" Xander warned.

"I'm already in a fight with her." Rose whirled around in a lightning-fast motion and slugged Buffy, sending her tumbling out the door into the dusty midway.

While Buffy writhed on her back, Rose sprang out of the trailer and landed on her throat, snarling like a wild animal. It took every ounce of Buffy's strength to keep the dark-haired woman's teeth from her throat, but the Slayer finally pushed her off and rolled free.

Both women jumped to their feet and circled each other warily. Fortunately, the carnival was still closed, so there weren't any witnesses to this fight, except for Xander.

"Come on, Buffy," Xander pleaded. "You're taking this thing too far! Fighting doesn't solve anything. If only you had told me how you felt about me, and that you were so jealous—"

"Jealous?" Buffy asked in amazement. "Xander, I only wanted to talk to you for a second."

"You couldn't leave me a message?" he wailed.

Rose finally doubled over, laughing. "You two are a real pair! It's been fun, Xander, but I've got to go to work. If you want to ditch this confused teenybopper for a real woman, you know where to find me, and what time." With that, Rose stalked into her trailer and slammed the door shut behind her.

"Confused teenybopper?" Buffy muttered angrily.

"You *are* confused!" Xander shouted, waving his arms in exasperation. "And you're acting like a teenybopper. First you bust into Rose's trailer, assault my date, and then you say it was for *no reason*!"

Buffy lowered her voice. "I did it to save you."

"*Save* me!" he shrieked. "You saved me from the one thing in the world I *least* want to be saved from!"

"Your love life is not the issue," Buffy said. "Your life—"

"My life? These people have been real nice to me and Willow. And they haven't done anything to you! Sure, maybe they try to make a few bucks from the locals, but that makes them *normal*! You're the only one who's acting crazy around here. These people are not monsters."

Buffy grabbed his sleeve. "Come with me to the library. Let's sit down with Giles and—"

"The only monster is *you*!" Xander snapped, yanking his arm away from her. "It's not part of your job description to ruin my dates."

He stormed off toward the midway, and Buffy chased after him. "When are you supposed to see her again?"

Xander covered his ears. "I'm not hearing you—you're not here!"

"Where's Willow?"

"I don't know, and I wouldn't tell you even if I did know!" He turned and glared at her. "You didn't want me, Buffy, so mellow out."

• • •

As Xander stalked off, Buffy stood dumbfounded in the middle of the deserted carnival. *Boy, I sure messed that up*. Not only had she failed to save Xander, but she had driven him toward the enemy. Of course, the enemy was shapely and pretty, so it didn't take much to lose Xander. Even if she found Willow, she doubted she could make her believe that the carnies were really werecoyotes.

The only real evidence she had was a chewed-up dog collar. The rest of it was just hunches and gut instinct. It was even possible that she was wrong, in which case she may have lost a good friend for nothing.

Could Xander be right? Was part of her reaction caused by jealousy? Being cute and cuddly, Buffy had always taken boys for granted, and that was fine in her previous life. Since becoming the Slayer, however, her love life had gone down the garbage disposal. Normally, this strengthened her bond with Willow and Xander, who were hopeless in romance for other reasons—but since the carnival they had suddenly gotten hot love lives. All Buffy had was a weird, majorly dangerous job whose pay stank.

She took a deep breath and tried to squelch the feeling-sorry-for-herself routine. Fighting evil had to be its own reward. Even though she had alienated one of her best friends, Buffy had learned one thing: Rose was unusually strong for a human. Her strength and agility made her a match for Buffy, or even a vampire. Once again, that was a nice thing to know, but it didn't prove anything.

The Slayer brushed the dust off her shirt and jeans, then began to stroll nonchalantly out of the carnival. When she had entered, there were a handful of carnies working and hanging out—she had asked one of them how to get to Rose's trailer. Now they were gone, except for one.

Hopscotch, the man with the coyote eyes, stood watching her from the deck of the Tilt-a-Whirl. His craggy face looked full of suspicion and disappointed at the same time, and he was wiping his hands on a grimy rag. Buffy felt like asking him a few questions, but she had picked enough fights for one day. She put her head down and hurried on her way.

Maybe Giles would have some answers.

CHAPTER SIX

Buffy wandered into the darkened school library and found Giles hunched over a table full of old books. Only one small desk lamp was turned on, and he had six books open underneath it. His nose was buried inside a large coffee-table book full of colorful paintings, and he was rapidly scribbling notes.

"Hi," she said, causing him to lift his chin and finally acknowledge her presence.

"Hello!" he answered cheerfully. "Spurs Hardaway turns out to be a fascinating character—just the sort of person to live in Sunnydale. Um, how are Xander and Willow?"

"They're fabulous, I guess." Buffy shrugged and slumped

into a chair across the table from him. "Xander's mad at me, and Willow's disappeared. Even her mother doesn't know where she is—only that she won't be home until late tonight. Of course, neither one of them wants to hear anything from *me*."

"What do you mean?" Giles asked in alarm.

"I mean we can't count on them this time. They're on the other side, giving aid and comfort to the enemy."

Giles nodded thoughtfully. "I presume you still think that the carnival workers are the werecoyotes?"

"Yes, but I don't have any proof, except for a dog collar," Buffy muttered. "Xander is really ga-ga over his carnival babe, and Willow is in the clutches of a super-hunk with lots of smooth lines."

She could tell that Giles was trying to phrase his next remark delicately. "You seem awfully certain about this, but it is *possible* that the carnival folk are harmless."

Buffy rolled her eyes. "You haven't met them. Even if they're not werecoyotes, they're far from harmless."

"But that's a decision Xander and Willow should make for themselves."

"Duh! I know everybody thinks I'm playing Mrs. Brady, but I know what I know . . . or what I feel." Buffy tossed her honey-blond hair. "Enough about Xander and Willow—what did you find out?"

"This will give you some idea of how popular Spurs Hardaway was." Giles picked up the coffee-table book he was reading and set it in front of her. Buffy had thought it was a book of paintings, but now that she got a closer look, she saw that it was a collection of old theatrical posters.

On the left page was a colorful painting depicting a long-haired mountain man surrounded by wolves, buffaloes, bears, and mountain lions. Below this was a scene of Indians on horseback circling a flaming covered wagon.

Banner headlines on the poster proclaimed, "Spurs Hardaway and the Thrilling Magic of the Wild West! Witness the Vicious Indian Attack! Gasp at Animals Never Before Seen in New York! Relive the Magic and Romance of the West!"

On the right page was another heroic portrait of Spurs Hardaway, this time wrestling a bear. Below that was an illustration of what looked like a rodeo parade, with lots of bespangled cowboys and Indians. At the bottom of the page was a scene of Spurs and a mountain lion inside a golden cage. But the writing on this poster was all in French.

"That's from his triumphant European tour in 1889," Giles said, pointing to the French poster. "By all accounts, Spurs Hardaway put on a magnificent show, with a cast of more than two hundred cowboys and wild animals. It was a combination rodeo, stuntman, circus, and magic act."

"So he was the Siegfried and Roy of his day."

"Who? Listen to this—his most famous magic trick was to climb into a cage, have the cage covered with a velvet curtain, and then turn himself into a wild animal! There are eyewitness accounts of Hardaway turning himself into a wolf, a mountain lion, and a bear."

Buffy narrowed her eyes at the Watcher. "Just because he did that trick doesn't mean he *really* turned into a wolf or a bear."

"*Au contraire*," Giles answered triumphantly. "Spurs Hardaway claimed that he really *could* turn himself into a wild animal, a trick he said he learned from the Plains Indians. At the time, his critics dismissed this claim as mere publicity, but what if he were telling the truth? We know that skinwalkers exist, and there were reportedly other performers in his troupe who could turn themselves into animals."

"Wow," Buffy said, getting a queasy feeling in her stomach. "But it could still be a trick—magicians do it today."

Giles shook his head. "Not like Spurs Hardaway did it. He did this trick everywhere—in circus tents, stadiums, saloons, even in jail cells. Turning oneself into a bear or a wolf is not a simple trick—you need a proper theater with a stage that has a trapdoor. Do you remember the badges on his tombstone?"

"Yes."

"In his youth, Spurs Hardaway was an Army scout and a federal marshal, and he spent many years living among the Indians. That was before they learned to be wary of white men."

"So he took Skinwalking 101," Buffy said. "But what is his connection to Sunnydale?"

"In 1895, he retired here, although his Wild West show kept touring without him. In fact, Spurs owned a great deal of land in the area—he was one of the founding fathers of Sunnydale. Suspicious, isn't it? I think he knew that he was right on top of a tremendous source of occult energy, although he may not have known how to access it."

"But he was mortal. He did die."

"Yes, and that's highly suspicious too." Giles paused for dramatic effect. "On his eighty-first birthday, Spurs was shot to death in his home—with a silver bullet. His murderer was never caught."

Buffy rose to her feet and began to pace. "You know, it's not much of a leap from being in a Wild West show to being in a carnival. City after city. Bad food after cheap food. Sawdust. Stuffed animals. It's the same kind of job, really, only the scam is different. Suppose the carnies are his followers from way back when, and they're still touring. Only now they can't do a Wild West show—p.c. police and all—so they have to do a cheesy carnival."

"It makes sense," Giles agreed.

Buffy frowned. "No, it doesn't. Most of them are too young. They're hardly older than me."

"Not necessarily," Giles said. "They could derive tremendous power from skinwalking. Throughout the ages, shapeshifting has been regarded as an advanced shamanistic skill. Anybody who has mastered it has undoubtedly mastered other spells, and the ability to look young could be one of them. When he died, Spurs Hardaway was said to look no older than a man of forty, even though he was eighty-one."

The Watcher's jaw clenched in anger. "They've taken a

formidable power from the Native Americans and have completely perverted it. It's possible that they could be very skilled sorcerers."

"And they keep their secret safe by living in a carnival," Buffy added. "Always on the move, going from town to town—so nobody knows that they never grow old."

"Exactly! But they are mortal. We know that they can be killed by the traditional silver projectile."

Buffy frowned at that notion as she continued to pace. "Yeah, I know we could kill them, but they aren't exactly vampires. I mean, they aren't running around ripping people's throats open. They attacked *me*, but that's because they know I'm onto them. Otherwise, they've only done small stuff, minor vandalism."

"Are you saying, after all this urgency, that these were-coyotes aren't dangerous?"

"That all depends. As carnies, they'll take your money and seduce your friends," Buffy said bitterly. "As coyotes, they'll eat your dog and dig up an old grave—but we can't *kill* them for any of that. We can't even go to the police, without giving them a good laugh."

Giles pushed his glasses up the bridge of his nose. "I see what you mean. They have behaved badly, but not that badly. Plus, there's the irksome problem that we don't have any proof."

"If only we knew why they're back here in Sunnydale. Why now? What were they doing in the cemetery last night, looking for bones in their old boss's grave?"

The Watcher suddenly looked grim. "There's one thing I forgot to tell you—about Coyote Moon. I did some calculations, and *tonight* is a Coyote Moon. Also, it's exactly one hundred years since Spurs Hardaway was murdered. Perhaps, like a vampire, he can be resurrected one hundred years after his death."

Buffy let out a low breath. "Last night, the freaky coyotes did look like they were doing some kind of ceremony."

"We'll never know if any of these theories are true unless we observe them firsthand or find irrefutable evidence."

"Coyote skins," the Slayer said. "If we're right, each one of them has to have his own coyote skin. I've got to find out for sure."

"*We've* got to find out," Giles said forcefully. "I insist upon coming with you. There's no more useful research I can do here, and four eyes are better than two."

She pointed to his glasses and smiled. "You should know."

"What can we bring? I may have a few silver bullets in the weapons locker."

Buffy winced. "Let's try not to kill any of them, okay? Some of them are kind of cute. Besides, if we can get proof, at least we can tell Willow and Xander to stay away from them."

She gazed worriedly out the window and saw the burning embers of sunset stretching across the sky. "I only hope Willow and Xander are all right."

"Ante up, boys," Willow said, forming her gigantic pile of poker chips into several neat stacks. The tiny trailer was smoky with tobacco and incense, but Willow figured she had won about two hundred dollars from the carnies so far. She could stand the smoke a little while longer, if they could stand the heat.

She shuffled the deck. “Shall we keep it five-card draw, deuces and one-eyed jacks wild?”

“How are you winning so much?” Lonnie grumbled. “You didn’t tell me you were a poker shark.”

Willow grinned. “Well, I do quite well against my family when we’re playing for Monopoly money. I guess that skill carries over into real money. Poker is a mathematical game, after all, with probabilities and risk factors that can be calculated. Money management is also important.”

An old carny with strange, rheumy eyes scowled and picked up his pathetic handful of chips. “Cash me out. I can’t beat this poker witch! Next time, Lonnie, don’t bring no ringers into the game.”

“Hey, Hopscotch, I didn’t know!” the blond-haired hunk insisted. “I loaned her five bucks so she could play a few hands. Who knew?”

Willow cheerfully counted the old man’s chips and gave him $3.75. “It was a pleasure meeting you.”

“Right,” he grumbled. “I’m going outside to keep a lookout for that vandal before we open up.”

“You have a vandal?” Willow asked in alarm.

The old man gave her a sneer. “Just someone who wants to screw things up for us. We’ll catch ’em.”

"Why don't you tell the police?"

Hopscotch rubbed the gray stubble on his chin. "We don't hold with outsiders knowing our business. In the carnival, we have our own brand of justice."

"I see," Willow said with a nervous smile.

"Come on, *deal*!" growled one of the players, a bare-chested young carny with long dark hair. Hopscotch waved and ambled out the door.

"You didn't ante up," Willow said, and the young man scowled and tossed two fifty-cent chips into the pile. Willow shuffled the cards and dealt to him, Lonnie, a third carny, and herself. She decided not to be so ruthless; maybe she would even give them some of their money back.

"Remind me never to play strip poker with you," Lonnie said with a wink.

Willow blushed. "Okay, I won't let it cross your mind."

"We might as well be playing strip poker," the guy without a shirt muttered. "Any more hands like this, and I'll be lucky to have my underwear."

"I can only give you fifty cents for your underwear," Willow joked. "I think that's more than generous."

Lonnie laughed. "I'll give you two cents."

Still smiling, Willow picked up her cards and saw two queens and a two, which was a wild card. Even before drawing any more cards, she already had three queens. *No sense denying it,* Willow thought cheerfully, *it's my lucky day*.

• • •

Xander snored loudly as he lay in his bed, sleeping through dinner. He had asked his mother not to wake him—not even for food—because he had a date planned and he needed to rest up for it. As he grinned in peaceful slumber, Xander dreamed of blue tattoos on creamy brown skin.

When Buffy and Giles strolled into the carnival at sunset, it seemed like a ghost town just coming to life after a long slumber. One by one, the neon lights twinkled on, and the towering machines grumbled to life. With creaks and groans, the mighty arms of the Octopus and the Ferris wheel began to rotate, lighting up the sky with sweeping rainbows of color. French fries, corn dogs, and fry bread bubbled in vats of grease, lending a homey smell to the air. Surfer music blared from crackling speakers.

It was as if every night were the same, just a continuation of the night before.

Buffy noticed families with children roaming around the kiddie rides, but most of them would be gone in another hour or so. The carnival after dark was a world of young people, shady people, and night people. Giles stood beside Buffy, gaping at the gaudy attractions and the milling crowd of teenagers.

"Oh, my," Giles muttered. "Western civilization is in more trouble than I thought."

Buffy sighed. "Well, nobody forces the kids to come here. We do it of our own free will."

"Terrifying," Giles agreed. "So where do we begin searching in this den of depravity?"

Buffy lowered her voice. "Time for a fashion check. I'm afraid we have to sneak into somebody's trailer, as I don't think they carry their coyote skins in their back pockets. I know where Rose's trailer is, but first let's see if she's working at the moment."

With Buffy leading the way, they strode down the midway, ignoring the barkers who kept trying to lure them into rides and games. She kept her eyes open for Hopscotch, who was probably spying on her from the shadows, but she didn't see the old carny. Perhaps he was actually working tonight, since there was a big crowd and all the rides were whirling at once.

As they walked, Giles gaped at the rides, the games, the food stands, and the people. When he saw a young girl eating a huge spool of blue cotton candy, he followed her for several strides. Buffy had to grab his arm and drag him back into the real world.

"Did you see what she was eating?" Giles asked in amazement. "It looked like . . . like ectoplasm!"

"What's ectoplasm?" Buffy asked.

"The nebulous material from which ghosts are made."

"Oh, it *tastes* like ectoplasm too," Buffy said. "Only with lots of sugar."

"It can't be good for you," Giles concluded.

"Does any of this look like it's good for you? This is one

of those places where you can be a kid and an adult at the same time. That's why teens love it."

Squinting through his glasses, Giles surveyed a row of busy game booths. "I see what you mean about the carnival workers looking rather young and fit, but perhaps that's not unusual. Traveling all the time, living off the land—this would be an occupation for young, fit people."

"I know!" Buffy snapped with frustration. "And maybe it's a coincidence that there's a pack of coyotes running rampant in Sunnydale at the same time. Maybe it's a coincidence that they were digging up Spurs Hardaway's grave, and that he died a hundred years ago today. That's why we have to convince *ourselves* of what's going on before we can convince anyone else."

"Is that your real hair?" a voice barked over a loudspeaker, "or are you wearing a muskrat on your head?"

"We're here." Buffy held out her hand and stopped Giles as they neared the dunking machine. The same clown she had dunked last night was on duty, and he was making fun of an older man wearing a toupee. Also on duty was his partner, the dark-haired vixen Rose. As usual, she was exchanging soggy softballs and sexy pouts for crisp dollar bills, while making fools out of a long line of men.

"Xander's new girlfriend is hard at work," Buffy said.

Giles peered through his glasses. "*That* is the young . . . woman who is interested in Xander?"

"See what I mean?" Buffy asked. "That's just one too

many coincidences. Last night, it seemed as if all the carnies were trying to pick up local kids."

"Onerous behavior, to be sure," Giles said, "but they could be normal lowlifes instead of shape-shifting lowlifes. Unless they commit a crime or we can get proof of what they are, we really can't do anything."

"So let's get our proof." Buffy steered the librarian toward the rides, away from the dunking machine. Taking a circuitous route to the rear of the carnival, they wound up behind the neon lights and painted facades. Back here, the paint was chipped on the beat-up trailers, noisy generators, and smelly garbage cans. It was like the dark slum hidden away from the warm city lights.

With Rose's nondescript trailer in sight, Buffy and Giles crept through the shadows. Hearing voices, they crouched down behind a pile of lumber. They listened warily as two teenagers walked past, taking a shortcut to the parking lot.

"Okay," Buffy whispered. "You stay out here and do what you do—watch—while I go inside. If anybody looks like they're coming to the trailer, knock on the side, then split. I'll get away as best I can, and we'll meet back at your car. Okay?"

Giles gulped and nodded. "I was just thinking that we could be arrested for this."

"Somehow, I don't think this group is big on calling the police. Here goes." Buffy stood and tried the door of the trailer. It was locked, so she grabbed the door handle and snapped it off, as if it was a dried twig. The door of the tiny trailer swung open, and she had to duck to enter.

Once inside, Buffy thought about putting on a light, but she could see fairly well. Through a grimy window, the swirling neon rides splashed a kaleidoscope of colors onto the opposite wall. It was just enough light to see by.

Buffy tried to ignore the weird smell, which was either incense or Rose's cheap perfume. Her eyes scanned the cluttered walls and shelves, but she didn't think that Rose's coyote skin would be hanging in plain sight. *I could never live in this tiny trailer,* Buffy thought. *There isn't any closet space.*

When her eyes hit upon the old wooden sea chest, she knew it was the only possible hiding place for the skin. She bent down to open the trunk and discovered that it had a strong padlock holding the clasp shut. If she had all the time in the world, she could probably loosen the lock without anyone knowing it, but she didn't have all the time in the world. Every second counted.

Buffy gripped the case in one hand and the shackle in the other and pulled the lock apart with a loud *sproing*. A small spring shot across the room, and the lock crumbled to pieces in her hands.

The lid of the old sea chest creaked loudly as she lifted it, and she plunged her hands into the silky contents. It seemed to be full of clothes—only they weren't clothes exactly, more like fancy costumes with fringe and sequins. *Maybe Rose moonlights as a go-go girl,* Buffy thought. Her fingers dug deeper into the pile of fancy clothes, looking for only one thing.

She finally touched it deep at the bottom—the greasy fur of an old pelt! Just as she was about to pull it out and inspect it, a frantic pounding sounded on the wall of the trailer. That was Giles's signal—somebody was coming! Buffy hoped that the Watcher would get away, but she was not about to leave without her prize, her proof.

Then she heard another sound, even closer. From somewhere at the back of the trailer came a low, rumbling growl. The animal could be a coyote, but it sounded bigger—much bigger. And *inside* the trailer.

A shadow loomed in front of her as the unseen beast lunged for her throat!

CHAPTER SEVEN

With no time to think, Buffy lifted the chest and used it as a shield, and the snarling beast crashed into it, splintering the wood and knocking Buffy backward. As slinky go-go outfits cascaded all around them, Buffy and the monster rolled on the floor. She fought to keep the pieces of the chest between them, but the beast was strong and determined. No matter what she did, she felt its hot breath on her throat.

With a karate cry, she punched the creature in its thick, furry neck, causing it to yelp with pain. Keeping on the offensive, Buffy kept punching and kicking until she propelled the beast away from her, then she rolled to her feet and dove out the door.

When she looked up from the ground, she saw four pairs of legs surrounding her. Rough hands grabbed her and dragged her to her feet, and Buffy recognized most of the carnies: Lonnie, Hopscotch, Rose, and the guy who ran the basketball booth. She looked worriedly behind her, but the ferocious beast that had attacked her was nowhere in sight.

Rose, however, looked really ticked off. "That's *twice* today you've broken into my trailer!"

With a swift motion, Rose swung her fist and buried it in Buffy's midsection. After the fight with the beast, she was tired. As the air rushed out of Buffy's lungs, she slumped to the ground—she was such dead weight that the three guys couldn't hold her up. They dropped her into the dust. For several seconds, Buffy could do nothing but gasp for air.

"And you!" Rose said accusingly. "You're supposed to be protecting my place. What happened?"

From the corner of her eye, Buffy saw Rose addressing a four-legged creature standing well inside the doorway of her trailer. It wasn't a mystery beast, it was a big black dog—husky, like a rottweiler. She had been attacked by a watchdog, not a watchmonster.

"He did his job," Buffy groaned. "He caught me by surprise."

"What is your problem, anyway?" Lonnie muttered, turning her over with the point of his boot. "What are you looking for, besides trouble?"

"My boyfriend—," Buffy answered, hoping they would believe her.

"That's bull!" Rose snapped. "He's not here, and you know it. You were snooping around again."

"What should we do with her?" Hopscotch asked, pushing painfully on her shoulder.

Lonnie knelt down so that his eyes were level with Buffy's. "Listen to me, you little snoop. You stay away from us, starting right now, or you'll never see your friends again."

Buffy glared at him, knowing he could probably make good on that threat. She thought about trying to escape, but she wasn't in any condition to put up much of a fight. "Why don't you go chase your tail? Or scratch your fleas?" she asked. "We have enough trouble in this town without your kind."

"And what is *our* kind?" Lonnie asked with a sneer. It was as if he was daring her to say what she suspected about them. Well, Buffy wasn't going to fall into that trap. She was gathering information, not giving it out.

"Listen, call the police on me if you want," Buffy said defiantly. "If you're not going to do that, turn me loose."

Lonnie smiled, looking again like the charming ladies' man she had met the night before. "Buffy—that's your name, right? You know, Buffy, I think you got us all wrong. We're just young kids, not long out of school, just trying to make a living and see some of the world. As for Willow and Xander, why don't you relax and let them have some fun? They're here of their own free will."

"Is that important?" Buffy asked.

Lonnie scowled and rose to his feet. "I don't know what

we should do with her. Maybe we should lock her up somewhere until . . . after."

"Watch her, she's awfully strong," Rose warned with a knowing glance at Buffy. She shoved her dog back into the trailer and tried to lock the door. "She broke my lock clean off."

"I've got a safe place for her," Hopscotch suggested. "The big tool chest in the utility rig. She should just about fit."

"I don't want to be kidnapped!" Buffy said, pretending to struggle. She started at Rose. "Just let me go home—you can have my stupid boyfriend!"

Rose chuckled. "Thanks. I've already got him. And I have big plans for him too."

Lonnie looked at Hopscotch and nodded. Buffy should have reacted quicker, but she was still trying to get her wind back. She didn't see the wrench in Hopscotch's hand until it came flying through the air, cracking onto the back of her head.

As blackness and pain engulfed her senses, Buffy slumped face-first into the dirt.

Giles paced in front of his car, wondering what had become of Buffy. Had she been caught inside the trailer? Had they called the police on her? Now he felt guilty about giving the signal and running off, but he had only been following her orders. She was the Slayer—always risking her life in order to keep other people safe. He feared that someday that policy might backfire on her.

He checked his watch and saw that it had been twenty minutes since he had left Buffy inside the trailer. She had said they would meet at his car, but that presupposed that both of them were coming. Buffy was obviously not coming, at least not quickly.

A young couple walked by, and they glanced at him suspiciously, as if thinking: *What is this middle-aged guy in a tie doing hanging out in the parking lot of a carnival?* Giles smiled reassuringly at them, and they hurried along their way. *Maybe I should be more inconspicuous,* he decided. He unlocked the door of his car and climbed behind the steering wheel.

But ten minutes of sitting in the car only made him more nervous than before. He didn't like sitting in the car, because he couldn't *see* anything. *What if Buffy forgot where the car was parked? What if she's wandering around, looking for it?*

Giles jumped out and started pacing in front of his car again. He scanned the swirling lights of the carnival for any sign of the perky teenager. Every other teenager in town seemed to be in attendance at the gaudy attractions, but not Buffy.

After a few minutes, Giles took a handkerchief out of his pocket and wiped the sweat off his neck. As he did, he surveyed the dark hills behind the vacant lot, and he saw something even more disturbing. The full moon had just started to rise, and it glowed bloodred in the night sky.

Coyote Moon!

Even though they had no real proof of the existence of werecoyotes or a plot to resurrect Spurs Hardaway, the sight of the moon filled Giles with dread. Bold and bright, it seemed to challenge the very lights of the carnival. By midnight, it would be fully risen in the night sky, and it would be bone white. Giles found it hard to watch the red moon without thinking that evil was abroad on this hot summer's night.

Now forty minutes had passed since he had left Buffy inside the trailer, and that was more than enough time to wait for her. Giles resolved to disobey orders and go look for her, starting with Rose's trailer.

Two minutes later, he was once again in the shadows behind the midway, stalking Rose's darkened trailer. Nothing appeared amiss—it looked exactly as he had left it. As if he owned the place, Giles walked briskly to the door and tried the handle. The lock was broken, but the door had been wired shut with a metal clothes hanger.

Without warning, something large crashed against the door on the other side, barking and growling ferociously. Giles staggered away from the trailer, nearly falling into the dirt, as the beast inside continued to growl and carry on. *Whatever is in there,* he thought, *it isn't human, and it isn't Buffy!*

He looked around, worried that the loud barking would surely draw a crowd. No one came to investigate, but still he scurried away, feeling cowardly and helpless.

Back on the brightly lit midway, Giles wandered for a while, looking for Buffy, Willow, or Xander. All he saw were the callow youths of Sunnydale and the creepy youths who ran the carnival. He did pass two uniformed police officers, who were drinking coffee and eating huge cinnamon rolls, but what could he tell them?

Excuse me, officer, one of my students has disappeared while breaking into a locked trailer, looking for proof of were-coyotes.

No, Buffy had gotten herself into whatever trouble she had gotten herself into, and she would have to get herself out. Giles tried to tell himself that she was the Slayer—she would know what to do. But these weren't garden-variety vampires, such as those she had fought dozens of times—these were sorcerers, shape-shifters! They were potentially more powerful than vampires.

Giles kept walking through the carnival, determined not to leave until he found Buffy.

Buffy awoke with a massive headache clamped to her skull like a baby alien. Either she was in total darkness or she was blind. When she squirmed painfully, trying to work out the kinks, she discovered that she was trapped inside a thick metal box about two feet by four feet.

As terror overcame her, Buffy tried to struggle and shout. She didn't get far, because her hands were tied behind her back and her mouth was taped shut. About all she could do was kick her feet against the sides of the box, which seemed as solid as a steel coffin.

Buffy kicked and kicked, until she was gasping for breath. She stopped, thinking that she had to be careful or she would use up all the air in this small enclosure. Buffy smelled oil and grease, which she assumed were all over her clothes and hair by now. *Great! Now I'll need a pro-vitamin mud treatment to even begin to restore my hair.* Of course, that wouldn't matter much if she died in this metal crypt.

Worse yet, she had failed Giles, Willow, Xander, and all the other local kids who were in danger. She had failed to stop the werecoyotes, who were now free to have a coming-out party for Spurs Hardaway. That dog in the trailer—it might not have been a dog at all but a man wearing a dog skin! With this scary gang of skinwalkers, there was no telling what was real and what wasn't.

She began kicking ferociously on the side of the box as she squirmed to free herself. All of this frenzied activity made her throbbing headache worse, but she wasn't going to just lie here and die—

Bang! Bang! came two loud raps on the wall of her prison. "Quiet down in there!" a muffled voice shouted.

Buffy stopped thrashing, but she continued to work quietly on the ropes binding her wrists. Unfortunately, she had been tied up by strong people who knew their way around ropes and knots. In her awkward position, she couldn't exert much force on the ropes, and she couldn't budge them.

With her lips, tongue, and teeth, Buffy began to work on the tape spread across her mouth. She had always wondered whether her tongue had extraordinary strength too, and apparently it did. Very slowly, she worked the tape down from her upper lip until she had a small gap through which she could talk.

"Let me out of here!" she yelled.

The banging came again. "Shut up in there!"

"No!"

A moment later, the lid of the box opened, and the silhouette of a man looked down at her. "Listen," he hissed, "I could fix you so that you'll never talk again! All it takes is a little snip-snip on your tongue. But if you promise not to yell and cause a ruckus, I'll take off the gag. Believe it or not, missy, I *want* to talk to you."

Buffy recognized the voice—she was pretty sure it was Hopscotch. She wasn't in much of a position to bargain, so she nodded and mumbled, "Okay, I'll keep quiet."

He lowered the lid, plunging her back into darkness. She had no reason to trust the old carny, but there had been a weird desperation in his voice, as if he, too, needed help. At least, by opening the top of the box, he had let some much-needed fresh air into the box and her lungs. The fresh air even helped clear her headache a little bit.

To her relief, the top of the box opened again a few minutes later. This time, Hopscotch had a flashlight, which he shined into her face. She closed her eyes and didn't see his big hand coming down to her mouth until he ripped the tape off her lips. Buffy yelped.

"Sorry," he muttered.

"Yeah, thanks. Now I won't have to wax my mustache for a while."

"Hey, nobody forced you to snoop around."

Buffy sighed. "I shouldn't have broken into that trailer, I know it now—but love makes you do silly things! Why don't you just let me go, and we'll forget all about that, and the fact that you kidnapped me?"

"Are you *really* just a lovesick teenager?" Hopscotch asked with a suspicious glint in his eye.

Some instinct told Buffy not to lie. "No," she answered. "I mean, Xander is a friend of mine, but I'm more worried about his *life* than his love life."

"You're smart," Hopscotch said with respect. "You *see* things. I remember you from that first night—there was something about you."

"You don't mean that first night when we met here, do you?" Buffy asked.

"No, when I met you on the street, when I was running with the pack. The others think all humans are worthless fools, but not me. After all, *we* were once human."

Bingo! she thought. "You guys are werecoyotes—skinwalkers."

Hopscotch chuckled. "Hoo-boy, you got it all figured out! We've been roaming this country for a century now, and nobody's guessed our game until *you* came along. You can fight, too. I still got bruises from where you kicked me the other night. So what's *your* story, missy?"

"Since we're friends now, why don't you let me out of here? Then we can sit around and have a regular conversation."

He shoved the flashlight in her face. "Tell me what you are, or I'll shut you up permanently."

"Okay," Buffy said, wincing from the light. "I'm a . . . a witch! I run this town, and I don't want any competition."

Hopscotch roared with laughter. "I *knew* it! I knew you were one of us. Like the freaks always say, 'One of us! One of us!'"

"Yeah, I'm a freak like you," Buffy agreed. "So why are you here? And what has it got to do with Spurs Hardaway?"

"Can't put anything over on you," the old carny said, his eyes lighting up. "Did you know that tonight is the Coyote Moon?" He looked as if he was going to howl in excitement.

"Listen, I don't really care what you do as long as it doesn't harm other people."

Hopscotch frowned. "As a witch, you should know that sometimes you can't avoid that. If we're going to bring Spurs Hardaway back from the dead, we need a blood sacrifice, and lots of it."

"Preferably young and pure," Buffy said.

"Yeah," the old carny agreed. "That's the general idea. Luckily, you can still find some in a small town like this. It's best when they come of their own free will."

"Okay," Buffy said. "I'll forget I ever heard about this stuff. Just get me out of this box."

"You're lying." Hopscotch sneered. "You won't let us kill a bunch of your friends so we can raise the meanest, evilest skinwalker who ever lived."

"Okay, maybe not," Buffy conceded, thinking furiously. *Now I know their plan for sure.* She suddenly realized that this conversation wasn't an accident—Hopscotch wasn't just lonely for a little company.

"Listen," she said. "Either you're one of those bad guys who likes to brag, or you don't really want Spurs Hardaway raised from the dead."

His voice took on a hard edge. "Do you know what it's like to live for a hundred years in a seedy road show?"

"No. Unless high school counts."

"It's pitiful," the old carny muttered. "No home, no family, no good food, no good mattress, no bathtubs."

"No manicures," Buffy said.

But Hopscotch wasn't finished. "There's nothin' but grease, gas fumes, and ten thousand towns, each one more boring than the last!" He snorted a laugh. "For the ones who have stayed young, there's fun in making whoopee with the locals, but I gave that up a long time ago. I'm a hundred and seventy-five years old!"

"You don't look a day over a hundred," Buffy insisted.

His wrinkled face looked wistful. "Now the only fun I have is when I put on my skin and run with the pack. Sometimes I think I should just run off and *stay* a coyote. I'm really tired of fixing that stupid Ferris wheel."

"I bet. But won't things get better after Spurs comes back?"

"Not for me."

"Why not?"

"'Cause I'm the one who shot him dead."

"Oh, bummer," Buffy said. "And he knows this tidbit?"

"He was there."

"Right. Then you might as well get me out of here," Buffy insisted, "because we're partners now."

A look of doubt flashed across Hopscotch's craggy features, and Buffy feared that he would slam the lid on her prison, leaving her to die. Finally, he reached down and hauled her out with strong hands and arms.

When he set her on her feet, she got her first good look at her surroundings. She was in the van area of a large equipment truck, with tools, spools of cable, electronic gear, and other stuff strapped to the walls. She had actually been stored in a large metal tool chest welded to the floor. The grimy tools from the chest were now in a pile at her feet.

The only light came from a naked bulb over their heads. The only way out was the closed door at the back of the truck, and the old carny stood between her and that door. In his hand was his favorite weapon, a massive wrench that Buffy knew only too well.

"Don't try nothin'," Hopscotch warned.

"I'm still tied up," she said, motioning to her hands behind her back.

"And you're gonna stay that way."

Buffy sat on a spool of electrical cable and stretched her stiff legs. “It must’ve taken some guts to kill Spurs Hardaway. Why did you do it?”

The old man scowled. “Because we were doing all the work, keeping his Wild West show on the road, and he was taking all the money! He was hardly paying us enough to live on and to feed the livestock.

“I’d been with Spurs since his first rodeo, in 1858, and I didn’t want to kill him. But he could be a mean old coot. I always had that silver bullet in my Derringer, just in case he didn’t see reason.” Hopscotch shook his head sadly. “He didn’t see reason.” The old man trailed off in thought.

“So how do we stop Spurs from coming back for another curtain call?” Buffy asked, hoping to keep Hopscotch in the present.

Hopscotch smiled. “*We* don’t. *You* do.”

“Me? Where are you going?”

The old man gave her a crooked grin and opened a red toolbox. Slowly he pulled out a ratty coyote skin and draped it over his shoulders, putting the moth-eaten animal head on top of his own head. Buffy didn’t like the way those dried, dead eyes stared down at her.

“I’m not sticking around,” Hopscotch vowed. “I’m heading for the hills. If you fail, Spurs will come after me, but I’ll lead him a merry chase. If you stop them, you’ll break the spell, and we’ll all live free. For the first time, we’ll have control over our lives.”

"But how do I do it?" Buffy asked.

"How do I know? *You're* the witch." He started to unbutton his grimy work shirt, then stopped. "There is one more thing you should know. Spurs was buried with his grizzly bear skin, and he knows how to use it. He's the only white man I ever seen who could turn himself into a bear. You've got to *be* the animal, and Spurs was a nasty ol' grizzly bear, with supernatural powers."

"Great," Buffy muttered. "Hey, before you go, at least untie me!"

Hopscotch squinted suspiciously at her, then pulled a hunting knife out of his boot. "Turn around."

Buffy didn't like turning her back on the armed carny, but she didn't have much choice. She turned and held her breath. A moment later, she felt the knife slice through the ropes, and her hands swung free.

"Thanks," she said, glancing back at him and massaging her sore wrists.

"You might want to turn around again, unless you don't mind seeing something really weird."

"I've seen weird before."

She had seen weird before, but never quite like this. Hopscotch stripped naked, except for his coyote skin, then from his toolbox he took a bundle of dried leaves all tied together. He struck a match and lit the bundle. In a few seconds, the truck was filled with cloying smoke—Buffy could smell sage and cedar among the pungent odors.

While he sang in a strange language, Hopscotch smudged his body with the burning torch until he looked like a grilled fish. Then the old man got down on his hands and knees and began to writhe to his own silent drums, still singing, sometimes growling. The coyote pelt rode his back like a furry parasite, and Buffy was startled to see the hairs on the pelt start to rise, as if alive. His singing grew more guttural and animal-like.

When she looked back at the man, he was no longer a man, but something in between man and beast. He twitched and growled, and his bones and muscles crackled as they changed shape. The smoke seemed to form around the writhing figure, helping him de-evolve into a wild animal. She could swear that the walls of the truck were glowing as magic filled the small enclosure.

By the time the smoke lifted, a coyote with familiar yellow eyes stood before her.

"Impressive," Buffy said hoarsely. All she could think about was Spurs Hardaway coming back and morphing into a giant, supernatural grizzly bear.

Acting like a scruffy dog that had just stolen dinner off the table, the coyote padded to the door and waited for her to come over and open it.

"Hmmm," Buffy said, crossing to the back of the semitrailer. "A skinwalker might make a good boyfriend. When you need a guy, you'd have a guy, and when you didn't want a guy, you'd have a pet."

The coyote snarled at her.

"It was just a joke," Buffy explained. She opened the latch and lifted the door at the back of the truck. The coyote stuck its nose out, sniffed the air, and leaped into the darkness. By the time Buffy looked out the door, it was gone.

The Slayer jumped to the ground and crouched down. She was lucky to be alive, and she knew it. She could easily be dead, if she hadn't run into the only skinwalker who didn't want to see Spurs Hardaway rise from the grave. She couldn't afford to underestimate the gang of shape-shifters again—they were real, and without free will, they were dangerous.

Keeping low and in the shadows, Buffy ran to the vacant lot next door, where most of the cars were parked. She hoped that Giles had followed orders and stayed with his car, because she certainly didn't want to go back into the carnival to look for him.

Be there, Giles! Please be there!

His boring car was there, but he wasn't.

"Giles, you idiot!" Buffy muttered. She looked at the full moon high in the sky and gulped. It wasn't red, only slightly pink, but Ol' Coyote Moon looked as if she meant business.

Buffy glanced at her watch and saw that it was ten o'clock—she had been unconscious even longer than she thought. There were only two hours left before midnight, and she didn't have a clue where her friends were or how to stop these monsters.

Somewhere a coyote howled, and it sounded as if it was laughing at her.

CHAPTER EIGHT

By ten o'clock, the Saturday night crowd at the carnival was bigger and rowdier than ever, with tons of people laughing, eating, and shrieking. Willow wondered where they had all come from. Maybe the carnies had put up posters in the neighboring towns too.

She and Xander sat outside a hamburger stand, eating a gigantic plate of greasy french fries and watching the parade along the midway. Whirling rides, bright lights, and blaring music—it was an immortal town, springing up over and over again all over the country. The carnival probably hadn't changed much since Willow's grandparents had gone to it, which was the eeriest thing about it.

With all the frenzied activity designed to mesmerize the senses, Xander still kept looking at his watch.

"Two more hours," Willow said. "And looking at your watch won't make the time go any faster."

"Would it help if I set my watch ahead?" Xander asked, grinning at his own foolishness. "Can you believe it, Willow? It's happening to *us*—a real summer romance!"

Willow sighed. "I'd rather have a romance that lasted summer, fall, winter, and spring." *And happened* between *us,* she thought.

"But that's not a summer romance," Xander insisted. "A summer romance is something special, because it blazes like a comet across the sky and then fades out. The thing that makes it special—that makes everything move so fast—is that a summer romance is doomed to end."

"How poetic. And you don't have to take Rose home to meet your parents," Willow added.

"They wouldn't understand our love," Xander declared, sounding quite tragic.

"Oh, yes they would," Willow said with a laugh. "All too well."

She straightened suddenly. Something in the crowd caught her eye—an older man in a totally unhip cardigan sweater and wool slacks. Before she could get a closer look, he blended into the crowd and was gone.

"What's the matter?" Xander asked.

"I thought I saw Giles."

Xander laughed. "Giles? At a carnival? I don't think he goes out on Saturday night, but if he did go out, it would be to a planetarium or a slide show at the museum. Not to a carnival."

"Yeah, you're right," Willow admitted. "I've been looking for Buffy, but I haven't seen her, either."

"She won't be back, not after the way she embarrassed herself. That girl is just so certain that she's right all the time, she'll never admit it when she's wrong." He laughed and slapped his knee. "What a ditz, thinking these nice people are *werecoyotes*!"

Willow laughed uneasily. "Yes, it is a little silly, isn't it? Say, do you want some ice cream?" She quickly changed the subject.

"Sure." Xander fumbled in his pocket and pulled out a wadded-up dollar bill. "See, I've got some money left."

"That's okay, I've got plenty of money."

"Oh, yeah?" Xander said. "How much?"

"Three hundred dollars."

Xander spit a french fry halfway across the midway. "You've got three hundred dollars? What did you do, pawn your computer?"

"No, I played a little poker with Lonnie, Hopscotch, and the boys. I cleaned them out, as they say. I even paid Lonnie back, with interest."

"Wow! Were they mad at you?"

Willow frowned puzzledly. "No, it was like they didn't

care. I have a feeling that they don't really have much use for the money they make here. I mean, what are they going to do with it? They can't own very much stuff, traveling around all the time."

"Yeah, what a romantic life," Xander said blissfully. "It's almost like they're monks—or samurai warriors—on a holy quest."

"And what exactly is that holy quest?"

"To have fun, to bring people pleasure! What higher calling could there be?"

"I suppose," Willow said doubtfully. She wished she were having more fun, and that Buffy were having fun with them. Waiting until midnight to go out on a date with a strange guy from the carnival was not her idea of fun, if he was a great kisser. With all the money in her bag, she and Xander could have more fun than anybody, if she could just get his attention.

He was looking impatiently at his watch again, and she knew that it was a hopeless cause. How could she compete with somebody like Rose and a summer romance?

Suddenly, she felt strong hands massaging her shoulders, and she turned to see tanned, brawny forearms. She looked up to see Lonnie's smiling face, perfect dimples, and curly blond hair.

"Hi, Lonnie," Xander said cheerfully. "I hear our little Willow cleaned you guys out at poker."

"Yeah," Lonnie said with amusement. "I always knew she had hidden talents."

Willow tried not to blush. “Good cards and money management, that’s all. What’s the plan for tonight?”

Xander cut in, “I know I’m meeting Rose back at her trailer.”

“No, that’s changed,” Lonnie said. “I talked to Rose, and we want to double-date with you guys again. We haven’t seen much of Sunnydale, so we thought we might do some sightseeing.”

Willow didn’t know whether to laugh or cry at the crestfallen look on Xander’s face. The only sights he wanted to see were on Rose’s immediate person.

“That’s great!” Willow said, trying not to sound too relieved. “At midnight?”

“We’ll try to close early tonight,” Lonnie answered. “We’ll make an announcement at eleven o’clock to say we’re going to close at eleven-thirty. We’ll say it’s fire marshals or something like that.”

“Why close early?” Willow asked.

Lonnie shrugged his perfect shoulders. “We’re a little shorthanded. There’s been an emergency, and some of our guys were needed elsewhere.”

“Was anybody hurt?” Willow asked worriedly.

He stared off into the distance and seemed to be studying the crowd. “Don’t worry your pretty little head—we can handle it. You guys just hang out around here, and we’ll find you when it’s time to go.”

“Okay,” Willow answered cheerfully. Lonnie waved and wandered off in the direction of his dart booth.

"Nice guy," Xander muttered, "but I'm getting a little tired of double-dating."

"Yeah," Willow said, trying not to show how relieved she was. "I wonder what the emergency is?"

"He said not to worry about it." Xander jumped to his feet and clapped his hands. "Hey, you've got three hundred dollars! That might even be enough to win a stuffed animal. Want to try?"

"Sure!"

Willow stood up and gazed into the night sky, where a lovely full moon was rising over the merry-go-round. She felt like grabbing Xander's hand, but she knew that would be pushing it. She was content to blend into the fun-loving crowed with him.

Everything is going so well tonight, Willow thought. *Why am I so worried? I can't be concerned about Buffy. If she wants to miss out on all the fun, that's her business.*

"Come on!" Xander said, rushing off toward the games.

"Okay!" Grabbing her bag, Willow hurried after her beloved.

This stinks, Buffy thought as she loitered in a dark corner of the carnival and watched laughing teens trump past, crunching candy apples and slurping Cokes. Not only were they all having fun, oblivious to the danger around them, but time was slipping away. The Coyote Moon edged higher and higher in the night sky.

Where are you, Giles? She couldn't go out into the bright neon and look for him, as she didn't want the carnies to know she had escaped. She couldn't stay put, because the chances were slim that Giles would just happen to walk past this one spot, between the ticket booth and the Porta Potties. She could stand in another spot, but her chances of finding him wouldn't be any better.

Since his car was still in the parking lot, Buffy reasoned that Giles still had to be there, looking for her. Either that, or he had been captured and stuck in a tool chest too. That probably hadn't happened, because the carnies had no way of knowing that Giles was with her. They would think he was just a slightly confused parent looking for his wild kids.

She hadn't seen Xander and Willow, either, which had her twice as worried. *I'm never gonna let those two out of my sight again! Whoa, girl!* She caught herself. *Don't take a parental trip!*

She had to do something—but what?

Amid the din of blaring music, clattering rides, and shrieking teens, she heard a gravelly voice. It was the clown on the dunking machine, taunting a customer. "You throw like a girl! In fact, you throw like my *grandmother*!"

Hmmm, Buffy thought.

Keeping to the shadows, she worked her way behind the rides, the food stands, and the game booths. Luckily, the dunking machine was in its own corner of the carnival, removed from the other games because it needed forty feet of throwing room. The redheaded girl was on ball duty instead of Rose, and Buffy wondered where the sleaze queen could be. Was she with Xander?

There's no time to worry about that now, Buffy told herself.

Crouching low, she moved along the fence to the rear of the dunking booth. Most of the flimsy structure was made out of plywood and two-by-fours hammered hastily together, and she had no problem removing a board and slipping under the back wall.

She heard the gravelly voice of the clown—he was making a joke about Sunnydale boys and sheep—and she saw the back of his multicolored fright wig and striped shirt. He looked dry, which was in her favor. Next Buffy located the target disk and the mechanism it tripped. Moving cautiously in the darkness, she ran her hand along the levers and springs until she found the hinge that actually dropped the clown into the water.

He was only a few feet away, just above her. She could smell his earthy, animal odor, and *he* got to take a bath a lot more often than the rest of the carnies. Now that she knew all about the cult of werecoyotes, it was hard to think of any of them as being human. They didn't even smell human anymore.

She waited until he paused in his usual litany of taunts and insults, and then she said quietly, "I want you to announce something."

He put his hand over the microphone, looked down, and growled, "Who's there?"

Still crouching in the shadows, Buffy reached up and shook the platform he was sitting on. “I’ll dump you if you call for help.”

“Okay, okay! What do you want?”

“Say, ‘Librarian, return to your car.’”

“Hey, come on, I’m working here!”

“Do it!” Buffy shook his platform again, and the hinges groaned ominously.

“Okay.” The clown removed his hand from the microphone and declared, “Here’s a public service announcement. Librarian, you better get back to your car. Pronto.”

He looked down and growled, “Happy?”

But Buffy was already gone. She scurried under the loose board, rolled to her feet, and dashed toward the parking lot. Usually, when they faced danger, Giles was a frazzled ball of nerves, certain they were going to get killed at any moment. She had to hope that he was nervously paying attention to everything around him.

When Buffy saw two carnies working on an air compressor dead ahead of her, she pulled out her barrettes and shook up her hair so that it fell in her face. She lowered her head and slipped past them, walking slowly. If they looked at her, she wasn’t aware of it, but she listened carefully for voices and running footsteps. When she heard none, she finished her leisurely stroll to the parking lot.

Get your Nikes in gear, Giles! We need to keep ahead of the pack. Buffy paced nervously for a few moments until she saw a familiar figure cutting across the lot. She waved, and he quickened his step.

"Thank goodness," Giles said, clasping her hands. "Are you all right? You look terrible."

"It's the carnival-chic look," Buffy answered, fluffing her stained, ratty hair. "Hey, weren't you supposed to stay by the car?"

"Surely not all night!" Giles protested. "I knew that something had happened to you, and I had to go look. What did happen to you?"

"First something bad, then something good, I think. I found an unexpected ally." She crossed to the other side of the car and waited for him to unlock the passenger door. "Get in, and I'll tell you about it on the way."

"Where are we going?" Giles asked, fumbling for his keys.

Buffy looked warily around the dark parking lot. The flashing lights of the carnival splashed off the hoods of the cars and trucks, twisting into psychedelic shapes. The music seemed distant and tinny, and it felt as if they were alone. But were they? Scrawny canines could be slinking between the oversized tires, stalking them.

"Unlock the car. Hurry!" Buffy ordered.

Giles jumped to attention and opened his car door. He started to get in just as a brown-and-white coyote bounded onto the roof of the car behind him.

"Duck!" Buffy shouted.

He dove into the driver's seat as Buffy sprang up and slid

on her stomach across the roof of the sedan. Fists flying, she smashed into the coyote as it lunged for Giles, and the impact threw them both into the car door next to theirs.

Buffy fell on top of the coyote, which twisted and squirmed desperately while trying to chomp Buffy's jugular vein. Her crucifix necklace flopped out of her shirt, but it didn't do a bit of good. She had to slug the canine viciously until it was unconscious and limp, something that was repugnant to her. It was so much like a dog!

Buffy jumped to her feet, tossing off the coyote like a smelly fur pelt. She didn't even wait to see what became of it, because she knew that its buds could be nearby, ready to pounce. Buffy scurried to the passenger door, yanked it open, and dove in.

"Drive!" she said breathlessly.

Still shuddering, Giles started the car engine. "Where?"

"The cemetery."

"I was afraid you were going to say that." Looking around carefully, Giles backed the car out of the parking lot. He drove as if he were afraid he was going to run over a coyote wherever he went.

Buffy didn't relax until they were on Main Street, headed back into town. The carnival was far behind them, and it was tempting just to forget about it and hide under the bed. But she couldn't do that, even though she felt out of her element fighting these four-legged Lon Chaneys.

"Why the cemetery?" Giles asked.

"Here's the short version," she began. "I was captured, but I got lucky and got turned over to Hopscotch. Have you seen him? He's the gnarly one. He's also the one who shot Spurs Hardaway."

"Really?" Giles remarked. "So he doesn't want to see Spurs come back. How much help will he be to us?"

"None. He turned himself into a coyote and took to the hills." Buffy frowned worriedly. "I can't say I blame him. I'm not sure how to stop them, but I know there's one thing we've got to do—get the bear skin."

"A rug?" Giles asked in confusion.

"No, the bear skin that was buried with Spurs Hardaway. We've got to open his coffin and get it out. The last thing Sunnydale needs is an evil sorcerer who can turn himself into a giant supernatural grizzly bear!"

"No, I suppose you're right," Giles said glumly. "And Willow and Xander?"

"I haven't seen them. Have you?"

The Watcher shook his head. "No. But perhaps they stayed home."

"You got a peep at Rose. Do you think Xander would stay home?"

"No, and Willow would stick close to him, if she could."

"She's got her hands full too," Buffy muttered.

With a grave expression on his face, Giles steered the car onto another quiet suburban street. "We're getting close to the cemetery. What's the plan?"

"We've got to check here first," the Slayer answered, "to make sure they haven't started the masquerade party yet. You stay in the car, while I go scope things out. If it looks clear, we'll get some shovels at my house and steal Spurs's bear skin. To be on the safe side, maybe we can dismember his corpse."

"Silver!" Giles said worriedly. "We've got to get some silver bullets."

"Only as a last resort. I think we can stop them without killing anybody." She opened the car door and slipped out. "You wait in the car—no more rogue warrior stuff. Honk if there's trouble."

"Will do," Giles answered, nervously surveying the quiet street and moonlit cemetery. He quickly locked the car door behind her.

Buffy jogged toward the fence, preparing to leap over the iron spears that surrounded the cemetery. As she was about to go airborne, a horn honked frantically behind her. Buffy pulled up at the last second and crashed noisily into the fence. She turned to yell at Giles, when she saw him pointing frantically down the street.

The Slayer whirled around to see a beautiful Irish setter come charging down the street with three coyotes yapping at its heels. When the frightened dog zigged to either side to escape, the coyotes deftly cut it off and kept it running down the middle. The setter was bigger than the coyotes, and just as fast, but it was obvious from its shiny red coat that it was a house pet, no match for the snarling predators, which would run her down sooner or later.

Buffy saw Giles get out of his car and start waving at the oncoming coyotes and their prey. “Shoo! Shoo!” he yelled.

Once again, it was coyotes behaving badly but normally. As soon as they saw Giles, they broke off the chase and loped into the shadows, where they watched from a respectful distance. The poor setter ran breathlessly toward Giles, and Buffy moved to head it off.

“Come here, girl,” Buffy said, holding her arms out to the frightened animal. The dog lunged gratefully into her embrace, and Buffy rubbed its silky coat. The animal was shivering and panting so badly that it was hyperventilating.

“Oh, you poor girl,” Buffy said sympathetically as she kept the three rotten coyotes in view.

“How do you know it’s a girl?” Giles asked.

Buffy shrugged. “I don’t know, something about her.”

“Do you suppose those three are normal coyotes?” Giles asked. “They don’t seem as aggressive as the other variety.”

“I don’t know,” Buffy admitted. “We shouldn’t take any chances. I thought I told you to stay in the car.”

Giles pouted with indignation. “It’s difficult to stand by and watch a beautiful animal like that get mauled by coyotes!”

“Yeah, I guess so.” Buffy petted the setter’s neck, which is when she realized that the dog had no collar or tags. Maybe it had lost its collar during the chase, getting it caught in a fence. A desperate dog could easily squirm out of a collar.

Then Buffy noticed something else—the dog’s smell. It was as if it hadn’t had a bath in a while. The warning hackles on Buffy's neck were just starting to rise when the dog whirled around with a vicious snarl and chomped her forearm.

"Aaagh!" Buffy screamed, trying to get the dog's powerful jaws to unlock from her arm.

Giles recoiled in horror at the sudden and ferocious attack, and he didn't see the three coyotes as they wheeled on their haunches and charged across the pavement. It was a concerted attack, with two of the coyotes rushing Giles and one coming to aid the dog. Only Buffy had discovered too late that it wasn't a *real* dog.

If they had the right skins, the shape-shifters could turn themselves into any *animal!*

Buffy watched helplessly as two swift coyotes pounced on Giles and drove him to the ground. When the third coyote lunged for her, she lashed out with her free hand and spun it around like a hairy boomerang. But the sweet Irish setter still had her arm in a death grip.

Giles's screams rent the air as the supernatural shape-shifters mauled him!

CHAPTER NINE

With a dog that wasn't a dog trying to gnaw her arm off, Buffy got good and mad. She leaned down and bit the setter brutally on its tender snout. With all her might, she tried to chew that weredog's nose off.

When the creature yelped and let go of Buffy's arm, she swung her other fist like a sledgehammer. She crunched the setter on the top of its head, and the beast went limp and slumped to the ground. The Slayer jumped up and booted the unconscious animal about ten feet.

As the setter rolled into the ditch, it took on the momentary appearance of a girl with red hair—Rose's relief at the dunking machine! Somehow the monster shook off the blow and became a harmless-looking dog once again. There was no time to gape at this weirdness, because Giles was still getting mauled.

Two of the attackers were now dazed, but two more were wrestling with the librarian, trying to rip their way through his sweater. Buffy charged across the pavement and flew into them feet-first; the canines went careening twenty feet and landed in a heap. She caught movement from the corner of her eye, and she spun like a top and smacked the first coyote as it tried to sneak up on them.

Crouching protectively over Giles, Buffy kept the four beasts in view. They were dazed and wary, but they knew enough to snarl in anger.

"That was a nice trick you pulled on us!" she said angrily, shaking her fist at them. "I bet if you had a human skin, you could even be human again!"

The canines snapped and snarled at her, but they were cautious now that they had lost the element of surprise. Buffy glanced down at Giles, who was covered in blood but alive. He groaned, rolled over, and picked up his glasses.

"The car!" she ordered. "Get in the car!"

"Gladly," the bloody librarian muttered as he crawled on all fours to the door of his sedan. While the coyotes circled them, Buffy feinted phantom blows at them and Giles hauled himself behind the steering wheel. With a trembling hand, he pulled the door shut.

Glaring at the monsters, the Slayer backed slowly toward

the passenger door. She gripped her wounded forearm, which was starting to throb with pain.

"I've had it with you hairballs! I really have!" Buffy warned. "I don't care about the anti-fur movement—I'm going to stitch all of you together into a fur-lined trash bag!"

The coyotes growled bravely at her, but they didn't attack as Buffy slipped into Giles's car. Why should they attack? They had won, driving the intruders away from the cemetery and safeguarding their ceremony. They had used trickery to do it, but that was the way of coyotes.

Giles started the car engine and tromped the gas angrily, sending the coyotes scurrying. He had a lot of scratches and bloodstains on his shirt, but he didn't appear to be badly injured.

"Can you drive?" she asked.

"I'm shaky, but I think so." Giles frowned at the tooth marks on Buffy's arm. "We should go to the hospital. We probably both need stitches."

She gulped. "We're not going to, like, turn into were-coyotes, are we?"

Slowly the car pulled away from the curb, and Giles shook his head. "No, this isn't a curse, like the typical werewolf account. These people studied and worked hard to become shape-shifters, and they've had more than a hundred years of practice."

Buffy turned to look for the werecoyotes and the were-setter, but they had disappeared into the dark landscape of the cemetery. She gazed into the sky and tried to find the moon, but it was too high overhead—the roof of the car blocked it. *Just as well,* Buffy thought. Exhausted, she slumped into her seat and tried to ignore the throbbing pain in her arm.

"I know a doctor who could patch us up," Giles said. "That way, we won't get bogged down in red tape at the hospital."

"Good thing, because we've got to get back to the carnival by midnight," Buffy said, gritting her teeth. "We need to head off Willow, Xander, and whoever else they have on a leash. Maybe *you* can talk some sense into them. Hopscotch said they had to come of their own free will."

"Which they're doing." Giles shook his head with frustration. "Our foe is crafty and dangerous, and they know *you're* the only one who can stop them."

"So what else is new?" Buffy asked with a shrug. "What's spooky is, when they're animals, they act like real coyotes. When they're in that wild state, we should be smarter than them."

"You mean, they should have some weakness we could exploit?"

"Yeah. We need to start using trickery too, or the next mayor of Sunnydale is going to be a werebear."

Giles nodded gravely and kept driving through the deserted streets, while the skull-colored Coyote Moon beamed down on them.

"Due to a request from the fire marshal, the carnival will be closing in five minutes!" a voice announced on the loudspeaker. Willow looked up, recognizing Lonnie's drawl. There were groans from the paying customers all around her, who were not done partying. Although it was twenty-five after eleven, the midway still boasted a sizable crowd.

"If you have any ride tickets left, come back and use them tomorrow!" the friendly voice suggested. "The rides and games will shut down in five minutes. Good night, and thanks for coming!" With a crackle of static, his voice cut off, and the surfer music cut in.

"At last!" Xander grinned with delirious happiness, as he hugged the gigantic stuffed tiger he had won. Willow knew that it wasn't a tiger he imagined he was hugging—it was a Rose. She tried to keep the jovial smile plastered to her face, but it was hard.

Having fun at breakneck speed, they had returned to the carnies almost sixty dollars of the poker money she had won. But it was worth it for the good time they'd had, playing the games, riding the rides, and eating too much junk. If only life could be this simple—just she and Xander out on a date, acting like a regular couple. Why did they need Lonnie and Rose?

For one brief, shining moment, Willow wondered if she could whisk Xander away before Rose showed up to turn him into Silly Putty.

"Xander," she said hesitantly. "What if Buffy is right, and there is something wrong with these people?"

He smiled pleasantly at her. "Hey, Willow, you know what? If you're getting cold feet and want to back out, go ahead. You've got enough money to call a cab." Xander reached into his pocket, fished around, and pulled out a quarter. "Hey, I'll even call the cab for you!"

Willow tried not to pout. "You want me to go, so you won't have to double-date."

"Bingo. I like Lonnie, but we don't need him, either. Rose and I can party by ourselves, if you know what I mean."

Willow cleared her throat. "Has it ever occurred to you that this summer romance might come with certain trade-offs? I mean, nothing else is *free* at this carnival."

A momentary look of concern passed over Xander's face, and he tried to hide it with a nervous chuckle. "Now, what could you be thinking of?"

"Come on," she insisted, "spill it. What's it going to cost you?"

Xander rubbed his jaw thoughtfully. "Let me ask you something, and I want you to give me an honest answer. Where do you think is a good place for a guy to have a tattoo?"

Willow frowned. *First a mustache, then a tattoo? Can a Harley be far behind?* She gestured with her hands as she tried to improvise an answer. "Someplace nobody would see it. Maybe on your . . . around your . . . on the bottom of your foot!"

"Ow!" Xander groaned at the very thought. "What we do for love."

Willow sighed and looked around at the hubbub of excited teenagers trying to catch a last thrill before the vacation ended. Those who hadn't come with dates were pairing up, or trying their best to pair up. Cliques of boys and girls had suddenly become smaller and tighter.

She looked at Xander, thinking that the hardest part of the evening was still ahead of them, when she would have to watch him and Rose paw each other. She would also have to be pawed by Lonnie, while Xander was nearby, which was confusing and strangely titillating. But it still seemed wrong, as if there was a scam she hadn't figured out yet.

Willow lowered her voice, which was hardly necessary in the crush of carnival-goers. "You know, Buffy has supreme gut instincts. What if she's right—what if there really is something wrong—"

"The only thing wrong with Rose is that she's leaving too soon," Xander sighed, dewy-eyed.

"I'm serious."

Xander smirked. "Hey, I think it's great to have Buffy jealous of *us*, for once. I think it's good for her to be cut down to size. I notice that she had enough sense to stay away from the carnival tonight and not make a fool of herself anymore. If we're in such danger, where has Buffy been all night?"

"I don't know," Willow admitted. "I guess there was nothing to it."

Xander suddenly sprang to his feet and waved frantically. "Over here!"

With a corn dog revolving slowly in her stomach, Willow turned around and got even sicker. Rose came strolling toward them, wearing a tight leopard-patterned dress, fishnet hose, and spiked heels. Men's heads swiveled, and their eyes followed her like the wake of an ocean liner. She was carrying a very large clasped purse—maybe it contained her bowling ball.

"Why don't you get your tattoo on your forehead?" Willow suggested.

"Good idea," Xander said, not even hearing her. He was totally oblivious to everything but Rose, who sauntered toward them in slow mention.

When she got closer, Xander slammed the stuffed tiger into Willow's arms to make room for the stuffed carny. "You look beautiful!" he gushed.

He tried to wrap his arms around her, but she teasingly pushed him away. "My public is watching. There will be time later."

Willow swallowed hard. "You dress is . . . stunning."

"Thank you," Rose answered. "I got this outfit in a burlesque house in Abilene."

"Beautiful," Xander repeated.

"They still have burlesque houses in Abilene?" Willow asked puzzledly. "I thought that burlesque houses went out of fashion in the 1950s."

Rose gave a throaty chuckle. "It's not really active, more like a burlesque museum."

"You mean, some old stripper used to wear that outfit?" Xander asked, obviously impressed.

Rose smiled. "You might say that."

"Where are we going?" Willow asked cheerfully, desperate to change the subject.

"I don't know," the carny replied. "Let's wait and see what Lonnie wants to do. He's the one who has the pickup truck. Xander, poor baby, you might have to ride in the back, in the bed of the truck."

"No problem," Xander said bravely. "If I get any boo-boos, will you kiss them and make them feel better?"

"Yes, my baby," she cooed, patting his cheek.

The corn dog wanted to escape from Willow's stomach, just as she wanted to escape from Rose, but neither one got the wish. It was clear that Xander would go anywhere with Rose, even if he were tied to a chain and being dragged by the truck.

"So you want to see the sights of Sunnydale?" Xander said, tapping his chin thoughtfully. "That could be a pretty short trip. There's the Bronze, which is a cool club, even though they let everybody in. Then there's a crummy mall, one lone coffee shop, and the slot-car races—they might still be open. And we have the usual collection of historical sights."

"Historical sights," Rose said, lifting a dark eyebrow mysteriously. "I've always gotten turned on by old places."

"Really?" Xander said excitedly. "There are some ancient ruins on Flagpole Hill—probably *cavemen* left them."

"It's an old army depot," Willow corrected him. "From World War Two."

"That was a long time ago," Rose said wistfully. She gazed up at the moon that was high overhead. "But it won't be much longer."

Before Willow could question that odd statement, the colorful lights on the Octopus blinked off, and the Ferris wheel creaked to a stop. One by one, the mammoth machines of the midway stopped spinning and went dark. The rock music faded out, and the speakers blared nothing but static. Even the calliope on the merry-go-round went silent. Lights on the poles stayed lit to help people find their way out, but the carnival was dying down.

"Thanks for coming, everybody!" Lonnie said over the loudspeaker. "We'll be open every day from six p.m. until midnight. Come back and see us!"

For the first time that night, it was quiet in the carnival as the customers picked up their posters, stuffed animals, and dates and began to file out. Several of them waved to Rose, who waved back. *In this strange, fake town,* Willow thought, *Rose really is a celebrity.* When the carnival closed, it was almost as if she had no identity, unless she wore a stripper's costume from the 1950s.

Although the carnies were cute, Buffy was right—they were *weird.*

Willow was suddenly struck by an irrational burst of fear and guilt, and she felt like running for the exits along with the other customers. But she looked at Xander making goo-goo eyes at Rose, and see realized that he would need protection.

For one thing, if he came home with a grotesque tattoo, he would probably be grounded for months.

She heard cheerful whistling, and she turned to see Lonnie striding toward them. He was also dressed for going out on the town—carny-style—with a white cowboy hat, fancy rodeo shirt, silver belt buckle, clean jeans, and shiny cowboy boots. In his hand was a grimy duffel bag. Willow wondered if he thought they were going to a square dance, or maybe the gym.

"Lonnie, my man!" Xander said, trying to sound like one of the gang. He had almost perfected the carny slouch, but it would be years before he could grow the facial hair. Every time Willow saw Lonnie, he looked hairier, which was also distressing.

He put his arm possessively around her slim waist. "Hey, are we ready to party, or what?"

"We were just trying to decide where to go," Rose said. "Xander mentioned some historical sights."

"The truth is, our historical sights aren't too exciting," Xander explained. "Unless old cannons really turn you on."

Lonnie laughed. "Sometimes they do."

"What's in the bag?" Willow asked nonchalantly.

He hefted and old duffel bag. "Just something to make the party even more lively. I'll show you later."

"You know what I like?" Rose asked with a twinkle in her dark eyes. "Cemeteries."

Xander laughed nervously. "Is that right? Cemeteries, huh?"

"I hear this town has a really cool old cemetery," Lonnie said.

Willow piped in, "How about the old courthouse? It's a classic example of Greek Revivalism."

Lonnie turned to her, his blue eyes piercing hers. "After the cemetery, okay? We're the guests, right?"

"Right!" Xander said, shooting a warning glance at Willow. "The cemetery is dark and quiet—fine with me!"

Are you forgetting about the last time we were in that cemetery? Willow wanted to scream. But she said nothing. After all, Lonnie and Rose couldn't be vampires, as they were up all day like regular people. They drank root beer, not blood.

"The truck's this way," Lonnie offered, steering the slender girl between the dark fun house and the boarded-up ticket booth. "Xander and your stuffed tiger will have to sit in back. You can sit up front with me."

"Okay," she said meekly. Willow really wanted to run for the hills and escape this weird double date, but Lonnie had her firmly in his grasp. Behind her, Rose giggled, and she turned to see the carny and Xander nuzzling each other as they walked.

It wouldn't be nice to break the date now, she rationalized. *There are too many other people involved.*

Despite her fears, Willow followed Lonnie through the deepening shadows behind the false fronts. Twenty feet ahead of them loomed a beat-up pickup truck, and she was about to climb into it and go to a cemetery with an itinerant laborer who worked at a carnival. At least they would be in a familiar neighborhood, and Xander would be along.

This date isn't hopelessly insane, is it?

As they neared the truck, Willow gazed at Lonnie in his white cowboy hat, and he gave her the double-dimple smile. She sure hoped he was the good guy he appeared to be.

In a small office on the first floor of a charming two-story house, a kindly country doctor still practiced medicine. The white-haired physician put on the last pieces of tape over a butterfly bandage that covered a cut too shallow to stitch. Then he covered Buffy's entire forearm with a protective sheath of gauze and taped it down.

Dr. Henshaw smiled wearily. "That will hold for tonight, but you'll have to come back tomorrow to have the bandage changed."

"Okay," she promised, glancing nervously at the watch on her opposite wrist.

"And be careful," the doctor warned. "No physical exertion, or you could rip out the stitches. That goes for you, too, Giles."

The librarian nodded gravely. He had a protective bandage stretched across his chest, where he had received most of his wounds. He grimaced in pain as he pulled on an old flannel shirt the doctor had loaned him.

"Those tetanus shots could also make you drowsy," Dr. Henshaw said. "Better go home to bed. You know, in forty years of medical practice in this town, I've seen some strange things, but I've never seen anyone who had coyote bites."

"We were in the wrong place at the wrong time," Buffy said with a helpless shrug. "We tried to save a dog from being attacked—dumb thing to do."

"Yes," Giles said, buttoning his shirt. "Thank you, Dr. Henshaw, for seeing us at this late hour."

The old country doctor stood and stretched. "Think nothing of it, Giles. You've helped me so many times to find obscure journals and pamphlets." He turned to Buffy and explained, "I have an interest in holistic turn-of-the-century medical cures, and Giles is a font of knowledge."

"Isn't he, though?" Buffy agreed, jumping to her feet. "Thanks a lot, Dr. Henshaw, but we've got to get going. Past my bedtime, you know."

The doctor escorted them to the front door. "Take a painkiller to keep the swelling down. Remember, I want to see both of you tomorrow."

"Believe me, we'll be very happy to be around tomorrow," Buffy assured him.

"Yes, indeed," Giles agreed. "Until tomorrow."

They hurried out the door and down the steps. Buffy felt a little woozy from all the medicine, but she tried not to think about it. With a final wave to the doctor, they jumped into Giles's car, and he started the engine.

"You've got to take me home," Buffy said as she settled into her seat.

"Are you done for the evening?" the Watcher asked in horror.

"Not yet. I feel burnt out, but I'm hanging in there. I need to go home and get a weapon."

Giles squealed the tires pulling away from the curb. "What kind of weapon would you have at home?"

"A werecoyote weapon," she muttered. "And you've got to find something that will work against them too. Our usual bag of tricks—stakes, holy water, crucifixes—doesn't do much. And don't tell me you're going to plug them all with silver bullets. Our friends will be hanging with them, and we're not going to turn this into a summer action movie."

"I've been racking my brain, trying to think of something," Giles said as he tooled down the quiet, tree-lined street. "There is one possibility. I've never told you this, but I used to raise hounds—for the fox hunt."

"But of course."

"At home, I have a high-pitched dog whistle, the kind that humans can't hear. I wonder if it would work on coyotes . . ."

"Who knows? It's worth a try. With this whistle, you could call them over from someplace else, right?"

"Theoretically, they would come to the whistle blower. But coyotes are unpredictable." Giles slowed down to take a corner.

"But if any of them were human, they couldn't hear it and wouldn't know what was going on." Buffy pointed. "My house is coming up."

"I know. Please be quick getting your secret weapon."

Giles coasted to a stop in front of her middle-class abode, which looked dark and slumbering this close to midnight.

Buffy slipped out the car door and shut it quietly behind her. She padded up to the front door, got out her key, and let herself in. Luckily, her secret weapon was in the dining room, which was near the front of the house. If her mom heard her at all, she would simply think she was coming home. *Knowing Mom, she'll save the lecture for tomorrow.*

Less than a minute later, Buffy got back into the car. She was wearing a clean jacket and hiding something underneath it.

"Let me see," Giles said eagerly.

Buffy grinned and held up an elegant silver carving knife with an *S* engraved on the handle. "I always knew the sterling silverware would be good for something."

Giles frowned worriedly. "You'll have to get awfully close to them to use that."

"Every time I see these coyotes, I get close to them. We're like a deodorant commercial."

"Next stop, my house," Giles said, twisting the steering wheel.

Five minutes later, the librarian came running out of his tiny bungalow clutching a brass whistle, which hung from a chain around his neck.

He jumped into the car, panting for breath. "I actually looked for silver bullets, but I couldn't find any. Remind me to order some."

"From the Monster's End catalog, right?" Buffy asked. She looked grimly at her watch. "We can still get to the carnival by midnight. Go to warp drive."

The Watcher slammed his car into gear and sped away from the house. After a few minutes of rather swift driving for Giles, they roared up to the vacant lot that was hosting the carnival. There were lights—but only a few—and only a handful of cars were parked on the lonely country road. None of the rides was running, and the place was deserted except for a few stragglers. In the dark, the odd towers, structures, and wires looked like some kind of alien prison.

"What's the deal?" Buffy asked, jumping out of the car. She looked at her watch. "What time have you got?"

"Five minutes before midnight." Giles also got out of the car and stared in disbelief and the silent machines and dark booths. Two hours ago, this ghost town had been bursting with screams, music, and teenage hormones. Now it was dim and drained of life, like a corpse.

She saw some kids hanging out at an old convertible, just watching the stars, and she yelled over to them, "What happened? Did this place close early?"

"Yeah, at eleven thirty!" one of them hollered back. "Stupid fire marshals."

"Oh, man!" Buffy muttered. "They're alone with Xander, Willow, and those other lovesick fools."

"Thank you!" Giles called politely to the kids in the convertible. "Are there any people still working here?"

"I think most of them left too."

Buffy gazed upward and saw the Coyote Moon hanging high in the black sky, glowing like a Japanese paper lantern. The face on it seemed to be laughing at her.

CHAPTER TEN

Just what they needed after gorging themselves on junk food all day was some more junk food, so Lonnie drove the rusty pickup truck to the Dairy Queen. Even though Willow was flush with money, Lonnie insisted on paying. Armed with swirled and dipped cones, the rambunctious double-daters headed for the cemetery, with Willow sitting in the front seat between Lonnie and Rose.

Thanks to aged shock absorbers, Xander was bounced pretty hard in the bed of the truck. But he had the stuffed tiger for padding.

Willow had to admit that she felt better after the stop for ice cream, even though her overworked stomach balked at processing it. Getting ice cream was just so wholesome that it made up for going to the cemetery. She noticed that Lonnie didn't eat much of his dessert either.

His duffel bag sat between Willow's feet, and she was sorely tempted to unzip the zipper and look inside. From what she could tell by poking at it with her toes, the bag contained clothes, or maybe a blanket. *Yes, a blanket probably would be part of the proceedings.* Willow licked gingerly at her ice cream.

On the other side of her, Rose devoured everything including the sugar cone.

"Hungry?" Willow asked.

"Always," Rose purred. As if a curious thought had just occurred to her, she looked appraisingly at Willow. "You know, you could be half cute, if you would develop some style."

"Other people have told me that," Willow said. "My friend Buffy—"

"Grrrr," Lonnie growled under his breath.

"Pardon me?"

"Nothing," Lonnie said. "Just clearing my throat. Say, is this where we turn?"

Willow nodded. "Yes. You seem to know your way around Sunnydale pretty well."

"You bet," Lonnie answered with a laconic grin. "I saw it all when I was putting up posters and passing out handbills. Do you know the best way to get into the cemetery?"

"You can usually squeeze through the gate, if it's even

locked," Willow answered with a knowing grin. *Or, if you're a Slayer, you can just jump over.* "It's the third drive on the right, behind those trees."

As the headlights of the truck sliced through the hedges around the cemetery gates, Willow saw several other cars and trucks parked in the street. "That's funny, there are other cars parked here."

"Maybe other people had the same idea," Lonnie muttered.

"Somebody's probably having a party," Rose suggested. "See, that house across the street is all lit up."

"Yeah, that's probably it," Willow agreed. "Are you sure you want to do this—it's not too late to see the courthouse."

Lonnie chuckled and turned off the engine. "I'm sure. How's your ice cream?"

"Great," she lied.

"Good." Lonnie grabbed his bag at her feet, opened the door, and stepped out. Warm, flower-scented air flowed into the truck cab.

Rose patted Willow's hand reassuringly. "Don't worry, honey, we won't bite. Much."

Grabbing her oversized purse, she oozed out of the car and held her hands out to Xander. "Hey, baby, we ready to party?"

"You bet!" He crawled over the stuffed tiger and vaulted out of the truck into her arms. They kissed disgustingly for several seconds, until Rose shoved him away and sauntered toward the gate. Xander loped after her like a puppy.

Willow was frozen in the truck, knowing that she had a chance to back out but only if she took it right now. *Why the cemetery? Whatever happened to parking on lonely country roads?*

Lonnie stuck his head in the window, and Willow jumped. "It's such a beautiful night," he drawled. "Come out and sit with us for a while. Howl at the moon."

Willow laughed nervously. "It's just my stomach—it's a little upset from all the junk food."

"I promise I won't feed you anything." Lonnie smiled charmingly.

"Okay, for a little while." Willow opened the door and stepped out.

With Rose in the lead, the foursome walked up to the wrought-iron gate, which was already open a crack. The padlocked chain that normally held it shut was nowhere to be seen.

"Oh, they stayed open just for us," Rose said with amusement. The gate creaked open as she pushed her body against it. Xander stumbled after her, his libido totally in charge.

"This looks like an old cemetery," Lonnie said, his hand warm and active on Willow's back, massaging her fears away. "Is anybody famous buried here?"

She thought about that question as she strolled through the gate. "There was Herbert Jeremiah, who invented the bathing cap, and I think there was some old rodeo cowboy. Many of the town's founding fathers are buried here. You know, Sunnydale is a lot older than it looks."

"I'm sure of that," Lonnie said, shutting the gate behind them. "That rodeo cowboy—where might his grave be?"

"Well, if he was really famous, he's down in the hollow, where the mausoleums are." Willow tried not to shiver as the surveyed the bleak landscape of tombstones, gnarly trees, and little mansions for dead people. *And undead,* she thought, remembering the last time she and Xander had been lured to the mausoleums by dates. At least there was plenty of light, with the full moon casting a silvery glow over the spooky proceedings.

She looked for Xander and Rose and saw them on the fresh-cut lawn, wrestling playfully. As they tussled and rolled about, they looked more like two puppies than two lovers, and Willow hoped that Rose thought of Xander as a younger brother. In the next instant, that hope was dashed as the wrestling degenerated into a lip-lock and embrace—right there in the cemetery, under a full moon.

Lonnie's hand tightened around her waist, and she let herself be dragged along the sidewalk. Despite his amorous clinch, he seemed to be in a hurry to get deeper into the cemetery—and to keep her close. Willow gazed back at Xander and Rose, who were still writhing in the dew. If she ignored reality in favor of fantasy, she could insert herself into Rose's place. But she would still prefer someplace dry.

Without warning, the petite carny tossed Xander off as easily as if he were a bedsheet. He rolled about twenty feet down a hill and crashed into a tombstone, while Rose jumped to her feet, laughing.

She was fixing her dress as she walked past Lonnie and Willow. "He's a frisky one, all right. Let's go see that big white spire down there."

Willow broke away from Lonnie to see if Xander was all right, but he came loping toward them. From the goofy expression on his lipstick-smeared face, she could tell that he was still lobotomized.

"Wow!" was all he could say as he staggered past them.

Angry and sad, Willow had a sudden urge to kiss Lonnie in front of Xander, and her face must have broadcast that loud and clear. Lonnie hovered closer, and she sensed that earthy, animal smell about him. Before she had a chance to meet his tender lips, Willow wrinkled her nose and sneezed!

"Sorry," she said with a sniffle. "I must be allergic to something. I don't understand it—I'm usually only allergic to dogs."

Anger flashed on Lonnie's handsome features, then he tipped his hat back and was once again charming. "Lots of stuff growing around here, especially ragweed. Let's catch up with them, okay?"

As long as Lonnie was being a gentleman, Willow wasn't going to be frantic about this strange site for their date. In many respects, it was better to be with a gentleman than a raving maniac like Xander.

A fleeting shape caught her attention before it vanished behind a tree trunk. It was too low to the ground to be human—it had to be a dog or some other kind of animal. *Maybe that's why I sneezed.* Willow hoped it wasn't a skunk. She watched the tree, but she didn't see any other sign of movement.

Then she heard voices, and they weren't coming from Xander and Rose, who were only a few feet ahead of them. The voices were coming from down in the hollow, where mausoleums and fancy tombstones decorated the city of the dead.

Rose had mentioned a white spire, and there not only was one, but about ten people were milling around it. At first, this was reassuring to Willow, because they were obviously living people. But the more she thought about it, the stranger it seemed that they would go to a cemetery at midnight and find a bunch of people already there. Once again, she told herself that the carnies couldn't be vampires. They lived in the sun; they ate corn dogs.

"You weren't kidding," Xander said puzzledly. "There really is a party here."

As they strolled toward the gathering, Willow realized that half of these other people were carnies and the other half were local kids. They were all on a mass double date!

She turned to Lonnie and asked, "What's going on?"

"It's just something we do in every town," Lonnie said with a shrug. "We don't know if there'll be a decent club or a park, but every town has a cemetery. So we just have a party there one night after work."

"You could've told us," Xander muttered. If anything, he was more disappointed about seeing all these people than Willow was. She hoped that he would go home disappointed.

"Oh, lighten up," Rose said, running a red-lacquered fingernail under Xander's chin. "The more, the merrier."

Doing a quick count, Willow saw there were exactly seven carnies and seven local kids, counting the four of them. Among the carnies were the red-haired woman and the dark-haired guy she had whipped at poker. Apparently, the old guy, Hopscotch, had not been able to get a date.

The carnies sat about on the tombstones with studied indifference, while the local kids looked awkward and confused. Whatever they had expected to happen this night, it wasn't hanging around in a cemetery, staring at one another. But as long as Xander's plans were upset too, Willow wasn't going to complain too loudly.

"What do we do now?" she asked. "Charades? Kevin Bacon?"

"We'd like to put on a little show for all of you," Lonnie announced. He nodded to his fellow carnies, and they climbed down from their perches and formed a rough line in front of the grave under the white spire. All of them were carrying some kind of bag or purse, and one of them lit a bundle of dried leaves. A pungent, spicy smoke filled the dark hollow in the cemetery.

Willow and Xander drifted closer to each other. From the side of his mouth, Xander whispered, "I hope they're not going to try to scare us."

"They already have," Willow answered. "I'm ready to bolt when you are."

"Let's see what happens."

"A hundred years ago," Lonnie began somberly, "a great man lived in this town. His name was Spurs Hardaway, and this is his grave. He was a showman, like us. In fact, you might say he was our inspiration and guiding light."

Lonnie exchanged a confident look with his fellow showmen. "Spurs enjoyed all types of sports; best of all, he loved to hunt. In honor of Spurs and his favorite pastime, we do a little show that we call the Coyote Dance. Tonight we have the perfect audience and the perfect moon gazing down upon us. Let us begin with a song."

Willow wouldn't exactly call it singing—not those strange whoops, cries, and guttural groans. The carnies looked properly spooky as they swayed and twitched in the silvery moonlight, surrounded by tombstones. All of the local kids were now bunching together, as if they were on the opposite team, waiting for a kickoff.

"Well, their singing bites," Xander murmured, "and their dancing is not much better."

"I'm ready to go when you are."

As the smoke from the flaming torch swirled around them, the carnies began to remove their clothes. It wasn't a sensual striptease—just people ditching their clothes, as if they were about to take a shower.

Xander grinned at Willow. "Hold on, things are looking up!"

A few other kids giggled, but the possessed performers paid no attention to them. They continued stripping, singing, and swaying—as if no one in the whole world were watching them. That was the most disturbing part of their act. Just when Willow thought things couldn't get any weirder, they reached into their duffel bags and pulled out old coyote skins, which they draped over their shoulders.

Xander looked at her and shrugged. "Costumes."

"This is too weird," Willow said, "I'm outta here."

She started to walk away from the twitching carnies, with two more local girls right behind her. Before they got ten feet, they were stopped short by the sound of low growls. The three girls stared in horror as half a dozen coyotes leaped upon tombstones and paths, cutting of their escape.

She heard gasps and shouts from the others, and she whirled around to see the seven dancers down on their hands and knees, trembling and growling as if possessed. The smoke swirled around them, making them look as if they were changing shape. As Willow stared more intently, she realized they *were* changing shape.

They were morphing into coyotes!

Triumphant howls echoed all around them as the coyotes cut loose in unison. She now realized that they were surrounded by at least fifteen coyotes. That didn't even count the ones writhing on the ground, turning *into* coyotes.

His eyes wide with fright, Xander sidled closer to Willow. "Next time, I'll listen to Buffy."

"Been there, thought that," she admitted.

A deep groaning sound came from behind them, and Xander, Willow, and the teens whirled around to see the grave under the white spire start to shudder. The earth and withered flowers crumbled away, as if an earthquake had gripped that grave and no other. They heard splintering noises—as if the coffin under the soil was also breaking apart.

Suddenly, several coyotes attacked the grave and began to dig furiously, trying to free whatever was in there. Trembling, Willow lifted her eyes to read the name on the grave: Spurs Hardaway.

Some of the other teens tried to make a break for it, and they were instantly surrounded by vicious coyotes. Snapping and growling, the canines herded them back into a frightened huddle. When one boy didn't move fast enough, a dark brown coyote lunged and bit his calf. Shrieking, he hobbled after the others. The number of coyotes had doubled, and Lonnie and his friends were . . . gone.

Everywhere Willow looked, there was something horrible going on, especially behind her. Thanks to the frantic digging of the coyotes, the grave was open, and something was pounding its way out of its coffin. Chunks of rotted wood flew outward, and skeletal fists reached toward the sky.

"Release me!" groaned a low voice that wasn't remotely human.

From the full moon overhead came a bright beam of light, which struck the sphere at the top of the white spire.

It exploded as if hit by lightning, and sparks and debris flew everywhere. Willow ducked to the ground, and she was sorry she did, because now she had a level view of the open grave.

She gaped as a grotesque, worm-eaten corpse rose slowly from the pit. The monster was wrapped in a ragged bear skin, complete with rotted head. Smoke, leaves, and wind swirled all around this gruesome apparition as he threw his skull back and cackled.

"Ladies and gentlemen, it's good to be back!"

The coyotes howled and yipped triumphantly, while the teens whimpered in terror.

"Okay, guys," Xander said, backing away from the zombie astride the grave. "You scared us—that was really . . . something! Can we leave now?"

The coyotes seemed to laugh, and the gruesome corpse spoke in a hollow voice. "Not yet. You haven't seen my best trick."

Crunching like a pile of bones, the monster slumped forward and was completely covered by the ratty bear skin. The mangy pelt looked a million years old. As he coyotes yipped and yowled and the teens wept, the old bear skin swayed back and forth. Lightning crackled in the sky, and the moon turned a horrid shade of red.

Willow blinked because she couldn't believe her eyes. Black hairs on the back of the pelt began to rise and twitch. *Must be static electricity,* she thought.

Xander gripped her hand, frightened. "It's all our parents' fault for moving to the Hellmouth."

"I know," Willow said.

For some reason, the coyotes stopped howling and they began to look around, puzzled. A few of them even loped off toward the street, and the others trailed after them, uncertain what to do. The terrified local kids seized the moment and ran like jackrabbits in the opposite direction. Willow was about to do the same when she heard a roar that was so thundering it shook the trees to their roots.

She whirled around to see an enormous grizzly bear rearing over her and Xander. It had to be at least ten feet tall—a thousand pounds of teeth, gristle, and muscle! The primeval monster roared again, sounding furious and very, very hungry.

"Say no to fur!" a voice shouted.

Willow and Xander flopped to the ground as a lithe figure came bounding through the air behind them. It was Buffy! Doing gymnastic flips, the Slayer flew over their heads and smashed into the chest of the grizzly bear. The beast roared in outrage and staggered backward, clawing at something shiny in its fur.

Willow realized that Buffy had stabbed it with some kind of sword—she could only see about two inches of the handle. With a loud grunt, the Slayer hurled herself into the grizzly one more time, knocking it back another ten feet. The bear's enormous bulk smashed into the white spire with such force that the whole thing teetered, crumbled, and fell. Tons of white marble came thundering down around the wounded animal.

Buffy rolled away at the last moment as the entire monument imploded into the earth. The bear's anguished growls became strangled human cries—then nothing at all—as chunks of marble crushed the creature. After a few moments, a haze of dust and a sickly stench of death rose from the grave, but nothing else.

Xander instantly turned to Buffy. "Hey, we believed you the whole time! We were just keeping an eye on them, because you were, like, nowhere to be seen."

"Thanks," Willow said. She didn't have enough breath left to say more than that, but she really meant it.

Buffy sighed. "I hope my mom doesn't check the sterling silver." She snapped her fingers. "Giles!"

The three of them jogged across the cemetery and out the main entrance. In the street, they found Giles sitting in his car, with about twenty coyotes clawing at the vehicle. He had his window down a crack and was blowing on something—but making no sound.

He saw them and Buffy waved. A moment later, Giles started up his engine and drove off slowly, with the coyotes bounding playfully behind him.

"Too bad," Buffy said. "I think your dates have dumped you—for a guy with a dog whistle."

"Why be *coyotes*?" Xander asked, totally confused. "Isn't it fun enough being humans? Especially when you look like *that*?"

Buffy shook her head. "It's a long story. Let's get a

good night's sleep and meet tomorrow morning. We can all go together to see them. Now that they don't have a leader, maybe we can talk some sense into them."

"Will you walk us home, Buffy?" Willow asked.

The Slayer smiled and put her arm around her friend's shoulder. "Sure. Was he at least a good kisser?"

"Yeah." Willow grinned.

AFTERWORD

Buffy, Willow, Xander, and Giles drove out to the vacant lot about noon the next day, but they were too late. The carnival was gone—every bolt, compressor, and stuffed animal. In the spot where the Ferris wheel had stood the day before, there was nothing but the ashes and dying embers of a large bonfire.

When they stopped to poke around the fire, they noticed the charred remains of several animal skins. That seemed to have been the purpose of the fire—to burn the skins.

"Hopscotch said that the spell would be broken if we stopped Spurs Hardaway from coming back," Buffy remarked. "Maybe now they're free to live their own lives."

"Human lives, let's hope," Giles added.

"I hope they find peace," Willow said.

Buffy felt eyes gazing at her back, and she turned to see a lone coyote standing high on the hill behind the vacant lot. She waved at the old coyote, and it turned and loped away.

Night of the Living Rerun

Dedicated with love to my wife, Lydia.

With much thanks to David and Bobbi, Lisa and Liz, that Whedon guy, and the cast and crew of *Buffy*, especially Ken Estes for doing that video playback thing.

I'd also like to take this opportunity to say hello to my mom, my stepfather, my mother-in-law, my brothers, their wives, my nieces, my cousins, their spouses, their children, my aunts, my uncles, and everybody else associated with family values.

CHAPTER ONE

Nothing ever changed in the Master's lair. Nothing of importance, anyway.

Oh, a few minions and undead assistants always came and went, but they fit into the nothing-of-importance category.

The Master had lived in these dreary, monotonous tunnels for nearly thirty years. By now he was deep in the process of going stark raving mad, simply from the razor-sharp dullness of virtually everything.

The Master felt he was living beneath his station. He felt like a giant, gilded cockroach, scurrying up and down the tunnels in perpetual search of an exit which did not exist.

That was on the good days. . . .

Lately the Master had become less prone to shout. For this his lowly, sniveling minions were infinitely grateful—the echoes made their ears bleed. The Master rarely shouted when a plan was going well. And recently he had bragged often about devising his most subtle, devious plan ever.

Keep in mind, the minions never saw the Master actually working on a plan. He never did *anything.*

The minions clung to the faint, doubtlessly futile hope that the Master's current plan, whatever it was, would succeed beyond his wildest expectations.

Then, the Master would be gone. Out of here. Splitsville from the Lair. At long last striding the surface of the Earth like a primordial god from the lower depths. Badder than Mars, more twisted than Hades.

On Earth the scene would be chaos, as the population found itself as close to the lower depths of the spiritual underworld as one could get without actually being there.

Thus preoccupied with a personal reign of terror of mythological proportions, the Master would have little time to devote to the insignificant minions minding his former prison.

So that down here, in the place where nothing ever happened, the unworthy minions could walk off the stage of history forever, and never have to do anything again.

Looking back, Buffy realized the entire adventure had begun long before she'd ever realized it. When had it started? When the Master had begun his manipulations? Had it begun with the idea of the exhibition? Or when Mom had moved to Sunnydale?

Maybe it had begun with the creation of *The Moonman.* Or perhaps with Prince Ashton Eisenberg's Prophecy of the Dual Duels. Maybe the Salem witch trials were the true beginning. It was odd to think that certain events of 1692 could have such a direct bearing on events in 1996. If stranger things had happened, Buffy did not want to know what they were.

For Buffy personally, it had begun with the dreams. At first they consisted only of a few images that recurred now and then. They had been going on for a few weeks when one afternoon in the library, Giles, from out of the blue, suggested Buffy write down her dreams first thing every morning. "Before you even get out of bed!" he insisted.

"Why?" Buffy asked, thinking of those images. "And why now?"

Giles shrugged. "Other Slayers have kept dream journals. It might help you get in touch with your inner warrior." He handed her a notebook. "This should do quite nicely."

"For me? Giles, you shouldn't have."

"You're welcome, Buffy."

"Maybe I don't want to get in touch with my inner warrior. I can't be the Slayer *all* the time. Sometimes, I just want to go to sleep and forget all about this last-stand-against-evil nonsense." She stopped when she saw her friends' faces. "Forget it. Bad idea. Never mind."

"I think she's trying to say she wants a life," Willow said, typing in a series of commands without looking up from her computer screen.

"A life? Whatever do you mean?" asked Giles, taken aback at the enormity of the concept.

"Yeah, Buffy, whaddya mean?" Xander teased. "We have times, don't we?"

"Buffy, is this some kind of career thing?" Willow asked.

"A motivational problem?" Giles asked, raising one eyebrow.

Xander perked up. "A good action movie will make you forget your troubles. There's a new Jackie Chan–Jim Carrey team-up. We can go together. Tonight."

"No thanks," said Buffy, taking the notebook. "I was just under the delusion that if I kept a few private thoughts to myself, I'd have an actual private life someday. Guess I should have known better."

"You are the Slayer for this generation," said Giles, in all seriousness. "A private life is out of the question. And as the current Watcher, I should know."

"Giles, you need to get out more," Buffy said. Then she looked at the cover photo on the notebook. "Who's gramps?"

"That's Sigmund Freud," said Giles in his best you-should-already-know-this-too tone. "I thought his example as a pioneer in the exploration of the human mind might be inspirational."

"Oh yeah. He had a thing about cigars, didn't he?" Buffy

handed the notebook back to Giles. "That's okay. I think I can find my own inspiration."

"As you wish," said Giles coolly.

When Buffy got home, she found her Mom unpacking a box. "New shipment?" she asked.

"Look at these! They'll fit in perfectly with the new show." Buffy's mom held up a notebook. The photo on the front was of a sculpture of a man composed of squares and rectangles. "This is the great sculptor V.V. Vivaldi's masterpiece *The Moonman.*"

"Cool!" said Buffy, admiring it. "I just so happen to need a new notebook."

"Then it's yours. But tell people they can see the original at the gallery."

Before she went to sleep, Buffy dutifully put the notebook and a pen on the nightstand beside her bed. She was out like a light the moment she put head to pillow. Her sleep was deep, deeper and colder than any she'd previously known.

When she awoke, she discovered she'd already written down her dream.

The images themselves creeped her out. There was a pulpit lying in a heap, as if smashed by a giant club. Maggots swirled around the feet of a guru whose face had been seriously rearranged. Graves burst open with blasts of lightning, young women danced in the moonlight, and people or things passed by on the wind, only to go nuts and attack her.

Okay, so they weren't exactly the sort of dreams she'd thought she'd be having, but they were interesting, and they sort of made sense if you happened to be a Slayer.

But one image had struck her as being out of place—not really the sort of thing she'd associate with being Buffy Summers, a modern Slayer—but there it was: the moon, with a huge meteor heading directly for it!

Every morning she wrote down her dreams from the night before. After about a month she reread what she'd written to see if anything struck her as noteworthy.

She was surprised to find that while some of the images were indeed random—as you'd expect in a dream—others had an internal chronological order.

The story in the dreams began through the image-distorted eyes of a little girl learning how to sew with her hands and how to cook using a huge fireplace in the kitchen. Soon she learned how to gather chestnuts and berries from the woods, and how to grind wheat for bread. When she grew older, she took to preparing the meat. Evidently she'd taken rather well to that chore, because there were a lot of images from the girl's point of view like plucking geese and chickens and cleaning fish.

Eventually the girl reached adolescence. While the other young women were being courted by the eligible young men of whatever village this happened to be, Buffy dreamed of taking over the household hunting chores. She sensed a tragedy had happened to the head of the household that had necessitated this, but she couldn't be sure.

Her dreamself could use an ax and a knife, and a flintlock rifle whose powder had to be lit with a match before she could fire it. She was a good shot, and Buffy dreamed of bringing down turkeys at a hundred and fifty yards as well as geese and duck on the wing. She was also adept with the bow and arrow, and used them not only for hunting but for fishing as well.

There were images of people interspersed with all this sewing, cooking, and hunting. Buffy had no idea who they might be, though it was reasonable to assume they were friends and family.

Around the time the girl was fifteen, the nature of the images began to change. Violently. Indians killed most of the friends and family she'd glimpsed in previous dreams, and those images were interspersed with images of herself killing Indians in return. And, as time passed in the dream, of killing all sorts of abominations. Vampires. Zombies. Demons disguised as Quakers, Indians, or British aristocrats. Stuff that struck Buffy as being rather usual. Only the time period was different.

One night, without warning, the dream became a single coherent narrative. It began with Buffy's dreamself in the middle of the square in a strange village on a starry night. Patches of ice-hard snow were on the ground. The clean, neat square was illuminated by a series of oil lamps. At one end stood a huge wooden church, its position in relation to the shops and offices designating it as the most important place in the community.

In the center of the square was a gallows. A group of angry men in plain black suits pushed a young man wearing a cleric's collar toward the steps leading up to the hangman's noose. A few of the men carried old-fashioned flintlock rifles, the kind where the powder and bullet were loaded separately. Occasionally, when the young man wasn't moving fast enough, they prodded him with the rifle barrels.

Buffy looked down. Her dreamself sat astride a horse; across the saddle lay her flintlock, loaded and ready for bear. A muscle twitched in her wrist. She calculated how fast she could reload, and how many men she might shoot if they rushed her.

She sighed; such an approach was not worthy of the righteous. She fired her flintlock. Into the air.

Some of the men gasped, others denounced her or shook their fists, but none made a move toward her. Her hands and powderbag were a blur as she reloaded faster than any had ever imagined possible.

She pointed the weapon directly at the man at the forefront. "Forgive me, gentlemen, I usually refrain from interfering with matters of justice—"

The man was large and fat, but clearly possessed great confidence and personal power. He looked up at her defiantly. Behind his brave smile, however, lay profound fear, though whether it was directed at Buffy's dreamself or at the situation in general was a little hard to tell. "Samantha Kane. I might have known. You are tardy once again."

"I was delayed."

"By the presence of evil, I presume?"

Samantha Kane shrugged. "What is evil in your eyes, sir, is not necessarily evil in mine."

She lowered her flintlock and got off her horse. The crowd of men whispered furtively among themselves. Samantha Kane did not care. She knew they thought her unusual. Women in this day and age did not ride horseback, they did not travel alone, they were not marksmen, and they never, *never* were feared by common rabble. Such women would have been accused of witchcraft, found guilty regardless of the mitigating circumstances, and hanged.

Yet no one dared accuse Samantha Kane of witchcraft. Her reputation precluded that. "It is good to see you, Judge Danforth, though I wish the circumstances were more pleasant."

"Circumstances are never pleasant in these perilous times, Goodwoman Kane. You are well?" He looked at her kindly, the fear in his eyes replaced by a great weariness.

"I am well. And you, my friend?" Samantha regarded this Judge Danforth as an ally, though she still harbored suspicions about him.

"Well enough to carry out my sad duties. This poor wretch has just been pronounced guilty of practicing the rites of a warlock and of consorting with a witch. The sentence is to be carried out immediately."

"Immediately?"

Danforth shrugged and frowned. "Normally those found guilty of consorting with the devil are given twenty-four hours to contemplate the error of their ways and ask for forgiveness, in the hope that their soul may be redeemed. But this wretch"—the judge sneered—"was a protégé of mine. I had high hopes that he would one day become a righteous leader of the community and would save many souls. It saddens me greatly to see how far he has fallen."

Samantha looked the "wretch" in the eye. They were golden, sensitive eyes, and she found herself liking them.

"Your name, sir," Samantha demanded.

He regarded her coldly. "I am the Right Reverend John Goodman. And you are Samantha Kane, the witch hunter."

"Among other things." She noted his clothing was filthy as a result of his imprisonment, but he still wore the white collar of the clergy despite his fallen status. His face was bruised and his long red hair was matted. She supposed he was holding up pretty well for a man who was about to be hanged.

"You people," Samantha said to the crowd, and especially to a man pouring whale oil over the wood, "just wait."

"Why?" sneered one, who obviously thought her no different from the rest of the witches.

Samantha grabbed him by the frills of his waistcoat, pulled his face close to hers, and growled softly, "Because it is not a good night to die." She released him, then looked around. "Your 'warlock' can die tomorrow night just as easily."

Judge Danforth took her by the arm and drew her gently away from Goodman and the crowd. "Are you defending this man?" he asked patiently. "This *devil worshipper*?"

"I know I missed Goodman's accusation and trial because I was away dispatching abominations in New York," said Samantha, flashing on an image of the natives rising from their burial grounds to attack a town meeting, "but I have reason to suspect you and the others have been duped. I would know more."

Shocked, Danforth said, "First, Goodman denounced a woman as a witch. Second, after we debated the evidence and came to our decision to try the woman, he was nowhere to be found. He only reappeared after she'd been found guilty and was scheduled to be punished. Third, soon after he visited her in the witch dungeon, she made good her escape. The witch is still at large. What more evidence is needed to conclude he is in league with the devil?"

"How righteous is the tribunal who sanctions the execution of an innocent man?" Samantha shot back. "I would know more!"

"For instance?" Danforth asked.

"Was this witch accused on his word alone? Or are there others who believe this woman in league with the devil?"

Danforth's mouth curled up. He nodded to a man Samantha recognized as Sheriff Corwin, who in turn nodded to the man Samantha had pushed around. "Bring out the girls," said Sheriff Corwin, "bring them out immediately and show her the devil is not in New York, nor Williamsburg, nor any other place people believe him to be. It is 1692, and the devil is here in Salem."

Salem in 1692! Buffy almost jolted awake. This past Slayer had operated smack in the midst of the witch hunts in Salem, Massachusetts. It was one of the most notorious incidents in early American colonial history. Buffy had learned a lot about it from renting horror films.

The man Samantha had pushed around glared at her. "This is your fault, woman. You deny me justice."

"If what you want is just, it will not be denied," Samantha replied. "Now please, sir, do as you have been asked."

"This is Joseph Putnam," said Judge Danforth. "His daughter Heather is one of the girls he must fetch to satisfy your curiosity. Go, man, and let us do what must be done."

He went. Samantha barely noticed. "It is not mere curiosity that causes me to question your wisdom."

"Though that is certainly true in part."

"Yes."

Samantha and the men waited in silence. Fireflies flew everywhere, reflecting in the eyes of the angry crowd. Goodman stood calmly, unmoving, looking at her. A breeze ruffled his long hair. Samantha was impressed by his bravery. She felt that under different circumstances, they might have been friends.

She saw no reason why she should not fight for his survival. After all, was she not charged with protecting the innocent as well as eradicating abominations?

"He is the one!" cried out a young girl hysterically. "He is the one responsible for my delirium!" The material and workmanship of the girl's dress marked her as a member of a wealthy merchant family, yet the sleeves were tattered and many stitches were torn. The girl's eyes were wild, and fresh red scratches marred her ivory complexion.

Samantha recognized her as Heather Putnam. She noted the tips of Heather's fingers were bloody; the girl had injured herself, an indication of contamination by the devil himself if ever there was one.

Back in the present, Buffy ascribed her condition to hysteria, pure and simple.

Heather and two others approximately the same age and in the same general condition were bound at the waist by a single rope. Putnam and four other men were required to hold the rope in order to drag them in the desired direction. Having brought them this far, the men were now obliged to hold the girls in their place to prevent them from lunging at Reverend Goodman and, presumably, scratching out his eyes.

Putnam's mind was not on his job. He stared mournfully at his daughter and occasionally wiped a tear from his eye.

Danforth shook his head in pity at the girls. Goodman, on the other hand, muttered a prayer for them. The men in the crowd regarded them with horror.

"He is responsible! He is the one!" the girls said. "He is responsible!"

"I thought you said the slave woman was responsible for your condition," Danforth protested.

The girls got very quiet. Heather frowned, deep in thought.

The other two pointedly looked at her, as if silently asking for direction. Heather nodded. Then, almost in unison, they proclaimed, "The slave is responsible too! Tituba is the one! Tituba is the one!"

"Do you see?" Danforth calmly asked Samantha. "They are all quite mad. And very easily confused. Each and every one. Obviously the work of the devil."

Samantha's sharp retort formed in Buffy's mind, but the dreamworld of the past was suddenly obliterated in a flash of red light, and Buffy realized, with a groan, that she had fallen out of bed.

"Buffy!" shouted her mother from down the hall. "Are you all right?"

CHAPTER TWO

Buffy began her morning ritual of tai chi exercises at the first sign of dawn. She tried not to think about her dream. What had seemed so supremely exciting now seemed vaguely unnatural. Obviously the best thing to do would be to relax, so she could face the day with a clear head.

That decided, Buffy checked out her appearance in the mirror on her dresser. And practically fainted: There was a bruise the size of Kansas on her forehead.

Later, at breakfast, Mom was preoccupied with advertising the V.V. Vivaldi exhibition at the gallery (which she was sure would bring in a lot of business), but she did find time to make it clear—for the umpteenth time—that Buffy's pretty skin wasn't going to keep its pure, youthful quality too long if she kept banging it up all the time.

Buffy shrugged, absently tossing her butter knife into the open dishwasher.

The dishwasher happened to be across the kitchen. The butter knife had sailed through the air end-over-end and landed handle up.

It was followed in quick succession by the rest of Buffy's silverware. Each piece landed perfectly in the rack. Buffy paused, twirling her steak knife in one hand like it was a baton.

Mom sat there silent and slack-jawed. "Buffy—?"

Buffy remembered she had an audience. "It's, ah, something we've been learning in Home Ec." She threw the steak knife.

And missed. Completely.

It landed in the sink. Buffy picked up her glass and moved toward the dishwasher.

"Ah, wait a minute there!" interrupted Mom. "Why not do the rest the old-fashioned way."

"Oh, we never throw the dinnerware."

Her mother looked relieved.

"Not until next semester."

Buffy walked to school under a cloud. She'd been so distracted by the dream that she'd gotten sloppy and let her mother see something that reminded her of when Buffy had burned down the school gym—a big *no-no* in the mother's manual. Mom had said a thousand times that if she caught Buffy doing anything that smacked of that kind of trouble again, she would ground her indefinitely.

Buffy believed her. She didn't want to have to explain to Giles that she couldn't save the world from a wave of enraged soul-eaters because she was chained to her bedpost.

The only silver lining in her cloud was the knowledge that soon she could confide to Willow about the dream. She wanted to tell Willow first because Giles would just try to explain it all away with facts and theories, and something about the experience was simply too fantastic for that. Buffy didn't want to spoil it yet.

The only problem, as it turned out, was Xander, who knew their schedules better than they did and hence did not miss an opportunity when it came to finding one of them. Today he simply would not go away when Buffy and Willow made it clear his presence wasn't welcome at the moment.

Consequently, Buffy was probably harsher than necessary when she finally told him to get lost.

"Why?" Xander asked. "We always study in the library together."

Giles cleared his throat but refrained from looking up from the massive, dusty tome he'd been studying since they'd come in.

"You too—out!" Buffy pleaded. "Willow and I need to be alone."

"We do?" said Willow.

"Yeah, You know, girl stuff: hair, nails . . ."

"Clothes, boys," Willow quickly added.

Giles closed the book and said with mock resignation, "Come along, Xander, I guess even a Vampire Slayer needs a private moment once in a while. Besides, this will give us a chance to discuss certain astrological portents we need researched."

"Right now?"

"Why dally where we're not wanted?"

"I'll want a complete report later!" said Xander over his shoulder as Giles led him away.

"He must think you want to confide in me about your personal life," Willow whispered, barely containing her excitement. "Is it about boys? You do want to talk about boys, don't you?" She was visibly crestfallen when Buffy, who suddenly had second thoughts, countered with:

"Well, no. I need to talk about history."

"You're kidding."

"No. I've got some questions about colonial times. I'm afraid I haven't always been paying attention in class."

"So what else is new? You've been daydreaming about boys, right?"

"No, I've been taking catnaps because I've been up all hours of the night keeping the world safe from the scum of the nether regions."

"Oh, now I understand why you're so interested in history all of a sudden," said Willow, her sigh indicating her reluctant acceptance. "We are, after all, having a big test this afternoon."

All the blood drained from Buffy's face. "This afternoon? Today? Or this afternoon, tomorrow?"

Willow checked her watch. "Today. In about twenty minutes, to be precise."

"What kind of test is it?"

"Probably multiple choice, or in your case, multiple guess. That way it'll be easy for Mrs. Honneger to grade. She likes doing homework about as much as we do."

"So, why don't you ask me a few questions?" said Buffy, trying to relax. Tension always worked against her when she was trying to recall facts for a test, though strangely, it always seemed to help when the situation called for arcane vampire lore or sophisticated combat improvisation.

"Okay, what year was Plymouth Colony founded?"

"1620!"

"Who founded it?"

"The Puritans, who were fleeing religious persecution in England."

"And what did they want?" Willow asked, her eyes narrowing.

"A place where they could enjoy religious freedom. But that's where they sorta screwed up. 'Cause the only religion they allowed was their own. Dissenters were punished—banished! Did you know that?"

"I knew that. What was the name of their colony?"

"The Massachusetts Bay Colony."

"What kind of government did they practice?"

"A theocracy, meaning government by interpretation of the religious scriptures. Preachers had quite a bit of influence, since officeholders always had to look to them for approval."

Willow pursed her lips. "Buffy, you *have* been studying, haven't you? On the sly, right?"

"Uh, right."

"What can you tell me about the witch trials of 1692?"

"Not too much," said Buffy. "A group of girls about our age became afflicted with convulsive fits; short-term hearing, seeing, and memory loss; and strange bruises and marks on the skin! The local doctors didn't know what to call it, so their diagnosis was witchcraft! By the time the preachers, judges, and sheriffs got involved, there was a full-scale panic. At that time, anything that couldn't be explained was blamed on the supernatural!"

"Mrs. Honneger never told us that!"

"Did you know that one of the first people to be accused was a slave named Tituba, who on dark and stormy nights fed the girls tales of possession and the walking dead? Tituba survived, actually, because she repented. Mrs. Honneger thinks the girls were faking their symptoms, but the problem could have been entirely medical or psychological in origin! Or maybe they just wanted the attention!"

Buffy became pensive. "You know, if you put together the changing social and political structure of the colony with the people's view of a world where the devil and his demons were actively conspiring against them—then the Salem witch trials were almost inevitable. Besides, hysteria over witches had been going on in Europe for a couple of centuries, and there they were burned at the stake, rather than merely hanged."

"I wouldn't worry too much about this test if I were you," Willow said.

Just then Giles stalked back in, followed by Xander, who was barely keeping his mirth to himself. Giles wore a stern expression on his face.

"I hope you ladies are through with your little talk," Giles said, "because I suspect a situation is brewing right under our very noses."

Buffy sighed. "Another emergency? No prob. I can probably fit it in between history and math."

Xander giggled.

Giles looked at him sternly. "This isn't funny. The human race could be doomed to extinction."

"I'm sorry," said Xander, in tones that indicated he really wasn't, "but you're getting all worked up about a prophecy made two hundred years ago by some guy even you admit was insane."

"He doesn't sound too reliable," said Willow as Buffy gestured at Xander to stop snickering. Which Xander did, but with difficulty.

Giles cleared his throat, then plunged right ahead. "I have been studying *The Eibon*. It is the most notorious book of prophecies ever written, with the possible exception of two lost books referred to in that great cycle of East Indian mythology, *The Mahabharata*. Unlike those two lost books, however,

The Eibon is still with us. An early copy is almost always in the possession of the Watcher, passed down from the previous occupant of that post.

"You've heard, of course, of Nostradamus, Cayce, Criswell—the great seers of modern Western thought who saw far into the future and then wrote it down, in the hope their wisdom would be handed down to subsequent generations. Their major predictions tend to be deliberately vague, so it's possible to draw many different meanings from them. Some people, for instance, believe Nostradamus predicted the advent of the airplane and tank as weapons during World War I, while others believe the same verse refers to the approach of the tropical weather phenomenon known as *El Niño*. Personally, I think they're both wrong, but nobody's been asking me my opinion lately."

"Is that such a surprise?" asked Xander, unable to resist the line. He was mildly frustrated when everyone pointedly ignored him.

"Greatest of all was the mad Austrian heretic Prince Ashton Eisenberg V, who lived from 1692 till 1776. Toward the end of his life, when he was imprisoned in the Bastille in Paris—thanks to being caught in the midst of some indiscretion—he wrote a book of prophecies unparalleled in their precision. When he writes that the snake-brother's army shall devour the parasitic brother's army in the New World, for instance, he's obviously referring to the American Civil War, nearly a century later."

"Obviously," agreed Willow.

Caught up in his lecture, Giles continued, "Prince Ashton's most famous prediction is known simply as Eisenberg's Prophecy of the Dual Duels. It's the vaguest of all his predictions. Roughly translated from its pidgin German, it says:

There came a time when the planets and stars
were in harmony
A time when that which was before, shall be again,
And that which was done, will be done again.
A time when a great beast shall crawl onto
the land,
A beast beyond defeat but not beyond loss
A beast who shall be vanquished by the pure in
heart.
Such a time shall come again
As surely as the stars will once again be in
similar harmony.
And at this time another beast shall rise,
A beast different in body but same in spirit
And like his brother of old he shall strive
To steal the moon, to consume the sun, and to
walk the earth.
To see if he might strike a dagger into the heart
of destiny.

"Interesting, wouldn't you say?" Giles eagerly awaited their response.

"Actually, the word I was thinking of was far-fetched," said Xander.

"I think I'm leaning toward Xander's point of view on this one," said Buffy. "Tell me again how accurate this guy was—"

"—on matters other than this great beast thing," Willow suggested.

Giles smiled weakly. "There are some who believe Prince Ashton Eisenberg predicted night baseball."

"Before or after the invention of satellite television?" Xander asked smartly.

"Before."

"Wow," said Xander breathlessly. "He *was* good."

"So when did the first great beast try to walk the earth?" asked Willow.

"The beast in question was an abomination called the Despised One. The Despised One tried to rise from the nether-regions sometime around the year of Prince Ashton's birth—"

"1692!" exclaimed Buffy.

"And it happened somewhere in the New World. Now, I grant you old Ashton was certifiable, but he is a towering figure in occult studies because so many of his prophecies have come true. He claimed the ghost of the Despised One communicated with him occasionally and discussed strategies to shift the traditional balance between good and evil. Ashton approached occult rather scientifically, so when a routine examination verified the beast's information, he realized the strategy could be repeated, but only at particular times, when rather specific conditions are met.

"I don't know about most of the conditions, but the stars are getting right. And that means we could be in the midst of it and not even know it yet."

"1692," said Xander soberly. "That's the year of the Salem witch trials. Which happens to be one of the subjects we're being tested on in history class today."

The bell rang, indicating study period was over.

"A test which is right about now," said Willow.

The moment Buffy laid down her pen in history class, she knew she'd aced the test. Answers had come to her so easily she'd had to force herself to slow down, just in case Mrs. Honneger had thrown a few trick questions into the mix.

After midnight that evening, she snuck out of the house to foil an insane circus clown's plot to infest the Sunnydale rat population with piranha DNA. The clown, it seemed, held a grudge against the town after some environmental mishap he had suffered during his youth.

Buffy was successful—but not until the clown had been devoured by his own creations. Unfortunately, while eluding the horde of mutant rodents by crawling through a flooded basement, Buffy came down with a serious cold.

By the time the rats lay dead in a giant heap before a statue of the blindfolded lady justice, Buffy could barely breathe, and she was sweating like she'd done an intense workout on a hundred-degree day.

Immediately after sneaking back into the house, she took a cold shower to try to get her temperature to drop. Once again she was out the moment her head struck the pillow. Her hair was still wrapped in a towel and her body didn't seem cooler by even one degree.

Her mind fell through a sea of holes. It landed on an infinity of nothingness.

And she was back. Back as Samantha Kane, intrepid witch hunter in 1692 Massachusetts; but the Salem gallows, the angry men, and Heather Putnam and her co-conspirators were nowhere around.

Samantha was alone, on horseback, in the crossroads of two trails in a daylit wood. She had followed the escaped Sarah Dinsdale's footsteps to this point, but now they had suddenly disappeared.

No matter, Buffy heard Samantha thinking, *she'll reveal herself another way. They always do.*

Samantha's mount was jittery. Her own horse was spent, so she'd borrowed this mount from Judge Danforth, but it wasn't used to being ridden as hard as Samantha needed it to.

The rays of the setting sun reflected off something down the eastern fork. Samantha jerked the reins to get the horse's attention, then rode it roughly to the place where she'd seen the glint.

Buffy mumbled in her sleep, "The way you're treating that mare, it's a wonder she doesn't throw you in a briar patch."

Samantha dismounted and lifted a bright orange piece of cloth shaped like the letter *W* from where it was caught on top of a bramble bush. It was the mark of the witch—customarily sewn onto the clothing of a devil's consort once sentence was passed.

One thing was obvious: Sarah Dinsdale had taken the eastern fork.

Samantha spurred her horse onward. Night fell quickly this time of year, and the Slayer knew she must find Sarah soon, or she would lose her under cover of darkness.

But by late dusk Samantha realized the witch had left no further evidence of her passing this way; indeed, if she had taken this direction in the first place.

Samantha brought her horse to a halt and fumed. Flummoxed by a witch! She felt very stupid, which made her very, very angry.

Suddenly the walls of the dream shifted a few hours into the night. The seventeenth-century Slayer sat by a campfire. She was alone, without a captor to keep her company; even the corpse of a witch would have been an improvement, because then Samantha would have had her satisfaction to keep her warm.

The forest was quiet, devoid of insect noises and animal calls, and it was still—no breeze rustled the leaves, no animal wandered about. Not even the owls hooted in the trees.

Samantha knew this silence was unnatural. The forest was a live, vibrant place. It was this quiet only when the presence of some malevolent force made it so.

Samantha yawned. She had been traveling nonstop for the past three weeks and had expected to rest once in Salem. She needed time to refresh herself, and to think. It didn't appear she'd have it anytime soon.

She tore off a piece of dried meat with her teeth, sat on a log, and watched the fire. Samantha didn't regret being the Slayer of this time—in fact, she rather enjoyed ridding the earth of unclean abominations—but she disliked the lonely nights.

She thought of roads she might have taken, opportunities seemingly offered up by God's will millions of years ago. In truth, only eight years had passed since Samantha had first embarked on the quest, but each year seemed like a lifetime.

Suddenly—what? A sound of some sort, but it ceased almost the moment it began.

It had happened there, in the brush.

Samantha picked up her flintlock—she'd refilled the powder just this morning—and with her other hand took a torch from the fire.

Her every sound was accentuated, from the crunching of pebbles underfoot to the soft rustle of a branch she shifted to get a better look at the place from which the sound had come. None of those noises, however, could match the pounding, pounding, pounding of her heart. She was convinced the thunder in her chest and temples could be heard all the way to New York.

A cluster of leaves and twigs near the ground moved.

The thunder stopped; Samantha's heart felt like it had

collapsed. But a bittersweet taste in her mouth forestalled the fear. It was the taste she always got when she knew she was in the presence of an abomination. Every chance she had to rid the Earth of one of those infernal things made her thrilled to be alive. And every thrill erased a thousand regrets.

She moved in, wishing for a third arm so that she might hold forth her rapier as well.

She shook the torch and yelled. Not the most cautious move, but certain impulses toward danger were among her more self-destructive traits.

The move worked. Fortunately or not—mostly not, from Buffy's perspective. Because *it* darted out! And it was charging full out like a giant spider, weaving from side to side with every step, yet never wavering from its basic direction: straight toward Samantha Kane!

It leapt, grabbing Samantha's throat with gray, decomposing fingers that were amazingly strong. They squeezed Samantha's neck. *Hard.*

Samantha dropped her torch and her pistol and grabbed *it* by the stump at the end of its hand. Actually, that's all it was—a disembodied hand, but it was one that could move of its own accord, with a will of its own. Samantha couldn't pry the fingers loose. Her face and lungs felt like they were about to explode.

She suddenly remembered her knife. She began butchering the hand. Tearing off the skin was easy; the hand was about the size of a rabbit, and Samantha had skinned plenty of those.

She whittled away at the muscles, yet the bones of the fingers squeezed just as hard on their own. They had no need of muscles—exactly the sort of thing Samantha had come to expect from such sorcerous vileness.

One by one, she cut the finger bones from the hand. Lacking even a palm, the fingers still tried to hang on to her throat. Samantha had to break them off with her own hands.

She seethed with anger and shivered in disgust. With the simplest of lures, the witch had drawn Samantha into a trap. This really gnawed at Samantha's pride—she was the best hunter and tracker in the northern colonies who didn't wear war paint and worship like a heathen, and she'd been tricked like a novice.

Samantha noticed her mount was nervous and was trying to pull its reins free.

She picked up another torch from the fire and somewhat impulsively, but with a growing sense of horror, peered deeper into the bush.

Other body parts approached: Another hand walked on fingers. One full arm and the two halves of another rolled toward her. At least the head was still attached—though to a limbless torso. That meant the head and torso had to pull themselves forward with the use of the neck, teeth, and chin, a process that had wreaked havoc with the corpse's freshly decaying flesh.

The eyes looked toward Samantha. The head tilted sideways so it could speak more easily. "Samantha," the broken mouth said. "I've come for you. Wait for me. . . ."

Now Samantha knew what had happened. Sarah had used her witchcraft after coming upon, and perhaps butchering, this pitiful wretch. Then she had placed a spell on the pieces to find and kill Samantha.

Samantha took aim at the center of the head with her flintlock. She fired once, and the disembodied head's skull and brain exploded in all directions.

That didn't stop the other body parts, though. They were still coming for her, as quickly as they were able.

Obviously the time had come to leave. Samantha kicked out the fire, got on her horse, and lit out with all possible speed, using only the moonlight to guide her.

CHAPTER THREE

The gathering was a spontaneous event to which everyone had been invited. It was being held in a giant cavern on the outskirts of the Lair, lit by fires whose embers burned farther below than anyone wanted to know.

Any normal person would have found the heat outrageous, yet those here thought it rather comfortable. The crowd focused their attention on the stage, which featured a podium, a microphone, and a picture of the Master that took up the entire rear curtain.

Equally spontaneous was the deafening roar the crowd made at the behest of a few minions when the Master walked onto the stage. Bathed in a spotlight, the Master took a few bows, waved at a few demons he had a professional relationship with, and then basked in the general adulation.

The entire affair was climaxed by the unexpected appearance of the biggest, baddest fallen angel in the hierarchy of evil—Old Scratch himself! He presented to the stunned, humble Master a plaque inscribed TO THE MASTER OF EVIL, EXCEPTIN' OLD SCRATCH HIMSELF.

"Sire! Does this mean you're setting me free?"

"Not a chance, skull-face," Old Scratch said, drawing a big laugh from the crowd. "Now go away, boy, you bother me!"

The crowd roared, seeing the Master wallowing in his own hotheaded despair.

The Master reached out for the hooves at the end of Old Scratch's legs. Don't do it! I beg you! Just tell me what you want to do to me and I'll inflict the same unspeakable punishment on somebody else! Please!"

Old Scratch did not respond. He did not even use that hideous gurgle of boiling hot blood reserved for any cowering servant who had committed the most serious transgression. In fact, come to think of it, there weren't even those great, rock-hard hooves about. The Master could not find them to grab.

The Master took a chance and looked up. Old Scratch was nowhere to be seen. The crowd, the lights, and the stage were gone. The Master was back in his underground prison, wallowing on one of the tunnel floors. He had been asleep. Dreaming. A nightmare.

The Master chuckled as he stood up. The cheap irony did not escape him. He too had been using dreams to serve his ends. He thought it excellent that his own subconscious had reminded him what powerful, unpredictable forces dreams could be.

The others, however, wouldn't be so lucky. They didn't have his unique insight into the unnatural order of things. And because they lacked this knowledge, the Slayer, her Watcher, and her chattering lackeys would be dust, and he would rule his rightful realm once more.

The Master laughed until the echoes rang up and down the tunnels like a scream from an infinite abyss. Even his minions, who had thought they were immune to most effects of complete, abject fear, quivered in their three-toed boots.

Xander and Willow caught up with Buffy on her way to school. Childhood friends, their conversation often revolved around matters Buffy couldn't possibly relate to.

Today, their preoccupation with their kindergarten days left her free to brood over her dreams. Given all that Giles had said, the dreams had to be regarded with suspicion.

What she'd revealed to Willow about her knowledge of the period was only the beginning. Buffy found she knew things about the people of Salem and North Salem that couldn't have been learned from any history book.

Including the inner joy that had surged through Samantha Kane when she'd slain her first vampire.

They were only a few blocks away from the Sunnydale High rear entrance when Buffy became vaguely aware of someone trying to get their attention.

He was a late-middle-aged man in a baggy old suit, with a bow tie and a battered old hat. He carried a large, old-fashioned flash camera.

"You're that newspaper reporter I saw on TV last week," said Xander before the man could open his mouth. "The one who believes mad cow disease was caused by the ghosts of buffalo who'd been forced to cross the Atlantic for Buffalo Bill's traveling Wild West Show in the 1890s!"

"No, no, it's more complicated than that," the man replied defensively. "My words were taken out of context."

"This gentleman shows up a lot on the Channel Three News 'Conspiracy Theory of the Week' slot," Xander explained to the girls. "I forget his name—"

"Darryl MacGovern," said the reporter.

"He also broke the story to the supermarket rags about the outbreak of three-legged frogs in Spokane, Washington," continued Xander. "And he claims the animated TV show *Teenage Mutant Two-Fisted Possums* is actually propaganda created by aliens to prepare us for what they look like when they invade the planet."

"I never said that!" protested MacGovern. "Not exactly, anyway!"

"So you work for Channel Three?" asked Willow, trying to be casual.

"No, they just use me for their conspiracy segment whenever they can't find anything else suitably outrageous."

"So, if you only do TV part-time, who else do you work for?" Buffy asked suspiciously.

"The *Clayton Press*," said MacGovern. "Well, to be honest, I used to work there. The publisher fired me three weeks ago. Apparently he found my frequent appearances on a show about conspiracy theories compromised my integrity as a reporter." He snorted. "As if such a thing were possible."

"It's a cruel world, but sometimes it's a fair one," said Xander.

"So what brings you to Sunnydale High?" asked Buffy innocently, though she had a bad feeling about this.

"A story!" said MacGovern enthusiastically. "One so fantastic the paper'll beg me to come back. But I'll have enough name-value recognition to start my own exposé show."

"On Channel Three?" Willow asked.

"No! On the Occult Channel!" MacGovern exclaimed. "I'll make cable after this!"

"You may smell a story," said Buffy, "but I smell a *rat*!"

MacGovern leaned in to her. "Perhaps you can help me. I understand a lot of peculiar doings have been going on in Sunnydale lately."

"No kidding," said Buffy dryly. "Nobody told me!"

"Things are pretty quiet around here," said Xander. He and Willow yawned.

"I have this talent for stumbling across things that defy

rational explanation. The frustrating part is, no matter what I do, no matter how careful I am, I can never get to the bottom of a story without losing all my tangible proof!"

"So why are you here?" Willow asked with a smile. She couldn't help herself; she thought this guy was funny.

"A few weeks ago, I realized I was coming out of a cloud. Something had been nagging at my natural curiosity for months, yet I'd been unable to verbalize it. I mean, it's my business to know whether or not something's any of my business. Understand what I'm talking about?"

Buffy got a sinking feeling, as if her stomach were being thrown over a ravine with the rest of her soon to follow.

"In fact, I realized I'd heard a whole lot of unsubstantiated rumors about things that were happening in Sunnydale. So after about sixteen hours pondering the situation from the vantage point of conspiracy theory pages on the Internet, I did some research in the files of the *Clayton Press* and other major suburban newspapers in the vicinity. And you know what I found? Of course you don't. I discovered nothing."

The three teens looked at one another in confusion.

"Nothing?" Willow echoed.

"Exactly! And that's the whole point!"

"No kidding," said Willow sympathetically. "You look a little pale. Have you been taking all your mineral supplements?"

"No. Listen, no town has *nothing*. Everybody has *something*. Something to hide. Something to deny—"

"No, we don't!" Xander tried.

"Yeah," Buffy echoed. "We don't have nothing. . . ." She trailed off. "Where was I?"

An awkward silence passed between the reporter and everyone else. Buffy stewed, betrayed by fate in the form of a nosy flat-footed reporter, yet she had to struggle to conceal her emotions. The tendency of most people not to believe what's right in front of them, which had enabled her to live a semblance of a normal life, was now playing tricks with her. She could only wonder how many people might be noticing, for the first time, the events that had recently occurred in Sunnydale thanks to the existence of the Hellmouth below.

"So what are you trying to tell us?" asked Willow aggressively—which was unusual in itself.

"Nothing!" MacGovern answered forcefully.

"So you're telling us you're going to hunt for nothing?" Buffy spoke slowly as if to a child.

"Exactly!" MacGovern seemed excited someone finally understood. "I'm going to find this nothing and expose it as something!"

"Uh-oh, gotta split!" said Xander suddenly. He took MacGovern's hand and pumped it vigorously. "Gonna be late!"

"Can't miss homeroom!" said Willow.

"Nice meeting you," said Buffy, leading the others away. "Good luck finding nothing."

• • •

"So, Giles, still searching for portents of things to come?" Xander asked briskly as he entered the library with Buffy and Willow. They often stopped by right after school just to see if anything was going down.

"*The Eibon* is nothing to joke about," replied Giles sternly.

"What else do we know about this Prince Ashton Eisenberg besides the fact he was two tamales short of a full plate?" Willow asked.

"Reliable sources say he died as a result of spontaneous combustion," said Giles, "that is, his body burned up of its own accord, without benefit of fuel or match."

"Fascinating," said Buffy. "But we've got a problem."

"You first," said Giles with a smile.

"Okay." Quickly she told Giles about their encounter with Darryl MacGovern.

"It's bad, isn't it?" Xander asked.

"It's worse—it's disastrous!" Giles exclaimed. "This MacGovern character is a veritable *stalkerazzi*, well-known in legitimate scholarly occult circles as a complete pest. He never rests until he gets his story or meets a total dead end, whichever comes first."

"At least we can always use Xander as a decoy until we can throw him off the scent entirely," said Willow with a sigh.

"Thanks a lot," said Xander.

"It's a good plan," said Giles, "but I bet MacGovern is just a pawn in some greater game. He may be only an insignificant red herring, sent to throw us off the real scent while the real pieces come into play."

"Maybe we should introduce him to the Master," said Xander. "Then MacGovern will start bugging *him* for an exclusive."

"We could," said Willow, "but that would be wrong."

"Giles, what did you mean by 'You first'?" asked Buffy.

"Last night I had a dream that disturbed me greatly," Giles replied.

Buffy literally bit her tongue.

"It was so vivid, so real—it was unlike any dream I had ever experienced. After all, it had a coherent narrative—at least, as much as the events it portrayed allowed it to be."

"Were these actual historical events?" Buffy asked.

"As near as I can determine, yes," said Giles. "I was clearly dreaming about a past life. I have long suspected I might be the reincarnation of an earlier Watcher or two, but never in my wildest flights of fancy did I think I might be spiritually related to the legendary late-seventeenth-century Watcher Robert Erwin."

"What were you doing in the dream?" asked Willow.

"Not very much," said Giles. "I'm afraid I had succumbed to a raging fever and was delirious. Robert Erwin thought the fever had supernatural origins, which I tended to agree with."

"Oh, come on!" said Xander. "The supernatural can't explain everything! Maybe he was just sick!"

"That is possible, but I remember his paranoid ravings

quite clearly," said Giles. "Anyway, Erwin was under the care of an innkeeper and his wife in Boston. Of course he was worried about what the late-seventeenth-century Slayer was up to."

"Who was she?" asked Buffy dryly. She thought she would like to hear what Giles knew before offering collaborating evidence.

"Her name was Samantha Kane, and she made quite a reputation for herself. She was described in letters and certain official writings as a sort of Joan of Arc type, in that she could perform with ease tasks formerly thought only the province of men."

"I like her already," said Willow slyly.

"So do I," replied Giles. "Unfortunately it seems that poor Robert Erwin was unable to assist Samantha Kane as he so clearly desired to. He died of his fever, and she disappears entirely from the historical record around 1692, during the height of the infamous Salem witch trials."

CHAPTER FOUR

Sure we should be doing this?" Buffy asked Giles as she deftly deflected a thrust of his *kitana*—a Japanese practice sword—with her staff. "Aren't you worried that MacGovern might be spying on us?" shifting her weight, she swung her weapon sideways, taking Giles's feet out from under him.

He landed heavily on his back with a satisfactory thump. "Of course," he gasped. He rolled over and coughed. "But he'll probably attempt to verify his facts before trying to sell the story to his editors. After all, he needs to fill an entire show and be prepared to go on some cable news channel to defend his story."

She reached down to help him stand. "Where did you learn that move?" he asked.

"From an old movie on TV," said Buffy proudly. "I think it starred somebody—Flynn, or maybe what's-his-name . . . Lancaster, I forget which. Are we done?"

"No, we must complete the session." He rubbed his back and groaned. "As difficult as that might prove to be."

"Okay! But don't say I didn't warn you—I've been watching a lot of old movies lately."

"I was afraid of that." Stiffly, Giles assumed a fighting position. "This is called a wombat stance—"

"Looks more like a drunken squirrel to me," Buffy giggled.

He sliced sideways with the *kitana*. When she avoided it—easily—he grabbed her arm, twisted around, and tried to throw her over his shoulder. But she was too fast. Using their momentum, she landed on her feet, pivoted around to face him, and grabbed him by the collar. With one smooth movement she threw herself backward and, with the help of her foot on his chest, she threw him across the room.

Buffy picked up her staff as she leapt to her feet, ready for his next move, exactly as she would do had she been facing a genuine foe. "Can I go home now?" she asked pleadingly.

"No," Giles groaned. He reached out for a helping hand, which pointedly did not arrive.

"What is the point of this lesson?" she asked.

"Perseverance," said Giles, pulling himself to his feet. "And patience against an opponent who doesn't know when he's been beaten." He tried to jab her with the *kitana* handle.

She dodged the blow easily, grabbed his wrist, twisted the

kitana from his hand, elbowed him against the chin just hard enough so he knew she could do it, and then sent him flying again.

He slid across the top of the desk like a stone skipping across a lake, and then hit the floor.

Fortunately Giles wore elbow, knee, and chest pads whenever he worked out with Buffy, but now he considered just buying a padded suit to cover every inch of his body. "I am convinced, Buffy, that if demons and other ghouls don't do in this particular Watcher someday, his favorite Slayer will manage to do the job for him."

"Sorry about that. I really want to go home today. By the way, what was that stance again? The wombat?" Buffy attempted to imitate the stance Giles had taken.

Giles blinked until he got her into better focus, then said, "Hold the right arm higher. The left leg out a little more—"

"Walk me home?" Willow asked Xander at the gate to the school grounds.

Xander shrugged his shoulders. "Sure. Why not? Why does Giles insist on giving Buffy combat lessons?" he asked casually. "She keeps mopping up the floor with him."

"Somebody has to do it, I suppose," Willow replied. "Maybe Giles just wants her to keep her edge."

"Yoo-hoo! Yoo-hoo!" called out a woman's voice from a street to their left.

Willow and Xander turned to see a man and woman getting out of a gigantic Hummer with tires that looked big and wide enough to ride the surface of Mars, if need be.

The man was in his mid-forties an wore and ill-fitting designer suit; he was just now getting out of the driver's side. The woman, who was about a decade younger than he, wore a stylish, modern blue power jacket and skirt. She'd been so intent upon reaching Willow and Xander she had left the passenger door open for the man to close. "Kids! You go to Sunnydale High, don't you? May we have a word with you?" she called out insistently.

"I bet I know what she wants to find out," whispered Willow.

"This is too weird," said Xander.

"Thank you, this will just take a few moments. My name is Lora Church," she said, holding out her hand. Her hair was short and brown, her face round, attractive, and cheerful. "This is my husband, Rick. Your name is Willow, am I right? And you must be Xander?"

"Yeah, how did you know?" asked Xander, who found it somewhat difficult to take his eyes off her.

Willow nodded suspiciously. She didn't like it when Xander noticed beautiful strangers, be they from afar or close up. But then Rick Church looked into her eyes and she found herself holding her breath.

Managing to possess the illusion of danger while acting like a perfect gentleman, Rick Church said, "Well, Xander, we have a mutual acquaintance. She suggested you and your beautiful young friend here might be able to fill us in on the many unusual occurrences in Sunnydale."

"Really!" said Xander dryly. "Actually, it's not the number of occurrences but the lack of them that I find the most interesting. Nothing ever happens in Sunnydale. People don't even run red lights here."

"So who's our mutual acquaintance?" asked Willow.

"A ghost," said Rick. "You don't really know her, though she knows very well who you are."

"Explain," said Willow simply.

"On those nights when there really isn't a whole lot to do, my husband and I hold séances," said Lora. "We call up dead acquaintances or family members, just to see how they're getting along in the afterlife. Or we call up historic figures at random. We think of our séances as spiritual fishing expeditions. We've been pretty lucky. We've spoken to the spirits of Cleopatra, Alexander the Great, Victor Hugo."

"All in English?" asked Xander.

Rick laughed weakly and looked at Willow as if she were the only woman in the entire world. "It's been well documented that called-up spirits tend to speak in the language of the séance holders, whose minds they must be filtered through. Well, last week, we bumped into someone who claimed to have been reborn and was living in Sunnydale."

"If the spirit was reborn, then how come you reached it on the astral plane?" asked Willow immediately.

Rick blinked; he hadn't been expecting that question. "Why indeed? But who else could be in two places at the same time, if not a spirit? This spirit distinctly mentioned you, young lady."

"What did she say?" asked Willow.

"Not much," said Lora. "Spirits rarely do. She intimated that the two of you have a lot in common with us, and suggested—most strongly—that we look you up."

"Which we did," said Rick. "So what do you think of that, Willow? Your fame precedes you."

Willow had the distinct feeling this charming man was an utter fruitcake. "Gee, I'm flattered, but, hey, I told my mother I would help around the house after school. We can talk later."

"Fair enough," said Rick. "When? Soon, I hope. Surely it shouldn't be too much trouble to fit in a cup of coffee—or a milk shake—with Rick and Lora Church, occult mavens extraordinaire." He bowed slightly, gallantly. "You might have the rare opportunity to take part in one of our supernatural adventures."

Willow decided that in the final analysis, the fruitcake was still charming. "How about tomorrow," she suggested.

"Excellent! Same time, same place? I trust that will give you enough time to do a background check on us via the Internet?"

Willow grinned. "Plenty of time. I mean, uh, that'll be fine. C'mon, Xander, we've gotta go."

Xander still couldn't take his eyes off Lora. So Willow

took him by the arm and pulled him away. Lora and Rick waved good-bye at them.

"By the way," called out Lora, "where can we find Rupert Giles?"

"In the library. Where else?" Xander replied, flattered to have been asked.

"Xander!" Willow hissed.

"Oops. Sorry."

They walked. Willow was relieved to be alone again with Xander, but it still bothered her that the Church couple had asked for Giles. Considering everything that was going down, perhaps she should have been more curious.

Lora Church and her husband opened the library doors the instant Giles flew out—backward! He missed them both completely, landing rump-first on the hard tile floor. Lora grimaced at the impact.

"Ooh! That had to hurt!" Rick said.

"Ouch!" was all Giles said after hitting the floor. He didn't have time to say anything else, because he was still sliding across the hall.

From inside the library, Buffy shrieked at what she'd done, and she ran into the hall between Rick and Lora, without noticing them.

They realized immediately this lithe slip of a girl was responsible for the commotion. "Hey! Wait up!" Rick cried out as he and Lora followed Buffy to where Giles lay unconscious and unmoving, except for a few twitches now and again.

Buffy knelt beside him and felt his pulse, then put her ear to his chest. “Come on, Giles, I know you’re alive,” she said. “I can hear you wheezing.”

“Wait, young lady, I know first aid,” said Rick, gently pushing her aside. He had already taken off his jacket and was putting it under Giles’s head. “Giles! Are you comfortable?”

Giles shook away three or four of the zillion cobwebs clogging his brain. “I make a pretty good living,” he croaked. Then he groaned. “I need a cup of instant coffee.” Suddenly, he woke up, getting his bearing. He looked at them all suspiciously. “Who are you?” he demanded.

“I’m Buffy.” She peered closely at Giles, trying to determine whether he really didn’t remember her.

“I know that! I’m talking to *him*!”

Rick bowed his head slightly. “Rick Church, pleased to make your acquaintance, sir, and this is my wife—”

Giles gasped. Suddenly he had recognized her . . . from somewhere. A few seconds passed. He gasped again. “Lora—?”

“You know each other—?” said Rick in surprise.

“Hello, Rupert,” Lora said. “It’s been a long time.”

“Hello, Lora,” said Giles, his eyes going all misty and sentimental. “Nice to see you.”

Xander listened; Willow talked. It was a sunny afternoon, the air was warm and exhilarating, and he could barely keep his mind on what Willow was saying.

Eventually he concentrated hard enough to gather that her computer had crashed the night before and she'd stayed up till three fixing it. Willow detailed every method she'd used to find out which program had corrupted the others as if Xander should have been fascinated by the process. As it was, he could barely understand. . . .

Wait a second! Xander thought. *Normally I'm only too happy to listen to Willow. But something's calling me, like a songbird from over the next hill. . . .*

Then he heard it: the sharp *crrrack!* of a bat striking a baseball dead-on, and the cries and cheers of young boys playing around the next corner. Willow was three steps behind before she realized he'd sped up.

"Sorry, Willow, I know I promised to walk you home, but I just realized—"

"Oh." She was none too successful at hiding her disappointment, but it didn't matter because Xander didn't notice. "What's that?"

"It's spring, and in spring, a young man's fancy turns toward—"

"Yes?"

"Baseball."

"Oh."

"See ya!"

The sandlot game was in its fourth inning when Xander asked to join one of the teams. Xander couldn't hit the broad side of a barn with a baseball from a yard away, but one team needed a right fielder—the position least likely to see any action, making it the position for which Xander was most perfectly suited.

Willow watched Xander play until it became apparent Xander would ignore her completely, because that's how boys were supposed to treat girls when they were playing baseball.

So she walked a few blocks to a small park and sat down on a bench. She would read Jane Austen's *Sense and Sensibility* until the game was over. Maybe then Xander would be interested in walking her the rest of the way home.

The distant noise of the game barely made a dent in her consciousness as she became lost in Austen's comedy of nineteenth-century English marriage, death, and manners. She was jolted back to the present by the sudden knowledge that one of Xander's teammates—a huge blond with more muscles on his arms than she thought possible—was trying to get her attention.

"Earth to Willow! Come in, please!"

"What—?"

"It's Xander! He's been hit on the head!"

"Oh no! Poor Xander! Is he hurt?"

"With him it's kinda hard to tell. A fly ball hit him on the head and knocked him out. He's been wacky ever since, calling your name, calling other people's names."

"Such as Mom? Dad? Giles? . . . Buffy?"

"No. He's talking about someone named John Kane. And

who else? Danforth. Corwin. Ever hear of any of these people? 'Cause I sure haven't."

But Willow was already running away. She was out of breath and utterly exhausted by the time she reached right field. The two teams were gathered around Xander. One of the smaller guys poured water from a plastic bottle on his face. "Let him breathe! Let him breathe!" she yelled despite her burning lungs.

The boys parted to let her through.

"Xander! Are you all right?"

Just then he woke up, sputtering water. "Willow! I just had the strangest dream!"

"Terrific—he's awake, folks!" shouted the short guy. "That's three outs!"

"It's good to meet you too," said Rick Church, shaking Giles's hand. "Although I must admit I'm surprised I hadn't heard about you until recently," he added, staring at his wife.

Buffy grinned at Giles's red-faced embarrassment.

"Mrs. Church and I were together on the Oxford debate team, Buffy," said Giles.

"And that was only the beginning!" said Lora happily.

Giles looked at Rick, directly and honestly. "Yes, but after we graduated we lost touch, as university teammates are so inclined to do."

"I never would have guessed," said Rick dryly.

Giles was escorting Buffy and the Churches into the library, then seemed to think better of it. "Would you care to join me for a cup of coffee in the teachers' lounge? I feel the need to freshen up."

"But what about me?" Buffy blurted out.

"I think the combat lesson is over for today," said Giles. "I've really had enough punishment."

"You're teaching *her* combat?" exclaimed Lora. "You *have* changed!"

Giles cleared his throat. "Not as much as you think. In the ways of combat, Buffy is the instructor, while I am just the pupil."

"She's teaching *you*!" Rick laughed.

Buffy opened her mouth to reply, but Giles stifled her by putting a hand on her shoulder and steering her away, while saying to Rick, "She has a gift, remarkable for one so young. Now why don't you two wait for a moment? Buffy usually offers me a few private words of encouragement after my lesson, and today I desperately need to hear them."

Rick snickered. "Sure. We'll be right here." He watched them make a turn down another hall and then said to his wife, "What did you see in *him*?"

Lora smiled, remembering the young Giles fondly even as she said, "How am I supposed to know? I was young and impressionable. Besides, remember that truck stop waitress you told me about once? What did you see in her?"

"That was completely her idea. I had nothing to do with it."

"A likely story. Anyway, it doesn't matter. Since meeting you, I never thought of Giles at all until the ghost suggested we see him while we were in Sunnydale."

"Now I'm happy." He pointed at his lips. "How about another smooch?"

Meanwhile, Buffy was letting loose with a barrage of questions about Giles's personal life. And even though Giles tried to impress Buffy with the fact that his pre-Watcher existence was none of her business, he nonetheless couldn't help remarking, "It's like seeing a ghost, only I've seen ghosts and they're not nearly as attractive. She has such wonderful—" He cleared his throat. "Buffy, I have no idea what Lora and this Rick Church fellow—"

"Her husband," Buffy pointed out.

"—are doing here, but I will find out. I wouldn't be surprised if it has something to do with the Eisenberg prophecy."

"Why? Maybe she and her husband are just passing through town."

"I suspect this ghost they spoke of is helping them overcome the spell of forgetfulness too. Besides, did you notice something profound about the connection between Lora and me? I think you would call it 'cosmic.'"

"Why would I do that?"

"It wasn't quite as if we were actually destined for one another, like genuine soul mates, just that we shared the feeling we'd shared something, sometime, somewhere, where there was a place for us. Then, for no apparent reason, we drifted apart. But it's gratifying to know something of that feeling remains to this day."

"I don't call that 'cosmic.' It's more like *Cosmopolitan*."

"I wonder what she wants."

"Now, that's the suspicious Giles I know," said Buffy, already walking away.

He frowned as he watched her go. *I'm not just suspicious of women,* he thought defensively. *I'm suspicious of everyone!*

With a sharp intake of breath he realized that he was even suspicious of his dreams. Although it behooved a Watcher to be paranoid, he couldn't help wondering if he was going too far.

But when he returned to Rick and Lora in the hall, they'd been having an intense discussion that ceased the instant he walked in. "Well, Lora, this is certainly a pleasant surprise, but you didn't come all the way to Sunnydale from wherever it is you're living now—"

"Carmel," she put in helpfully.

"—just to look me up," Giles continued.

"I should hope not," said Rick slyly.

"We'll probably have more privacy there."

"The teachers' lounge is that way," said Giles. "We'll probably have more privacy there."

On the way, he and Lora tried to catch up with each other. Twice Lora mentioned her surprise that he had not been married, not even once, during the last two decades. Rick remarked that he'd been married and divorced enough times for all three of them.

"You must be rich," said Giles.

"Not anymore," said Rick.

Inside the lounge, Giles led his guests to a corner furnished with pieces purchased from the Salvation Army. "So really, people, why are you here?"

Rick and Lora suddenly became quite serious. "A ghost named Sarah Dinsdale suggested we come see you," said Rick.

CHAPTER FIVE

By the time she turned onto her block, Buffy felt pretty good inside, thanks in part to her plan to take a nap as soon as she made it home in the hopes of learning about the fate of Samantha Kane.

Suddenly her good feeling evaporated. What was that huge van with the satellite dish on top doing across the street from her house?

On both sides of the van was painted a large, garish logo: a column of frogs falling from a clear blue sky. Buffy recognized it as the hallmark of the syndicated show dealing with paranormal phenomena called *Charles Fort's Peculiar Planet*. It aired on Channel 13, appropriately enough, every weeknight at 11 p.m. The subject matter ranged from giant ants in the Amazon to the ghosts of aliens on a space shuttle. Buffy usually watched it for laughs, but she wasn't laughing now.

Especially when the show's top reporter, Eric Frank, got out of the passenger side and, microphone in hand, headed toward her front door!

"Sarah Dinsdale, eh? Never heard of her." Giles sipped his cup of coffee. Today the coffee machine in the teachers' lounge was producing an especially bitter product, and he fought to maintain a neutral expression lest the Churches think he was uncomfortable with the subject matter. He had played dumb for a while, a skill he'd picked up through necessity while dealing with the education bureaucracy on both sides of the Atlantic.

"Funny," said Rick with a smile. "She seems to have heard of you." He sipped his coffee and immediately stopped smiling.

"I don't see how," Giles replied casually.

"Oh please, Giles," said Lora impatiently. "You were always interested in the occult. It's all you ever talked about."

"I'm afraid you have me confused with someone else," said Giles indignantly. "I'm interested in books and movies and art."

"Humph! You never had time to see any movies unless they starred Christopher Lee or Peter Cushing," said Lora.

"Do I detect a trace of resentment?" chuckled Rick.

"Sweetums," Lora cooed. Nevertheless, she continued the attack on Giles. "The only books you ever read had to do with paranormal subjects such as spontaneous combustion and psychic detectives—and the art, good grief, the art! It was all primitive stuff and usually had been handled by witch doctors first."

"Ever do any research on UFOs?" Giles asked in all innocence.

"Don't change the subject," said Lora. "The ghost of Sarah Dinsdale sent us to see you. And that's why we're here."

Giles sighed. He'd forgotten how stubborn Lora could be when she felt like it. But that was part of the problem. Over the years, he'd forgotten almost everything about her, but now that she was in his presence again, memories and emotions were resurfacing like salmon jumping up a waterfall.

"All right," said Giles. "What does this Sarah Dinsdale want with me?"

"I'm glad you asked!" said Rick briskly, his eyes darting this way and that. He lowered his voice. "Is this place bugged?"

"I should certainly hope not!" said Giles, hoping he was right.

"Good. What I am about to tell you, most people would find somewhat extravagant—perhaps unbelievable. But I assure you, every word is true."

"Or close to it," added Lora.

"Lora and I used to look forward to our weekly séances, when we'd sit in our darkened den to call forth the spirits of the dead."

"There were no portents the night Sarah came—subjective or otherwise—that the upcoming séance would contain a few unpleasant surprises," said Lora.

"No sudden flashes of lightning in a clear sky," said Rick. "No white owls in the trees, not even an old-fashioned chill up the spine. I had my hopes, too. Cleopatra had intimated she'd be back for a return engagement, and lately we'd snared a few ladies-in-waiting from the court of King Louis XVI of France."

"Those weren't ladies," said Lora. "I myself was hoping Nijinsky, the great ballet dancer, would drop in again, though in a mood less neurotic than before."

"You just like what you see in his eyes," said Rick jealously.

"You just like Cleopatra's—," Lora began, before Giles interrupted and reminded them of the story they were supposed to be telling. "Of course," said Lora. "You can imagine our surprise when, having done this hundreds of times before, the séance conjured up all sorts of atmospheric effects, such as flickering candlelight, creeping fog, and a stench so repulsive I won't begin to describe it to you."

"I have no problem doing that," said Rick. "It smelled like a thousand dead skunks piled on top of one another, lying on a bed of liver and castor oil. We couldn't have failed to notice it if we'd tried."

"I got ill," said Lora.

"Big time," said Rick deliberately. "Luckily, I'd taken an antacid before dinner—for my ulcer, you know. When the ghost of Sarah Dinsdale appeared above us, we couldn't have been less in the mood for occult explorations. But there she was, nonetheless."

"She was the scariest ghost I've ever seen," said Lora. "Most ghosts are pretty alienated from reality to begin with—they say purgatory gets on a specter's nerves—but this one was frightening, paranoid, and utterly confident in her spectral dignity. You never knew how she'd respond to any one of your questions."

"She blamed the smell on us, too," said Rick resentfully. "Said we weren't conjuring her up correctly. I took umbrage at that."

"It wasn't long before she began asking *us* questions," said Lora. "And she insisted on answers! Threatened to go back if we didn't talk. Well, you never let a specter go away if you can help it. It just isn't done in polite society."

"Of course," said Giles. "What did she want to know?"

"Where you were," said Lora. "How you were faring on this mortal coil. Things of that nature."

"I had never heard of you, of course," said Rick.

"What did she say, exactly?" asked Giles impatiently.

Lora answered, "She said you had a good head on your shoulders. But then she implied you'd lost it before and that you might again if you weren't careful."

"This is all very interesting," he said guardedly, "but how seriously am I supposed to take this warning? Especially since I've never heard of the ghost before and have no idea what she could possibly be talking about."

"This is not the first time we've heard a dire warning or received a vague, almost nonsensical clue that's required action on our part," said Rick. "In the past, we've solved murders long set aside by the authorities. We've also added significantly to our stock portfolio by taking advantage of what spirits have told us about the immediate future. It all depends on the situation."

"We don't know exactly what Dinsdale was talking about," said Lora, "so we don't really know what we might have to do. But when the clutch comes, we'll be there for you."

"Yes. Well, ah, thank you, but that won't be necessary," said Giles. "I may seem a little awkward occasionally, but I think I can take care of myself."

"So long as you don't have to fight any teenage girls," said Rick with a smirk.

"Buffy is not just a teenage girl, she's—" Giles caught himself; he'd almost let his pride cause him to spill the beans. "She's a black belt, a gifted brawler in the most profound sense of the word."

"She can't guard you as well as we can," said Rick.

"I've no doubt whatsoever, but I feel pretty safe," said Giles, which was definitely untrue, but he had to maintain a facade of not taking them seriously. "Besides, there are times when—*ahem*—a man must do what a man must do, and I'd rather be by myself when I do them."

"We're still going to be close by," insisted Rick. "We're very good at this bodyguard thing. We've had lots of practice."

"Ever lose any of your charges?" Giles asked.

"We don't talk about that," said Lora tensely. "There were extenuating circumstances. How were we to know there'd be a killer shark in that lake?"

"Our failures have been few and far between," Rick said. "Barely worth mentioning, in fact."

"Well, I feel safer already," said Giles. He sipped his lousy coffee, barely noticing the taste. He suppressed the sudden urge to excuse himself and go home for a nice, long nap.

"Sorry I left you for a baseball game," said a still-woozy Xander as Willow walked him home. "I just wanted to be a *manly* man."

"And *baseball* is the way to prove your manliness?" asked Willow, clearly confused at his logic.

"Yeah. You know what it's like to be one of the few who can actually remember all the strange doings in Sunnydale, to know you've performed some pretty brave—"

"Or foolhardy," interjected Willow.

"—actions, and to want everyone to know about everything: the doings and the actions. But you can't, so you'd settle for just being a normal person who can do normal things like playing baseball—"

"Or having a girlfriend," said Willow, leading him on, although she knew in advance it wouldn't do any good.

"You want a girlfriend?" Xander asked, surprised.

"Never mind. Tell me about your strange dream."

Xander cleared his throat. "Well, to begin with, it seemed so real. I feel like I can recall every detail. But that wasn't the strangest part."

"Go on."

"Remember Giles's dream that took place in the seventeenth-century Massachusetts Bay Colony? Mine appeared to happen at roughly the same time. But even that wasn't the strangest part."

"Xander, get to the point."

"It's embarrassing. I dreamed I was a girl. Or rather, a woman. A full-grown adult woman."

"I always knew you had a feminine side," said Willow, smiling.

"*I* didn't!" Xander exclaimed.

"Boys rarely do. Perhaps you should tell me exactly what happened."

They sat down on a bus stop bench and he began talking. At first he was reluctant, but as he got going, he couldn't help himself. Besides, if he couldn't trust Willow with the dream, then who could he trust?

At first the dream was like all dreams—series of mixed-up images, half-profound, half-absurd. All the images resonated with the power of real life, only they had little to do with the experiences of a teenage boy growing up in sunny Southern

California. They had more to do with the experiences of growing up a young girl in seventeenth-century New England.

The images included reading the Bible at home, feeding the farm animals, growing the vegetables, and going to church. Apparently the young girl went to church quite frequently, as did practically everyone else in the vicinity. Only she didn't like it.

This is where the images took on a different character. Before, everything was bathed in light. Now the dream settings became rather dark—more pleasant, occasionally, but always dark. During these parts of the dream, the young woman felt much more free, as if she was finally in control of her life after a long period of imprisonment. Xander tried not to exert his will or even his thoughts. He just let the dream unfold.

The images included several of walking through a forest of exquisite, pristine greenery teeming with everything from huge colonies of insects to squirrels, skunks, and hedgehogs. The bears and wildcats, Xander somehow knew, had been pushed out by the Puritans some time ago, though of course a few always ventured into the farmlands hunting for sheep and goat.

The young woman walked through fields of purple wildflowers. She harvested wild mushrooms and dug up mandrake roots in the forest. She searched for stones and metals by the streams. She slew frogs and mummified them, and then she went into caves and slew bats. Those were mummified too, according to ritual with the muttering of spells and chants.

The young woman traveled to these places during both day and night, but she especially enjoyed those nights when she was alone. It was then that she danced beneath the moon, communing with nature on a level so primitive and barbaric it horrified Xander.

Finally the dream returned again and again to those times the young woman spent at church, concentrating on the appearance—but never the words, apparently—of the charismatic young preacher, John Goodman. She saw in him potential that she saw in no other man, the potential to be a worthy life-partner in marriage.

Of course, they were apt to disagree over what type of marriage ceremony might be appropriate.

By now the bond between Xander and his dream alter ego was so strong Xander didn't know where he ended and she began. Conversations, memories, books read—it all blended together. Xander was becoming a new person. In a new time.

Xander knew exactly when and where he was: in Salem, Massachusetts, in 1692. His name in the dream was Sarah Dinsdale, and she was most definitely a witch. Up until a certain point she had avoided being victimized by the hysteria—which was ironic, because while she was fairly convinced most of those accused were innocent, she herself was *guilty, guilty, guilty*.

It was a situation that Sarah must have felt inevitable, because she was strangely calm when the church scenes faded out and the courtroom sequence faded in. She stood in chains in the square pen the courtroom reserved for the accused; a large orange *W* was sewn on her dress.

The stern, robed Judge Danforth regarded her severely. Nine angry men sat in the jury box. Sheriff Corwin stood in the back of the courtroom. Cotton Mather, the famed scholar and witch hunter from Boston, stood at the prosecutor's table asking questions of a pale, nervous John Goodman, who sat fidgeting in the witness chair.

The first question Mather directed at Goodman was, "And when did you first hear the unholy call of this Sarah Dinsdale?" His words echoed in Xander's mind like reverb at a rock concert.

Sarah Dinsdale suddenly shouted, "I object, your honor! That question is prejudicial and implies I have already been found guilty!"

The people in the court were shocked—she had dared to speak without the permission of the court! Sheriff Corwin grumbled something about Sarah being mighty darn guilty in his opinion.

Judge Danforth glared down sternly at Sarah Dinsdale. "Nothing would please me more if you were found to be innocent of those crimes of which you stand accused," he said, his tone belying his words. "But do not forget you are forbidden to speak, woman. You would do well to be silent, lest the crime of casting a spell on a member of the court is added to your long list of crimes."

"What do you mean by 'prejudicial'?" Mather inquired, idly scratching beneath his wig.

Judge Danforth seemed satisfied with Sarah's silence. He gestured for Goodman to break his. Goodman cleared his throat, apparently with some difficulty because he took quite a while doing it. Meanwhile, Mather folded his arms and drew himself to his full height. He had been waiting for this moment for some time and was impatient with Goodman's delay.

Finally Judge Danforth cleared his throat. Loudly. He and Goodman looked each other in the eye, and suddenly Goodman knew what to do.

He spoke. "It was during winter," he began softly, "and I was thinking of the pagan holiday then being observed by those citizens of the Old World, the very ones who persecuted we Puritans for not practicing religion properly. I happened to be walking by the modest home of Goodwoman Dinsdale. And I confess, I did think about her of my own free will."

"And what exactly," asked Mather, "did you think about her?"

"I thought it odd that such a pleasant young woman, so lovely and so hardworking, so obviously capable of running a household, was unwed. And at her age too."

"One might say the same about you, sir Goodman," said Mather easily. A few women in the courtroom giggled, but Judge Danforth's stern look quickly put a stop to that.

Goodman blushed, and this pleased Sarah Dinsdale, although at the moment things did not look promising between them. "In any case, passing by Miss Dinsdale's house, I perceived the distinct odor of mincemeat pie."

The audience gasped. It was forbidden to bake mincemeat pie in the winter, because in Europe the baking of mincemeat pie was a major part of celebrating Christmas, which Puritans believed was a pagan holiday.

"I knocked upon her door, and when she opened it to greet her guest, I pushed my way in. And that was when I saw, much to my chagrin, that Sarah Dinsdale was already among the damned."

"I see, my son," Mather said almost tenderly. "Then what course of action did you take?"

"The only one available. I denounced her. I had no choice. For in her kitchen I saw mummified bats and parts of frogs. I saw roots and other ingredients from the recipes of Old Scratch himself! I knew then and there she was unclean—that she was a witch!"

"A witch! A witch!" shouted many in the court, until Judge Danforth's threat brought a renewed sense of order to the proceedings. During that time Goodman could not look Sarah in the eyes, but she could look in his. And she liked what she saw there.

For there was no hate and no pity in John Goodman's eyes. There was only guilt—guilt that he was the one who had been forced, in his view, to denounce her.

"Since then, knowing she is a witch has made no difference. I cannot get the heinous female out of my mind. She haunts my dreams, she occupies my every waking thought. Surely she has cast a spell on me; she has looked upon me with her evil eye and devoured my soul."

Sarah could not resist a smile. Hearing those words had made worthwhile all the suffering she'd endured the past few weeks in the witch dungeons controlled by Sheriff Corwin.

Sarah was still smiling, inwardly at least, when the scene shifted slightly and Xander heard and saw, through her eyes, Judge Danforth pronouncing the death sentence: She will hang by the neck until she is dead! Sarah was confident this would never happen, even when Judge Danforth remarked that he would like to see Old Scratch save her now.

"Not Old Scratch," said Sarah. "Just a close personal friend."

The people in the court erupted with shouts of shock and anger. Sarah surveyed them with a regal, contemptuous air, and Xander couldn't help wondering if it was true that if you dream of your death, then you really die. He was afraid he would find out when the scene next shifted. . . .

. . . Only instead of cutting to the gallows, the scene cut to Sarah Dinsdale sitting contentedly in her dungeon cell, chained to the wall. A visitor arrived, sitting down on a three-legged stool on the other side of the bars.

It was John Goodman.

It was obvious he was coming as close to her as he dared. He fidgeted nervously and couldn't find a comfortable way to sit. He clearly wished he was anyplace else but here within these cold, damp stone walls, which were stained with the blood of accused witches who had confessed upon pain of torture; presumably the poor women had already gone on to receive their "just rewards."

Sarah, for her part, couldn't make up her mind how she felt about John Goodman's appearance here. She knew she should hate him. But his reaction to seeing her prepare her witch's stock had only been true to his nature, and even now something in his eyes reminded her why she'd desired his attention in the first place.

"I've come to say good-bye," Goodman finally said softly.

"Are you certain you haven't offered me one last chance at redemption?" said Sarah defiantly.

"You should repent," said Goodman flatly.

"Why? To ease your guilty conscience?"

"I did not choose these feelings I have toward you, Sarah Dinsdale. I do not hold myself responsible."

"Then who is responsible for them?"

"I think you are."

"It is true I cast a spell over you, Reverend John Goodman. But my spells are too weak to last this long. Perhaps my spell merely revealed an emotion that was already there."

Goodman's complexion wavered between becoming red with anger and pale with fear. He smashed his fist against the bars of Sarah's cell. "That is impossible! I could not—cannot—have these feelings toward a proven witch of my own volition! Release me from this curse! I beseech you!"

Sarah threw back her head and laughed. She also bumped her head against the stone wall, but she tried to hide that and concentrate on her laughter instead. "My most profound apologies, Reverend, but I can no more release you from your heart than I can free you from your conscience."

Goodman stood and nodded grimly. "Then that is how it must be. You are damned. I pity thee."

"I have never knowingly harmed another. I have used my powers only for good, only to help others. How then can I be damned?"

"Because your powers are derived from Old Scratch, and He corrupts all good that He touches."

"There are many ways to be damned, John Goodman, as I suspect you are about to find out." She grinned wickedly. At the moment she had no doubt which of the emotions she felt toward Goodman was dominant. "Perhaps there is a last wish I may grant you before I go forth to be damned."

"I would"—he cleared his throat—"appreciate it greatly if you would cease visiting my dreams, so that I may sleep in peace."

Sarah laughed again; never had she tasted a victory so sweet. "There are things not even a witch can do."

"May you face your death bravely," said Goodman as he turned to leave.

"The least of my worries," said Sarah casually as the scene shifted slightly and a rat sniffed about on the stool where Goodman had been. Sarah, still chained against the wall, looked down at her feet where several other rats sniffed about. She was not afraid of the rats. Their presence here meant she was no longer alone.

Through the bars she could see the moon setting in the sky; it would be dawn soon. A terrible stench permeated the air. Things became damp with the coming of the early morning fog. A wolf howled, an owl hooted, someone in an adjoining cell screamed. Two of the rats began fighting over a discarded piece of bread.

Through it all, Sarah felt relieved. Help was on the way. He did not disappoint her.

She just saw his face for an instant, a flash from a reality whose existence she could barely grasp. She sensed the face's terrible green complexion; its horrible fangs; its dead, remorseless eyes—eyes somehow capable of peering into the deepest reaches of her soul.

She liked feeling exposed that way. How could she fail to trust the Despised One?

The scene in the dream shifted again, to when Sarah had already escaped and was running through the forest. The forest was pitch-black, clouds hid the moon, and the ground was covered with bush and thicket, yet Sarah made her way with ease, as if she was doing nothing more difficult than navigating through her own house in the dark.

She was exhausted. All she wanted was to lie down on the cold earth and sleep.

But if she did that, then she might as well give up and die, and she could not do that. Not while the Despised One was waiting.

She ran to him, deeper, deeper into the forest until she vanished in the night and Xander woke, returning at last to his own reality. The dream had seemed like a four-hour epic on television, yet he awoke to find he'd only been out for as long as an extended commercial break.

Upon hearing the full story, an awestruck Willow discovered she was practically speechless—emphasis on *practically.* "My goodness, do you realize that your dream and the one Giles said he had both took place during the Salem witch trials?"

"I like to think mine was a little better. Yeah, and maybe they are connected. Even *I* can see that."

"We must find out more."

Xander yawned and stretched. "Yeah, I could use a nap. Maybe I'll dream the next part of the story. Should be easy enough, don't you think?"

"I have a better idea. What are you doing tonight?"

CHAPTER SIX

I have often wondered," said the Master aloud—to no one—"what it is like to dream, or to sleep. Is that the essence of humanity?

"Or perhaps I just want to eat, and drink. True, I have feasted on human flesh and occasionally have even devoured a human soul, but I wonder about real food. Scrambled eggs, for instance. With ketchup and maple syrup on top. Or a Virginia ham. Or perhaps what I really want is a simple cup of tea. If I had a cup of tea, would my cares drift away? After I consolidate my control of the surface, one of my first acts will be to find out. Hey! Minions!"

The black things who were his minions scurried around his

feet. "Master! Master!" they said in squeaky voices, not quite in unison. "Speak, speak! Instruct us, and we shall serve. We ask for nothing more."

The Master yawned. "Bring me the spirits!"

"YES MASTER! RIGHT AWAY MASTER YOU BETCHA MASTER," they said, then scattered immediately in all directions. A few even disappeared into the walls.

Moments passed. Or was it hours? The Master decided he didn't care. When time no longer matters, the amount of it is irrelevant as well.

The point was the spirits showed up. Alone, without a minion escort, which meant the minions were still looking for them. Typical. Two of the spirits emerged through a wall, another rose up from the floor, and the fourth descended from above. In this form they resembled black semi-transparent shower curtains.

They hovered and merely listened to the Master's words; in this form they could do nothing else.

"The pieces of the puzzle are in place at last," said the Master. "All the planets, in all the upper and lower dimensional planes, are in proper alignment. The stars are positioned favorably. The fortune reading by candle wax went well, as did the readings by bone dice and tarot card. Only the reading by the spilled entrails of a small rat fared poorly. Even so, the situation is close enough for celestial work.

"Things could be better on the ground. It would be preferable if everyone involved was an actual reincarnation.

"But I am satisfied that by influencing the thoughts of four occult chasers, I have brought to Sunnydale"—he shuddered at the mere mention of such an innocuous, happy word—"proper temporary receptacles for you, the four souls who served the Despised One so poorly three hundred years ago. It would have been nice to rely on more proven talent, but you, Heather, have been adequately devious during the séances called by that amateur Church couple. A good beginning, a good beginning for you all.

"Remember, the entire point of this operation is its predictability. Soon the four of you will have the opportunity to correct the mistake you made more than three hundred years ago. Were you capable of such things, I know you would be thrilled.

"Now depart. Begone. Skedaddle! You know what to do. And when the time is right, you shall do it, or the suffering you have endured so far shall be but a prelude to the pure hell you existence will become."

And they were gone.

The Master was again alone. In time his minions would return and scurry around his feet, apologizing profusely for yet another failure on their part. It didn't matter. Soon he would never have to tolerate their ineptness again.

Buffy had spent the last thirty minutes waiting for Eric Frank and his crew to leave. But they were obviously too stubborn to leave.

Every once in a while Frank, the anchorman who often went out in the field to conduct the most sensational interviews, knocked on the front door. Each time he stalked back waving his arms about and shouting something at his crew . . . at the house . . . at the trees . . . at anything he happened to see. Maybe he thought someone was really at home and was just refusing to answer the door. But every week on this day Buffy's mom took an invalid neighbor out for a drive, and Buffy didn't expect her home for another hour, at least.

Buffy had seen *Charles Fort's Peculiar World* many times, and she'd thought it was pretty stupid every time. Frank's dim-witted staff must have finally picked up shreds of information and fragments to learn there'd been some funny goings-on in Sunnydale. Paranormal goings-on. And they must have grasped that Buffy was the connecting thread, despite the spell of forgetfulness that had been cast over the town.

So if Frank interviewed her mom, he would ask her how she felt about her daughter being the Slayer for this generation. Then the footage would be broadcast on syndicated TV for the duration of cable—severely impairing Buffy's ability to have a normal life.

Eventually Buffy tried to think of ways to fool the reporters into abandoning their stakeout. She reasoned she could call their cell phones, pretend to be a talent scout from CNN, and send them off on a wild-goose chase. But that required knowing their numbers, which she did not.

She could get their numbers, but that would require time. Definitely not a good idea.

Now, if Willow were here, she would whip out her trusty cell and hack into their e-mail in about thirty seconds. Unfortunately, Willow wasn't here, and she wouldn't likely be happening by unless Xander happened to drop off the face of the earth.

Then suddenly things changed. Buffy simply *had* to go inside to use the nearest available facilities, and she wasn't going to let a bunch of TV clowns stop her. She figured they wouldn't get any usable footage on her, not if she walked straight in.

Besides, not one of their stories on vampires, wasp women, and heap monsters had been remotely accurate. Why should they suddenly start being credible with Buffy Summers?

Eric Frank stood leaning against the back of the van, huffing and puffing about something, when he suddenly saw Buffy coming. He sprang to life. "Guys! Guys!" he hissed, loud enough for the world to hear. "That's her kid! Maybe the brat will spill something!"

Buffy was so stunned she stopped in the middle of the street, forcing an oncoming car to swerve around her. *Spill something?* she thought. *I'm "her kid"—"the brat"? They must be here because they think—ohmigosh!—Mom!*

Like a gigantic mother hen from a Japanese monster movie, Buffy strode boldly up to Frank, stuck her finger in his face, and yelled, "What do you want with Mom? Get out of here! Leave her alone!"

Eric Frank's response was deliberate obtuseness. He put his microphone in Buffy's face. And he looked down that long, slim nose and asked, with snooty politeness, "Good afternoon, young lady. Might I inquire why you are so defensive? Does it have to do with your mother?"

"Defensive? What do you mean, defensive? Neither one of us has anything to be defensive about!"

"Ah, so you deny the obvious. So tell me, Miss Summers, what exactly is your mother's relationship with the supernatural? And why are you covering for her? Don't you understand she is involved with heinous forces of evil?"

"What are you talking about? What heinous forces? Look, why don't you ask her?" *Uh-oh.* She'd just realized: a) what she'd said, and b) who happened to be recording it for the gratification of millions. She smiled weakly at the crew.

"We tried to ask her, at the gallery," Frank explained in insincere tones. "But she refused to speak on the record. And when she spoke off the record, she politely but emphatically suggested our next destination. We think she's under the influence of the insidious art deco sculpture from the Bronx."

"What?"

"*The Moonman.* The famous sculpture by the modern Italian master V.V. Vivaldi, who died under mysterious circumstances during the fascist reign of Mussolini. I don't like it, myself. According to the story, it wound up in Mussolini's possession, whereupon everything promptly went downhill for the Italian dictator. Of course, he did choose the wrong side during World War Two. Just before he was hanged by his angry subjects, Mussolini blamed his entire downfall on a curse placed on *The Moonman* by Vivaldi. And he was just the first."

"I suspected as much."

Frank turned away and then looked at her from the corner of his eye, like a huffy history teacher. "An art speculator snatched the statue from the hands of the American forces right after the war. He died, but not before he sold it to someone else, who died, who sold the statue to someone else, who died, who had willed it to someone else, who died . . . you get the idea."

"So what's Mom got to do with it?"

"The point is that a local art gallery, *managed by one Joyce Summers*, is putting on a tiny exhibition concerning V.V. Vivaldi. This statue is cursed. Everyone who's owned it, or has been responsible for it, has died, usually before their time. Tell me, Miss, *ahem*, Buffy. I'll give you one last chance to come clean to our audience of millions of mild-mannered Americans. Is there something *you feel you must share* about Joyce Summers's—your mother's—extracurricular activities?"

Buffy bristled. "I beg your pardon?"

"So you're confirming your mother is under the insidious influence of Vivaldi's infamous *Moonman*?" Frank asked, pushing it.

"Hey, Frank, why do they call it *The Moonman*?" the soundman asked snidely.

"It's not actually from our moon, is it?" asked the cameraman just as snidely. Buffy got the impression those two's opinion of the show was about as high as hers.

"Vivaldi thought it was," Eric Frank said in exasperated tones.

"Hey! Why don't we put it on the show?" asked the soundman, laughing.

"Are you guys always this wrong about everything?" Buffy demanded, staking her entire credibility on her ability to be as off-base as possible. "I think you are. I've seen your show. To be honest, Mr. Frank, it's pretty preposterous stuff."

Eric Frank turned quite pale and glared at his crew, who were laughing at him. "You don't trust me because of the way my hair looks, right?"

Buffy tried not to laugh. "Exactly," she said sympathetically. She pushed her way between Frank and his crew. "I'm sorry, boys, but I really gotta go!"

The crew laughed some more, but suddenly they spotted something and became totally serious. "Hey, Mr. Murrow," said the soundman, facetiously referring to a legendary TV newsman from the 1950s. "Over there! In that Hummer!" He pointed toward the huge vehicle. "It's Rick and Lora Church!"

"Hmmm. Looks to me like they're headed toward the gallery," said Buffy, even though the Churches were actually headed *away*.

She'd been counting on the probability that the three strangers to Sunnydale would be too unfamiliar with the streets to recognize that fact—a slight risk that proved justified when all three began loading the gear into the van in a bumbling, comical fashion. Within a few moments a very satisfied Buffy watched the van with the falling frogs logo disappear after the Churches.

Naturally she was very concerned that Mom had gotten herself involved with a cursed artifact of some sort, and under normal circumstances she would have gone to the gallery immediately. But today circumstances were far from normal. Curses, dreams, and coincidences were running amok in Sunnydale, and she was certain they were connected to Prince Ashton Eisenberg's Prophecy of the Dual Duels.

Only one man could help her fathom that connection.

Rupert Giles. She would have to see him.

In a few minutes.

CHAPTER SEVEN

Giles lay down on a couch in the library and wiped a line of perspiration from his forehead with a handkerchief made damp from the number of times he'd used it during the past hour. Buffy and her friends had never seen him this casual before: The buttons of his shirt were undone, he'd kicked off his shoes, and his feet were on a table. Of course, at the moment he had a temperature of a hundred and one, and he had just taken a few aspirin to reduce the fever.

"We should get you to a hospital," said Buffy.

"It wouldn't do any good," said Giles. "My illness isn't medical, or I should say, isn't scientific in nature. No rational person can help me now."

"Thank goodness," said Xander. "That means we might have a chance."

Giles coughed. "All right, the time has come for us to try to get this straight. Three of us—Buffy, Xander, and myself—have had dreams linking us to past lives that all coexisted at the time of the Salem witch trials. We are not necessarily reincarnations, but all these past lives interacted with one another, much as all four of us interact today. The fact we are all having these dreams of the same people, the same events, at the same time is inescapable. There must be some significance, if not reincarnation then some joining of purpose. So let us, for the sake of argument, assume that we *are* them for right now."

"You are a Watcher named Robert Erwin, which stands to reason since you're a Watcher now," said Willow. "And Buffy is a Slayer named Samantha Kane."

"And I, for reasons I cannot possibly understand," said Xander, "have been dreaming that I was a woman named Sarah Dinsdale, a tried and convicted witch who just happened to be as guilty as sin."

"Furthermore," said Giles, coughing again, "because you are having the dreams of Sarah Dinsdale, we know the spirit Rick and Lora Church know as Sarah is likely the spirit of an imposter. Because the spirit of Sarah is within you, and can be nowhere else."

"So is this spirit in the employ of all the nosy people who've been bothering us?" asked Willow.

"Undoubtedly," said Giles. "But I suspect the nosy people are unwilling dupes."

"Obviously the next step is to learn more about what happened to Sarah Dinsdale," said Willow.

Xander stretched and yawned. "Great. I could use a few Z's. I've been told"—he looked at the girls meaningfully—"that I don't snore."

"Your teddy bear talks?" asked Willow.

"We do not have time to wait for you to dream," said Giles. "We must . . . how do you Americans say it? . . . cut to the quick on this one."

"I think you mean 'cut to the chase,'" said Buffy.

"Exactly," said Giles, suppressing another cough. "We must hold a séance. Willow, please retrieve the candles and the holy water from the locked cabinet behind the desk. Xander, on the shelf over there is a book called *Séances for Fun and Profit* by Rick and Lora Church. We need it. Buffy, I fear I must ask you to get something gross again."

Buffy gulped. "Okay."

Ten minutes later she returned from the morgue, with a vase filled with someone's ashes. "I suppose I'll have to take this back, too, in the morning."

"Hopefully, sooner," said Giles. "Thank you, Buffy. I must say, it always amazes me how you get in and out of these places so quickly."

"I could to it," said Xander, "if she could only show me how she does it."

"That's all right, Xander," Buffy said dryly. "I'll be glad to keep on doing it."

"I am grateful," said Giles. "Now, in this book Lora describes the preparations for a do-it-at-home séance. She keeps it simple; the only exotic requirement is this demand for the ashes of the cremated. The curtains are drawn? Good. Now we must hold hands."

But he began coughing badly as he reached for Buffy and Willow. Everybody waited for him to be done. He sat at the head of the table, with Xander opposite him. The library was dark—Xander had switched off the lights—but for the candles, which were placed on the table to make the points of a pentagram, what Buffy called the occult design of choice. The wax formed the pentagram itself.

"I'll be fine," he said. "Obviously Robert Erwin had been very sick throughout the duration of this event, so obviously I'll be just as sick."

"What are you saying?" asked Xander.

"Merely that"—*cough!*—"what happened to our past lives during the event probably has . . . no, *must* have some bearing on what happens to us during this one."

"I get it," said Xander. "Like on television. Repeats always end the same."

"Once again, your logic is abnormal," said Giles. "But that is, in a roundabout way, the point."

"Well, this is one rerun where the ending's in doubt," said Buffy. "Whoever is setting up this repeat action must want a different ending, because there weren't any questions about a 'Despised One' on our history test today."

"Even so, if Sarah Dinsdale ends up being burned at the stake, I'm going to allow myself to feel very, very nervous, understand?" said Xander.

"The witches were hanged, not burned at the stake," said Giles. "We're not dealing with total barbarians here. The Puritans were as civilized as anyone else at the time. Furthermore, Sarah Dinsdale's name is not among the victims. She did not die as a witch."

"What happened to her?" asked Xander.

Giles shrugged. "After her escape, she disappeared. Whatever happened to her, her name is erased from history."

"That may be," said Buffy, "but from what I've seen, Corwin and Danforth weren't above exacting a little street justice."

Suddenly an incredibly bright light flashed from the nearby hills, followed not long afterward by a prolonged blast of thunder that rippled through the air.

"Funny, the weather babe said the skies would be clear all week," said Xander.

"I think we're about to experience an autumn New England storm," said Buffy. "The next time I sneak out, I'm grabbing some mittens."

"Let the séance begin," said Giles, controlling his cough as he and Xander took hold of the girls' hands. "This shouldn't be too difficult, since we know Sarah's spirit is already with us. We just have to bring it out."

• • •

The language recommended by the Churches' book basically updated traditional séance chants. Since the spirits of the dead responded not to the sentiment but to the language of the caller, how something was said wasn't nearly as important as *what* was said.

The Churches believed the "swami" of the séance should have all the slickness of the average infomercial host. Giles spent about twenty minutes laying down a sales rap to the spirit of Sarah Dinsdale, telling her it would be in her karmic self-interest if she revealed herself to the living.

Buffy, Xander, and Willow concentrated with all their might.

Meanwhile, the rains came softly creeping in on the very fringes of their collective consciousness, which became stronger with every passing minute.

They felt no breeze, yet the candles flickered. Sometimes the flickering coincided with the thunder. Sometimes it coincided with the quivers up their spines.

The vase stood in the center of the pentagram. The participants in the séance tried to visualize the ashes inside, to imagine their texture, their smell, their taste.

Gradually the contents became easier to visualize. The energy among between the four participants grew to a powerful current. The thunder overhead shook the entirety of Sunnydale High. Everyone's bodies felt lighter, but their minds became heavier. Forming thoughts was becoming more difficult as their content grew foggier. Meanwhile, Giles's voice droned on and on until it was just noise in the background.

Suddenly Xander stiffened, practically into a state of rigor mortis. Giles gasped and finally clammed up. Either at the same instant or a second later—Buffy couldn't be sure which—an incredible bolt of lightning struck a tree near the school with catastrophic force. A startled-out-of-her-wits Willow broke the chain with both hands, and Buffy listened detachedly to the wood and fire sizzling in the rain.

Buffy opened her mouth to say something when the thunder roared directly overhead; she couldn't even hear herself think, much less speak.

Xander, meanwhile, managed to remain stiff and to shiver as if he'd been dipped into ice water. He groaned. Willow leaned toward him, but Giles silently indicated she restrain herself. Which she did, but not without worry.

Buffy noticed the flash of light that had hit the vase inside the pentagram had yet to fade. If anything, it now glowed more intensely. Clearly the ashes of the dead had absorbed the magical energies released by the lightning bolt.

Outside, the rain slowly extinguished the fire. The lightning had sliced the trunk in half, and a column of ashes and smoke rose up from the wound. It was normal for the sidewalk and the road right outside Sunnydale High to be deserted this time of night—except when there were school activities such as ballgames and dances—but tonight the normal state of affairs seemed foreboding, as if reality itself was about to take a hike.

Xander already had, spiritually speaking. Buffy had been too busy concentrating on the subtle shift in the tone of their surroundings to notice that Xander had loosened up. Although still in a trance, he managed to stand of his own accord in a distinctive posture, with a definite personal body language.

Unfortunately, it was not his own.

It didn't take a rocket scientist to figure out who Xander was acting like. In Buffy's dreams Samantha Kane had yet to encounter Sarah Dinsdale, but the adventuress and the witch must have had a face-to-face at some point, because Buffy recognized Sarah with the gut-certainty of genuine memory.

Buffy's emotional reaction was the same as Kane's must have been too, because at that moment she hated the entity in Xander's body, loathed it with all her heart. She hissed and made a move toward Xander.

"Buffy! Xander is not an enemy!" hissed Giles. "He is merely possessed!"

"We better have him back when she's gone, otherwise Dinsdale's going to pay!"

"And how will you find me," asked Xander, "in this world or another?"

Giles's mouth dropped open. "Sarah Dinsdale?"

Xander shook his head as if to brush aside his hair. "At your service. I see I have been called. I'm not surprised. It was inevitable I would rank among the Summoned one day."

"You sound like you've been involved in séances before," said Willow.

Xander—or should we say Sarah—looked around at the library in wonder and spoke almost offhandedly. "Of course, but always one of the callers, never one of the called."

"Who have you called in the past?" Buffy demanded. "The Master?"

Sarah visibly deflated. "I have never heard of the Master. In my day I called, to my eternal shame, an evil entity known as the Despised One. My sole defense is that I was but a lonely, wayward mistress of the dark arts, and I had been told he would soothe my great loneliness."

"We need to know something," said Giles. "About you and Samantha Kane."

Outside it began to drizzle. Lightning flashed. The air in the library chilled.

Sarah hung her head in shame. "I understand. But what could you possibly want to know about Samantha Kane, other than I am the one primarily responsible for her death?"

Giles put himself between Buffy and Xander/Sarah. "Everything! It has been prophesied that tonight what has been done will be done again, and the official record is too sparse for us to prevent it from being done successfully this time."

"Ah, you speak of the prophecy. I did not realize the time had come."

"How do you know about Eisenberg's Prophecy?" Giles demanded.

Sarah looked at him as if he was truly naive. "We spirits have to know these things. Now I am truly glad that you called. I do not possess the means to help you in any material way, but I can provide you with information."

"That will be immensely helpful," said Giles. Outside, the drizzle had turned into a steady downpour. The fire had finally been extinguished, and a brisk, sustained wind began to build, shaking the trees and stirring the puddles.

"Why don't you start with what happened after you tried to kill Kane with that dead hand?" Buffy asked with a sneer. She knew she should be more dispassionate, but she couldn't help herself.

"I had thought I had merely called up one corpse, that of a seaman who had died and been left there long before. But to my shame, I had not realized my ability to call forth the dead was beyond my control. I had inadvertently called up others—many others. Indians who had fallen from a white man's plague. Settlers who had died from a harsh winter and mothers who had died in childbirth. Souls not yet at rest."

"My grasp of the details is vague, because I was not actually there and know only what other spirits have communicated to me. But I do know that the risen corpses found and attacked the vengeful ones from Salem seeking to recapture me."

"That's not in the history books!" exclaimed Willow.

Sarah smiled and shrugged. "Such incidents rarely are." Obviously whatever misfortune befell those men gave her pleasure, however much she may have suffered since.

Xander/Sarah walked to the window and looked outside. "Strange. I was making my way through the forest to a place feared and avoided by all savages, be they Puritan or Indian, when storm clouds rolled overhead and it began to rain, exactly as it is now.

"It was still raining when I finally reached my destination near the mouth of the Danvers River, not three hours before the dawn. At first I thought I was early, because the site was deserted. Not until I'd actually stepped foot on the site did I suspect all the ambitions and dreams of the last few years might have been part of some massive mistake on my part, for this place could not possibly have been prepared by men."

"How so?" Giles asked.

"Suddenly, with definite boundaries, the forest was clear-cut. Not even a stump remained where the great trees once stood. In their place stood thirty massive slabs roughly forming a horseshoe structure; more slabs lay on top of them, indicating either an entrance or a boundary—I did not know which.

"The slabs were gray, but they glowed with an incandescent blue neither the night nor the rain could dim. I knew, with the instinctive surety only one with my occult abilities could command, these slabs were not formed on Earth. But where? My wonderful instincts, I confess, did not provide me with a clue until I spied a small break in the storm clouds, through which shone the light of the moon."

"They were moon rocks!" exclaimed Willow. "But how?"

"One small step for the Despised One," said Buffy, "one big bite for mankind."

"Certain meteors found in the Antarctic originated not from deep space, but from Mars," said Giles. "They were chunks knocked off the Red Planet with the impact of giant meteors. They spun around the solar system until they were captured by Earth's gravitational pull. Obviously the same thing could have happened with moon rocks."

Buffy immediately flashed on her vision of the moon being hit by exactly such a giant meteor . . . of a huge crater being formed, and of great slabs hurtling out into space.

Xander/Sarah walked back to his place at the table. Buffy noticed his hips moved with a distinct feminine rhythm. "I stood in the rain, cold, hungry, and miserable, and waited. For the first time I wondered what I was doing there. At the moment I had no idea of the suffering my spell was causing, or of the fact that my body was already acting as the conduit for supernatural forces.

"As I waited there was little else for me to do but watch the storm. It was the most powerful I'd ever seen. Even the distant thunder was deafening, the distant lightning blinding. I wandered about aimlessly inside the rock edifice. I noticed the closer I walked to a slab—any slab—the more I felt strange energies stirring inside me.

"Suddenly I was struck straight on by a lightning blast. So great was its force I should have instantaneously burnt to a cinder. Yet, miraculously, I remained whole, bound by a blue light that held me high in the air like a fish caught in a net. I was immobile, and incapable of coherent thought.

"I could only watch helplessly as four people emerged from the forest at four different points before me, and I despaired at the extent of the trap that had been set for me—"

"How the mighty have pratfallen, eh, Sarah?" taunted Buffy.

Xander/Sarah whirled angrily at her and gestured. "Although my current male reincarnation is unpracticed in harnessing occult energies, I can still muster the strength to cast a terrible curse. I can smell the self-righteous smugness of the Slayer in you, girl."

"All right, stop it, you two!" said Giles. "We must get to the bottom of this before we run out of time."

"Let me guess," said Buffy, "the four people were Cotton Mather, Judge Danforth, Sheriff Corwin, and Heather Putnam."

"Yes, how did you know?"

"Slayer intuition."

"They were indifferent to me; I was no better than a wheat fetish or a berry potion in their eyes. Their talk revealed them at last as secret worshippers of the Despised One who had spent the past several months dutifully following his instructions, like the mindless sheep I'd always expected them to be. I just hadn't suspected the sheepdog would turn out to be the Despised One.

"Poor Cotton Mather actually thought his bargain with the

Despised One would prove a boon for mankind. By sacrificing his soul to Old Scratch when he convicted the innocent of witchcraft, he hoped to turn others, many others, to the Good Word; and then the Almighty might forgive him and send his soul to Heaven.

"I truly believe that if the Despised One's plan had succeeded, poor Cotton Mather would have been among the first to be eaten."

"Cottonmouth," Buffy whispered aloud to no one in particular.

"I watched with wonder and horror as the four sheep performed the ceremony for calling forth the Despised One. It had never worked for me, but I'd always been alone. Alone, and manipulated. These people believed they were acting of their own free will.

"A multifingered fork of charged white light struck the standing slabs in a sustained eruption. I twisted about in my blue prison and watched the archway of power reaching down from the sky like the wing of a great cathedral. This lightning did not die in an instant; rather, thanks to invisible sources of might, it was continuously renewed.

"Meanwhile, the storm intensified. The wind howled like anguished wolves. The rain came down in buckets, yet still could not extinguish the curious blue flames that had engulfed the slabs. The four worshippers held hands and performed a slow, unsavory dance. I felt their polluted souls rising above their bodies—I felt my mind's doors of perception widening in a manner I did not approve of. And all because of the power of that dance.

"I realized then that when it came to serving the needs of the Despised One, I was a rank neophyte. Surely he had thought me no better than a pawn, while these four were utter professionals.

"Suddenly they began to chant. A thousand invisible pin-pricks skewered my body like so many thorns. My every nerve was in agony. Yet the cuts and bruises I had sustained during my flight healed completely. Even the scars that might have lingered disappeared. Indeed, the occult energies mended and cleansed my clothing as well. Obviously the Despised One desired that his offering be presentable. But then my blood began to flow. I screamed; yet I heard no sound. This unholy place had rendered me silent."

"This is really exciting," whispered Willow to Buffy.

"Not when you consider that according to Eisenberg's Prophecy, this ceremony is going to be performed again, somehow," said Giles.

"Where's he going to get the moon rocks?" asked Willow.

"Yeah, Sunnydale is in the wrong part of the solar system to get moon rocks," said Buffy. Then she reconsidered. "Uh-oh. No, it isn't." She tapped the cover of her dream notebook.

"Will you people be quiet? Have all manners and propriety been lost in this future age?"

"Blame television," said Buffy. She happened to glance at the glowing vase as Sarah continued.

"The ground beneath the dancing fools transmuted as if by alchemy. Alternating between a bright crimson and a soft pink shade, it became translucent. From above I easily saw the flames of the underworld.

"The four worshippers brought their dance to a climax and fell to their knees. 'The Despised One comes!' they shouted in unison. 'Soon his presence shall be known to the entire world, and the entire world shall turn upside down!'

"The storm intensified to gale force. Trees fell as if cut by an ax. The earth shook. The pale blue lightning became stronger, hotter, and the thunder even louder and more dissonant. Winged creatures with claw and fang flew in formation in the clouds.

"My thoughts sank in a chasm of helplessness. I believed the world wasn't turning upside down so much as it was dissolving in a pool of chaos.

"The worshippers rejoiced as suddenly a single green webbed hand protruded from the translucent, bloodred soil. The Despised One had arrived!

"Indeed—He had risen! He stepped up onto the solid earth as if he'd already conquered his greatest foe! Even from my distant vantage point, he was the ugliest creature I'd ever seen. His body looked like a cross between a dragon and a giant worm. His mouth was devoid of lips, and his nostrils were missing a nose. And those teeth! My arcane studies had informed me of a species of fish that lived in the southern hemisphere, a voracious, carnivorous fish with two rows of sharp, pointed teeth. These the Despised One's resembled.

"I could tell the entire world was going to be in for a cataclysm of biblical proportions, and there was nothing I could do about it. There was nothing anyone could do about it.

"Except for Samantha Kane. Surely her arrival could not have been as silent as it seemed. Doubtless the storm had concealed the sound of her horse's gallop. I am certain I was the first to spot her, and I trust my reaction was not so great that I inadvertently warned any of the others.

"In any case, they appeared most surprised when her horse bolted between them. Heather Putnam and Cotton Mather were knocked to the ground, while Sheriff Corwin and Judge Danforth were simply too stunned to react. I do not blame them. Had I been in their position, I would have been equally surprised.

"As Kane's horse galloped past the Despised One, she jumped from her saddle and threw herself directly on top of him. They both fell, but Kane fell on top. Keeping the startled Despised One pinned with her weight, she stabbed him with the hunting knife she held in one hand and poured holy water from the bottle she held in the other. She doused his face. Even in the rain and the confusion, I saw the steam rise from his head; I saw those terrible features disintegrate into a formless shape even more terrible; and I heard screams so horrible I would have felt pity had they come from anyone, or anything, else.

"The Despised One undoubtedly lacked the experience at

physical combat that Kane demonstrated, but that did not prevent him from fighting back. The two fought furiously as they rolled in the mud, while the others, lackeys that they were, did nothing except look to one another for direction. In vain, of course.

"Then it was over: Kane had achieved victory. But at such a cost.

"For they both rolled into the transmuted ground an instant before it closed. Before they disappeared, I saw the Despised One sink his fangs into her shoulder and rip out a huge mouthful of flesh. Kane had surely been bleeding to death before the earth closed up around them."

"You don't seem exactly broken up about it," said Buffy.

"Why should I? Does she not live on in you, after a fashion?"

"As do you in Xander?" Willow asked Sarah.

"I stand corrected. The essence of Sarah Dinsdale indeed resides, temporarily, in this being called Alexander Harris, but I would not call it living. Even so, it is superior to being bound by the confines of nonexistence. I suppose you would like to hear, now, what happened after my occult prison disappeared and the four worshippers fled to resume their charades of respectability?"

"I'm not sure we have time," said Buffy as an especially loud thunderclap resounded above the school. She noticed that the vase with the ashes inside was trembling, as if it and it alone were caught in an earthquake.

"I think we'd better get out of here," said Giles.

"Can't I just throw the vase in an open sewer or something, like in the movies?" Buffy asked.

Giles reached out to touch it, but drew his hand away before he actually did so. "Too hot."

"Darn," said Buffy, "and I'm all out of hand lotion. You're right. Okay, I'm outtie. Xander? Or should I say, Sarah? Are you with us?"

"All right, I've heard quite enough," someone said from above them.

Xander/Sarah was a little slow on the uptake, but the others all turned toward the person just in time to be blinded by a camera flash.

"MacGovern!" exclaimed Buffy, trying to blink away the spots in her eyes. "How long have you been standing there?"

"Long enough to learn that you four are part of a religious cult bent on world domination!" said MacGovern. His face was red and he was breathing hard. Buffy was about to protest when he flashed another picture, this one of Xander.

"What heinous sorcery is this?" Xander/Sarah cried, backing into a chair and falling down.

"It's the *science* of the fourth estate, young man, er, madam," replied MacGovern, both defiant and confused. "And now that I have my proof, the entire world will know what's going on in the Sunnydale High library!"

"No, you shouldn't report this!" Giles protested. "If people actually believe you, the media will keep her under constant surveillance!"

"Summers should have thought of that when she tried to take over the world!" MacGovern replied.

"Buffy! Quick!" said Willow. "Hit him over the head! Maybe it'll knock some sense in him!"

"It's too late for that!" said MacGovern, trying to get past them to the front door. "Stay away from me. It's my First Amendment right to be trespassing here!"

Suddenly the vase exploded. Everyone was engulfed in ashes. Everybody was immediately grossed out, too—everybody except MacGovern, that is. He was inundated with one of the four blue shower-curtain-esque fields of ectoplasm revealed in the aftermath of the explosion. The blue field outlined his body until it was completely absorbed. The others did not notice because they were still grossed out, and because the effect was disguised by the brilliant flashing of another lightning blast striking the school grounds. This time they heard the distinct sound of a wall crumbling.

"We've been undone!" Giles exclaimed, staggering backward onto a couch as if felled by a hammer. Already the perspiration brought on by his fever caused the ashes to run down his face. He looked like a crying clown with too many eyes.

"What makes you say that?" asked Willow. "Is it your fever?"

"Has something happened we should know about?" asked Buffy, who was always a little suspicious of Giles's tendency to withhold information until the last possible moment.

"I believe so," said Giles. "Whoever's manipulating present events to fulfill the Prophecy of the Dual Duels used the mystical forces focused on the vase during our séance to pry open a gateway between the dimensions of the living and the dead."

"You know, it always amazes me that you're able to say so much without taking a breath," commented Xander.

If Willow tried to contain her excitement, it was lost on the others. She did restrain herself from throwing her arms around Xander, though just barely. "You're . . . yourself again!"

"Who else?"

"Time check," Buffy advised.

Xander did. He was wearing a cheap wristwatch he had purchased at a hamburger joint. "Hey! It was only eight! Where was I? Oh no, I wasn't a girl again, was I?"

"'Fraid so," said Buffy. "We were about to give you a makeover."

"Your identity crisis will have to wait," said Giles with a cough. Then, nodding toward MacGovern: "We've more pressing problems."

Xander finally noticed the reporter standing there. "Ah, I don't think we're talking to MacGovern anymore."

The girls automatically took a few steps back from MacGovern. Giles cringed momentarily. Xander sneezed.

Holding his flash camera like a weapon, MacGovern breathed heavily and glared at each of the foursome in turn. A noticeable change had come in his posture. He stood straighter, with his shoulders held high. With a shrug he tried to make his jacket appear a better fit—a hopeless effort. He looked down imperiously at them, easy enough to do from the upper level.

"I know you!" exclaimed Buffy. "You're Cotton Mather. Where's your blood?"

MacGovern/Mather scowled. "I do not know your meaning, sinful one."

"The blood that's supposed to be on your hands!"

He chuckled. "Oh, very good." He inspected the reporter's hands, which at the moment were his own. He appeared to enjoy it. "It is there. These hands are not nearly as clean as MacGovern might wish."

"So Mather's your name, eh?" Xander asked. "What's your—?"

MacGovern silenced him with a gesture. "Don't. You have no idea how many times I heard that phrase in purgatory, where the imagination runs the gamut from A to B."

Buffy was unimpressed. "Still a good question."

MacGovern/Mather smiled like an angel. "I have returned so I may do my bit, however modest, in unleashing the underworld onto the Earth. It's time for what's currently called a hostile takeover."

"Come on," said Xander, "what's the race of mankind ever done to you?"

"Exist."

"So you're a little bitter," said Willow, trying to be helpful, "and you've had a bad experience these last three-hundred-plus years. But that's no reason to have such a negative approach right now."

Mather drew himself to his full height and pointed his finger straight toward her nose. “Silence, woman! I am not an open book for you to read.”

“Doesn’t matter,” said Buffy quietly. “We already know how you’re going to end.”

“And you too, unfortunately,” snapped back Mather. “Well, I must retrieve an important ingredient for the upcoming resurrection. Bye!” He gathered his arms before him and dove toward a closed window, intending to smash right through it. He stopped at the last possible second, startled practically out of his wits.

“The bars are made of metal in these newer buildings,” Giles pointed out. He couldn’t resist a smile, even in his condition.

“Curses!” Mather exclaimed, and before they could guess his intentions, he leapt over the railing and landed on the table, square in the middle of the pentagram, knocking down two of the candles. Lightning flashed, followed by deafening thunder, and all the lights in the library cut out for several moments, enough time for lightning to flash yet again. Buffy spent the time stamping out the two flames.

Thus giving Mather the time to jump down and dash out the front door.

“Next time we have a séance, Giles,” said Buffy, “you should remember to lock the front door from the inside.”

“Point taken,” said Giles, just before throwing up.

CHAPTER EIGHT

The black raincoat she'd borrowed from Giles was much too big for Buffy, but at least it had a hood and protected her somewhat from the continuous rain. Though she was on the verge of becoming totally out of breath, she continued running toward the gallery, where she hoped to prevent MacGovern/Mather from obtaining V.V. Vivaldi's *Moonman* statue.

She ran through an open shopping center, across a small park, and through a ritzy neighborhood. Normally when she had this great a distance to make across Sunnydale, she broke down and asked Giles for a lift, but right now he was running a temperature of a hundred and four and was taking a cold shower in the boys' locker room. Xander's job was to take care of Giles, while Willow was searching the Internet hoping to find some kernel of information about Prince Eisenberg, *The Eibon*, V.V. Vivaldi, or anything else that might prevent tonight's events from becoming an absolute rerun of the past.

Buffy hated prophecies. Especially this one. Normally she didn't like to admit to herself that she needed help—even when she knew she did—but she had no problem making an exception in this case. It was too bad Angel wasn't around. He often showed up whenever he was afraid she would get in over her head, but tonight he was nowhere to be seen. She supposed even a conscience-ridden vampire had a social life; that is, if he wasn't out raiding a blood bank somewhere.

At least the raincoat was doing its job. Without her boots, though, her feet were soaked and felt wrinkled to a wormlike state by the wet.

Her Slayer instincts were doing their job too. She knew the Hummer following her belonged to the Churches. They were good at their work too. Every time she took a shortcut or deliberately went down a narrow alley impossible for them to get their Hummer through, they always picked her up a short distance down the line.

Buffy had the distinct suspicion the Churches might be more heavily involved in this affair than they'd intended. She also wondered if they were aware of the other set of headlights—belonging to a van—following them. Probably. They were undoubtedly used to occasional media attention by now.

Even so, if she couldn't prevent *The Moonman* from being stolen, then her task was to keep the four former worshippers of the Despised One from doing a reprise of their "unsavory" dance. She figured that if she could prevent one major element of the original incident from fitting into its proper place, then the entire prophecy might wash away with the smog and pollen in the storm.

Buffy was just a half mile from the gallery when she finally spotted MacGovern/Mather. He was drenched. He shambled down the center of the street, which tonight was devoid of traffic thanks to the terrific storm; everybody with a semblance of common sense—or no bodily repossessions—was staying home.

She was glad to be able to slow down. Her heart was beating so hard that she was surprised he couldn't hear it, even over the frequent thunder. Still, she edged closer to him, and they were both approximately a hundred yards away from the gallery when Buffy spotted her mother's car parked outside. Naturally. As if it wasn't bad enough she was willfully participating in a scenario that may have killed her in a past life, her mom might discover her daughter is secretly a key player in the eternal struggle between good and evil. *Can you be grounded for eternal life?*

There was only one thing to do, and that was take the bull by the horns and face the situation.

"Mather!" she called out.

MacGovern/Mather stopped and turned. He had been

carrying his flash camera the entire time, and it was as drenched as he. Rivulets flowed from the brim of his hat, and his cheap coat clung to his cheap shirt like plastic wrap. "What do you want? Do not think of interfering," he added, answering his own question.

"Why? Afraid I'll die before my time?" said Buffy, trying to maneuver close enough for an effective attack.

"Doesn't matter when you die, so long as you do. In fact, should you die before the ceremony, so much the better. Reduces the chance of a complication."

"Hmm. It's nice to know you're afraid of complications."

Mather growled and hurled the flash camera at Buffy. She dodged it with ease and it shattered on the sidewalk, exposing the film. It appeared MacGovern's luck would be consistent, in the short-term at least. Buffy couldn't help but laugh.

Mather's reaction was unexpected. Mainly because it was MacGovern's reaction. "Hey, what's so funny?" he asked indignantly. His imperious posture momentarily deflated, only to resume its unnatural height as he said aloud, "Leave me alone. Stay suppressed like you're supposed to, and you might live through this night. You, on the other hand"—now he looked at Buffy—"haven't got a prayer."

"Other hand? Sounds to me like you're having trouble keeping the *upper* hand."

Mather, again firmly in control, looked around at the sleek, modern buildings, then glared directly at Buffy. "We knew how to handle smart-mouthed young vixens in my day."

"Burned them at the stake?"

"We were kinder, gentler executioners; we merely hanged them. The barbarians in Europe, they burned the witches!"

"I knew that. I just wanted to hear you deny it." She bent at the knees, bringing forward a branch the size of her arm she'd picked up in the park.

Mather stepped back. Way back. "I deny anything if it's a lie." Lightning flashed behind him, and his shadow cut across the road.

A few blocks down, a Hummer came to a stop and turned out its lights. Then it came forward.

"Deny *this*!" said Buffy. Taking advantage of the distraction, she broke the branch in half—into two pointed stakes—and rolled straight at him, shooting with the force of a bowling ball. Her legs got a little tangled in the raincoat, but otherwise the maneuver went all right.

Mather laughed. She sprang at him, cocking her right arm to drive the stake into his heart.

Or where a heart should be.

Mather dodged the stake with ease. "I once possessed a martial arts master," he explained while he kicked her in the stomach.

Buffy managed to deflect most of the blow, but it still delivered quite an impact. She landed on her back, in a manhole up to its rim with water. She rolled out of the way a second before Mather landed on top of her feetfirst. She hit him with the bottom of her foot, at the kneecap. His leg crumbled out from under him, and she kicked him in the face.

He grabbed her leg, twisted it—thus twisting her—and sent her flying headfirst into the door of a parked Honda. Luckily the door bent easily.

But she was in the process of standing before she even touched the ground. She turned and threw an underhand stake toward his eye.

He avoided it, knocking it straight down to the ground, but he fell down, which definitely hadn't been part of his plan. He grabbed the stake and threw it back at her.

She caught it.

"Slay me and you slay MacGovern," Mather said. "Possession isn't permanent. Sooner or later I'll have to return control to MacGovern."

Buffy raised her eyebrows. MacGovern/Mather was right. She would have to be more careful.

"How do I know you're not lying?" she asked.

"Maybe my journalist half is talking!" He turned and ran directly toward the gallery.

Buffy could have caught up with him easily—possessed though he might be, he still had the legs of an old man—but she was momentarily stymied. How should she proceed?

Her mind was made up when Mather, trying to avoid a huge puddle, brazenly climbed over the hood of Joyce Summers's parked car.

Buffy dashed toward him with murderous intent, but she

came to an abrupt stop and slipped and fell onto another car the moment she saw her mother coming out of the gallery.

Mom wasn't alone. With her was the cleaning lady, Pat, who held a bucket filled with cleaning tools in one hand, and with her other hand balanced a mop over her shoulder. Pat was about four and a half feet tall and weighed nearly 150 pounds; she resembled a fire hydrant.

"Why, Mrs. Summers, how good it is to make your acquaintance," said Mather with a definitely smarmy air. He offered to shake her hand.

"Mister, are you all right?" Buffy's mom asked, peering out from under her umbrella. "You look a fright!"

Buffy watched what happened next in a car mirror. The moment Mather made a false move, the stakes would start to fly!

"Look a fright?" exclaimed Mather. "I am a fright!"

He grabbed Mrs. Summers by the wrist and yanked her toward him. She spun into his arms and he held her in a bear hug. It had taken only a second.

But it was long enough for Buffy to expose herself and cock back her right arm. She had her eye on the nape of his neck.

Joyce had hers on his foot. She stamped it with the point of her high heel.

Mather yelled and released her, thus giving Pat the cleaning lady a clear shot with her mop. She caught Mather upside the head and he staggered away from them, toward the stairs leading to the gallery.

"The gallery is closed, sir," said Joyce Summers, who had already gotten her cell phone from her pocketbook and was dialing 911.

"That depends on your perspective," Mather replied. He had steadied himself by the time he'd reached the top of the stairs, and when he turned toward the front door he broke out into a full run, giving the others the distinct impression he would try to run straight through it. Instead, he veered at the last possible instant and ran straight into a window. No iron bars! Glass and wood shattered as he disappeared into the gallery. A slew of alarms went off, but Mather obviously didn't care.

No respect for the human body whatsoever, thought Buffy, moving down the line of parked cars. She had to follow Mather, regardless of whether or not her mother spotted her. *Besides, if I live through tonight I can be grounded forever, for all I care. In fact, I could use the rest.* But it would be better if her mother didn't see her. See pulled the hood closer.

"Shouldn't we go after him?" asked Pat, raising her voice to be heard.

"No, leave the heroics to the professionals," Joyce replied. "Hello? 911? I'd like to report a break-in."

Thanks, Mom, thought Buffy as she took advantage of the moment, the darkness, and all the alarms and dashed across the sidewalk with the fleetness of a cat in hunting mode. She realized her dilemma had gotten worse, if that was possible. Now she was faced with the choice of either stopping Mather before the police came or letting him be arrested for attempting to steal the Vivaldi *Moonman*. Either way, Darryl MacGovern, streetwise but unlucky reporter, would take the rap.

Buffy found the upraised path along the side of the gallery so narrow she had no choice but to walk directly under the rain that rolled off the rooftop like a waterfall. It was like getting hit in the head with a succession of buckets of water. But at least it enabled her to see inside.

Most businesses leave at least half the lights on after closing to discourage unwelcome visitors. The gallery was no exception. Buffy saw through a window, and through an open door beyond, into a room where a drenched Mather was examining the podium upon which stood the *Moonman* statue. Naturally it looked just like the statue on Buffy's dream notebook. Like a standing jigsaw puzzle of a man with a broken face.

Buffy broke the window with her elbow, reached inside, and opened it. Normally she wasn't so up-front about breaking and entering, but she figured tonight she could make an exception because the alarms already made it sound like the whole city had been struck by a giant earthquake.

But by the time she reached the podium, Mather had already knocked it over and taken the statue. She looked down the hall just in time to see him closing the back door behind him.

Then she looked up the hall just in time to see the first policeman coming in.

He had a flashlight. She could almost feel the beam hitting the back of her head as she pulled up her hood and ran toward the back door. He called out for her to stop.

He fired one shot into the air—at least, she hoped it was in the air—so she zoomed from the gallery rear exit with an extra burst of speed. Mather was nowhere to be seen, which was a problem, but she had to make sure the same thing could be said about her before the policeman's backup arrived.

Near the fence in the rear were two bushes just far enough apart to provide her with cover for a few moments while she thought of her next move. She dove in.

And landed right on top of Mather. They bumped heads so hard she saw stars.

By the time Buffy recovered enough to think straight, Mather was already gone—he'd probably climbed over the fence—and the rear of the gallery was now crawling with police.

Actually, there were only two who were inspecting the grounds—two too many under the circumstances. Buffy had no choice but to lie low, hugging the mud while the rain poured down. Her only consolation was that she was behind enough cover so the cops couldn't see her when the lightning flashed.

By the time the police were gone and it was safe for Buffy to climb over the rear fence, Mather was nowhere to be seen. Any trail he might have left behind was by now washed away. To make matters worse, neither the Hummer nor the van was visible. One would have thought that Eric Frank's face would be everywhere, looking for angles on the theft of the infamous *Moonman* statue.

Buffy refused to give up, however, and she trotted down the street looking for a sign.

CHAPTER NINE

But first, a phone call to the library.

She just hoped Giles was still conscious enough to hear it ring.

Buffy's heart sank when Willow answered.

"Giles is so hot he's practically steaming," Willow said. "But he's not getting any worse. According to the Slayer histories, Robert Erwin didn't die until a few days after Sarah Dinsdale's escape, so we think Giles will be okay until . . . after . . . well, you know . . ."

"Believe me. You haven't mentioned Xander."

"That's because he went looking for you."

"I thought he was supposed to—"

"Buffy, he's as much tied up in this as you are. No one wants you to face this alone."

"Yes, but I'm hoping to keep Xander and myself separated, to change the equation, so to speak."

"Oh. I take it he hasn't found you yet."

"Well, if he went to the gallery, he might have been distracted by all the police running about. Have you found anything yet?"

"No. I've been racking my brains, but I have no idea where a ceremony with a false Stonehenge setting can take place in the Sunnydale area. At the moment I'm in a forum with some British witches who claimed to have erected the original Stonehenge in a previous life. They're a little confused, though, on which of the three major building periods they were involved with—"

"And the weather?"

"All the weather sites are confused. There was no indication anywhere in the atmosphere that the Pacific Coast was going to be hit by a storm this large and fierce. Flash-flood warnings are in effect from Seattle to San Diego."

"Get me some cold medicine. I'll be back eventually." Buffy sneezed. "See you."

"Ciao," Willow said weakly, and then they both hung up.

Buffy tried to think of what to do next. She was tired and cold and worried, and she was barely able to hold in check her anxieties about her role in the prophecy. Were Slayers supposed to die until one of them finally got it right, or did they always die? Perhaps the best thing for her and Xander to do would be to screw things up completely by leaving town, where they couldn't possibly be affected or drawn in.

But then again, maybe things would be even worse if they did. That was the trouble with fate. You never knew when you had reached another fork in the road.

On the other side of the street were two empty lots that despite being prime land had gone unused for Sunnydale's entire history. The rain showed no sign of easing up.

Buffy thought seriously about giving up and just going back to the library. She didn't even know where to head first.

A car passed, splashing up a huge wave. Until that moment, Buffy's knees had been dry. She made up her mind. She was halfway across the road when she came to a dead stop.

For a few seconds she had no idea why. Her survival instincts occasionally compelled her to do things without knowing why. Usually in retrospect she realized her senses had picked up on something her conscious mind hadn't noticed. Such as the moving mound in the mud in one of the empty lots.

Another car approached, forcing Buffy to finish crossing the street. She veered in the direction of the mound. She twirled the stake in her right hand. No doubt about it—something underground was approaching her. It couldn't be good.

Whatever senses it possessed, however, were severely limited. It went right under the sidewalk and disappeared for several moments. She imagined it—a giant, carnivorous worm? a deadly multi-bladed machine?—hitting the underside of the asphalt several times in an effort to break through and restore whatever dim bead it had on her.

The mound revealed itself again. It moved away from the sidewalk in a different direction; the two lines in the dirt formed a V.

Buffy hurled a stake at the moving mound. The stake spun like an axis, glistening in a lightning flash, and stuck straight up in the dirt. It quivered for a few moments, then rose straight up in the air. At least, that's what it looked like.

Until the zombie's head rose out of the ground, quickly followed by the rest of its body. At that moment Buffy would have gladly traded all the stakes in creation for one good minute with a surface-to-air missile launcher.

The zombie turned to face her. Its face was pretty rank: Most of the skin had been scraped off underground. It wore buckskins and its putrefying hair was tied in ponytails; once it had been a warrior. When it growled, a strip of rotten skin fluttered where its Adam's apple should have been.

Once the warrior had lost an arm at the elbow. With that lost arm he'd held a hatchet. The zombie held that same arm, which was holding that same hatchet, right now.

It advanced.

Buffy sighed. That missile launcher sure would have saved a lot of time. As it was now, dispatching this zombie would take a few minutes longer.

So she became the missile, launching herself at it feetfirst. She was betting that it couldn't move very fast without accelerating its decay, and she was about half right.

It grabbed her feet with its remaining hand, but it had to drop the forearm with the hatchet to do so.

It still couldn't stop her, really. She buried both her feet into its chest up to her ankles. Bone cracked big-time and Buffy winced; the experience was like jumping from a diving board onto a giant snail.

They both went down in a heap, with Buffy on top. The zombie fell badly, breaking apart under the combined impact of Buffy and the sidewalk. Buffy fell almost as badly, hurting the small of her back. But that didn't stop her from rolling away from the pieces of the zombie as quickly as possible.

A putrefied hand clung to her raincoat. Buffy broke its fingers in half one by one, and then stamped her foot on the hand until it was mush. The fingers still crawled toward her like worms. The rest of the zombie was attempting the same. A shoulder scooted, the head rolled, and the one standing leg hopped. Their intentions did not look good.

Buffy knew she couldn't just leave them because that head was bound to bite somebody before it got itself kicked in, but as she waited for a car—and its startled driver!—to pass by, she got the distinct impression somebody else was growling at her.

She turned to face a fieldful of zombies rising from the earth.

They seemed to have no leader and no mind, group or otherwise. They simply shambled toward her, apparently with no other intention than just killing her.

This was bad, more than just a tough jam. Buffy remembered the dream of Samantha Kane being menaced by parts of a zombie, not to mention Sarah Dinsdale's story of what happened to the men trying to recapture her. They had been set upon by a horde of zombies. *Like a gaggle of geese,* Buffy thought grimly.

She got ready, stooping to a fighting stance. It might take a while, but she was sure she could eradicate them, with or without the stake she'd dropped. She changed her mind when four zombies scooped up the parts of their fallen comrade along the way and ate them. (The one without a lower jaw stuffed pieces of the foot, including a shoe, down his throat.) She had decided to look for the nearest bulldozer or any other piece of equipment that would help her mash these things as flat as possible, as quickly as possible.

Seeing nothing of potential help in the immediate vicinity, she took off into the alley between the empty store and a deserted office building and climbed over a wire-mesh fence into a dark, wet grade school lot and ran as fast as she could.

On the other side of the lot she slowed down and saw the zombies still following her, though they had no hope of maintaining her pace, much less overtaking her.

Buffy waited until most of them were halfway across the lot, and then she climbed over the fence and landed on the sidewalk. Across the street lay Sunnydale Central Park.

She had an idea. It was risky and broke every Slayer rule in the book, but that had never stopped her before. So that there would be absolutely no chance they'd lose sight of her, she sauntered into the park as if on a Sunday stroll. Now she was entering well-lit territory. The sidewalks and open spaces were so bright the rain glistened like sunlight on the sea, and even the tops of the pines were lit. Luckily the weather was so bad even the delinquents who usually hung out there had gone home.

Buffy turned around (though she kept walking backward) and saw the zombies shuffling across the street. Tires screeched and a car crashed into something nearby. Buffy tensed. All the zombies she saw were still coming toward her, but she had no idea if she was drawing them *all* away or—

Someone screamed. Gunshots were fired. There was a second car crash.

No, some zombies had definitely become distracted. *Curses!* Now she had to double back to make sure no one was being eaten.

She began to make an arc, but when she reached a pedestrian lane at the edge of the park leading back across the street, she stopped and let out a little cry of frustration.

And no wonder. Coming straight toward her was another zombie army, though this one was dressed more like the Spaniards from the early days of California history, complete with metal helmets and chest plates. Obviously they were going to be more difficult to stomp to death than the army of zombies already chasing her. It appeared checking up on whoever was in the automobiles would have to wait, perhaps indefinitely.

Currently on the same wavelength, the two sets of zombies simply flowed into one great stream; they still followed her just as relentlessly, just as mindlessly. They weren't even fazed when one was struck by a bolt of lightning and turned into cinder.

Buffy kept about a hundred yards between herself and the zombies. She stayed in sight. She tried not to put too many barriers between herself and the shambling creatures because she wasn't sure they possessed the smarts to navigate past them. When she ran through a tennis court, she was sure she'd been right: Some zombies went through the openings, but others tried climbing the wire-mesh fence rather than going around it. Most succeeded, incidentally, but a few fell all the way down and broke apart upon hitting the ground. The ones that still had legs and torso attached gathered themselves together as best as they could and straggled behind.

Three-quarters of the way through the park Buffy sighted the town gazebo in the middle of an open stretch of ground. According to legend, a brass band had played in the gazebo every Sunday until the advent of the Jazz Age, and the people of Sunnydale gathered on the grounds to listen and do all the other things people of small towns were supposed to have done during the glorious "Past."

The notion of resting and getting out of the rain for five

minutes was appealing. Indeed, with the way the zombies were advancing toward her, maybe she could take a catnap.

She was just bounding up the stairs, however, when she realized that all of a sudden she wasn't alone.

Of course, neither were the startled Cordelia and the second-string halfback she was making out with, the snotty Augie Duluth. "Buffy!" exclaimed Cordelia as she broke away from Augie and tried to hide how disheveled her hair and clothing were. "Invade personal space much?"

"Getting out of the rain?"

"You can't! I'm busy!" Cordelia replied as an undeterred Augie pursed his lips, grabbed her, spun her back to him, and attempted to suck face with all the finesse girls usually expect from members of the football team.

Buffy's stomach turned: She didn't find Augie attractive in the slightest. Then, with a rear glance, she remembered why she'd come here in the first place. The zombies were nowhere to be seen—not yet—but their distinct growl was faintly audible, if one knew what to listen for. "Cordelia, I think it's time you blew this gazebo!"

"I beg your pardon?" Cordelia exclaimed.

"All right! My little dew flower!" Augie exclaimed, just before he planted yet another big wet sloppy kiss on her.

Somebody better throw this dog a Milkbone, thought Buffy. "The police are coming!"

Cordelia jumped away from Augie as if he'd given her an electric shock. "What?"

"I'm sorry," said Buffy sheepishly, "but I've gotten into trouble with the law. They're on their way," she added, pointing to the trees.

"Why should I go?" Cordelia asked. "I didn't do anything wrong."

"Just think of the social black eye you'll get if the word leaks that you were hanging with a known felon."

"Don't tell me you burnt down the *Sunnydale* gym too," said Augie with a laugh.

"Only the boys' locker room," said Buffy. "All those smelly gym socks needed was one spark and . . . *poof*!"

"You said you're in trouble with whom?" Cordelia asked. At last the full implication of what Buffy was saying had sunk in and she was genuinely shocked.

Buffy saw the first pair of zombie legs become visible beneath the distant foliage. "You'll read about it in the papers tomorrow. Just trust me and go!"

"She's right, babe," said Augie. "See you around, my little jailbird," he said to Buffy as he took Cordelia by the elbow and attempted to escort her down the steps.

But Cordelia was reluctant, and she glared at Buffy. "You're involved in more funny business, aren't you?"

"You don't want to know."

Suddenly energized, Cordelia slapped a surprised Augie several times on the arm. "What's keeping you? Let's go!" She grabbed him by his varsity jacket and practically dragged him into the rain. "You're so slow!"

"That's not—"

"Shut up!" Cordelia hissed.

Buffy sighed with relief that they were finally going. She hated to admit it, but at the moment she envied Cordelia, who for all her faults was at least living a normal teenager's life.

And then, of course, there were the zombies, who had already lived theirs. The army shuffled down the hill toward the gazebo. A few slipped and fell, knocking others over and breaking off more than a few limbs in the process. Their chorus of growls was not inspired by the self-inflicted carnage or by the carnage they hoped to inflict on Buffy—they just came out spontaneously.

"Oh Romeo, oh Romeo, about time you showed up." Buffy had no idea if any of the zombies had enough brains left to be taunted, but she'd noticed a couple of them veering off in the direction Cordelia and Augie had taken. She needed them all to follow her, without exception, if her plan was to work.

The zombies did. Buffy leapt off the gazebo, landed on the first stone of a raised path, and headed out the park past a baseball field and a deserted public building. Well, at least she hoped it was deserted. It certainly appeared closed for the night, which was good, because in a few minutes she wouldn't be able to deal with any strays.

She crossed the street, by now so drenched that she thought nothing of fording the water overflowing the gutters on either side.

Buffy reached the border of a well-groomed field that was

off-limits to the public. Beyond the field was a well-lit building surrounded by an electrified fence covered with barbed wire. During the few seconds Buffy glanced that way, the building's lightning rod attracted no less than three bolts.

Then, without trying to be too circumspect about it, she ducked into an underground tunnel. It was a two-way road, with each lane just large enough to handle a Mack truck. The parking lot it served was more than two hundred yards away, below the other side of the well-groomed field. There were no doors, no emergency exits. The only way in or out was at either side.

Buffy hesitated, thought of something, then dashed back out into the street. Sure enough, the zombies showed every sign of missing her, of wandering by. She put two fingers to her lips and whistled loudly. She waved. "Hey! Adoring masses! This way!"

She went back into the tunnel, pausing until she saw that the zombies were following her this time. Then she ran. The zombies' growls echoed eerily throughout the tunnel; they rang in her ears like curses. The farther she went into the tunnel, the narrower and darker it seemed. It was all Buffy could do to refrain from running full-tilt to put as much distance between her and the zombies as possible. When she saw the guard in the booth up ahead, she knew she had to slow down.

Slow down and try to think of a way to save him.

Perhaps the best approach, she thought, would be an honest one. "Hey, mister!" she called out.

Uh-oh! The "mister" was a woman. A *police*woman. She got out of the booth, where she'd been reading a paperback novel. On one side of her belt hung a nightstick, while on the other hung a holster heavy with the biggest sidearm Buffy had ever seen. The officer was in the process of pulling her gun from its holster when she saw that she had been startled by a teenager.

"Girl!" exclaimed the officer. "What are you doing out on a night like this?"

"I'm being followed. May I borrow that?" Without waiting for an answer, she freed the nightstick from the officer's belt.

"Hey!" she cried at Buffy.

"Relax," said Buffy, pointing the nightstick down the tunnel. "I just need to make a point."

The zombies shuffled into view, their zombieness further distorted by the parking lot's lights. The policewoman gasped in disbelief. Buffy got the balance of the nightstick and then threw it briskly, just like a butter knife, at the foremost zombie.

The stick went through its forehead like a hot blowtorch through a gallon of ice cream.

Still the zombie approached. The fact that most of its brains had been pushed out of its ears had no effect whatsoever on its overall performance.

The officer screamed, and Buffy didn't blame her; most people went about their daily business unprepared for confrontations with formerly dead people dropping body parts.

"Better run," Buffy suggested. "I'll be right behind you."

They backed up into a heavily fenced parking lot.

Buffy quickly scoped out the situation. She stood at the border of the lot where the police and guards kept their civilian vehicles. Buffy knew the place would soon be swarming with cops, thanks to the officer's continuous screaming.

Buffy smiled to herself. *Life could be good, after all.*

She turned to the approaching zombies—the one with the big hole in its forehead now brandished the nightstick awkwardly, but no less threateningly—and whistled at them again. "Hi, boys, new in town?" she called out. "My name's Buffy, and I know how to show you a real good time."

The zombie with the hole in its forehead still had two good dead eyes. It growled so deeply parts of its neck fluttered out and hit the blacktop with a sickening *plop!* Another zombie nearby scooped up the debris and stuffed it into its mouth, swallowing several of its own teeth in the process. Even though all the zombies weren't out of the tunnel yet, their leaders—that is, the ones who happened to be at the front or close to it—advanced toward Buffy.

Buffy backed up some more. The idea was to lure the zombies as far as possible into the parking lot, an idea which, now that she thought about it, was working better and faster than she'd ever anticipated. All the zombies were now inside, and she had no choice but to slow down, because the zombies were trying to maneuver her back against the wall.

Buffy tried to circle around using a couple of parked

automobiles for interference, but while they couldn't exactly taste flesh and blood, the zombies were becoming excited, in their own detached way, about the prospect of soon feasting on the meal that had thus far eluded them.

Buffy slammed back against a van. Zombies approached to the front of her. To the right of her. To the left. She looked down to see a blackened hand reaching out from beneath the van, groping for her. She ground her heel on the hand with all the might she could muster, turned, jumped, grabbed the luggage rack, and swung onto the top of the van.

A zombie was already crawling up to greet her. She kicked it under the chin. The head lifted completely from the torso with a *rip* that echoed throughout the underground lot. She turned and kicked another zombie in the chest.

Oops! My fault!

This time when her foot went into a zombie's chest, this one helped keep it there by grabbing her ankle with both hands and twisting it. Buffy had to twist her entire body to keep her leg from being broken. Her greatest fear at the moment was that she would fall off the van, but she managed to stay on the top, landing face-first with her outstretched palms absorbing most of the impact. She drew in both her knees, then kicked with both feet, sending the zombie flying into three zombies scrambling over one another in their efforts to get to the top.

The four zombies fell in a heap. At that moment Officer McCrumski entered the area ready for the night shift. He saw a young woman clinging to the top of his partner's minivan. "Hey, what are you . . ." He trailed off, his breakfast sandwich falling to the pavement. He fumbled for his gun.

The zombies didn't care. Those who weren't climbing up the van simply turned toward the thin blue line.

Uh-oh! Buffy rolled off the van, on the opposite side of the policeman, the moment he began firing. This gave her protection from the bullets but not from the zombies who happened to be on the other side. They caught her before she hit the ground and immediately tried to pull her apart or eat her, whichever was easier.

Wonder if Prince Ashton predicted this, Buffy thought sardonically as she kicked off the face of a zombie trying to bite her ankle. She twisted and jabbed her elbow into another one. It got stuck between the creature's ribs. She hooked her elbow in deeper and then yanked with all her might; her fist struck another zombie on the sternum with such force that it pressed against the spine and all the organs in between squished out the other side.

Only to be caught and eaten by other zombies.

Buffy and the zombies holding her fell down in a heap. She fought herself free and grabbed a headless, legless torso and tried to use it as a shield against the other zombies. That part of the idea was good, but the fact that the arms were still attached and quite active made for a bad complication. The arms reached backward and tried to pull her hair out. Buffy wound up bumping the torso against attacking zombies as she tried to pull off the arms and hide behind the car parked next to the van.

Meanwhile, the zombies advancing on Officer McCrumski were literally cut into pieces by the bullets. One dropped a shoulder. One chest was hit hard enough that it split in half, right down the middle.

McCrumski emptied his revolver without thinking. Now he held a smoking gun against an invasion of . . . *Mutants,* he thought. *Probably rejects from a drug research program.*

He took another look at the advancing perps, threw his empty gun at them, and bolted for the station house.

Buffy half-crawled, half-ran behind the line of parked cars, heading for the nearby access road to Route 13. She needed to lead them away from the station before anybody got a good look at them. Once she did that, she had to disappear herself. Without a quarry they should return to the cemetery. *Brain-dead lemmings,* she thought.

The manhole ahead presented some interesting possibilities.

With what felt like the last of her strength she whirled and threw the torso she'd been using for protection at a zombie who'd so far managed to gain on her. The zombie caught the torso and began nibbling at what was left of the neck. Meanwhile, Buffy summoned just enough energy to lift the manhole cover and push it away.

She crawled into pitch darkness, into the sewer. She closed the cover behind her.

The sewer tunnel was tall enough to permit her to stand as she walked. Since she couldn't see anything, she simply picked a direction.

After a while her gag reflex kicked in to such a degree that she was afraid she would vomit everything she'd eaten since the age of six. Her only consolation was a sliver of light in the distance, an indication, perhaps, of another manhole leading out of this tunnel.

She hoped it was still raining. Right now she smelled worse than all those zombies put together, and getting drenched yet again would be a blessing.

CHAPTER TEN

It was your average manhole cover. It filled in the hole leading to the sewer, and didn't collapse whenever a car, truck, or what-have-you ran over it. At the moment it lay there in the rain, doing its job, while not far away a steady barrage of gunfire testified to the ferocity of the zombie attack on the police force.

A couple of fingers, whose nails desperately needed to be redone, poked through the holes in the manhole cover. They slipped back down the moment before they were run over by a passing automobile.

A few more moments passed, and then the fingers poked through again, more gingerly this time. They pressed down, hard.

The manhole cover moved with a sudden jerk. It lay in the middle of the street while Buffy Summers stuck her head through the hole and made sure no more traffic was coming. Then she crawled out on her hands and knees and, with a weakness she found frightening, pushed the manhole cover back into place.

It lay there, once again doing its job, while Buffy dashed to the sidewalk and tried to ignore the fact that right now *she* was the only source of the incredible stench causing her to gag. She fell onto her knees, tried to catch her breath, and spent a few luxurious moments feeling the rain wash away the grease and grime from her clothing.

Well, she hoped no one at the police station had gotten hurt—no one who was still alive, anyway. And while it might have been bad heroine form to desert the police, she really hadn't been in much of a position to help. Her main concerns were her mom and the prophecy. In that order.

Next to the underpass was a popular truck stop called Billy Bob's Steak House, famous for having, as its slogan said, "the fastest food in the West." *But hardly ever in the way Billy Bob intended,* Xander was fond of saying.

Even so, in the storm the Steak House's neon lights promised temporary shelter. She wondered how much they charged for a cup of coffee.

Buffy had never eaten there—it didn't exactly cater to the social ambitions of high school students—but judging from how packed the parking lot was, the food must be popular with people passing through town. Especially truckers—for several semis, some with their engines still running so the drivers wouldn't have to waste time warming them up, sat in the largest wing of the parking lot.

Another wing was filled with approximately forty less specialized vehicles, plus about ten motorcycles belonging to members of a local club. Buffy slowed, forgetting for the moment she was in the middle of a thunderstorm, when she noticed a familiar Hummer. The Churches' Hummer.

Parked right beside it was the van with the raining frogs logo painted on the side. The Churches and the crew of *Charles Fort's Peculiar World* were evidently having a bite to eat here.

Buffy scowled. Could it be that Cotton Mather, in the body of Darryl MacGovern, and with a certain purloined statue fashioned from moonrock in tow, was sampling modern cuisine in the company of Judge Danforth, Sheriff Corwin, and Heather Putnam?

Buffy had to contact Willow at the library and find out if she could confirm that the showdown was fated to happen here, at a country steak house.

She sneezed. Suddenly Buffy saw her own future, all by herself: She was going to spend the next three or four days in bed, nursing a cold of Olympian proportions. If she lived through tonight, that is.

She looked through the Hummer's windows. She saw an unfolded map of Stonehenge in the backseat, lying right next to one of the gallery's notebooks with the picture of

V.V. Vivaldi's *Moonman* statue on the cover.

Buffy moved to the van and looked through the rear window, where she saw something definitely exceptional: the cameraman and the soundman sitting in the back trussed up like turkeys, gagged, blindfolded, and lying amid their scattered equipment. It was easy to see what had happened, even if they, as Buffy suspected, did not. Possessed by one of the loose spirits, Eric Frank had overcome them.

And had gone inside. Every sense Buffy had rang like a bell. This was it. Everything was going to happen again. The manipulator of events was going to rise, just as the Despised One had attempted three hundred years ago. Truly a case of a living rerun.

Only people usually know in advance how a rerun turns out, Buffy thought. *But not tonight. Tonight it's going to be him or me, but not both!*

Buffy grimaced. She took off her raincoat, wrapped it around her fist, and pulled back, aiming for the window. She knew she had no choice but to start the festivities by freeing the crew.

Or maybe she did have a choice. Sure, she was obligated to free them, but nothing in the prophecy said anything about people standing around taking pictures.

She could free them later.

Good. The fewer distractions, the better. Looked like the crowd was up to capacity inside, which amounted to approximately one hundred and fifty other distractions.

Billy Bob's was boomerang-shaped, like an urban bus stop, but with one wing, that of the restaurant itself, vastly lengthened. That wing had three long, wide picture windows providing Buffy with a pretty good view of the layout despite the distance between them. There were booths, all filled, at the windows, a long bar at the rear where the truckers ate, and round, wooden tables in between. Part of the kitchen extended into the wing, and the chefs handed the busy waitresses their meals through a large portal.

Neither Frank nor the Churches were in view, and neither were, come to think of it, Darryl MacGovern and *The Moonman*. But not all booths were visible. They undoubtedly sat in one of those.

She couldn't help noticing the portions were huge. Her mouth watered at the odors that not even the storm could wash away. She made a mental note to have lunch at this place after it was rebuilt.

Glancing at the short wing, which comprised a huge filling station and some facilities the truckers could use to tune up their vehicles, Buffy marched for the front doors. She kept a lookout for stray zombies on the way. Those creatures had been as singleminded as it was possible for a dead organism to be.

She slowed down as she stepped under an awning—at last, relief from the rain!—and assumed the demeanor of a distressed girl who'd been caught in the storm. She wrung out her hair, but since she was soaked from head to toe, that hardly made a dent in her overall dampness.

She walked to the swinging doors and was about to push one open when someone on the other side opened it before she did.

"Honey, are you okay?" drawled a waitress with a pile of red hair that reached out to Jupiter. She wore a canary yellow uniform, and had clearly been on her way outside for a cigarette break. "I didn't see you coming."

"That's all right," said Buffy cheerfully, but still acting distressed. "I didn't see you either."

"Honey, what happened to you?" the waitress asked.

"You know. Bicycle. Rain. The Weather Channel."

"That's a shame, honey."

"Is there a place where I can dry off?"

"Better than that, there's a place where we can put you in a waitress uniform while your clothes dry. How's that?"

Buffy grinned. "Perfect."

The waitress's name turned out to be Edith. She took Buffy to a dressing room to the side of the kitchen opposite the serving portal. There the waitresses changed in and out of their "civvies." While the uniforms were perfectly presentable to the general public, they had a certain tackiness that made the waitress want to wear them in the world beyond Billy Bob's as little as possible.

Buffy understood how they felt the moment she put on one of the uniforms. The big white apron with its cartoonishly large bows on the back made her feel like she was dressed like a doll at a costume party. The fact that the yellow uniform's "small" size was still too large for her made the feeling worse.

And don't even talk to me about the hairnet. Way not*!*

But at least wearing the uniform might allow her to snoop around without being noticed. Furthermore, she had to make a call. After throwing her clothes in the washing machine with a bunch of clothes that looked as filthy as anything she'd seen in the sewer, she headed back toward the front door to make a call.

She still couldn't see in all the booths. Whoever was in the booth all the way to the end of the wing was in Edith's territory, and they seemed to be demanding a lot of attention from her. Buffy wondered what she could say to Edith that would make sense *and* would induce her to split this scene as quickly as possible.

Well, she'd think of something. First, she had to check in.

"Willow! What do you have for me?"

"Nothing!" came the slightly desperate reply. "What do you have for me?"

"I'm going to treat you to steak after all this is over!" said Buffy.

"Why? Save it for the vampires." Her voice was distant and distracted on the other end of the line.

"No, no, I mean steak as in Billy Bob's Country Steak House. That's where I am, and I have to tell you, I'm coming back when I have time to eat. Anyway, I think MacGovern and the three missing souls are seriously chowing down here, but I haven't seen them yet. Even so, this is where the prophecy's going to go down. I can feel it. Did you say you haven't found out anything?"

"Yeah, sorry, Buffy, but I've been in every techno-pagan discussion forum I can think of, and no one has any info remotely helpful."

"Figures, there's never a good voodoo priestess around when you need one. How's Giles?"

"Sick as a dog. He's got an ice pack on his head and his feet in a bucket of ice, but his temperature is bad. I may have to call an ambulance!"

"Any word from Xander?"

"He hasn't come back. I bet he finds you first."

"Right. I'll check in as soon as the fun's over. Ciao!"

Suddenly someone opened both the swinging front doors smack into her.

I've gotta work on this in-and-out thing, she thought, then stopped cold.

Xander.

But that was just her first impression. A closer look, focusing on his posture, revealed that Sarah had asserted herself and was definitely in control of Xander's body. Unused to walking in the body of a man, "she" stood and walked stiffly, very unlike Xander's normal gait, as if he had become a female mannequin.

Luckily, Xander/Sarah did not recognize Buffy. The

seventeenth-century witch might have known her as a participant in the séance, but the waitress outfit was an effective distraction.

But while Xander, to whatever degree he might have been self-aware, was no doubt concerned about Buffy's safety, Sarah clearly had other people on her mind. He/she strode purposefully down the steak house, weaving among the crowded tables.

Xander/Sarah stopped at the furthermost booth. She said something in an agitated manner, gesturing with an air suggesting that it had taken a lot of nerve.

The something must have been shocking, judging from how everyone in the immediate vicinity grew quiet and looked at Xander/Sarah as if he was a crazy person.

Buffy recognized that things were clearly coming to a head. Xander/Sarah backed up; the moment of determination and will had given way to doubt and fear.

Some guy stood and turned, frowning at Xander/Sarah with arms folded across his chest with the contempt only those who are utterly evil can bring to bear. The body belonged to Rick Church, but the stooped shoulders revealed the true personality to be that of elderly Judge Danforth.

"Pray to your betters, Sarah Dinsdale!" Danforth said in a booming voice. "Bow before us. Perhaps you'll give us reason to show mercy."

"Sarah? Who's Sarah?" asked some of the customers aloud to friends or those close by, and most everyone chuckled or giggled as they eyed Xander.

Only Xander/Sarah cowered before this man. The crowd might be amused but she was the only one who knew the truth: This man was about to call up the forces of darkness.

At the moment, Buffy was more afraid of the crowd. So far she'd tried to avoid doing her Slayer stuff before strangers, especially a hundred and fifty of them. This place undoubtedly had security cameras. That meant she'd really be doing her thing before the entirety of civilization as she knew it today.

People forget, Giles had once said. *Cameras remember. Forever.*

Meanwhile, Rick/Danforth became angry at the crowd. He seethed with anger barely contained, his emotions struggling with a strong disbelief factor. After all, he wasn't used to having the common rabble treat him with such disrespectful familiarity.

"You people are doomed," he said. "It awes me to see such ignorant buffoons embrace their destruction so enthusiastically. So be it."

He snapped his fingers. He waited.

Three other people rose out of the booth. On the surface they were Lora Church, Eric Frank, and Darryl MacGovern.

Almost. They didn't act like Lora, Eric, and Darryl. MacGovern/Mather held forth the Vivaldi *Moonman* in one hand like a club, just in case Buffy doubted he had possession of it. Lora's posture, meanwhile, had changed from that of a woman to that of an awkward adolescent, like Heather.

And Frank's obnoxious demeanor had changed into the stern malevolence of Sheriff Corwin.

And once again they had Sarah in captivity. Her talents would augment and complete their circle of power.

Buffy realized she never would have known this if it hadn't been for the dreams. The patrons had no reason to suspect the four standing were anything other than they appeared to be, two well-dressed yuppies along with two reporters with bad fashion instincts. And a guy named Sarah. The patrons had no idea what they were dealing with.

This is it, Buffy realized. *All the pieces are in place. Our rerun is imminent.*

Rick/Danforth's fingers snapped and produced the tiniest flash of light, so tiny Buffy was certain she was one of the few who caught it.

Buffy realized she couldn't wait any longer. She had to do something.

And then the zombies hit.

CHAPTER ELEVEN

The zombies were hard to miss. They came crashing through the front windows. A line of zombies marched double-time through the entrance, while another line came charging from the men's room and a third came from the ladies'. They'd evidently come in through the bathroom windows.

The first thing Buffy noticed about this army of the undead was that it was well-armed with the latest in assault weaponry.

Most of the zombies were derived from the corpses of old men, though quite a few had been young men, and a good number of corpses from both categories had been maimed before the ravages of decay had set in.

Buffy remembered there was a Veterans of Foreign Wars cemetery in Sunnydale. They must have hit an armory on the way over.

Needless to say, the crowd's reaction was immediate. People screamed and tried to scramble away, but a few of the zombies fired in the air. Lights burst and debris fell from the ceiling while the people screamed again and dropped to the floor—the way they'd seen innocent bystanders do in movies whenever there was gunfire in a crowded situation.

Only Edith, Buffy, and the possessed people were left standing; Xander/Sarah was still cowering.

Edith had realized she was one of the few still standing, and she'd also recognized that Buffy stood her ground like someone who knew how to handle herself whenever she was surrounded by massive armies of the undead. Though *how* she recognized that, Edith wasn't sure. She was sure, however, that she'd quit smoking the minute she got out of this alive.

Buffy pointed to the floor. Edith nodded, got down, and crawled out of the immediate vicinity while trying to be as inconspicuous as possible.

"What's next, people?" Buffy asked. "Turkey dinner?"

"I do not understand," said Lora/Heather. "Was that supposed to be humorous, child?"

Buffy bristled. She had her hands in fists and she made tiny steps back and forth, very indecisively. She would have had no problem doing something about the zombies—she might have even charged right in at the possessed people—but the presence of so many innocent bystanders was unprecedented in her experience.

I'm a Slayer, not a cop! she thought. "All right, Danforth—Rick Church—or whoever you are. You have what you want. All four of you. You have Sarah and me right where you want us. Why don't you send these zombies back where they came from?"

"Oh, my dear, I am afraid we need them," said Danforth unctuously. "In order to guard all these hostages. And I am afraid we need these hostages as well, to keep you towing the straight and narrow."

"We cannot afford unpredictable events during the ceremony," said MacGovern/Mather.

"Thanks for telling her, you imbecile!" hissed Frank/Corwin.

"Excuse me. I am a judge," said Rick/Danforth.

"Excuse *you*," said Buffy. "You're a man who doesn't know he's dead."

"What do *you* know about death?" snorted Lora/Heather.

"Been there, bought the T-shirt." Buffy gestured at the people. "Any one of these people might do something you hadn't planned on and screw everything up until the next time the stars or whatever are right for you to try again. So you'll have to wait—what? Another three hundred years? Deal with the wait."

"She is right," said Rick/Danforth.

"I agree," said MacGovern/Mather.

"Kill them all," said Lora/Heather to the zombies.

Buffy tensed; the time had come to do or die. She just wished things had gone a little better before she died.

"No!" said Xander/Sarah. "You must wait!"

"Why is that?" sneered Frank/Corwin.

"I cannot speak for whoever has brought us here now," said Xander/Sarah, "but the Despised One would not have appreciated the fact that you arranged for his first feast, then slew everyone before he had the opportunity to make the first bite. I can imagine how the current Master gets when his appetites are not sated. You must not kill them. You must allow them to wait outside, unharmed."

"I get it," said Heather. "When the Master rises, he will know what to do with them."

Which is not *going to happen,* Buffy added to herself. Then: *The Master, eh? What a surprise. His decayed hand is all over this.*

The four looked at one another. Buffy kept one eye on the zombie army, another on the hostages, and a third on the Freakin' Four. Were they silently communicating with one another?

Finally they turned to face Buffy and their captives. "I have made my decision," said Rick/Danforth.

"No!" said Lora/Heather. "*We* have come to our decision. Here we are all equals."

"I fear you have spent too long in the New World," said

Rick/Danforth sadly. "It has affected your mind."

"Death has a way of doing that," said Buffy.

"In any case," said Frank/Corwin, "the end result is the same. Buffy—or should I say, Kane?—we will let these people leave the premises only on one condition: that you surrender yourself immediately." He held a rope out to a zombie, who lowered its assault weapon, took the rope, and walked toward Buffy.

"Mind you, we did not say we would set the people free," said MacGovern/Mather. "The zombies will still guard them, and a few will remain behind to guard *us.*"

Reduction of odds. A good thing, Buffy decided. She was fairly positive no one noticed her bumping against a table as the zombie approached.

Other zombies, making weird growling noises that sent Billy Bob's customers down a spiral of terror, gestured with their weapons indicating the course the good citizens should take. Naturally the good citizens took it, some practically falling all over one another in their attempts to get out.

They all marched past Buffy while her hands were being tied behind her back. Everyone, whether they be fearful, stoic, altruistic, or among the injured, looked her in the eye. The zombies escorting them out did not encourage communication, but Edith was brave enough to muster a "Thanks, I won't forget this."

"You probably will," Buffy replied.

"Bet you a steak dinner I don't," said Edith.

"You're on," said Buffy.

"Silence!" said Rick/Danforth. "You, my young Slayer, are in no position to do anything."

"In fact," said Lora/Heather in conspiratorial tones, "we could ensure you won't be around to commit your treachery a second time by taking advantage of whatever instruments of torture the kitchen may provide."

"Slay them!" said Xander/Sarah desperately, turning to Buffy. "Why don't you slay them?"

"My hands are tied," replied Buffy. "And I try—whenever possible—not to kill my friends' bodies."

"You're not like Samantha Kane!" Sarah exclaimed.

"I'll take 'Duh' for two hundred," said Buffy dryly.

"I think the Master would rather devour this Slayer personally," advised Frank/Corwin. "I believe they have a history."

"So do we," said MacGovern/Mather, "in our fashion. Come here."

That order was directed at Buffy, but she did not respond until the zombie behind her pushed her with its rifle. "Keep your head on. I'm moving," said Buffy testily.

"And just how would you slay us, young Slayer, in the unlikely event you ever have a chance?" inquired Rick/Danforth as he walked around his prisoner, inspecting her.

"I would drive a stake through your heart." She could not help glancing at Xander/Sarah, who, though still cowering, had managed to slink to a chair.

"That wouldn't work on us," said Frank/Corwin with a laugh. "We're already dead."

"It would work on Eric Frank, though," pointed out MacGovern/Mather. "And that would seriously delay us."

Xander/Sarah nodded, as if she understood something. Buffy immediately got a bad feeling. While Buffy was reluctant to slay the living bodies of innocent people in order to thwart the heinous spirits of the dead, Sarah Dinsdale operated under no such personal restriction.

"Time for the ceremony," said Rick/Danforth.

"I think we need to fix the decor first," suggested Lora/Heather as she hefted a table over the bar.

"You got that right, woman! We need some ceremony room!" said Frank/Corwin as he kicked the table Sarah was sitting at with great gusto. The table smashed into other tables, sending them in different directions.

One of the remaining zombies happened to be in the way of a flying chair. The chair crashed into the zombie's putrid leg, which buckled and bent the wrong way, throwing the zombie off balance.

No one seemed to notice, not even the zombie.

"I need some more ceremony room!" Corwin shouted in delight. "Some ceremony room for the enlightened!" And he threw another table into the counter.

Xander/Sarah yelped as if bitten, then withdrew into herself as the four other possessed bodies commenced to tear up everything still standing in the steak house. Buffy couldn't blame her. This type of violence was so much more irrational than the kind found in the fight of good against evil.

The others threw themselves into the wanton destruction by ripping down those few things that had been left standing—jukebox, pinball machine, serving cart. And when everything was on the floor, the four of them worked together and threw everything up again. Maybe just to see how it fell into place.

"This is not enough ceremony room!" exclaimed Corwin in frustration.

Then they threw the stuff in the air again. Within a few moments Buffy realized there was some method to their madness. They were piling the debris with a definite pattern Buffy had seen before—in her dreams.

When she took into account the mess they were also making in the kitchen at the same time, she realized the piles were pale, smaller imitations of the stone slabs which had formed the boundaries the last time the ceremony had occurred.

"Hey, guys," said Buffy, "if the site in New England was a Pilgrim's Stonehenge, then is this a redneck Stonehenge?"

The possessed ones ignored her. Windows broke and the hokey sawdust that "flavored" the floor of Billy Bob's was stirred up. The rain began falling inside the steak house.

"Now is it time for the ceremony?" demanded Frank/Corwin.

"It is time," said Rick/Danforth. He walked into the kitchen. Or what was left of it.

The others followed, as did Xander/Sarah, meekly, and Buffy—but only because Frank/Corwin was pushing her.

They gathered around the grill. MacGovern/Mather carefully placed V.V. Vivaldi's *Moonman* sculpture on it, and the rock sizzled at once, filling the immediate vicinity with a terrible black smoke.

The four possessed ones chanted and danced. The moonrock glowed red-hot like a coal, only it remained whole; it did not, perhaps could not, burn. Even the heat generated by the grill was not enough to melt it.

"This is it," said Xander/Sarah. "He is coming! The Master is coming!"

Buffy thought she'd seen everything by now, but she'd never seen a mystical rupture in the space-time continuum before, where the boundaries between *here* and *there* vanished.

An altogether different kind of heat and smoke began to fill the room. The smoke curled out through the huge hole in the ceiling, while within a matter of moments the heat became suffocating.

"I'd forgotten what it was like to be human," said Rick/Danforth, trying to catch his breath.

"Quiet!" said Frank/Corwin. "The Master is coming!"

Indeed. A white hand whose skin combined the worst features of worms and reptiles rose up from the nothingness, followed by an arm wearing the sleeve of a dapper black jacket.

"How trendy," said Buffy. "Pale skin."

"Silence, insipid knave!" said Rick/Danforth.

"Have you no respect for your betters?" asked the Master. His head and torso had emerged. Both his hands were on the hot grill, no worse for the wear. He looked about wearing an expression of ecstasy. "I see you fixed the place up for me. How thoughtful."

"Would you care for a snack?" asked Rick/Danforth. "We thought you'd like to start with these two."

The Master looked at Buffy with a toothy grin. Buffy grinned back. *He* was the key to this whole nightmare.

At last the time to act had arrived. In the next few seconds she would know if she would live or die. *One thing is for certain,* she resolved. *Regardless of my fate, the Master will die. Again and again. Now I just need a distraction. . . .*

Buffy caught an unexpected movement from the corner of her eye. She turned to see Xander/Sarah holding an object while he/she rushed toward the Master with murderous intentions. "No!" Buffy exclaimed. "Use a *stake*! Not a *steak*!"

Sarah stopped in front of the grill and struck the Master several times on the chest and shoulders with the piece of meat.

The Master, halted in his emergence by this pesky human, took the steak from Sarah and held it gingerly between both fingers; he was clearly disgusted. "Do you realize how many nutrients were lost when they ruined this meat by cooking it?"

"Really? Looks a little rare to me!" said Buffy. Her hands were free—she had cut her bonds with the knife she had palmed earlier, when she'd bumped, seemingly accidentally, into a table. "Let's cut it."

She hurled the knife.

She was vaguely aware of Xander/Sarah showing a distinct lack of faith in her abilities by ducking, even though Buffy had planned on the knife missing him/her by a good half inch.

Indeed. The knife spun right on course and thrust deep in the Master's Chest.

"That's what I call a real steak knife!" said Buffy. "Game over."

The Master looked down in abject horror at the knife protruding from his body, but he couldn't bring himself to touch it. The sudden action broke the spell of the four chanters as they stopped in shock. The malevolent equilibrium dispersed and the gate between the *here* and the *there* began to disappear.

"You failed me!" he said to Rick/Danforth, the Master's voice rising in pitch. "I should have known. You're coming back with me! You're all coming back with me!" He held out his hand and closed it in a fist as if grabbing the four internal essences from thin air.

Then he fell back through the gateway.

The bodies of Rick and Lora Church, Darryl MacGovern, and Eric Frank fainted, collapsing into heaps.

"It's over," said Xander/Sarah. "Now I can leave this realm secure in the knowledge that I have made up for the evil I helped cause three hundred years ago."

"What about my friend Giles?" Buffy demanded. "Is he going to be okay?"

"His fever is already beginning of break, of that I am certain," said Sarah. "Farewell."

And Xander fainted too, adding his body to the heap made by the other four on the floor.

The "living rerun" part of the night of the living rerun was over.

We now return to our regularly scheduled program.

"Thank goodness," said Buffy. "Now maybe I can get out of this stupid outfit."

CHAPTER TWELVE

The rain ceased and the skies grew quiet. The wind still blew, but what came through the demolished steak house was warm and comfortable. After she had seen to it that everyone who hadn't started the evening as a corpse was still, Buffy rushed to the ladies' dressing room, which thankfully was still intact, pulled her clothes from the dryer, and changed. Then she returned to the kitchen and knelt beside Xander.

"Xander!" she hissed. When he didn't respond, she slapped him once.

His eyes opened immediately and he sat up. "Hey! That hurt!"

"Sorry, I had to make sure you were Xander. Are you okay?"

"Apart from a hot flash here and there, I think I'm fine."

"Phew!" exclaimed Darryl MacGovern as he rolled into a sitting position. "Where did all these dead bodies come from? They sure do stink!"

"What happened?" asked Eric Frank with a groan. His hair looked like he'd stuck his finger in an electric socket.

"How did we did get here?" asked Rick Church.

"Oh my gosh! I look a fright!" exclaimed Lora Church, checking herself out in the reflection of a napkin dispenser.

Buffy guided Xander to what remained of one of the walls. "What do you remember?"

"Everything," he said. "Up to a point. I still don't know what happened to Sarah Dinsdale after Kane put the kibosh on the Master. I'm afraid we both know what happened to Kane, though."

"But they don't seem to remember anything," said Buffy. "I guess when the Master yanked Mather and company from them, he took their memories, too."

"The Master didn't want anything to do with Sarah," said Xander. "I know that. She went of her own accord. But where?"

"Phew!" said MacGovern behind them, as the wind shifted and a certain potent stench from outside wafted in like the aftermath of a stampede of skunks.

"What are they doing with those assault rifles?" asked Eric Frank, pointing at pieces of zombies. He and MacGovern looked each other in the eye. "I smell a story here."

MacGovern, deep in thought, rubbed his chin. "You know, I think something paranormal happened here. I'd bet my reputation on it."

"You have no reputation," said Frank.

"Where's your crew?" asked Lora. "Shouldn't they be getting this on film?"

"Maybe they're in the van!" said Frank. "Let's find out!"

Let's go, mouthed Buffy to Xander, pulling him out the back door by his shirtsleeve. Then, once they were outside, "I think Eric Frank is going to have a difficult time explaining things to his crew."

"Really?" said Xander.

"Yeah, we'll probably read in the papers about how Billy Bob's was struck by a freak lightning storm," said Buffy.

"How will people explain all the dead . . . bodies?" Xander asked.

Buffy shrugged. "Mad corpse disease?"

Buffy and Xander found Giles and Willow sitting on the couch in his office.

"You made it, Buffy," said Giles, pleased, "but I hoped all along the prince's prophecy was just an educated guess. I knew if anyone could untangle the complex web of fate, it would be you."

"*Now* you tell us," said Xander. "Oh, and thanks for being glad to see me."

"Well, I am," said Giles, not understanding the reason for Xander's sarcasm. "It's just that Willow and I were having a conversation about what you would call 'stuff.'"

"You mean 'things,'" said Buffy.

"Exactly. 'Stuff.'"

Xander waved his hand above his head.

"Ah," said Giles. "I'm talking over your head." He grinned. "A momentous occasion. If the two of you must know, I was telling Willow of the flashes I had of Robert Erwin's life before he died of that mystical fever. And we were wondering how much free will we really have—how free we are to make the choices that matter to us."

"You're always telling me I should forget about my private life and concentrate on my destiny and duty as Slayer," said Buffy.

"It's true that destiny has selected you," said Giles, "yet I would hope in the coming years you will find more freedom of choice than even you could have imagined possible."

"I'll remember that the next time I have a hot date," Buffy replied. "Or *any* date."

"Willow, you're awfully quiet," Xander observed.

Willow was surprised to have everyone's attention suddenly turn to her. "I was thinking. And wondering."

"About?" prompted Xander.

"Well, it's just that sometimes people choose their own destiny, you know, as in I've chosen to assist you two"—she pointed at Buffy and Giles—"in saving the world from various despicable creatures. But you two believe that destiny has more or less selected you."

"Yes," said Giles, nodding gravely.

"So what's your point?" asked Xander.

"How do you really tell? What if you two have made some massive mistake and you're not really the chosen Watcher and Slayer, and that I haven't been fated to make the same mistake with you?"

"I think you're reading too much into current events," Buffy advised.

Willow pouted. "Maybe. I've felt like such a fifth wheel this whole time."

The others immediately tried to buoy her confidence, pointing out how invaluable her assistance had been so many times in the past. If that wasn't destiny, Xander asked, then what else could it be?

"Better a fifth wheel than someone walking around in your skin. Yeesh!" Xander shivered. "I'm glad she's gone. Is my hair all right?"

After everyone had said good night and Willow walked home, her spirits plummeted again. This whole adventure confused her. It indicated bonds between the souls involved, but no love. To make matters worse, her soul, apparently, was not involved. And if there was anything Willow desired in this world, it was a bond between her and Xander even deeper, stronger than the one they now shared.

That, however, was not in the cards. Willow arrived home seriously bummed, a solitary person apparently for all time.

After staying up to watch a movie on the Romance Channel, Willow fell asleep with tears in her eyes. To say she felt lonely and depressed would be like saying the night is dark, or outer space is big, or there are too may reruns on TV in the summer.

Even so, her sleep was deep, and it wasn't long before she dreamed.

She dreamed of running through a heavily wooded forest—thicker, more teeming with life than any she'd ever seen—during a frightening thunderstorm of a strength almost as great as the storm that had struck Sunnydale while she'd been awake.

In this dream Willow felt older, heavier, and distressed. She experienced a heartsickness so intense it was almost crippling. And yet some dread she could barely fathom propelled her through the woods, through the storm, toward a mysterious distant light that arced over the trees like a dome.

Whenever she noticed her clothing, though, she got the funny feeling she was no longer a she. For she wore a man's boots and a man's pants. The sleeves of the man's white cotton shirt were bloodied and tattered. Her breathing was labored, her every muscle ached, and her heart pounded at top speed.

A silent explosion, so odd its origin was surely evil, knocked Willow *the man* to the ground. When he got up, the storm had diminished and the distant glow was fading. By now the glow wasn't so distant—only a few hundred yards away—but the man was stricken with spiritual agony. He had a hunger that would never be satisfied, a thirst that would never be quenched. He felt as if his life was over, though he was still young and strong.

Then he saw Sarah Dinsdale—also dirty and disheveled—running through the wood. He called out for her to wait, but she paid him no heed. He ran after her. He did not catch up to her until they had left the wood and were running down the beach, and even when he was able to touch her she did not stop.

So he tackled her. He landed on top of her and they struggled until he had both her hands in his grip and she was unable to fight back.

"Go on! Finish it!" she exclaimed. Do what the others could not do and kill me! Isn't that what you always wanted?"

The man was so shocked he released her hands. "Absolutely not. Forgive me, but that was the last thing on my mind."

Something in his expression must have changed Sarah's mind about him, because she ceased to struggle and did not try to escape even though he was giving her plenty of opportunity.

"But you denounced me!" she said. "You denounced me before all of Salem."

The man stood, bowed his head in shame, and turned away from her. "It is true. I denounced you because I hated you. Rather, I thought I hated you. I did not know my own mind."

"A common enough affliction among men," said Sarah, "but presumably you know your mind today."

"Indeed I do. As I know my heart." He turned back toward her, and she read something in his eyes that changed her expression to one of awe, and of a fear more tender and vulnerable than any he had ever before witnessed. "I love you, Sarah Dinsdale. I ask for more than your forgiveness. I ask for your heart. I ask for you to be my life partner."

"I wish I could believe you, but I am a witch. That I admit freely."

"Granted, but I have learned that not all witches are evil, just as all preachers, I am loath to admit, are not as good as they might imagine."

She smiled and touched his cheek with her warm fingers. "Do not be dismayed to learn there is a bit of the devil in you. There is a bit of the devil in us all."

"I love you, Sarah. Come away with me. Let us leave this colony and go to Philadelphia. There we can change our names and no one will know of how you were wronged in Salem and of how I was the man who wronged you."

"You say that, knowing I cast a spell on you to make you love me?"

The man shrugged. "It made no difference. I would have come to love you in time, spell or no spell. So what is your answer? Will you come away with me? Will you marry me?"

"When you put it that way, how could I say anything but yes, John Goodman?"

And Sarah/Xander kissed John/Willow. The two souls had made their connection, and forged their future together.

Willow Rosenberg smiled. She would sleep soundly tonight.

Portal Through Time

TO NORMA, FEARLESS HISTORY TEACHER, MY STALWART COMPANION, MY MOTHER, FOR YOUR SUPPORT AND BELIEF IN ME. YOU GAVE ME MY LOVE OF HISTORY, WHICH SHINES THROUGH IN THIS BOOK.

Hearty thanks to Cara Bedick for all her editing work; to Elizabeth Bracken for her assistance in the early stages; to Debbie Olshan at Fox; to all the other writers, cast, and crew who have brought Buffy to life on the page and screen; to Jason, for his endless encouragement, belief, and support; and to Norma and our rainy visit to the Shiloh battlefield.

CHAPTER ONE

Los Angeles, 1995

Buffy Summers did not know she was about to die. She entered the gym for cheerleader tryouts, excited to show off the new move she'd perfected. For some reason, she was much better at acrobatic moves than the other girls. It just came naturally to her. And now, during her freshman year at Hemery High, she was trying out for the high school cheerleading team.

With a toss of her blond hair, she entered the gym, confident of placing on the team. She'd bowl them over, do her flips, and then go home and binge on pizza with her parents. When she came to school the next day, the tryout results would be posted.

The doors shut behind her as she entered the gym.

• • •

Ten feet away, two vampires crouched in the shrubbery outside the Hemery High gym. Gold and pink still glowed in the west of the newly darkened sky. They talked in whispers, orchestrating their attack.

The gym doors opened suddenly with a bang, and a stream of girls appeared, pom-poms in hand, tossing ponytails, talking in excited voices. The last one out was Buffy, walking a little slower, a small frown on her face. They knew she'd tried out for the team but didn't think she'd done very well. It was a low moment, a vulnerable moment, and though she was not yet an active Slayer, the vampires hesitated before attacking. They both knew her as the fearsome warrior they'd fought in 1997 during the Master's ascension. Victor, who'd been around since the Crusades, had barely escaped when the Slayer's attention focused on killing Luke at the Bronze. He'd slipped out the back door into the alley. Jason, much younger, was no less terrified when he'd glimpsed the end of his three-hundred-year life as Buffy fought her way through the horde of vampires gathered at the Bronze that night. Somehow, miraculously, he'd been shoved aside by another vamp, and Buffy had staked her instead.

But that was the future they'd left behind. When they returned later that night, everything would be different. If all went well, they'd kill Buffy, and the Master would reign supreme on the surface, rising to ever more power with each passing moon. Victor grinned at the thought of that glorious possible future. But the current reality was far more dire than that. The Master was dead, and Buffy triumphant. And so they'd crossed time itself, mouths eager to taste the blood of a potential Slayer. The Master would live, and the earth would tremble. The Hellmouth, writhing and alive, spitting out demons to swarm over the earth, would gape open, emitting darkness and chaos and things that fed voraciously on human life.

Victor leaned forward from his crouch behind the bushes, chancing a look at Buffy. She loitered by the stairs, still looking sad, and slowly made her way to the sidewalk. As soon as she turned her back, Victor would strike. He licked his lips, the anticipation of tasting a potential Slayer's blood making his stomach nearly sing with savage delight. He signaled for Jason to follow him, and they started down the sidewalk behind Buffy. Victor fought the rising fear back down into his chest. This was not the Slayer. Not yet. She was an ordinary human that he would destroy.

He and Jason had one simple assignment: Stab her. Slit her throat. Be sure she was dead. Then return to 1998, triumphant.

Victor slunk forward, still at a crouch, moving silently. Jason followed close behind, drawing his knife slowly from its sheath above his boot. Victor reached inside his jacket, felt the reassuring weight of his throwing knife in its holster. Buffy made her way down the street, unaware of their presence. They crept from bush to bush, taking refuge in the shadows of trees and hiding behind parked cars on the road.

Now Buffy walked only ten feet before them. Victor slid his throwing knife out of the holster and rose to his full height. Taking careful aim between her shoulders, he flung the blade with a powerful movement of his wrist. Expertly it sailed to its target, and Buffy Summers cried out in surprise and pain as it sank into her back. She stumbled, pitched forward, went off balance, and landed with a painful smack on the concrete.

Quickly Jason closed in, stepping over her prone body and grabbing a fistful of blond hair to lift her head. He moved his knife low, readying to draw it across her throat. Buffy spun suddenly, rolling over, then cried out in agony as the blade in her back twisted against the sidewalk, tearing her flesh as she landed on it. Her eyes teared in pain but still she fought, kicking at Jason.

Victor's feet turned to lead. There was some mistake. She was already the Slayer. She had to be. She kicked Jason in the groin and he sprawled to one side.

But no. That couldn't be right. It was 1995, and he knew that she would not be activated until 1996. He remembered Lucien warning him that she might still be strong, still quick on her feet. But she was not yet the Slayer.

Victor closed in, tripping Buffy as she rose to her feet. She crashed back down, and he wrenched the knife out of Jason's hand. Trembling, he lowered the knife to her throat, praying she wouldn't spring up suddenly, produce a stake, and drive it through his heart, turning him to dust. But she didn't. The pain in her back looked unbearable, and he could clearly hear from her labored breathing that he'd punctured a lung. She wheezed and coughed, striking him with her fists in his face and neck. He braced for the blows and moved in closer.

He thrust the blade into her neck and dragged it across her throat, slicing a deep wound that instantly welled and overflowed with sticky blood. He studied her face as she glared back at him with eyes full of hatred and anger. Buffy struggled and punched him as she suffocated. Then she managed to throw him off and get up, staggering down the street with her hands clenched tightly over the gash in her throat.

She lurched out into the street, trying to shout but unable to. She waved her arms, choked, and sputtered. The street lay empty. No cars. No people out walking. Her struggle for life went unseen.

Victor pulled Jason up from the sidewalk, and they watched as she rushed violently into a parked car and slumped over its hood, gathering strength to continue. But they could hear her rasping, failing breath, could see the warm sticky blood erupting out of her. She staggered forward into the street and fell. One elbow came up, trying to lift her, but her head hit the pavement for the second time. This time she lay still, arms splayed, the last of her blood pumping into the street, where it meandered into rivulets, rejoined in the gutter, and flowed away into the storm drain.

Buffy Summers was dead.

CHAPTER TWO

Standing in the center of the cemetery, the two assassins waited. Victor looked at his watch. Five minutes until the rendezvous. He searched the shadows expectantly for Lucien. He should be here, somewhere, observing at a safe distance. After all, Lucien didn't want to risk himself. He was the only one who knew how to work the arcane time magicks. And if they had not succeeded in killing Buffy, he would have had to work them again. But they had killed her. They'd killed the Slayer, even if she wasn't quite the Slayer yet.

As Victor checked his watch again, Lucien crept out of the shadows. Dressed in a white frilly shirt, black pants, and tall black boots, he looked more like a villain from a gothic novel than a devotee of the Master.

"We did it," Victor said to Lucien unnecessarily. After all, the spell caster had seen everything.

Lucien nodded. "And now we journey back to 1998 and see how we fared."

Jason frowned. "But she's dead. We did it. When we go back, the Master will have ascended safely. Chaos will rule the earth."

"Yes, yes," Lucien replied. "Maybe." He scowled with one eyebrow up, an expression that made Victor think of a million bad actors he'd seen in his lifetime. And the way he dressed made him look as if he'd just stepped off the cover of a romance novel. He was the Fabio of vampires, no doubt, and Victor couldn't deny that he knew his stuff.

Speaking in a language that Victor didn't recognize, Lucien uttered the words that would open the time portal and transport them back to 1998. At the end of the incantation, a tiny point of light winked into view in the air above them. It swirled, growing and growing in size, sucking in dry leaves, and lifting Lucien's hair to toss in the wind.

The spinning portal was ready for the assassins.

Victor steeled himself for the inevitable seasickness that accompanied the transportation. They all closed their eyes tightly against the brilliant, swirling vortex of light. It descended over them, and Victor felt the pricking of his hair as the portal began to draw him upward. His shirtsleeves tugged up toward the vortex, followed by his chest, and then his waist. He hovered for a moment, arms windmilling as he fell off balance. Then he was sucked violently up and through the whirling bright light, grabbing at Jason as Victor came up beside him. Sheer terror thrilled through Victor's chest, and he opened his eyes wide. They streamed with tears from the incredible velocity of forward movement. In spite of himself, in spite of centuries of playing tough, he held on to Jason tightly, letting out a piercing shriek as the speed increased. Then, just as abruptly, it stopped, spilling them out onto a parking lot in Sunnydale, 1998.

A very sunny parking lot.

Jason's hair caught on fire immediately, going up in waving tendrils of bright flame. Victor's hands smoked, his face suddenly bubbling and hot. He burst into a run with Lucien close behind, not caring what direction he headed in, as long as there was cover. Then, a few feet away, he spotted a manhole. Tearing off the cover with vampiric strength, he leaped feetfirst into the cool darkness. With a splash, he landed in fetid water that coursed by his feet. Not caring about the vile stench, Victor dropped and rolled in it, quenching the flames. Lucien landed next to him, splashing eagerly into the water as if they were at a luxurious spa and not a fecal-matter-strewn sewer. Victor rose to his feet and called for Jason through the small round hole above.

He heard screaming, his friend's unmistakable voice crying out in agony. Then nothing.

Victor turned to Lucien and cursed. "The day? You brought us back in the friggin' day?"

Lucien stood up on wobbly legs, brushing strands of something black and glistening off his once pristine shirt. "I didn't know . . . ," he said pitifully.

"What the hell? Don't you know your own ass from your arcane spells?"

Lucien said nothing, only stared on miserably.

"Are you really that clueless? What if we'd been transported right into daylight before we even killed Buffy? What if there'd been no cover?"

Lucien shook his head. "It was a risk. There's really no way to tell when it will be sunny and when it will be night."

"It was a *risk*?" Anger fumed inside Victor. "You didn't tell me or Jason anything about it!" He punched the curved sewer wall, then immediately wished he hadn't, as pain coursed up his arm. He liked Jason. They'd been pals since the Revolutionary War. Now he was dust.

"No one gambles with me like that!" Victor shouted.

Scowling, he chose an underground course to Lucien's lair and set off, feet splashing in the vile gray water. He didn't care how powerful Lucien was. He'd lost his best friend and almost become a toaster pastry.

Behind him, he could hear Lucien tromping in the water, quiet and thinking.

In less than ten minutes, they reached the lair.

Only it was completely different.

Where tables once stood, covered in books, maps, calculations, historical research, and candelabra, now rested a lush canopy bed full of velvet draperies and piled with soft pillows. A few pillar candles resting on pedestal tables gleamed in the confines of the cavern, creating shifting shadows on the wall.

"What the hell?" Victor asked.

"Something's not right," Lucien agreed. He moved forward, striding around the room and looking for clues.

For a moment Victor wondered if they'd walked into the wrong chamber. But he was sure it was this one. The cave formations were familiar, but nothing else was.

"We need to go topside, find out what's been going on," Lucien explained. "I expected the future to be a little different when we returned, so this could just be par for the course."

Victor was less hopeful. This all felt wrong.

Just as they turned to leave, a tall, attractive vampire strode into the room. He knew her—recognized her as one of the girls who was friends with Buffy. But she was a vampire now, brow creased and raised, fangs glistening.

"Ever hear of knocking?" she asked, frowning.

"Uh . . . ," Lucien began, then trailed off.

"Pardon us," Victor stepped in. "We are new in town, and wondered if you could fill us in on what's been going on in Sunnydale the last couple of years?"

The attractive brunette vampire placed one impatient hand on her hip. "The last couple of years?" she quipped.

"Why don't you take your skanky butts over to the library and do some research or something? You smell like a sewage treatment plant. And what are you doing in my place, anyway?"

Lucien trembled with impatience. "Has the Master risen?" he blurted out, all eagerness and no style. Victor couldn't believe he followed this guy. But if it meant putting the Master back in power, he was willing.

"The Master?" She furrowed her brow. "You guys really have been out of town. He was killed right after he ascended."

"By the Slayer?"

"Well, yeah, of course." After a moment she added, "Well, not really. You know, a former Slayer."

Lucien frowned in confusion.

The vampire shook her head, obviously pitying the sadness that was Victor and Lucien. "Clueless and styleless," she said. "It's bad enough I have to live in some stinky old cave because my parents' house has skylights all over the place. But I hardly think I have to chat about the weather with creeps like you." The other hand came to her hip, and she fixed them with a scowl.

"Please," said Lucien. "Please explain."

"Don't tell me you haven't heard of the Slayer and what happened to her?"

Lucien shook his head.

"Kafara. She came to Sunnydale to fight the Master, only her presence allowed him to ascend. He drank her blood and escaped. But some other vamps found her near death and turned her. Man, is she one mean vamp. I wouldn't want to cross her, and she's the only one you'll ever hear me say that about." She smoothed back an errant strand of brown hair and looked down at her nails. "Anyway, she dusted the Master that first night. Rose to power herself. Sunnydale's been great ever since. I used to think vamps were so gross, but I like being one."

"And the Hellmouth?" Lucien asked, pressing her for more.

"Closed. When the Master died. But that's okay. If the world had been overrun by beasties, there'd be less for us to eat, right?"

Victor smiled at her. "What's your name?"

"Cordelia," she answered. "But don't think you can wear it out. Don't ever come here again."

"Of course," Victor murmured. "Have you ever heard of Buffy Summers?"

"Who?" Her expression was blank.

"No one."

Lucien punched his palm with a fist. "Then why did it go so wrong?"

Reaching to take his arm, Victor said, "We're going, Lucien."

"But . . ."

"We're going," he said more firmly, leading Lucien out of the cave.

Darkness crept over them again as they returned to the

sewer tunnels. "I didn't count on that!" Lucien cursed. "I thought we'd just have to kill Buffy. I thought no other Slayer would be able to destroy the Master."

"And no other Slayer did. She was a vamp when she dusted him."

Lucien turned on Victor in the darkness and struck him hard across the mouth. "Don't say 'dusted' when referring to the Master. He was too important for such reckless terms."

Victor brought his hand quickly to his mouth, tasted blood there. His eyes narrowed, anger simmering inside him. Half of him wanted to pummel Lucien into the sewer brick right then. Lucien had struck him, he'd killed Jason, and they'd been unsuccessful. But he stilled himself, forcing calm to spread over his limbs.

"What went wrong?" he said through clenched teeth.

Lucien shook his head. "Maybe we need to go farther back. Kill Buffy when she's just a kid. That will activate a different Slayer. And perhaps that one will be ineffective."

"Perhaps? I don't like the idea of jumping back into daylight for a 'perhaps.'"

"Maybe not," Lucien answered, "but we're going to. And we need to find another assassin."

At that offhand comment, Victor raised his hand to strike Lucien hard, hard enough to rattle his teeth. But he restrained himself. Jason had been his friend for two hundred years, and Lucien treated him as if he could replace him by walking into an assassin mart and picking someone off the shelf. "We won't be able to replace Jason," he said instead of hitting him. "You lost one of the best assassins you could have gotten."

"Yeah, I noticed back there," Lucien retorted, and Victor remembered how Buffy had disabled Jason with a kick. But that didn't give Lucien the right to that dig. Every assassin had his off days. This time Victor did strike Lucien, hard across the face, an open-handed slap meant to humiliate the cocky spell caster. It worked.

Lucien roared with rage and shoved ineffectively at Victor in the confines of the sewer tunnel. Victor evaded his blows and sprinted down the length of the tunnel, outpacing him. "Looks like we have to start all over again!" he yelled back.

He heard Lucien's footsteps slow to a stop. "No," came his voice in the darkness. "I kept a backup of all my research. We only need to get it out of lockup and gather the next team."

"And what about the unique artifact? Where is it?"

Lucien's face contorted in anger. "Damn!"

This did not sound good to Victor. The artifact was what made it all work. When Lucien joined the artifact with his incantations, they could travel through time. Lucien had forged the artifact himself, fashioning it from two different unique relics rumored throughout the ages to hold the power of time travel. It had taken him considerable time just to locate and acquire the relics, and he had traveled as far as Tibet in his search. Once both relics were found, he had incanted and melted and wound the two pieces together to make the Wand of Wells, as Lucien called it. At first Victor thought he meant "wells" as in ancient, sacred places of worship. But it had actually been a tribute to H. G. Wells, author of *The Time Machine*. The wand itself was gorgeous—it gleamed silver along its jewel-encrusted length, and at one end a silver clawed hand held a luminous blue stone the size of a house cat. It wasn't exactly tiny. Not something you could put in your pocket. Of course, they couldn't have carried it with them anyway.

The way the magick worked was that the Wand of Wells always had to stay behind on a time jump. It served as a marker to the year from which the travelers departed. Without it, they could return to the Stone Age, or worse yet, to a time when the sun had gone supernova and there was no Earth at all. To ensure that it wouldn't get misplaced or stolen, they had bricked it up inside a wall in one of the crypts of the Sunnydale Cemetery. As long as it existed when they left a year, it would still be there when they returned, guiding them back to the correct year. It existed in a time bubble of its own. Even if they changed the past, the artifact would still be there in the alternate version of 1998. Even if the wall they'd bricked it up inside didn't exist anymore, the Wand of Wells would still be there, on that exact spot.

But while it was great at returning them to the right date and year, it wasn't so hot at returning them to the right location and time of day, as the previous sunlight incident had proven. They'd departed from Lucien's underground lair, but had returned two blocks away on the surface.

During their test runs, they frequently had to backtrack to the artifact's location. At least it would be there. It always was.

"Let's backtrack to the crypt," Lucien said. "This time we'll kill Buffy when she's a little girl."

CHAPTER THREE

Armed with backup copies of research, Lucien peeked at the artifact he'd constructed, preparing to open the portal. The Wand of Wells was still there, bricked up inside the crypt wall. They always checked for it, every time they readied to travel back in time. If it wasn't there, they wouldn't be able to return to 1998. Seeing it gleam inside its dark hole, Lucien replaced the loose brick, sealing it inside once more.

It had taken him months of constant work, with almost no sleep, to build the artifact and imbue it with arcane powers. At first he didn't even think it would be possible. But the more obsessed he became, and the more he read about time magick, the more determined he grew.

The Master, he knew, simply had to rise again. And though Buffy may have sent him plummeting down onto a sharp protrusion of wood and broken his bones to powder with a hammer, there was still a chance.

All Lucien had to do was travel back in time and kill Buffy so that she was not the active Slayer at the time of the Master's ascension. Only Buffy, he believed firmly, could have defeated the Master. Another Slayer in her place would not have the fortitude, the necessary skills. At least he hoped not. Unless she turned into an evil, power-hungry vampire. But they were about to erase this alternate future altogether.

He left the secret room, making certain it sealed behind him. Then he navigated down a narrow tunnel and entered his sleeping room. Just as he shut the door behind him, he heard shuffling in the corridor outside and pressed against the door, listening. His biggest fear was the Slayer discovering what he was up to before he had the chance to go back in time and kill her. He quickly breathed a sigh of relief, almost laughed. It couldn't be Buffy outside. They'd killed her. Her life had come to an end at the ripe age of fourteen, and if there was a Slayer out there, lurking outside his door, it certainly wouldn't be her. Not that he didn't feel that deep-down twinge of fear at the thought of another Slayer. It was just that he'd seen Buffy in action and knew she was practically undefeatable.

The shuffling grew louder. Then came a tapping at his door. He swung it open to reveal Victor standing on the other side, cleaning his throwing knife with a cloth. "Ready?" he asked, looking up from his task.

Lucien nodded. He'd just returned from Willy's, where he'd recruited the meanest-looking vamp of all the patrons for this little excursion. The goal this time was 1984. Buffy would be only three years old. Easy pickings. This would hopefully undo the mess he'd made and restore the Master again. He had given strict instructions to the Master's closest followers to keep them from turning any Slayer the Master killed this time around.

His warning had met with strange glances and humoring nods. Most of them didn't understand the power of time travel. They didn't even think it was possible. For them, this change in events, in which the Master was murdered by a vampiric ex-Slayer, appeared to be as it had always been. But for Lucien and Victor, because they'd been the ones traveling through time, events had changed around them, and they could still recall how the time line originally flowed. They were, in essence, in an alternate 1998, one that Lucien now hoped to alter even more.

"Where's the other assassin?" Victor asked, resheathing his knife. Lucien tried not to notice his clothes. Victor dressed the part of uncivilized ruffian. His leather jacket, at least two decades old, was scored in a dozen places from scuffles and fights. Before he could help himself, Lucien snarked, "Do you always have to dress so . . . low?"

"It's my lucky jacket," Victor said defensively.

"At least we'll be going back to a time period where you'll still be in style."

Victor poked Lucien's shoulder angrily with his index finger. "A time period when *I'll* be in style? You look like you raided Lord Byron's closet. Your clothes just announce, 'Hey, I'm a vampire, by the way. A dorky one.'"

Lucien waved him off. "We need to meet Gorga."

"Gorga? You got us a guy named Gorga? That sounds like a cheese or an enemy of Godzilla, not an assassin."

"Then you should get along perfectly." Lucien exited, closing the door behind him.

Twenty minutes later, in an alley behind the Bronze, all three vampires met. Monstrous, muscular, and bald, Gorga carried a battle-ax, a crossbow, and a sword sheathed in a belt. Lucien had a feeling Gorga hadn't quite wrapped his head around the fact that they were targeting the Slayer *before* she was the Slayer.

"She's a three-year-old girl, for God's sake," Victor told him, disliking Gorga from the start. But Lucien knew that anyone but Jason would have made Victor angry.

Reciting the proper incantations, Lucien opened the time portal. It sucked the three of them inside, whirling them uncontrollably faster and faster, careening into the past and across space.

They tumbled out into the early evening on a suburban street in 1984. The portal winked out of view. Lucien had gotten pretty good at determining where and when it would spit them out. While he wasn't able to pick a specific hour, he'd become more accurate at figuring out how to land in specific months and years. And for locations he could get within five miles of his target. And now here they were, in 1984 Los Angeles.

Lucien knew it was 1984 because just then a group of teenagers turned the corner. One wore a Michael Jackson *Thriller* jacket, black parachute pants, and a sequined glove on one hand. One teenager's hair, styled in a Jheri curl, positively dripped with shiny product. He produced a spray bottle from his jacket and squirted his Jheri with more "activator." A girl in the group had bleached-blond hair so big that it continually poked her companions in the face and eyes with stiff, hairsprayed tendrils. Her big hoop earrings could have comfortably slept five. Another of the teenagers wore a pastel blue blazer with a coral pink T-shirt underneath. On his feet were white slip-on canvas deck shoes with no socks. Lucien felt the pain deep, deep down.

Victor consulted a map in his back pocket, then replaced it. "Three doors down," he said. "On the left. Not bad, Lucien. I half expected us to land in Paris, going this far back." Sometimes, on test runs, they'd spent days just reaching their target location. Other times they hadn't reached it at all.

Lucien nodded. "I'm getting better." He didn't remind Victor of one of the first attempts, which had landed them in a yak herd in Burma for seven hours, knee-deep in dung, with no coats while Lucien tried to read the incantation as the ink ran during a rainstorm.

This was much, much better, Lucien kept telling himself as the teenagers passed and he stifled a shudder.

Victor forged ahead, not waiting for the others. The group of friends snuck looks at Gorga and his collection of medieval weaponry, but the vamps kept quiet. They were under strict instructions this time not to interact or otherwise alter the future. Their sole change would be to kill Buffy when she was a child.

As they neared Buffy's childhood home, Victor slowed, peeking over a chest-high wooden fence that framed her backyard. He laughed softly. "We're in luck. She's outside. Looks like they're getting ready to cook something on the hibachi. And she's alone right now."

They glanced up at the sliding glass door that led into the house. Inside, her parents milled around, cutting vegetables and pieces of meat. In the yard, Buffy played with a badminton birdie, tossing it around while she sat on the grass, giggling softly to herself.

Victor rummaged around in his other pocket and produced a stolen photo of Buffy as a kid. He compared it to the little girl. "It's definitely her. Make yourself scarce, Lucien. Meet you down the block."

"Then we can party like it's 1984," Gorga put in, shouldering his battle-ax.

Victor narrowed his eyes. "I really don't think you're going to need that thing."

"Split her in two. Split pea soup," the monstrous giant retorted.

Double-checking the house again and seeing her parents still inside, Victor vaulted over the fence, landing beside Buffy in the grass. Here was the Slayer, the woman he had feared since he'd come to Sunnydale two years ago. Amazing. As he closed in on her, she looked up at him, her smile fading to a frown. "Who are you?" she asked.

Gorga landed with a heavy thud next to him. He swung the ax up, then paused.

"What's wrong?" Victor asked.

Gorga looked down at the little girl. He couldn't kill her. He kept the ax poised but couldn't bring himself to swing it down.

"You're not having a change of heart, are you?"

Gorga relented, bringing the ax down gently beside him. He gripped the handle, meeting the little girl's eyes. "Not because I care," said the monstrous hulk. "Gorga is no softie. It's just that she's only three. How embarrassing is that? How will I describe this kill to the monthly Assassins Club?"

Victor shook his head. "How about, 'Man, that baby came at me with everything it had, but I still made the kill.'" He grabbed the ax out of Gorga's hands and swung it high. The ax blade flashed and swung down. With a sickening *snick* it sliced the little girl in two.

Gorga stood, unblinking. She hadn't even cried out. The badminton birdie, now spattered with blood, rolled out of her hand and described a small semicircle in the grass before coming to a halt near the hibachi.

Victor straightened up and looked at Gorga, who met his eyes. Then he waved one triumphant fist in the air. "Dangerous kill, man," Victor told him. Briefly he thought of beheading the vampire giant. Some use he was. But he decided against it. They might need him again. He handed back the ax, then sprinted up over the fence again. Gorga used the gate, opening and closing it silently behind him.

They hurried down the street. Victor heard the sliding door swish open and a woman's scream so powerful it caused his eardrums to thrum with vibration.

Buffy Summers was dead.

Again.

CHAPTER FOUR

Sunnydale, 1998

Thirty minutes later Lucien, Gorga, and Victor whirled out of the vortex into the quiet of night, crashing into a brick wall next to the Bronze.

Lucien leaped up, hopeful, eyes darting down the alley as if he expected a banner to be strung across the wall declaring, THE MASTER ROSE. ALL WENT WELL. WISH YOU WERE HERE.

But of course they'd have to ask around before they knew if they'd been successful.

Lucien chose the Master's lair as the first stop. They entered through the back of the mausoleum and started down the tunnels. They'd gone only a hundred feet before the tunnel abruptly ended in a cave-in. They tried the other routes in—a sewer tunnel Victor knew about, then a maintenance tunnel on the far side of town Gorga had used once. But all of them ended in cave-ins.

At Willy's, Lucien asked around and learned that a tremendous explosion had shaken that part of Sunnydale so vigorously that huge parts of it had collapsed. When one demon clammed up, not wanting to discuss it further, Lucien moved on to the next. Slowly the story came together.

When he probed about the current Slayer, he learned that her Watcher focused primarily on prophecies, and that he'd figured out that the Master could not ascend if he didn't drink the blood of a Slayer. So the Slayer, who came to Sunnydale specifically to stop the ascension, just sat in her hotel room and didn't go down to confront the Master at all. One night soon after, she and her Watcher dynamited the whole underground lair, burying the Master completely. One vamp who'd barely escaped witnessed the Master's skull getting crushed by a falling stalactite.

Lucien assimilated all of this, downing only half of his glass of blood as he sat at the bar. Anger simmered, then exploded. "Damn it! Why the hell isn't this working?"

Victor shook his head. "Something's wrong. It's the time line. It's as if the Master's destruction is ordained. We need a prophecy guy."

Lucien brought his fist down hard onto the bar, then winced from the pain. He knew Victor made sense, but the sheer frustration made him want to smash his glass and give up on the whole thing. But the minute he finished that thought, he knew better. He could never give up. He'd pledged his life to the Master and would not stop until he was resurrected.

But he couldn't believe this. What a mess of trial and error. So far none of the time jumps had worked. Originally, after several successful trial runs, Lucien had traveled back to 1937. The Master came to Sunnydale that year, intending to open the Hellmouth and invite the old demons to retake the earth. But a violent earthquake shook Sunnydale just as he was finishing his incantation, and he became sealed in a prison of his own making, trapped as the earthquake shifted land and created an impenetrable mystic wall.

At first Lucien thought the matter simple—he would travel back in time and warn the Master not to open the Hellmouth on that particular day. The Master could wait, be successful another day. But when Lucien interrupted the Master before he began the incantations, the great vampire didn't know Lucien. Lucien remembered with frustration that he hadn't entered the Master's service until 1942, when he needed more and more vampires to do tasks for him during his captivity. Lucien explained nonetheless about the earthquake and his subsequent imprisonment. But the Master had not only refused to listen, he was gravely insulted. No mere earthquake, the ancient vampire had reasoned, could trap him down here and disrupt his spell. Lucien obviously just wanted to keep the status quo. He was a coward, afraid of releasing the creatures from the Hellmouth. The Master ignored him and continued the incantations, ordering three vampires to drag Lucien out of the area, for his cries were distracting.

Shortly after Lucien reached the surface, escorted by the vampires into the night, the earthquake began. First a mild shaking shuddered through the earth beneath their feet. Then a more robust wave rolling through the bedrock set gravestones askew and knocked the vampires off their feet. The violent quake lasted a whole minute, then stopped, the rumbling replaced with the crying sirens of fire engines and police cars.

As Lucien wandered the smoldering rubble of devastated Sunnydale, he knew he had to think of a different way to help the Master. Stopping him in that moment, when the Master had traveled so far and researched the perfect incantation to open the Hellmouth, would be impossible. The Master could be stubbornly determined, Lucien knew. And so he quested on, feeling not discouraged but almost self-righteous. The Master may have turned him away in 1937, but Lucien was such a powerful devotee that he would struggle on regardless. His reward would be to see the Master free and the creatures of the Hellmouth overtaking Sunnydale—and then the world.

Now, sitting in Willy's, Lucien's mind wandered over these events. Why weren't his attempts working? Were the events written in stone? The Master's incarceration in 1937? His death in 1997? This couldn't be. If it were so, what was Fate's point in imprisoning him in 1937? Just to keep him trapped for forty years? To teach him a lesson? Why not just kill him in 1937? There must be a way, somehow, for Lucien to alter the events. Maybe he just hadn't gone back far enough.

Victor was right. They needed a prophecy guy. And Lucien knew just who to see.

Five hours later, Lucien and Victor sat in the waiting room of Zaaargul the Seer. They'd left Gorga at Willy's, needing a break from him. Victor put down the issue of *Celebrity Haircuts* he'd been perusing and exhaled impatiently.

"Is this guy even for real?" he asked Lucien. "He's got three *a*'s in his first name. That's such a cheesy 'creature from beyond' thing to do."

"It's not his first name, it's his *only* name."

"That's even worse."

Lucien turned to him, head lowered and threatening. "You got a better idea? Got another prophecy guy in your Rolodex of the Undead?"

Victor nodded. "Yeah, as a matter of fact. I say we kidnap this new Watcher, torture him, and make him figure out why we can't stop the Master's death."

"I wouldn't want to torture a Watcher," Lucien said. "Those guys can be brutal. You ever meet the last one?"

"Yes, at the Bronze. And he didn't seem so tough."

Lucien shuddered. "That was a front. Believe me. I knew that guy in the seventies in London, and he was one hell of a brutal guy. Ripper, they called him. The kind of guy you don't want your brood to go near when they're young. Or old.

Believe me, wherever that guy is, we're damn lucky we're not stuck with him as the Watcher."

Victor restlessly picked up an issue of *Make-or-Break Looks*. The cover lines read "10 Ways to Please Your Demon," "5 Surefire Makeup Cure-Alls to Cover Your Puffy Tentacles," and "1501 Two-Minute Hairstyles for the Undead." Victor flung that aside too. "Oh, come on! This guy's an evil prophecy reader, right? Well, how come he doesn't have any good magazines?"

"Because he's evil."

"Oh, yeah. See your point."

"And listen," Lucien added. "Don't insult him or anything, okay? I've heard things. I don't know if they're true, but I've heard things."

"What kinds of things?"

"Head-squished, dragged-to-the-bottom-of-the-ocean-to-rot-for-all-eternity, toothpick-in-the-eyeball kinds of things."

Victor shifted uncomfortably in his seat.

A few minutes later the receptionist, a gaunt vampire who looked like she hadn't eaten in a week, showed them in to see Zaaargul.

She closed the door behind them, and they stood before a massive mahogany desk with a green study lamp. Zaaargul sat at the desk, a bulky, vaguely octopus-looking creature with too many tentacles to count, and huge, luminous golden eyes with curved, horizontal pupils.

In one tentacle he held a quill pen, with which he filled in ovals on a lottery ticket.

"Hello," Lucien said.

One golden eye swiveled in its protruding socket, and a tentacle emerged from beneath the desk and motioned them forward.

Quietly they took the two chairs sitting before the desk. The unnerving suggestion to take the chairs came silently, unbidden into Lucien's head. He'd heard that Dracula could do that, but Dracula had a lot fewer tentacles and wasn't nearly as disturbing to behold. Next to the ticket an ancient tome lay open, its leather binding decaying, parchment pages stained and worn.

Several moments ticked by painfully. "I can tell you more of my situation, and then we can come back for the solution," Lucien offered, anxious to get out of there as soon as possible.

"Look. You do the waiting in my waiting room, not in here." He placed the quill pen back in its silver holder with one delicate tentacle. "I figured it out on your way here."

Lucien looked amazed. "From the little I told you on the phone—"

"Please don't interrupt. My time is valuable." From a small silver tray, Zaaargul plucked a slice of Gruyère from an array of cheeses and brought it to his beak, nibbling daintily. "A Slayer named Buffy Summers," he continued, "is prophecied to kill the Master toward the close of the twentieth century."

"Yes, and we killed her. Twice. I'll bet you've never even heard of her. Have you?" he added less certainly.

Zaaargul held up an impatient tentacle. "I assumed she was the destroyed Slayer you spoke of on the phone. Because you have now disrupted the flow of normal events, the prophecy is still trying to fulfill itself, using whatever Slayer is in her place, because she should be the natural Slayer during these years. In the unaltered time line, Buffy was born and should have become the Slayer. Her Watcher should have found her and trained her at an early age, so that she would be ready to become the Slayer when she was activated."

Lucien leaned forward across the desk. "But she was different. Her Watcher didn't find her until she was in her early teens. She lacked much of the usual training and discipline."

Zaaargul lowered his large, meaty unibrow over his yellow eyes. "That is not important now. Because Buffy was born a potential Slayer, and because all the other Slayers before her died just when they happened to die, she was activated at the perfect time to be the Slayer when the Master ascended." Zaaargul paused, opening a drawer and taking out a handful of sunflower seeds, which he munched down, shell and all.

Disgusting, thought Lucien.

"Therefore, if you want to disrupt this prophecy, your only chance is to disrupt the lineage of the Slayers. Take action in the past to ensure that Slayers are activated at different times. Therefore, when it comes to the years in which Buffy Summers is alive, she may never be activated at all. The prophecy of her killing the Master goes out of whack, and the Master goes free."

Zaaargul closed the heavy tome in front of him, then used several rear tentacles, much longer than his front few, to reshelve the volume carefully behind him on a massive bookshelf. He blinked, his large yellow eyes glistening and nearly hypnotic. Lucien flashed back to a time when he had stood in front of an octopus tank at the Monterey Bay Aquarium for hours, convinced that the creature held him in his power. Those glistening golden eyes were the same then. . . .

Lucien shook his head and was unnerved to see Zaaargul make the barest hint of a smile. A smug smile. Darn mind-control cephalopods. Lucien reined in his thoughts, considered what he'd learned. "So you're saying that I need to go back in time and either kill a few Slayers, or preserve their lives beyond the years they lived?"

Zaaargul nodded.

"I like the killing option better," Victor said, the first words he'd spoken since they walked in. "More room for creativity."

"So we kill some Slayers," Lucien agreed.

Zaaargul's skin flushed to an entirely different tone. The greenish parts turned gold, the reddish parts blue. "I suggest you choose the most documented Slayers. The more details you know of their tendencies and schedules, the better you can hunt them. Three or four of them should do the trick."

"Any idea who those were?" Lucien ventured.

"Not a clue. Not my area. Now," he said, waving a tentacle distractedly, "if you'll excuse me, I have others waiting."

Lucien jumped up. "Of course! Thank you!"

Victor got up too, with a little bow, and they backed toward the door. Something about those eyes . . . Lucien wanted to get out of there badly. He suddenly felt like a snack.

"And don't forget," added Zaaargul, "that you must go back and save Buffy's life. Twice. You must put the time line right again and then work from there if this is going to be successful."

Lucien licked his lips nervously. "Of course!"

Victor opened the door. "Say, do you always pick your own numbers, or do you ever do quick pick?"

Lucien couldn't believe this. If his heart could still beat, it would be skittering around in his chest right now like a kitten high on catnip.

"Quick pick, on occasion," Zaaargul answered. "Today I'm using the numbers for the date I spawned my daughter."

"Cool." Victor left the room, with Lucien treading on his heels. Lucien didn't relax until they were all the way out of that place, in the cool night air. He looked up at the twinkling stars, glad to be outside. "How will we choose which Slayers to kill?" he asked Victor.

"Simple." He glanced at his watch. "Three hours to sunrise. We find out where this new Watcher is holing up while they're in town, break in, and steal his journals."

"Sounds simple."

"If he's not there," Victor added. "I don't fancy fighting off the new Slayer tonight."

"Nor do I," Lucien put in.

"Let's do some recon."

A half hour later they'd tracked down the Watcher's hotel. Liam Folsworthy, a graduate of Oxford, they were told at Willy's, was not only an expert on prophecies, but knew a bit of Jeet Kune Do as well. Victor was not enthused. The last thing he wanted was some English Bruce Lee kicking his ass up and down the hotel parking lot.

The hotel room, though, was dark, and Victor wasted no time in bashing in a window after he'd checked the darkness inside for a sleeping form. The Watcher was out. He reached around to unlatch the hotel lock, and they slid inside. It was fortuitous, Victor realized, that the Slayer and Watcher *were* only visiting. It meant hotel rooms and not houses. They couldn't have entered Liam's house without an invitation, but a hotel room was public, and vampires, though without the right to vote, were still the public.

Lucien and Victor quickly moved to the bed, dumping out suitcases and clearing out drawers. In the bathroom, between two folded towels, Victor found the Watcher journals. He grabbed them, and they left without cleaning up. No reason to do that. In a few minutes they'd travel back in time again, and Liam Folsworthy might never be a Watcher after all.

With the Watcher journals tucked under Lucien's arm, they headed for the caverns beneath Sunnydale, where they would open the vortex once again, this time to save Buffy's life.

Three days later Lucien prepared for his most dangerous mission yet. He had never traveled so far back in time. He had spent the last few days making much smaller time jumps, but he told Victor to stay behind, not sure of the danger of someone meeting themselves in the past. He went alone, avoiding himself and pausing only to talk to Victor in both situations. In 1984 he'd stopped Victor and Gorga from leaping over the fence to kill toddler Buffy. In 1996 he'd stopped Jason and Victor in the bushes outside the Hemery High gym, before Buffy emerged after tryouts.

This last had the added effect of bringing Jason back from the dead, because Lucien warned Jason about the impending sunlight and told him which direction to run to get to the sewer. Lucien's effort was successful, and Jason lived. Victor had been in a good mood ever since. Saving Jason had been an unforeseen bonus, and Lucien played it up, making Victor think it had been as important to Lucien as saving Buffy. He didn't let Victor know it had only occurred to him at the last minute, because frankly, he was a little scared of Victor.

They had returned to a Sunnydale in which Buffy Summers was the active Slayer and the Master was dead.

But that was a temporary situation, Lucien knew.

He'd pored over the Watcher journals, surprised at all the detail, not just about the Slayers, but about many vampires, too, including Darla, Angelus, and the Master himself. After many sleepless days of study, Lucien at last narrowed down his search to four of the most documented Slayers: a Celtic warrior Slayer who lived during the Roman occupation of Britain; a Sumerian Slayer living in 2700 B.C.E.; an American

Civil War Slayer; and an aristocratic Slayer who'd survived the French Revolution.

He'd selected teams of assassins, including Jason and Victor, to tackle these time periods. The assassins received period dress and lessons on how to act, talk, and blend in. He didn't want them getting staked for standing out. They had to infiltrate each time period, find the Slayer, and destroy her.

When they were all finished, the Slayer lineage would be so off that Buffy would never be activated. Instead, the Slayer in her time period might not even journey to Sunnydale. And if she did, they could all band together to kill her. This way the Master could rise, instead of his bones being ground to dust.

Unfolding the incantations before him, Lucien checked them over and over. He'd made three copies. One for himself, one for Victor, and one that he would leave with Gorga in case they all failed. He checked again on the artifact. It was still there. Now he just needed to gather Victor and Jason, and they could jump back in time to kill the Celtic Slayer in 60 C.E.

CHAPTER FIVE

Buffy Summers was not dead.

But she did feel like she was. She'd dragged in from patrolling at four a.m. the night before, and she'd had trouble sleeping because of a painfully bruised shoulder. Buffy was the lucky Chosen One, the one girl in all the world with the power to fight vampires and other creatures of darkness. This usually meant long hours hunting around cemeteries, but occasionally it meant long hours hanging out at the Bronze, their local nightspot, hunting for vampires. Buffy greatly preferred the latter. Occasionally it even meant smooching with Angel, her vampiric love, in a graveyard. That might sound strange, a Slayer in love with a vampire, but Angel was different. He had a soul. Other vamps didn't, which made them free of conscience to do any evil thing they wanted. And they took full advantage of that. But Angel had pissed off the wrong gypsies by murdering one of their daughters, and they'd cursed him. His soul had returned to his body, and now he lived in eternal anguish over the terrible things the vampire demon had done in his soul's absence. He was always brooding and tormented, though occasionally he took a break to engage with Buffy in those graveyard smoochies.

But now Buffy sat in English class, slumping forward in her desk, able to stay awake only because of the semiconstant rain of paper pellets flicked at her by her best friend, Willow Rosenberg.

Her head began to sink down.

"Buffy!" her friend whispered sharply. "She's coming this way!"

Buffy snapped awake, ready to stake vamps, and instead saw something far more terrifying. Mrs. Niedermeyer stood at the head of her row, thumbing through a stack of handouts. "Today's quiz," Mrs. Niedermeyer said, "is on Thomas Hardy's *Tess of the D'Urbervilles*. I hope you all read your assignment this week. This covers the basic themes and plot points of the book. And if you rented the film instead of reading it, be warned that there are enough differences to cause you to get an F on this quiz."

Rented the film? That would have been a good idea. Less Cliffs-Notey, more entertainment value. But Buffy hadn't even thought of that. *Tess of the D'Urbervilles*? She thought she'd heard of it before. Vaguely recalled being handed a copy of it a few weeks ago and signing for it. She even remember seeing the book recently—probably beneath her bed—yes, that was it, under her new pair of boots. Or had she left it at Angel's?

Either way, she hadn't read it.

She hadn't even cracked it open.

The quiz landed on her desk, and Mrs. Niedermeyer turned to inflict her reign of terror on the next row of seats. Buffy looked down at the test. Thomas Hardy. Did he have anything to do with the Hardy Boys? She'd seen a few episodes of that old show on cable recently, starring hottie Parker Stevenson. Then she saw the date of the book's publication: 1891. This was definitely something different.

"Will," Buffy whispered to her friend. She gave Willow the best *help!* face she could muster, bringing her eyebrows up, frowning slightly.

"It's simple," Willow whispered back. "Just write down the most depressing answers you can think of. They're bound to be right."

"Okay." Buffy thought. She scanned the questions:

1. When Tess is forced to baptize her own dying infant, where does she ultimately bury the body?

2. When Tess confesses her unfortunate past to her new husband Angel, he leaves her behind, unforgiven, and moves to what country?
3. When Alec returns for Tess's hand in marriage, what does he use to bribe and coerce her into being his consort?
4. When Tess receives word that her mother is dying, which family member unexpectedly dies instead?
5. What crime does Tess resort to in order to ultimately escape from Alec?

Buffy blinked, taking in the story line, reading the rest of the questions. She got the full gist of this book from the quiz alone. Even with a love interest named Angel, which she could certainly appreciate, it sounded like the most depressing book she'd never read. Dying infants, lonely burials in neglected corners of graveyards, women forced to be with men they despised and hated, family members dying unexpectedly, families turned out into the street with nowhere to go, a woman neglected and then driven to murder. *What was this guy's damage?* The author clearly needed a side of depression with his morning depression.

She glanced over at Willow, eyes wide in disbelief.

"This is pretty bad," admitted Willow in a whisper. "His novel *The Mayor of Casterbridge* is downright cheery in comparison. It opens with the main character selling his wife and baby at a country carnival, and things generally get worse after that."

"Sounds uplifting. I'll get right to reading that one." Buffy glanced up at Mrs. Niedermeyer, who sat at her desk, busy grading homework.

She went back to the quiz.

Following Willow's advice, she wrote down the most depressing answers she could think of, getting quite creative at times, including making Tess into a homeless, impoverished seller of wilted violets. It seemed to fit right in.

The bell rang, and they all filed forward, placing their tests on Mrs. Niedermeyer's desk. She smiled at them all as they passed by. Buffy felt the hot burning of classic I Didn't Do My Homework Syndrome as she walked up. She plunked her test down on the pile and hurriedly left the room.

"So how was slayage last night?" Willow asked, falling in beside her. The Slayer was supposed to have a secret profession, but she wouldn't have lasted as long as she had without the help of her friends.

"Pretty uneventful. Maybe four vamps total."

"Any other vamps show up?" Willow shot her a meaningful look.

"Maybe," Buffy answered, immediately swept away in Angelness.

"Sounds like it was a good night."

Xander Harris appeared behind them, placing his arms

over their shoulders. "What sounds like it was a good night?" he asked.

"Buffy saw Angel last night. There were smoochies."

"Buff—the guy's dead. I just don't get it," Xander said, disgusted. She knew he was actually jealous. He'd been crushing on her since they met.

"Yeah, Buffy, what would you see in someone so gorgeous, gallant, and mysterious?" Willow asked.

"You know, Will, I just don't know." Xander was a goofy kind of guy, sort of awkward and a little fashion-challenged. But he was a good person, and he made her laugh. He and Willow had been best friends since they were kids. Willow often reminisced of happy times watching Xander do the Snoopy dance, which he apparently still did upon request. However, Buffy had yet to make such a request.

Since her arrival at Sunnydale High, Willow and Xander had become her best friends. Her Watcher, Rupert Giles, had initially been dismayed that her two new friends knew her secret identity as the Slayer. But they had bailed her out more times than she could count, and Xander had even saved her life once. Buffy shuddered involuntarily every time she thought about it. She'd gone to fight the Master, one of the most ancient and powerful vampires ever to exist. At the time he was trapped in the caves beneath Sunnydale. Despite a prophecy that she would die in the fight, Buffy had challenged him. He killed her. Bit her, drank her blood, then tossed her facedown into a standing pool of water. Her blood gave him the power to break free of his imprisonment, and he rose to the surface. Buffy had drowned. If it hadn't been for Xander and his CPR skills, she would have stayed dead.

Instead, because of her friends, she had lived and killed the Master.

His plans to open the Hellmouth, the evil portal that lay beneath Sunnydale, had been thwarted.

They had won.

So Giles didn't know what he was talking about when he warned her about her friends knowing. She wouldn't be here if they were in the dark, because there were a lot of other things in the dark that wanted her dead.

Of course, Giles would continue being annoyed by how many people knew she slayed vamps. At least her mom didn't know. Buffy wouldn't want her worrying about her daughter staying out all night, staking vamps, beheading demons, and generally getting all manner of supernatural goo on her new sweaters.

They reached the end of the hall and walked into the cafeteria.

"Anything interesting happen last night, aside from the usual vamp slayage?" Willow asked.

"You mean demony stuff?" Buffy asked.

"Yeah."

"Nope. Nothing like that. Just the usual. Fight, dust, brush off the clothes."

They filed through the cafeteria line, and Buffy got some

mashed potatoes and so-called gravy, which looked more like slime from a mucous demon than anything edible. "And this is why I keep the world safe," she told Xander. He'd selected the too-perfectly-square chicken patty that for some reason was gray.

"It's a noble job," he answered.

They chose a table and sat down. Willow had somehow conquered the lunch line and emerged with a rather fresh-looking tossed salad.

"Hey!" Buffy said. "How did you pull that off?"

"I bribed the cafeteria lady."

"With what?" Buffy asked.

"Told her I'd help her with her homework."

"She's not in high school," Xander pointed out. "She *works* for the high school."

Willow took a bite of the crisp lettuce. "Night school," she said around the mouthful. "She's studying to be a dental hygienist."

Maybe she feels bad about all the teeth the school food is ruining through malnutrition," Xander guessed.

"Probably," Buffy said, picking at her mashed potatoes with a spork.

"Good morning, all!" called a chipper English voice. Rupert Giles approached the table and pulled out a bright orange plastic chair. He sat down, the chair legs screeching on the floor as he drew the seat closer. "Oh, sorry."

It was a normal day.

“Hi, Giles,” chorused the other three.

Buffy smiled at him. “Hey, Giles. What’s up?”

“I’m not sure,” he said, placing the books on the table. As usual, he wore head-to-foot tweed, gray today. Giles was the school librarian, so he could pull off the look. He adjusted the wire-framed glasses on his nose and spoke quietly. “Something’s going on. Apparently there have been some very interesting thefts of priceless artifacts. The police have tracked the thief to Sunnydale, though they haven’t caught him.”

“What artifacts?” asked Buffy.

“Well,” Giles said, looking around to be sure no one listened, “I’ve been researching just that all morning. Both artifacts are reputed to have similar powers.”

When he fell silent, Buffy prompted him. “What kind of powers?”

“Time travel.”

“What?” chorused Willow and Xander.

“Time travel,” Giles repeated. “The first artifact was the Blade of Madrigon, reportedly able to slice holes in the fabric of time and space.”

“Holes you can crawl through?” asked Xander.

“Yes. Holes to the past. But supposedly you cannot climb back through once you’ve crossed over.”

“Not very handy,” said Xander.

“And the other one?” Buffy asked.

“Ah, yes. The other one is the Gem of Chargulgaak.”

"The Gem of Whosamawhatsis?" asked Xander.

"Chargulgaak. Throughout the centuries, it was rumored to transport people forward from the past to the present."

"Sounds like the noise you make when drinking expired milk," Xander said. "So you'd activate this Gem of Gargle-gok and poof, there would be Einstein? Or poof, you'd have Mozart standing in your living room?"

Giles regarded him sternly. "Well, perhaps not as easy as 'poof,' but in essence, yes. A person long dead could be brought to the future."

"Wouldn't they stink if they're long dead?" asked Xander.

"No, Xander," Giles said impatiently. "You would bring them forward from a time when they were still alive."

"Oh, gotcha."

"So why would someone want to steal these two thingies?" Buffy asked.

Willow faced her. "Imagine their power if they were brought together. You could open a hole to the past, climb through, then use the Gem to return to the future."

Giles looked at her proudly. "Exactly."

"And you think some beastie here in Sunnydale wants to use it for evil? What if it's just an eccentric art thief? Or it could be someone collecting them for the purposes of good," Buffy added hopefully. In reality, she wanted to spend the evening at the Bronze with Angel, instead of doing recon work.

"Buffy, how many times has a rare stolen artifact been

brought to Sunnydale for the purpose of cheering up denizens of retirement facilities, or finding homes for sad little puppies?" Giles asked her.

"Oh. Yeah. Good point." She glanced around to make sure no one overheard. "So where do I start?"

Giles related a news item he'd found earlier in the library. "The police traced the Gem to a warehouse near the Bronze, then lost the trail. Perhaps you could start there? Do a little reconnaissance after school?"

"Bronze. Sounds like a plan," Buffy told him.

"Wonderful." Giles stood up. "Now I'm going off campus for lunch."

"You're so evil, Giles," Buffy said, convinced now more than ever that her "mashed potatoes" were actually the excretions of a potato demon. Maybe it was a teeny tiny potato demon, who right now was actually living inside the viscous mound of white mush.

"Yeah," Xander agreed. "You're supposed to be one of the good guys, helping us fight the forces of evil."

"Yes," Giles said, cocking one eyebrow defiantly. "And I'm about to go fight the forces of evil at a nice little French bistro I noticed on my way to work."

He turned and left the room, waving good-bye over his shoulder.

Buffy looked down at her mashed potatoes and waited for the potato demon inside to install cable in his little mashed-potato hut.

• • •

Later that afternoon, as soon as dusk hit, Buffy set out. After two and a half hours of creeping through cemeteries, sewers, caverns beneath Sunnydale, and an endless series of warehouses in the Bronze district, Buffy had learned nothing. However, she had overheard more useless vampire gossip than she ever cared to. She dusted most of those she came across after listening in. Who knew the undead could be so boring? Most of them didn't know any good dirt at all. Especially nothing having to do with a gem or a knife. She even questioned some of them directly when she didn't overhear anything of interest. At first they were always swaggering and cocky. By the end, they quivered and pleaded. But none of them had heard anything about the stolen artifacts.

So then maybe some kind benefactor *was* going to use them to save the lives of unfortunate puppies?

Giles was right. No way.

She needed more info.

As she walked down the street in front of the Bronze, she heard a thud, and suddenly quick footsteps closed in on her. She whirled around. Angel stood before her.

"Hey," he said.

"Hey." He looked stunning, all darkness and mystery. *Play it casual. Don't let him see that your heart is fluttering out of control.* Willow was right. He was gorgeous. Tall, with short, dark brown hair and expressive eyes, he dressed completely in black, with a billowing trench coat. It wavered in the slight evening breeze. He looked the part of a hero, a warrior. And he was one fine kisser.

"Going to the Bronze?" he asked.

"Yeah. Giles had some hunch about these two stolen artifacts, but I've dug around everywhere and haven't found anything remotely related."

"You mean the Gem of Chargulgaak and the Blade of Madrigon?" Angel asked.

Her mouth almost fell open. She didn't let it. "Yeah, you heard about those?"

"It's why I was coming to see you."

Buffy felt a pang in the pit of her stomach. Oh. And here she thought it might have been just to see her. But he was in warning mode. She saw that now. A deeper furrow on the perpetually brooding brow. A slight downcast of the mouth. "What do you know?"

"A vampire named Lucien brought the two artifacts to Sunnydale. He joined them together to form a unique object, capable of—"

"Traveling through time?"

Angel gave a slight smile. "Yes."

"And his insidious plot?"

"To travel back in time and kill a Slayer."

"Why?" Buffy asked. "She'd already be dead."

"But he wants to murder her before her natural death."

Now Buffy's brow furrowed. "What would that accomplish?"

"It would mess up the Slayer lineage. Different Slayers would activate at different times."

She still didn't get it. Sounded more like an Ethan Rayne chaos plot.

"Buffy, he wants to keep you from being activated as a Slayer. That way, the Master will rise."

Her head started to hurt. "He can do that?"

"Yes. If he destroys the natural progression of Slayers, you won't be the Slayer when the Master rises and opens the Hellmouth."

"But won't whoever is the Slayer still stop him?" she asked.

Angel shook his head. "Not necessarily. The alternate Slayer could live in Zimbabwe, for all we know. Or she might not be able to defeat him. It's a problem, Buffy. You've got to stop him."

"How did you learn this?"

"Oh, the usual. Slinking around sewers. Lurking in warehouses. Keeping my ear to the graveyard dirt."

"Where is this Lucien?"

"In one of the caverns under Sunnydale, near where the Master was trapped. I tracked one of his lackeys to a fork in the tunnels but lost him afterward."

Buffy took a deep breath. "Okay. I'm going to call Giles and tell him this. See what he can dig up on the time travel capabilities of this new artifact. In the meantime, will you show me where you lost the minion?"

"Of course."

She sighed. No Bronze tonight. Just an evil plot to foil. But Angel was with her. Things could be looking up.

As they walked, Buffy leaned a little closer to Angel, taking in his scent. "Which Slayer are they going to kill?"

"I don't know. The bits and pieces I overheard were never that specific. Mostly just boasting, would-be assassins bragging that they were going to kill a Slayer."

"So they could choose any Slayer, in any time period in the past?" she asked.

"As long as it's before you were alive. That's all they need to do to alter the Slayer lineage."

"This is pretty insidious." Briefly she entertained the notion of an alternate future in which she was just a normal girl who could lead a normal life. Someone else would be the Slayer instead of her. She could have a conventional dating life, and her boyfriends might not get killed by rampaging demons at all.

Of course, would she have Angel then? And would she move here to Sunnydale? She would have had no cause to burn down the gym that got her kicked out of her former high school. She would never meet Willow or Xander or Giles. But she'd have fewer bruises.

Then again, she sort of liked saving the world from time to time, and Angel was right. The alternate Slayer might not even live in this country, might not learn about the Master until it was too late. Or worse, she could even get killed by the Master. Buffy did, after all.

Buffy called Giles at his place. She described the newly forged artifact and Lucien's plot.

"Insidious," Giles said.

"That's what I said."

"I'll see what I can dig up on this Lucien character. I may end up at the library later for some of my books."

"Okay, Giles. I'll come by there after I do a little recon with Angel."

"Be careful, Buffy. We don't know anything about this new player. He could be very dangerous."

Across town, deep under the streets of Sunnydale, Lucien got a paper cut and cursed. He tried folding the incantations again with one hand, bringing his egregiously wounded finger to his mouth.

"Our fearless leader," Victor remarked to Jason. Jason snickered.

"Shut up!" cried Lucien. He finished folding the papers, straightened his ascot, and smoothed his lapels. He looked like a character straight out of *The Importance of Being Earnest,* Victor thought. Didn't he know a Slayer would stake him on sight for being so out of date in his fashions?

Now composed, Lucien handed one copy of the papers to Victor, and one to Jason. "It's very important you hang on to these," he told them. "These are the incantations that will transport you back and forth through time."

"I remember the drill," Victor said impatiently. How many times had he endlessly traipsed through time while Lucien spoke one incantation after the other, honing their landing spots and times?

"This time it's different," Lucien snapped. "It's going to be dangerous in these places. These Slayers are active and trained. We're not killing them while they're still children. All of us may perish. Keep this copy of the incantations in case I am unable to speak them."

"You mean if you get dusted."

"Or toasted," Jason sneered bitterly.

"I've told you a million times I was sorry about that!" Lucien said in exasperation. "But yes. In the event of my death, you must continue on. I've written the incantations out phonetically. You have your copies, and I have mine.

"Now. First we go to Wales in 60 C.E. I've chosen appropriate clothing for all of us so we can blend in. I've worked and worked on this spell, so we're going to land right on the Isle of Anglesey. That was a tough one to calculate. Very tough. It took a lot of hard work."

Neither Jason nor Victor provided the compliment he was fishing for.

"Right. Let's change. We leave here in an hour," Lucien told them.

"You sure we'll land at night this time?" Jason asked. "I don't want to risk a repeat of becoming a Tater Tot."

Lucien threw his arms up in frustration. "You know I can't promise that. It's not that exact. I run the risk of daylight too, you know." He stormed around the cave, fuming.

"Why do I have to work with people who don't appreciate the subtlety of time travel and its alternate future capability? That is what this entire endeavor centers around!"

"We can appreciate the subtleties," Victor assured him. "We just want to avoid your errors."

Jason snickered again, and Lucien ordered them out.

As Victor left the cavern room, the incantations crinkling in his pocket, he shook his head sadly. How did he end up with such a wiener as a boss? It was downright dispiriting.

He and Jason meandered to their quarters, two little rooms off the main cavern that Victor had decorated with some stolen antiquities. On his bed rested their outfits. Two woolen tunics, woolen leggings, leather boots that laced up the front, and two heavy woolen capes.

Victor hated wool.

It itched. It was heavy.

Jason followed him in, eyeing the outfits. He picked up the moccasin-like boots. "No way, nohow. I'm not wearing these things."

"We have to look authentic."

"I don't give beans for authentic. I haven't taken off my lucky combat boots for fifteen years."

Victor looked down at his friend's feet. The combat boots, once black, were now worn, the brown leather beneath showing through in a dozen places. Jason had sewn and resewn the soles in place countless times. They smelled only slightly better than a compost heap on fire.

But he knew that Jason's insistence on wearing them would annoy Lucien, so he encouraged his friend to do so.

In their separate rooms, they dressed quickly, anticipating the hunt. They rejoined each other and checked their knife holsters. Victor had lovingly sharpened and oiled each blade to perfection.

They returned to the rooms beneath the crypt. Lucien was already in a similar outfit. Instantly he sized them up. "What are those?" he asked Jason impatiently, pointing to the boots.

"Those are my lucky combat boots."

"Well, they aren't historically accurate."

"Screw historically accurate," Jason countered. "They're my lucky combat boots. You can either live with that or send Gorga."

Lucien sighed. As much as Jason annoyed him, his intellect was a step above Gorga's. No. He would use the monstrous vampire only as a last resort, if all of them failed. "Very well," he said. "It's time to leave."

Angel stopped at a fork in the tunnels. "This is where I lost him."

Buffy bent low, looking for recent scuff marks in the cave floor. There were too many to count. "Looks like Free Burger Wednesday at the Doublemeat Palace. Dozens of people have passed by here. These passages are definitely being used for something."

They took the left tunnel, walking along a narrow passageway. The cave floor lowered, forcing them to bend as they walked. Buffy felt along the rough stone wall for any sign of a hidden door.

"We're under the cemetery right now, aren't we?" she asked Angel.

"Yes. Under the west side."

His underground geography was a lot better than hers, but then again, she could move around on the surface at all hours. Angel wasn't so lucky.

The tunnel ended at a large cavernous room. A dozen other passageways led off from there. They backtracked to the fork and took the passage on the right. Again Buffy felt along the narrow cavern walls for a ledge or crack, anything that might pass as a secret door. She found nothing.

They emerged into the large room for a second time. "I can see why you lost him."

Angel looked up at the ceiling, then around at the various passages snaking off into the distance. "I don't think he made it as far as this room. I would have seen him, whichever tunnel he took. I ran straight through the left tunnel and emerged here. He was nowhere in sight, and I'd been right behind him."

"So then back to the search for the secret passageway." They turned around, facing the tunnel they'd just taken.

Suddenly a bright light flashed out, blinding Buffy. She brought an arm up to shield her eyes. At first she thought it was a powerful flashlight. It played over the cavern walls. Then she spotted a crack in the tunnel wall. The light squeezed through that tiny space. It coursed blue, then silver, dancing in the dust kicked up from their movement.

It pulsed, then vanished.

Buffy raced to the spot, feeling again along the wall. Her fingernails slid into a barely perceptible crack. She traced the line of it down to the ground, then along the floor and up the other side. A small piece of rock slid to one side as her fingers grazed it. With the grinding of rock against rock, a square door scraped inward. The flicker of torchlight illuminated the room beyond.

Buffy entered, Angel behind her.

No one waited in the small room. One of the walls was brick, the others the limestone of the cavern. Tables littered with notes stood along three of the walls. A worn chair sat before one of them, next to a pile of Watcher journals. She leafed through them. Next to the journals lay a piece of thick parchment paper. An inscription was scrawled on it, in some strange language Buffy didn't recognize. There were numbers, though, and she read those: "60 C.E."

"Look at this," she said to Angel.

He joined her, peering at the paper. "Looks like they picked a Slayer. But I don't know what the inscription says."

"No," she said, pocketing it. "But I know someone who will." She continued her circuit of the room, gathering up any other notes she found. The rest of the material was books, charts, and magickal symbols. She'd have to bring Giles back here.

She stared at the walls, the floor, and the ceiling. Nothing here could have created that play of light on the walls. *Magick?* she wondered. She moved to the brick wall. "This looks like a foundation," she said, peering up.

"Maybe there's a mausoleum up there," Angel agreed.

"The flash of light . . ." Her voice trailed off.

"Yes?"

"Do you think that was the assassins leaving?"

"You mean in a portal?"

She nodded.

Angel's face turned grave. "We need to get to Giles."

CHAPTER SIX

At the library, full research mode was under way. Buffy and Angel strode in, greeting Willow and Xander at the large center table.

"You guys are here late," Buffy said. She glanced at the clock. Eleven p.m.

Willow gave a slight nod to Giles's office. "Apparently we don't need sleep."

Xander sighed and leaned back in his wooden chair. "Or social lives." He threw his pencil onto the table, where it rolled to a stop.

Giles emerged from his office.

"What'd you find?" Buffy asked him.

Her Watcher walked with a heavy book in his hand, thumbing through the pages as he moved. “It’s all quite fascinating,” he said. At the center table, he placed the book down, then referred to another one lying open beside it. “Very fascinating.”

“Share, Giles.”

“There is a record of a vampire named Lucien who hails from the fourteen hundreds. He was a master sorcerer, capable of the most advanced incantations. Not only could he perform spells and enchantments, he could create them.”

Buffy pulled out the piece of parchment from her pocket. “Like this?” She handed it to Giles. She told him about the books and charts they’d found in the little room, and about the bright flash of light that could have been a portal.

He studied the note. “Oh, my.”

“What is it?”

“Just a moment . . .” Reading the note and walking at the same time, Giles climbed the short flight of stairs to the upper stacks. Moments later he emerged again with a large, dusty volume. He read a few pages and returned to the table. “Oh, my.”

“Oh my what, Giles?” Buffy urged him.

“He’s created an incantation to go with the newly forged artifact. It’s written in an obscure Akkadian dialect. There are two spells here. One will transport the user and his companions to Wales in 60 C.E. The other will bring them back here, to the present.” He put down the parchment, then hurried into his office. Buffy heard file drawers opening and shutting, then a brief silence. He emerged, thumbing through some Watcher journals. "60 C.E., 60 C.E.," he mumbled, searching the pages. "Ah, here we are. The Isle of Anglesey, 60 C.E. The Slayer then was Incinii, a fierce warrior who defended her homeland not only from vampires, but from invading Romans." He looked up from the text. "She must be the target. We must stop them before they leave!"

Angel stepped forward. "It might be too late for that."

"What do you mean?" Giles asked.

Buffy cleared her throat. "We think the assassins already left in that flash of light."

Giles nearly dropped the journal, then looked at his watch. "Any moment now, history might change around us. If they succeed, the Slayer lineage will be disrupted, and the time line forever altered. We could all cease to exist at any moment."

"How do I stop them?" Buffy asked.

Giles looked down at the spell. "We must follow them back in time."

"Right on!" Xander yelled, leaping to his feet. "Time travel!"

Willow smiled too, excited at the prospect.

Buffy had a bad feeling, and Angel brooded next to her.

Giles turned to Willow and Xander. "I don't think it's a good idea for either of you to go. This could be a very dangerous endeavor. And time travel could be tricky—anything we do could forever alter the future. You could step on a beetle and cause a plague to wipe out all of Europe."

"What, like the butterfly flapping its wings in Central Park and causing a hurricane off the Eastern Seaboard?" Willow asked. She liked chaos theory.

"Exactly," Giles said.

Xander shook his head adamantly. "Oh, no way. I'm going. You guys will need an expert in time travel."

"Your expertise," Giles said bluntly, "comes from Arnold Schwarzenegger and Michael J. Fox movies."

"And that's bad?" Xander challenged.

"Oh, dear."

"Giles, look," Buffy said. "I could use all of your help. Who knows what I'm going to come up against in these places?" After a modest pause, she added, "I didn't exactly study a whole lot of history. I could get burned at the stake or something."

"That's no fun," said Willow. "I hate when that happens."

"Wait, wait," Angel interrupted. "What about this artifact? We don't know where it is."

Giles held up a finger, then pushed some books around on the table until he found the one he wanted. "Aha! This is what I learned about the power of the Gem of Chargulgaak. It does not travel through time itself. It acts as a marker, left behind in the present."

"What does that mean?" asked Xander.

"It means," Giles continued, "that Lucien would have to

leave it here in Sunnydale in 1998 when he journeys back in time. It would be the only way he could return."

"So then we find it and steal it?" Buffy asked.

"You didn't see it in the chamber?" Giles asked.

Buffy shook her head.

"That's strange. . . ." He took off his glasses, placing one stem in the corner of his mouth, then removing it. "Why would the artifact not be there? It must be there!" He paced around the room, then sat down on the table corner.

"Could he have hidden it?" Angel asked.

Giles shot to his feet. "Of course!" He snapped his fingers, then replaced his glasses. "He would have to hide it. If someone stole or destroyed it while he was gone, it would be disastrous." He met Buffy's eyes. "And we don't even need to find it to use this spell," he finished.

"What?" Buffy asked, bewildered.

"We know it's here in Sunnydale in 1998. Lucien would have to leave it behind." He waved the parchment. "If we use this incantation to travel back in time and stop the assassins, we, too, will return to Sunnydale in 1998. As long as it's here somewhere, we don't need to actually possess it to travel backward in time."

"This whole thing is very confusing," Buffy said.

Willow stood up. "No, I see what he means, Buffy. We just piggyback onto Lucien's spell. We say the incantation and poof, we travel back to 60 C.E. Then we speak the return incantation and we come back to Sunnydale in 1998. The artifact has to stay here."

"Wouldn't the assassins already have beat us to the Slayer?" Buffy asked.

"No," Xander told her, starting to get it all. "We need to think four-dimensionally." He pointed at the incantation. "As long as we use the same incantation, we enter at the exact same point in time as the assassins. They won't have a time jump on us at all, no matter how much earlier they left today. Even if they left last week, we'd still arrive at the same time. Like in *The Terminator*, Reese and the Terminator leave at different times, but arrive the same night—"

Buffy cut him off. "So we speak this incantation?"

Giles read it over. "We can give it a try."

"And we come back to 1998?" she asked suspiciously. "Not to Cro-Magnon times when I'm going to have to fight off pterodactyls for my food?"

"Would you wear one of those little deerskin bikini things that—," Xander began, but stopped abruptly when Angel cleared his throat.

"It should work," Giles assured her.

"I don't like 'should,' Giles."

Xander walked over to her. "Like the 'should,' Buff. Embrace the 'should.' This is time travel. A once-in-a-lifetime adventure."

Willow and Giles waited for her, eyebrows raised.

She stared at her friends, then exhaled. "Okay," she said. "When do we leave?"

Giles excitedly paced again. "We'll need supplies. And period clothing."

"We could raid the drama club's storage closet," Willow offered. "It's Saturday. They won't notice anything missing for a couple of days, and we'll be back by then, right?"

Giles again read over the spell. "We should be back only moments after we leave."

"Moments?" Buffy asked. "How many moments? You mean Angel and I could have stuck around and grabbed this guy when he returned?"

"Perhaps," Giles said.

"But wouldn't that mean that he would have been successful?" Willow asked. "Wouldn't their coming back mean they'd killed the Slayer, and then everything would be different?"

Giles regarded her gravely. "You may be right, Willow. The sooner we leave, the sooner we'll be outside of time ourselves. Right now, if they returned successful in their mission, we could all suddenly disappear. At the very least, Buffy may not be the Slayer. At the worst, the Master would be in power."

"We need to leave now, Giles," Buffy said, her stomach turning sour. "Will, go raid the drama club's closet. Xander, help her. We go now."

Twenty minutes later they rendezvoused in the library, all wearing clothes from a recent production of *Robin Hood*. The outfits weren't historically accurate, but the garments were heavy and woolen, with simple tunics, leggings, and capes. They were good enough on such short notice.

Giles, after practicing the incantation silently, realized it wasn't very specific about the time of day. They could arrive at sunrise, noon, or night. Buffy insisted that Angel stay there and dig up all he could on Lucien and his plot. Angel didn't like it, but he agreed.

He left the library and the four Scoobies gathered, with Giles in the center. He spoke the words aloud for the first time. A bright point of light fluttered into view in the air above them. The library shook. The bright point expanded, growing elliptical, and a wind kicked up in the room. The light swirled and glittered, the wind tugging at their hair and clothes. Buffy felt lighter and lighter, and then she sailed up through the air, her feet leaving the floor. Speeding toward the dizzying display of light, she held her breath and squeezed her eyes shut. Then, unsure of what lay on the other side, not even sure she'd live to see it, she hurtled into the vortex, careening backward through time.

CHAPTER SEVEN

Wales, 60 C.E.

Buffy felt her body decelerate suddenly. The brightness flashed and faded, spitting her out onto a sandy beach. She tumbled, landing against a large rock in the small of her back. Wincing, she looked up to see the vortex, spiraling in the air five feet above her. She rolled over onto her stomach, propped herself up on her elbows, and scanned the beach. No sign of the vamps at all. Giles said they would land at the same time. Was it possible they'd landed somewhere else? She tried to get up to run, do a cursory search, but her trembling legs gave out beneath her and she fell.

A flash of brightness pulled her attention back to the vortex. A dark figure appeared in the brightness. Then Xander, screaming, launched out of the light and tumbled to a painful stop on the beach. Dazed, her head feeling more like a pillow than a place with a working brain, Buffy crawled to him. Two more silhouettes appeared in the light, and the vortex ejected Willow and Giles simultaneously onto the rocks below. Willow landed rolling, managing to somersault up and onto her feet, where she stood, blinking, looking as if any minute she might fall over again.

Giles landed flat on his face, hitting his head on a rock. He groaned, cradling his skull and curling up onto his side. Buffy fought the woolliness in her head. It was day. She had been right to leave Angel behind. If the vampires did land at the same time, they might be dust now. She peered up into the heavily overcast sky. Or maybe not. She scanned her surroundings, searching for the assassins to no avail. Then she spoke to Xander. "You alive?" she asked.

He groaned.

"Good." She looked over her shoulder at Willow. "Are you alive?"

Willow swayed on her feet, eyes fixed on the spot where the portal was. "I think so. But I can't feel my head."

"It's still on your torso. Trust me."

Buffy crawled then to Giles, who continued to lie in a ball. She peeled his hand away from the wound to find a small red bruise forming. It looked minor, with no blood. Poor Giles. Always getting hit on the head.

"Don't say it," he warned her, reading her mind. He rolled

over, meeting her eyes. "I travel back in time to Roman-occupied Britain to face legionnaires and Druids, only to be done in by a rock."

"I think you'll live."

"Oh, good." Shakily he rose to his knees, holding his head again. "Anyone else feel like their head is full of sponge cake?"

Xander stood up on trembling legs. "I was going to say Ding Dongs, but that works too."

"Or matzo balls," Willow added. She slumped onto her knees.

"Giles, where are the vampires?" Buffy asked, rolling over on her back.

He scanned the beach, getting to his feet, his hands resting on his knees. "You looked when you first landed?"

"Yes. No sign."

"Interesting." He straightened up.

Her friends were up. Buffy knew she had to get up too. She tried to shake the gauzy feeling from her mind and slowly stood up.

"It's possible that Lucien worked out the time travel, but not the location travel."

Buffy narrowed her eyes at him. "What do you mean?"

"Well, the time magick may be very specific when it comes to what year we land in, but sketchier when it comes down to the location. The vampires may have landed at the same instant we did, but miles away."

Buffy scanned the beach into the distance.

"It's day, too," Xander pointed out. "Any chance they just went poof?"

Buffy looked up into the thick mass of roiling storm clouds above them. "I don't think so. These clouds would have protected them long enough to find cover. They would have smoked and been singed a bit, but I don't think we can count on total incineration."

On shaky legs, she moved to the nearest cluster of trees, then to a jumble of boulders, searching beneath them and in the darker places for any signs of hiding vampires. She didn't see any place that could have afforded them cover for long. Unless they went underwater.

She took in the scene before her. The beach behind them ended at a thinned tree line of oaks and pine, many of which had been cut down recently. Only a few still stood, thin ones. A misty rain began to fall, clinging to her hair in tiny droplets. In the distance a thin gray column of smoke rose up behind a nearby hill. Buffy turned around. On the opposite side of this ruined forest lay a narrow strait and an immense island full of tremendous old-growth trees. Beyond that lay an enormous ocean. Buffy wasn't positive, but she was pretty sure they should be on the *island* part of the Isle of Anglesey.

"Where are we?" she asked, brushing dirt off her woolen leggings. Her outfit was so scratchy that she couldn't imagine how people could have suffered in it for an entire lifetime. She pulled her thick cape closer around her shoulders as her breath misted in the chilly, wet air.

Giles swayed a bit but maintained his balance. He stared at the island momentarily, then removed his glasses. After wiping mist away from the lenses with a handkerchief, he replaced them. Squinting for a full minute at the vast forest on the island, and then at the ruined one on their side, he said, "Oh, dear."

"What oh dear?" Buffy asked, alarmed that she might be right.

"It seems we've landed on the wrong land mass. If I'm not mistaken, we are on the mainland, and the Slayer we seek is on that island there." He pointed to the land across the narrow strait.

"So it's possible the assassins landed in a different spot from us because they used a different portal?" She felt her stomach fall. "Then they might be on the island, already hunting the Slayer."

Giles regarded her with a grim expression. "Yes."

"Except that they'd have to find cover until dark, no matter how overcast it is," Willow added.

"Good point," Giles said, still wobbly.

Xander eyed the waterway. "It's not that far. Can't we just borrow a boat from someone?"

"I'm afraid it won't be that easy. You see those ruined trees there?" He pointed at the cut forest. "That's a sure sign of Roman occupation. The cuts look fresh, too, meaning they're likely still nearby."

"Like sitting around that fire?" Buffy asked, gesturing at the column of smoke.

"Oh, dear."

Xander lifted his eyebrows. "So? We just ask them if we can borrow a boat, right?"

"Not unless we want to be decorated in our own entrails or set on fire."

"What?" Xander cried.

"The Romans wouldn't take kindly to us being here. We made a choice to dress like British common folk instead of Roman soldiers because we'd be talking to the Druidic Slayer. The Romans would just as soon cut us down as help us."

"Oh, boy," Xander said, then squatted down.

Willow glanced around, then sat down herself. "I don't like this. I feel so out in the open."

"Yes," Giles said. "We should get some cover. Perhaps we can find a boat along the shore. I suggest we move along what's left of the trees, searching the waterline."

"Sounds good," Buffy said, already moving toward the oaks. Her head felt less woolly, more cotton candy now.

In a silent row, they slunk along the trees, keeping watch for any sign of Roman soldiers. The beach lay deserted. No fishermen. No boats. Just lots of sand and some bleached white driftwood. Buffy hoped Xander was right about the timing of the incantation, that if they repeated the same words the assassins had, they'd be deposited at the same instant in time. That meant the vamps didn't have a head start on them. If anything, since they landed in the middle of the day, Buffy and the others had the head start. The assassins, if they survived the daylight at all—which Buffy thought was probable under the heavily overcast sky—would have had to seek shelter. That gave the Scoobies the advantage for now.

The rain, though slight, began to accumulate on Buffy's woolen cape and tunic. A chill set in, and her teeth chattered. Frequently, she glanced back to be sure the others were okay. Willow was shivering more and more. Her fingernails were blue. Buffy wanted to find shelter, but she knew the vamps wouldn't be slowed down by wet or cold. The sky darkened in the east, and it grew increasingly difficult to make out the shoreline in the gloom. Still no boats. No people. The coastline was utterly deserted.

A half hour later, her leather shoes soaked completely through and her toes so cold she could barely feel them, Buffy stopped. Her woolen clothes, utterly drenched now, felt five times their original weight, pulling down on her shoulders. Her back and shoulders ached. She turned to watch the others catch up with her. It was completely dark. Now that night had fallen, the vampires would resume their search for the Druidic Slayer. If they had landed on the island, they had a significant head start. Willow's lips looked dangerously blue, and she walked as if in a daze. She was the last to reach them.

"We need to make a fire and get warm," Buffy told Giles. "The more night sets in, the colder it's going to get."

"We can't! The Romans will spot any flame," Giles reminded her.

Buffy gestured at Willow. "Look at her, Giles! She's freezing."

Giles studied Willow's face. She was no longer shivering, a dangerous sign of the onset of hypothermia.

"What about that fire?" Xander asked, pointing through the trees.

Ahead the shoreline angled inward, and firelight flickered in the tree branches there.

Willow suddenly shucked off her cape, then tried to strip off her tunic.

"What are you doing?" Xander asked her.

She didn't answer, just flung the cloak down on the wet ground, baring her teeth.

Giles picked it up, stilling her hands. "Keep it on. It's wet, but it'll still keep you warm." He draped the cloak over her shoulders.

"Follow me," Buffy said quietly, and they crept forward. Giles fell back, making sure Willow continued to walk.

"It was stupid not to wear modern clothes," he cursed, putting an arm around Willow. She remained silent.

Slowly they crept closer and closer to the fire, pausing often and stepping on pockets of sodden leaves to muffle their approach. Now the shoreline came into view, and Buffy's eyes filled with Roman legionnaires. Five bonfires blazed, embers floating up into the night sky. Dozens of battle horses paced and whinnied. More than fifty boats bobbed on the water, tied to other boats that had been dragged up onto shore. The men paced, talked, checked weaponry, and gazed across at the island. It was clearly a massive military operation.

"Oh, dear," Giles gasped.

"Not 'oh, dear' again, Giles. Stop it with the 'oh, dear.' What is it?"

"It seems we've landed at a most inopportune time," he whispered, drawing up next to her.

"These guys?" she asked, hooking her thumb at the soldiers.

"Yes. These guys. They must be the troops of Suetonius Paulinus."

"Sweet on us what?" Xander asked.

"Suetonius Paulinus," Giles corrected. "We've arrived on the same day that the Romans launched their largest, most destructive campaign against the Isle of Anglesey. Thousands of Druids were butchered or burned alive with their own torches."

Buffy stood speechless, gazing at the soldiers, then at the dark shape of the island across the strait.

"It looks like they're ready to launch the invasion within the hour," Giles went on. "They'd attack at night, of course."

Buffy narrowed her eyes at the shadowy island and could now see the faint flicker of firelight among the distant trees there.

"Wait, wait," Xander whispered. "So you're saying that we have to get over to that island while the Druids are made into crispy hash browns by the Romans?"

"It's highly likely," Giles told him. "We will have to steal a boat and arrive there at the same time as the invasion force. It's just the kind of chaotic cover we need."

Xander lifted his hand in protest. "Hold on, hold on. I am not going to steal a boat from a bunch of pumped-up Roman centurions."

"You don't have to," Buffy said. "I will." She eyed the bank, selecting the most shadowed part at the edge of the fires. Three boats floated away from the rest, tied to wooden posts in the ground.

"From what I remember reading about the invasion, some of the Roman soldiers forded the strait by swimming," said Giles.

Buffy looked poignantly at Willow, who still said nothing, staring down mutely at the ground. "But we can't do that, Giles. Willow can't get any wetter. We need to find her a fire. And those Druid fires across the way are going to have to suffice."

"We'll need to make them understand that we're here to help," Giles reminded her. "That may prove difficult."

"I'll leave that up to you, Mr. Linguist," Buffy said. "Now I'm boat bound. Wait here." She turned around a moment later. "Any chance my stealing these boats will mess up the future time line?" she whispered back.

Giles shrugged.

Not the usual Watcher prowess. She looked at Willow and realized that she had little choice. They couldn't swim, and every moment they spent dawdling here gave the vampires an advantage. With some soldiers swimming the strait, Buffy hoped the loss of one boat wouldn't alter the future too much.

She slunk off into the shadows, angling to emerge on the shore right next to the three boats. The men talked and laughed with one another, sometimes gesturing toward the island and exclaiming with upraised fists. Buffy couldn't understand a word of what they said. Giles would know, though. She crept forward slowly, a step or two at a time, pausing frequently to check the men, making sure none of them had turned her way or reacted to any noise she made.

Her shoulders and legs ached as she crouched and moved along. She thought of ditching the cloak, but wondered if she'd need it later. She kept it on just in case. Now she was only fifty or so feet from the boats and had to leave the quiet of the destroyed forest floor. The sandy beach stretched out before her, and she was grateful that the sand would absorb most sound from her movement. With the assistance of the din of Roman chatter and crackling from the bonfires, she stepped out onto the beach undetected, keeping just outside the edge of the firelight. Ahead lay the boats, now only thirty feet away. She moved more quickly now, glancing down the beach for an escape route in case they saw her. She'd lead them away from the others, down the beach, then cut into the forest again and hopefully ditch them.

But they hadn't spotted her yet, and now she was only ten feet from the boats. She eyed the stake and rope that lashed them to the shore. Buffy paused, glancing at the soldiers again. They continued to talk, poke at the fire, and check on their horses. They milled around restlessly, obviously awaiting orders to move.

Buffy reached the stake and silently untied the rope that lashed together the three boats. She walked a few feet to her left, pulling on the boats, hoping they floated free in the water and would be easy to tow. But they resisted, and she knew at least one of them was securely pulled up onto the shore. She turned to creep toward them, rope in hand, then stopped and pulled the wooden stake out of the ground and pocketed it. Could come in handy, and the Romans would be more likely to notice an unused stake.

Glancing at the soldiers again, she made sure they still took no notice of her. Then she reached the boats. Only one lay beached. The other two floated freely, bound to the first. She placed her hands on the cold, wet wood of the first and began to push it out into the water. It moved easily, and relief swept over her.

But just as it hit the water, it screeched on a rock and splashed loudly into the strait. Instantly the group of soldiers turned to her location, peering intently into the darkness. Then three of them took off toward her, shouting.

She had only seconds before they reached her. She leaped into the boat, teetered, and almost went overboard. Ducking down abruptly, she felt around in the bottom of the boat for an oar. Her hands closed around wet wood and she brought the paddle up just as the first soldier reached her. As he plunged into the water to stop her, she hit him hard across the face with the oar, knocking him flat onto his back. His friends reached him then, pulling his unconscious form out of the water.

Buffy thrust the paddle into the water and pushed off the bottom. Then she stroked with all her strength as the two other soldiers splashed out into the water in pursuit. One of them grabbed the edge of the boat just as she swung it around, and she stood up and slammed the hard edge of the paddle down onto his hand. He withdrew his fingers sharply, crying out in pain.

She began to paddle again frantically, gaining distance as the third soldier made a grab for one of the two boats she towed. She paddled farther out into the strait, alarmed to see a growing group of soldiers running to the assistance of the first three.

Now the third soldier grabbed solidly onto one of the towed boats. He threw one dripping leg over the side, then the other one, and he was inside the boat. Buffy continued to paddle, more interested in gaining distance between her and the growing mass of soldiers. She rowed hard, throwing her Slayer strength into it. She glanced over her shoulder. The Roman soldier in the other boat was reeling himself into her boat with the tow cable. He was only a few feet away. Buffy turned in her seat, raised the paddle, and sideswiped him over the edge.

He landed with a loud splash, and she returned to rowing. Now she looked back to the firelit shore and saw two soldiers getting into boats to pursue her. If more followed, she didn't know how she'd fight them all at once. She glanced along the beach in the direction where Giles and the others were and realized she'd lost her place. How far had she rowed? Was she past their location?

She turned and scanned the shore, then the banks of the island, looking for something familiar, something she had seen earlier and could use as a landmark. But the island was just a dark mass, with no detail at all except for the brief flickers of distant firelight.

She stopped rowing momentarily to check the progress of the pursuing Roman soldiers, a moment she dreaded. But they hadn't left the shore. They stood riveted to a spot on the beach. A man in gleaming armor stood before them, a red cape slung over one shoulder. He shouted at them angrily, then waved dismissively in Buffy's direction. The two soldiers climbed out of the boats and returned to the shore obediently.

Buffy turned and rowed a little farther, angling back toward the shore. She untied the other two boats, setting them adrift.

As she neared the shore, she heard Giles's voice whispering her name.

She rowed up onto the beach and stepped out of the boat to pull it onto the sand. "Over here!" she called, careful to keep her voice low.

Slowly three shapes materialized out of the gloom.

Giles walked with his arm around Willow, who stared at the ground.

"I got us a boat."

"I see that. Great work."

"Who was that guy on the beach in the cloak?" she asked.

"I believe it was Suetonius Paulinus himself, though I don't really know what he looked like."

"What did he say to them?"

"He told them not to waste their energy avenging a petty theft. They had to concentrate on the invasion."

"So this is the night," Xander said nervously. "And here I was hoping to make it to eighteen."

"You will," Buffy assured him. She studied Willow. "Willow?"

No response.

"We tried already. She's going into hypothermic shock," Giles told her.

"Then we need to leave now and get to a fire," Buffy said, taking Willow by the hand.

Together they moved toward the lapping water, steeling themselves for the boat trip. They were about to enter the stronghold of Druidism on the brink of invasion.

CHAPTER EIGHT

The boat glided silently toward the island, with Buffy's paddle making the only noise as it dipped into the water with each stroke. Xander found another paddle in the bottom of the boat and helped her make progress across the strait. She fought back the feeling of desperation struggling to rise inside her. Even now, the vampires could be killing the Druidic Slayer. They had to get across to the island fast.

The tide was moving out, making their progress easier, bringing them closer and closer to Anglesey. No doubt the Romans had the same plan. Buffy didn't know how long they had before Suetonius Paulinus attacked.

"Druids," Xander said thoughtfully. "Druids." He looked up at Giles as he rowed. "They're the ones who like trees."

"Yes, Xander, they like trees," Giles answered.

"And they built Stonehenge?"

"Well, actually, no, though they likely used it as a place of worship."

Xander's eyes widened. "Worship, yeah! Aren't they also the ones who commit ritual human sacrifice? I knew they were on my list of people I never wanted to meet."

Giles shook his head slightly. "Many ancient cultures practiced human sacrifice. The Maya, the Aztec—it was considered of vital importance. Besides, archaeological finds have produced many animal bones, but evidence for human sacrifice is far more scant on Anglesey."

"Scant? What about that guy they found a few years back? The one in the bog?" He dipped his oar in the water, propelling them forward.

"Lindow Man?" Giles offered.

Xander pointed his finger at him adamantly. "Yes. Lindow Man. Those bogs are bristling with bodies like that. Wasn't that guy ritually murdered in more than one way?"

"Three, to be exact. Bludgeoned, strangled, and throat cut. Plus, he was thrown into the bog, so that could count as four. Though he was likely already dead at that point, so you might not want to count drowning. Three was a sacred number to the Celtic peoples."

"Four different ways! Four! And he was one of their own,

wasn't he? A priest? I'd hate to see how they treat people they don't like." He realized he'd stopped rowing and resumed.

"Many religious groups throughout antiquity believed self-sacrifice to be quite noble," Giles explained.

"Maybe, but I seriously doubt the guy killed himself four different ways. That would be a bit challenging." Xander's voice rose. "What if they don't take kindly to us just barging in?"

"Lindow Man was found in England," Giles told him. "This is Wales."

"Oh, and you think they're kinder, gentler human sacrificers over here? You don't think Mr. English Druid and Mr. Welsh Druid get together for tea and chat about the latest guy they killed four times?"

"Well, I hardly think—," Giles started, but he was cut off.

"When was this guy killed?" Xander pressed.

Giles hedged a bit. Took off his glasses. "Well, archaeologists estimate that he was killed around 60 C.E."

"60 C.E.! That year sounds familiar."

"Well, yes. But as I said before, Lindow Man was killed in England."

Xander paused, getting more and more worked up. "What if *I'm* Lindow Man?" he said at last.

"What on earth?" Giles asked, exasperated.

"What if the guy who was *supposed* to be Lindow Man changed places with me, and I am the one destined to be sacrificed. They could drag me over to England and *bang*."

"Bang?" Giles repeated. "Yes, I see. Well, that's hardly

the case, because you're here now, aren't you?"

"Well . . . ," Xander assented, "I guess so. But time travel is wrought with paradox, my friend. Wrought." He watched a dark vortex whirl in the wake of his paddle.

"Boys," Buffy hissed through clenched teeth, "being quiet is an important part of sneaking."

"Oh, sorry," Xander said, reducing his voice to a whisper.

"Besides, ritual sacrifice is a religious rite," Giles went on quietly. "They wouldn't sacrifice just anyone at random. It's far more likely they'd suspect you of being a Roman spy scouting for the invasion and just outright kill you."

"Oh, great! Great! Way to be encouraging, Giles. And I suppose you'll just watch that happen, in your Watchery way."

"Shhhh!" Buffy told them again. "We're getting closer."

Scanning along the shore, she saw one section that lay relatively dark. No fires flickered between the branches. She pointed silently toward the area, nodding at Xander. He nodded back and helped her steer the boat in that direction. As they glided through the dark waters, the smell of salty sea air filling her nose, Buffy felt the blood thrumming in her ears. She didn't know what to expect once she was over there.

She hoped they'd be friendly, and that the few phrases Giles had learned would get their point across.

In the center of the boat, Giles sat with Willow, vigorously rubbing her arms in an effort to warm her up. Buffy put more strength into paddling, eager to get to a fire and to reach the Druidic Slayer before the vampires did—if she wasn't too late already. Images of the Slayer lying bleeding on the shore came unbidden into her head. She pushed the negative thoughts away.

As the shore came into view, Buffy saw a thick, dark grouping of trees—an excellent place to land in stealth. They were almost to the beach when Willow suddenly stood up, rocking the boat violently. For a second Buffy thought they were all going over, and she dug her paddle down, hoping to touch bottom. She did, and stilled the boat's motion.

"Will?" Buffy asked, turning in her seat to look at her friend.

Willow stared down at her with absolute hatred. "Shut up!" she yelled. "I don't want to hear a word from you!" Her voice thundered in the quiet of the night. Buffy didn't know her friend could yell so loudly, or sound so full of venom. Willow shrugged off her cloak as Giles tugged gently on it, urging her to sit back down. She reeled on him. "And you!" she shouted. "You thought I wouldn't figure out what you've been planning? You lured me out here to kill me!"

Xander leaned forward, pulling his oar up out of the water. "Will," he urged. "Please keep your voice down." He peered nervously at the shore.

"I will not!" she shouted. "You're all trying to kill me! Well, I won't let you!"

Before Buffy could lunge forward, Willow leaped overboard, landing with a splash in the dark water. Though it was shallow, she tumbled forward and was completely submerged.

She struggled, emerged, then managed to stand up. Without a glance back at the boat, she started splashing toward the shore.

"Giles?" Buffy asked, bewildered and scared that the Druids would suddenly learn of their presence.

"Hypothermia. It's one of the stages—delirium."

Buffy instantly began to row again, closing the last few feet to shore. Xander got into a crouching position, then jumped out and pulled the boat up on the beach.

As Buffy climbed out, she caught the briefest glimpse of Willow disappearing into the trees. Buffy moved forward silently, trying to follow, but a tree branch snagged on her cloak. She disentangled herself and moved forward again. She tripped on a root and went down hard on her hands, plunging into the cold mud and scratching her palm on a sharp rock.

She stood up, searching for a hint of Willow in the trees, but saw nothing but darkness up ahead. She crept forward again, this time checking her footing as she went. Behind her Giles and Xander cursed and crashed through the underbrush, making too much noise.

She turned to shush them but discovered they weren't there. Alarmed, she scanned the trees nervously. Where had they gone? And what had been making the crashing noise, then? Behind her lay only forest. She couldn't even see the shore, though she was sure she'd only progressed twenty or so feet.

"Giles!" she whispered.

No response.

"Xander, where are you guys?"

The wind sighed in the branches above.

She turned and pushed forward again, determined to find Willow and then plead with the Druids for a fire, even if she had to use English or draw stick figures in the mud of a shivering person and a warming fire.

Anything could happen to Willow out there in her delirious state.

Another root tripped her, and she pitched forward, barely keeping her balance. When she stood up, a branch tangled painfully in her hair, stopping her progress. She reached up, pulling strands free of the tree's hold. Then she continued on. Behind her the forest creaked and shuffled. Twigs snapped. Leaves rustled.

She spun around only to find an empty, shadowed forest behind her.

As she watched, the shadows shifted, moving from tree to tree. She whirled around. Dark forms beneath the trees darted away, out of sight, sliding along the forest floor and winding up the trunks of trees like shadow snakes.

Buffy steeled herself. This place was not going to spook her out. She was going to find Willow and the others. Then she was going to kick some vampire butt and be home before the Sunnydale Mall closed.

She pushed forward, moving tree limbs out of the way, shifting her eyes between the ground and the distance, searching for Willow. The wind in the boughs sighed more loudly, whispering over her head. Just as she looked up again to scan for Willow, she ran into a low tree limb, which struck her in the thigh. The branches caught in the wool of her cloak. She paused to yank the cloak free, and watched as shadows spilled down the sides of the trees around her, then advanced alarmingly fast, spreading over her.

Coldness hit her skin, and she backed away in a moment of unthinking fear. Then she wrenched the cloak free and started running. The trees bent and swayed, branches swinging down on top of her, catching under her arms, in her hair, snagging at her back. Root after root tripped her, and finally she went down hard, in a mossy patch. Darkness swept up over her and she flipped over, ready to kick her attackers.

Hands emerged from the ferns, arms from the undergrowth, lifting her up, up, until she stood, spitting dirt out of her mouth. And then the shadows stepped closer, dissolving into human form. Eight cloaked figures stood in a circle around her. They all wore medallions with the symbol of a tree.

"Look," she said. "I don't mean to hurt you. Unless you're evil," she added. "Then I probably do." She thought they might be Druids, though. Where was Giles?

They whispered to one another in a language she could not understand, pointing at her clothes.

Some decision made, they drew in closer, taking her arms, and pulled her toward the firelit section of the island.

"Wait!" she said, wondering if she should beat all of them up to escape. But then she decided that wouldn't go over well later, especially not while Giles tried to convince them she was there to help. "I had three friends with me! One of them is sick."

They regarded her with unmoving faces, clearly members of the Stoic-Villains-of-the-Month Club. Why did cloaked people always have to look so grim? Would it kill them to smile, or laugh at a good pun once in a while? Of course, Buffy herself rarely laughed at a pun, usually preferring to groan, especially if Xander was the perpetrator. Where was he?

As they dragged her toward the bonfires, Buffy craned her neck around, searching the woods for any sign of her friends. "Too bad I don't speak Druid!" she shouted for Giles's benefit, in case he lurked nearby. "Having a translator sure would be helpful in the land of cloaks over here!" When there was no response, not even a rustling of shrubbery, she added, "Well, off I go to the ritual sacrifice!"

Images of a wicker man on fire and her inside it flickered into her head. She forced them out and let the strangers lead her onward.

They meandered through the trees, which were quite well behaved compared to earlier. No branches snagging her clothes, no limbs in her hair. She imagined an eerie picture—the obfuscating Druids standing alongside her path, lowering twigs and branches into her way. Had they been there all along, hidden in shadow?

The flickering of a fire grew brighter and brighter, casting light on the trees around it. As they drew closer, the fire dissolved into four separate bonfires. Figures surrounded the fires, at least fifty people in robes, tunics, and cloaks.

And in front of the fire, with new dry clothes, sat Willow. She shivered now, a good sign, Buffy knew. It meant her body was warming up.

Standing up behind her were Giles and Xander, listening to the woman who appeared to be in charge of the group. Giles nodded, and then Buffy was within earshot. Everyone looked up as she and the Druids approached.

"Ah, Buffy," Giles said, walking over to her. "Are you all right?"

"Am I all right? How long have you been here?"

"Since we first landed. These people were kind enough to escort us over here."

"And the trees didn't . . ." Buffy could feel the immense oaks towering over her, weighing down on her.

"The trees didn't what?" Giles asked.

Buffy's voice felt tiny in the shadow of those ancient sentinels. "Nothing."

"Buffy! Hey!" Xander called as she approached. He gave her a little wave, grinning. Grinning a little too much. He was stuck in perma-grin, that expression he got when terrified on the inside and pretending to be brave on the outside.

"What's wrong?" she asked when she drew nearer.

"Nothing. Nothing," Xander said through clenched teeth. "Just keep smiling. Let's just hope that Giles here is getting through to them." He gave a little nod in the direction of a grouping of gray stones at the edge of the firelight. Something thick and red gleamed there, pooling in a small recess in the rock and spilling down the side of the forest floor.

Buffy did her best *probably nothing* shrug. "It may not be human."

"It's the 'may' part that bothers me," Xander said, still grinning like mad and nodding at the gathered Druids.

Giles resumed his conversation with the woman, who nodded and pointed down to the shore, where still more bonfires gleamed in the darkness. Buffy didn't know what they were speaking. It didn't sound like Latin. She didn't know what Druids spoke.

Giles gave her a slight bow, then joined them. "Fascinating!" he said. "Just fascinating!"

"What is?" Xander asked. "How long we've got before we're gutted as a sacred sign of worship?"

Giles shook his head. "No, Xander. Remember what I said about there being no archaeological proof whatsoever that the Druids practiced ritual human sacrifice on Anglesey."

"No proof? Before you said 'scant' proof."

Giles went on. "All we have supporting it is the Roman writing, and that could just be propaganda to make the Druids look even more the fearsome foes that they undoubtedly were. Besides," he added, taking off his glasses and cleaning the left lens, "even if they did, they wouldn't sacrifice just anyone. It would have to mean something."

“Oh,” Xander said, his voice momentarily cracking into a falsetto. “That’s no more reassuring now than it was the first time I heard that gem of Giles knowledge.”

“So what else did you learn?” Buffy asked. She regarded her Watcher in the flickering light. He looked tired.

“Well, the language is quite difficult. I tried several, wanting to avoid Latin, of course. I’m sure they speak it, but under the circumstances, I don’t think they’d react well at all to strangers showing up using the tongue of the Roman army. I spoke a bit of a Goidelic ancestor of modern Gaelic. I think they understood. They seem to be quite multilingual. Then I tried a variant of Old Welsh I know a little of, and that seemed to do the trick. At least, I think they understood me best when I used the more proto-British dialects . . . ancestors of Welsh, Cornish, and Breton—”

“Giles,” Buffy said firmly. “Point.”

“Ah, yes. I asked them about a powerful girl who lived on the island, someone who fought—”

Xander interrupted, holding up a protesting finger. “Hey, I thought Slayers were supposed to keep their vocation secret.”

“Well, yes. They are. If someone found out the identity of a Slayer, the vampires would hunt her tirelessly. That’s why I kept it vague.”

Buffy narrowed her eyes at him. “You? Vague?”

He ignored her barb and continued. “I asked her about a girl who fought unusually strongly, perhaps with almost supernatural strength.”

To their left, four men and a woman began chanting, holding thin branches. "And?" Buffy prompted him when he grew distracted.

"Oh, yes. She said the girl lived farther down the shore this way, and a bit inland."

"Can one of them show us? We need to get to her now. Every moment we waste here . . ." She let her sentence trail off.

"I could certainly ask."

"Tell them she's in danger and that you need to get there quickly."

"I will," Giles told her. "But they have their hands rather full with the upcoming Roman invasion."

"They know?" Xander asked.

"Indeed. They have spies on the mainland watching the Romans even now."

Xander nodded in appreciation. "Neat. Intrigue."

While Giles returned to the woman to talk, Buffy knelt down beside Willow, wondering if they should leave her by the fire. "Willow?" she asked.

Her friend looked up sheepishly. "I'm really sorry, Buffy," she said quietly. "I don't know what got into me. I could hear and see myself, and it all made sense at the time."

Buffy stroked her back reassuringly. "Giles said it was the hypothermia."

She pointed at the nearest Druids with her chin. "It's a good thing they found me. I was streaking through the trees, screaming. It was really weird."

"Did the trees . . ." Again she felt the weight of the dark forest at her back.

Willow raised her eyebrows. "Did they what?"

"Never mind."

Giles returned, and Buffy stood up. "They have a man who can lead us to the girl's cabin. She lives there with an older woman. Perhaps it's her Watcher."

Buffy turned to the woman and gave a little bow in thanks. The woman nodded. "Let's go."

Xander hesitated. "But what about Will?"

Buffy turned to her friend, deciding. "Stay here with her, Xander. I don't like the thought of splitting up, but Willow doesn't look good. I don't want her getting worse."

Xander's eyes filled with fear. "Are you crazy? I'm not staying here." He grasped Willow's shoulder. "*We're* not staying here. I don't want to be a large order of Xander Fillet with fries on the side!"

Willow touched his hand. "They're okay, Xander. I know it. We'll be safe." Then she turned her head toward Buffy. "But won't you need us?"

"Don't worry. We're going to fight vamps. I've done this a hundred times, and I don't want to worry about you."

The guide joined them, a stately-looking man with a long face, long brown beard, and a braid that hung down to his tailbone. On his arms he carried two dry cloaks, which he handed to Buffy and Giles. They nodded their thanks.

As they turned to go, Xander called, "Don't speak that

thingy without me! Don't leave us here. I miss my comic books. I miss central heat. I miss pie."

Buffy readied for the dark forest to swallow her. As she walked away, she turned one last time to see Xander sitting next to the fire, his arm around Willow protectively. Two Druids were staring at him, perched on nearby rocks, and Xander reached out with his free hand and patted the trunk of a nearby tree. "Trees good. Love the trees. Love Druids," he added, pointing at them.

Buffy hoped he didn't get them all killed.

For what felt like hours, Giles and Buffy followed the guide through the forest, following no visible trail from what she could see. Now and again the guide paused to consult the trees. He stopped at a huge oak, and later at a tremendous pine, staring up into their branches, as if navigating by the trees' location. Each time, he consulted the moss on the trunk, the way the branches hung, then chose a direction.

Buffy felt bad about leaving Xander and Willow behind. Normally, she was relieved when they weren't with her in battle. But in this strange place, nearly two thousand years before their own time, she felt odd and out of place. Anything could happen to them back there by the fire. Though she felt she could trust the Druids, she worried that the Romans would attack now and close in on her friends' location. They could be murdered as collateral damage of the invasion.

As she plodded through the dark and quiet forest, moving

more and more inland, her nervousness only grew. What if this whole trek through the woods was for nothing, and the girl they found was not the Slayer at all? Even if she was, what if they were too late? The vamps could have landed on the island and killed her by now. Buffy hoped the Druidic Slayer wasn't caught unaware, or distracted by the imminent invasion of the Roman forces.

As they crept farther and farther into the dark forest, Buffy once again felt the uncanny and eerie sensation that the trees surrounding her were alive. Of course, she knew they were alive in a plantlike kind of way, but this was more of a locomoting kind of way. They groaned and creaked, sighed and bent, their branches waving and lowering, raising and brushing against one another.

Her back burned as if hundreds of eyes dug into it, wooden eyes, ancient eyes. Unconsciously, she moved a little closer to Giles. "You feel it too?" he asked.

Buffy nodded, relieved that her Watcher also sensed it and that it wasn't her overactive imagination. Usually he believed her, even if he didn't sense anything himself. But occasionally, like the last time they had to deal with something creepy and wooden, namely a ventriloquist dummy, he hadn't believed her at first. But that had all turned out okay.

But that was just one creature made of wood.

This was an entire forest, and it moved around them, shifting and moaning.

Soon she smelled burning wood, and a small cabin came

into view. Out of a narrow chimney curled a long column of smoke. She didn't think she'd be so cavalier as to burn wood on this island.

The guide moved forward, signaling for them to wait outside. He knocked on the door. A woman in her thirties answered, looking weary. The guide exchanged brief words with her and then nodded, waving them forward.

Inside the small cabin, Buffy finally started to warm up. She stood next to the fireplace, reveling in its heat. Giles spoke with the woman, growing more and more excited as he did. Buffy couldn't understand a word. Was she the Slayer?

Finally Giles looked up to her. "She's a Watcher," he told her. "Her name is Eyra."

"Hi," Buffy said, giving her a little wave. She was younger than Giles, looked a little less stuffy. Buffy wondered what she was like as a Watcher. "So where's Incinii?"

"This will probably sound quite familiar to you," Giles said, "but she's disobeyed her Watcher and moved to the front lines to help ward off the Roman invasion."

"Hey, I hardly *ever* ward off Roman invasions," she countered.

Eyra said something to Giles in what sounded like Latin.

"She says we can catch her if we leave right away. She'll be with the group of warriors on the northernmost part of the resistance front. She has a brother among them." Just as Buffy was finally getting warm, Giles stood up. Eyra explained something at length to the guide, pointing out into the forest.

Then the guide made a short bow to Giles. Buffy waited for Giles to explain. "He's going to take us down to Incinii. We don't have much time."

"We never do," Buffy lamented, feeling a little sorry for herself. How many times had she passed up perfectly good shoe sales because she had to avert the apocalypse? How many school dances had she missed because some archvillain or another was ascending to power? Okay, maybe just the one, but still, her dress got totally ruined and she didn't get to dance at all. Now it was back to the creepy forest with no time to sit by the fire. Why couldn't this Slayer have lived in Hawaii? Or hey, maybe Fiji?

Seeming to read her mind, Giles said, "C'mon, Buffy," and waved her toward the door. He shook Eyra's hand warmly. Man, Giles was such a Watcher geek. Always wanting to swap notes with some other Watcher so he could see if Buffy was really as ill-behaved as he thought she was. But she did kick ass. And that was what was important.

And now she had some serious assassin vamp ass to kick.

"Can't she come with us?" Buffy asked.

Giles waved good-bye as he left. "She's waiting for an important communication. Once the beach falls under attack, she must get word to a nearby encampment."

Buffy looked over her shoulder as the door shut. It must be hard to sit home and wait.

They began retracing their steps back through the forest, but as they neared the shore, their guide branched off in a new direction. He turned and said something to Giles, then stooped low. Giles did the same, motioning for Buffy to follow.

"He says that the war party is just over that rise," Giles whispered, motioning to a small hill. "He's going ahead to find the Slayer."

The guide crept stealthily forward.

"Can't we go with him?"

"He says they're using magick up there, and he's not sure how it would react to our presence."

"That sounds ominous."

"Indeed. I suggest we wait here."

Buffy nodded and sat down in the wet, leaf-strewn dirt. She leaned against a tree. She peered up at the branches crowding out the sky. She played with the hem of her cloak. Time passed. The guide did not return.

"Giles, I don't like this." She rose to a crouch.

"Neither do I. Perhaps he had difficulties finding her."

"Or perhaps he ditched us," she offered.

Giles furrowed his brow. "I don't think that's the case. More likely the Romans have attacked, and he felt the need to stave off their advances."

"Or was killed."

Giles peered through the gloom toward the small rise. "Or that."

"I should check it out." She stood up, shaking the pine needles and leaves out of her cloak.

"Let's not separate here," Giles said anxiously. "I imagine getting lost would be enormously easy in this forest."

"Yes," Buffy answered, feeling the trees press in on her. They were listening. She knew it.

Together they crept toward the small rise, seeing the gleaming of firelight on the trunks of nearby trees as they approached. Soon they could hear murmuring, chanting, and then the slow, methodical slosh of paddles in water. As they crested the hill, a startling sight lay before them.

A circle of Druids stood to their left, hands raised to the heavens. They chanted around a stone altar. Blood pooled in a carved-out recess, glistening black in the weak firelight. They wore rough brown woolen robes and had blue spirals painted on their faces, arms, and hands. Long beards hung to their chests and navels. At the base of the hill gathered too many Celtic warriors to count, leaning on spears, gripping swords, stringing bows. Men and women alike stood in leather armor and metal plating over their chests and thighs. Buffy took in faces, arms, and legs painted with woad, a blue dye derived from a plant. Through these tense warriors shifted strange and eerie women with long, free-flowing hair and billowing robes. They wove among the fighters like snakes, slithering and passing between groups, touching a shoulder here, a head there.

The sloshing of boats grew louder, and Buffy strained to make out anything on the black water. With the dying storm had come calmer winds, and the surface of the strait lay glossy and black. Suddenly that stillness broke, and a line of turbulence on the surface stretched as far as she could see.

The Romans were crossing.

The strait came alive with a flotilla of flat-bottomed boats like the one Buffy had stolen. Loaded with men, the boats drew closer. She heard more frantic splashing and saw an entire row of horses swimming alongside the boats—the cavalry attempting to bring their mounts into battle. The men swam next to their horses, struggling under heavy armor.

Mere moments had passed since Buffy and Giles crested the hill. As the Romans approached, a rank of archers lined the bank and fired volleys of arrows. These hissed through the air, felling men in boats and splashing into the water when they missed.

Then the Romans gave up their silence and a single, voluminous roar rose up from their masses. Cries of rage and fear masked as bravado filled the silent night.

The Celts answered with a chorus of wild cries, whoops, trills, and shouts. More arrows cut the air, raining down on the Romans. The first boat reached the shore, and armored legionnaires poured from it, thundering across the beach to the Celts.

The battle had begun, and Buffy and Giles stood in the middle of it.

CHAPTER NINE

At once, the Romans leaped from their boats into the shallows, drawing their swords. Hundreds strong, they streamed onto the shore, shouting. The Celtic warriors rushed forward to meet them.

Buffy's mouth went dry. Raw battle unfolded before her, a cacophonous mass of voices and clashing weapons. To her left she heard the circle of Druids chanting, the sound increasing in volume. They lifted their heads to the sky, calling out, imploring. The trees swayed around them. Wind lifted the branches, sighed, and then roared in the leaves.

And then Buffy realized—it wasn't the wind at all.

The trees themselves moved, lifting earth-covered roots

from the soil. Snaking their way forward, the branches bent and swayed, closing in on the Roman invaders. The forest hissed and sighed. She took a step back, taking it all in, her mouth parting in astonishment. Her heel bumped against something solid and cold. She reached back and felt the reassuring solid mass of a granite boulder. Then it, too, shifted beneath her hand. The rough stone rotated and moved forward. She spun around, staring at it. The rock unfolded itself, lifting a stone head and bringing forth two massive stone arms. Leaning forward, the boulder pulled itself from the earth, sending soil and ferns spilling down the sides of the little rise. The stone was an ancient monolith, covered beneath centuries of dirt. The tip she had felt with her tentative hand was merely the very top. It continued to burrow out of the earth until it stood up, towering thirty feet above her. The lower stone parted into two massive legs. With a single step, it moved twenty feet off the rise, the ground shuddering beneath it.

Giles gripped her arm tightly. She turned to him as he pointed to a neighboring small rise. Another tremendous stone winnowed its way out of the earth there, soil raining off it as it emerged. Buffy had witnessed vampires crawling out of the dirt countless times. This sight left them all behind. The rocks broke and split along their masses, forming arms and legs and tremendous stone heads with fearsome eyes that gleamed red in the darkness.

The tree warriors closed in, now batting Romans off

the beach as if they were made of straw. As a third stone creature joined the first two, the Romans froze, gazing up in horror.

On the beach, the women with long, flowing hair screamed and ran, cloaks streaming out behind them. At their passing, the Celtic warriors worked themselves up into a frenzy. They rushed forward, stabbing the centurions and legionnaires while they stood in shock.

Buffy watched in awe as Roman after Roman stumbled and fell, not even fighting back. The sheer spectacle of the sight froze them to the spot.

Next to her the Druids chanted louder, their cries growing all the more intense and eerie.

On the beach, the same Roman commander she'd seen earlier stepped from a boat. His long red cape billowed behind him. He shouted at his men in Latin, shoved them and forced them into action. Some stumbled beneath his blows, others shook their heads slightly, then raised their swords once more. He strode through the ranks, yelling and berating his men. At once the invasion force came to life. Screaming, the Romans ran inland, clashing with the Celtic warriors.

The tree warriors crashed down heavy limbs upon the Romans, while the stone creatures crushed centurions into the soft mud of the shore. Buffy took in the chaos, the clashing warriors, the screaming, the women running with torches and inciting the troops, the forest come to life to protect its human denizens.

"How in the world are we going to find the Slayer in all this?" she shouted to Giles over the din.

"We need to find our guide. He knows what she looks like."

She looked down at the mesh of struggling bodies at the bottom of the rise. "And how do we do that?" she asked helplessly. Even as she said it, though, she caught a glimpse of a dark green cloak below. At the edge of the fighting, closer to the forest, their guide engaged in heated conversation with a young woman dressed in leather armor and coated with woad. He pointed to the top of the rise where Buffy and Giles stood. She followed his gaze, taking them in. Immediately she wheeled back around, shouting again at the guide. Shaking his head adamantly, he gripped her shoulders, and she shoved him away.

"That's got to be her!" Buffy yelled. "Come on!" Grabbing Giles's arm, she took off down the hill in the direction of the Slayer. But before she reached the bottom, two figures emerged from the clashing warriors. Dressed in cloaks and woolen tunics, at first Buffy thought they were other Celts. But then she noticed the footwear of the second. He wore twentieth-century combat boots.

As Buffy raced down the slope, her feet sliding in loose mud, the two figures reached the Slayer. In the din of combat, the girl did not notice them, just continued to argue with the guide. As Buffy shouted for her to turn, the vampires closed the distance.

Buffy slid and stumbled, righted herself, and sloshed desperately through the oozing mud. As it sucked at her feet, pulling one of her boots off completely, the closer vampire rushed forward. He pulled out a dagger and buried it deep in the Celtic Slayer's back.

CHAPTER TEN

Pulling her feet free, Buffy raced to the other Slayer. Incinii's eyes went wide, and she fell forward into the guide's arms. The two vamps spotted Buffy, astonishment on their faces. One actually shook his head in disbelief. She'd half expected them to run away. They'd murdered the Slayer, and Buffy had failed. Now their expressions changed. They looked at Buffy with hatred and contempt, arrogantly believing they could kill her, too.

But just as she reached the spot, she saw the Celtic Slayer stand up again, wheeling angrily on the two assassins. Quickly the guide readjusted Incinii's leather armor straps across her back. One of them had blocked the blow,

Buffy realized. Incinii was far from murdered. The guide pointed to Buffy, shouting at Incinii above the cacophony around them.

Incinii nodded at her and circled the vampires warily to join Buffy at her side. Clasping Buffy's forearm in greeting, she grinned and said something incomprehensible. Then both of them turned to face their enemies.

Now, with two Slayers bearing down on them, the assassin vamps didn't look so bold. They started to back away, eyes darting around to spot possible escape routes. Another stone warrior emerged from the darkness. The vampire in combat boots shuddered slightly as the creature stepped clear over him to reach the beach. His face contorted in fear, and he looked at his partner, eyes wide.

"Don't freak out on me, Jason!" said the other vamp, seeing the look in his cohort's eyes. "Let's just get this done." Then he turned to Buffy, his eyes sharp and keen, his body ready to fight. "I've killed you twice before," he said to her, "and I'm going to do it again."

"Thanks for volunteering," she told him. "I wasn't sure which one of you losers to dust first." She sounded brave, but inside, his words hit hard. What did he mean? Had she herself been one of the Slayers they tried to kill? She swallowed hard. Had they tried to kill her when she was just a kid? What had gone wrong?

"Victor!" Jason cried nervously, interrupting her thoughts. "This isn't the best place to fight!" He leaped back as a group of Celtic warriors crashed into him, struggling with three Roman centurions. A tree limb swung down, connecting with one of the Romans' helmets, opening it with a crack. Buffy saw blood spray over Jason. He blinked it out of his eyes, regaining his balance. "We're going to get squashed!"

"Just kill the Celtic Slayer. Finish our mission. That's all," Victor ordered him, not taking his eyes off Buffy. Jason raced forward to join the other vampire.

"Can't we take this fight somewhere else?" Jason shouted. "I have a bad feeling about this."

In her peripheral vision, Buffy took in the chaos around her. Off to her left, she spotted Giles crouching in the dense foliage. She hoped he wouldn't get himself squished. Beyond them, toward the beach, bloody bodies tangled and clashed. War cries and trills resonated in the air. Arrows whined and hit home. Swords clacked sharply against shields. Men screamed in agony. One boulder creature waded out into the dark waters and drowned the Romans as they tried to land.

It was not the best place for a personal fight. The vamp had a point.

But then Victor raced forward, bending low at the last minute and sweeping his leg out. His foot caught Buffy in the knee and she turned quickly, deflecting much of the blow. He leaped upright, thrusting his palm out and connecting with her chin. She reeled backward, struck a tree. Using it as a brace, she kicked him hard as he closed in again, connecting with his solar plexus. He bent over, gripping his chest. Buffy jumped up, grabbed hold of a branch, and swung, kicking Victor in the face with both feet. He stumbled backward, crashing down into the mud.

Next to her, Incinii struggled with Jason, who despite being scared was doing a damn fine job. Too good a job. He pinned Incinii against a boulder and produced a knife from inside his cloak. As Victor turned and threw a kick, Buffy leaped over his leg, landing next to Incinii. She struck Jason hard on the arm, then grabbed it and wrenched it around, snapping it at the elbow. The knife tumbled to the forest floor.

Incinii kicked him hard in the stomach, then picked up a jagged shard of wood from the ground. Strong arms clenched around Buffy's throat from behind. She slammed her foot down into Victor's instep, grabbed his arms, and flung him harshly over her shoulder. His head cracked against the boulder, leaving a smear of glistening blood behind.

He stood up, feeling the blood seeping from his scalp. "That hurt, Slayer!" he shouted.

"Good!"

Again he pulled out his knife, the one he'd stabbed Incinii with. "Let's end this!"

"I couldn't agree more," she retorted, glancing over at Incinii. She stood on top of Jason, who lay prone in the mud, spitting pine needles out of his mouth. She arced the wooden stake in the air, and then Victor rushed to meet Buffy. She snapped her head back to him, dodging out of the way and tripping him as he passed. He leaped back up, recovering more quickly than she expected, reeling and striking her hard in the kidney. She caught the flash of steel, saw the knife zipping in, and then the earth shuddered and rose up beneath them. They rolled, falling into the dirt.

The boulder with Victor's blood rose upward, two great eyes blinking open, taking them in. As Buffy struggled to stand up, a mouth rose into view, full of sharp stone teeth. Then a pair of massive shoulders, followed by a thick torso. The earth heaved up again, sending Buffy and Victor tumbling down the rising slope.

A few feet away, Jason threw Incinii off him, rolling over on top of her. She kneed him in the chest, flinging him away, and he slid down the loose mud. The stone creature emerged fully from the earth, glaring down at Jason. The vampire did not notice. Instead, he righted himself at the bottom of the slope, found his fallen knife, and marched angrily back toward Incinii.

A tremendous stone foot crashed down on him, pulverizing his bones. When the massive weight lifted, Buffy saw a disgusting tangle of flesh and splintered bone. Incinii jumped up, wiped mud out of her eyes, and drove the stake deeply into the mess. Dust billowed around her as she struck the heart.

Incinii looked up at the stone creature and grinned.

"Damn you!" Victor cursed, suddenly staggering to his feet. "Jason!" he shouted.

He dashed forward to his fallen comrade. Dust settled in the massive footprint, the only sign of his friend. Victor wheeled on Incinii, his eyes enraged. "Now I kill you for myself!" he shouted, rushing toward her.

A shadow fell over him as the tremendous stone creature raised its foot again.

Victor stopped short. He stared up at the massive rock, then back at Incinii. With one long glance at Buffy, he turned and ran full speed into the mass of clashing warriors. Buffy tried to follow, muscling her way through, but she heard Giles calling to her, urging her to return.

She pulled out just as a spear narrowly missed her. It wouldn't be the smartest thing to charge into the battle.

She ran to where Incinii stood, and Giles joined them. "We need to track the assassin on the other side of the struggle," he urged them. "We can't possibly fight our way through that. We'd surely be killed."

They stared at the continuing battle before them. The massive stone warrior stepped out onto the beach, joining its friends. "Let's go!" Buffy shouted, running along the edge of the skirmish. She hoped they could pick up Victor's trail on the other side.

Suddenly another vampire burst out of the bushes, closing in on the fleeing assassin. "Victor!" the emerging figure shouted. "Don't leave without me!" Buffy continued the chase. A few minutes later a bright flash of light brought her eyes to the sky. A vortex appeared about a mile away, spiraling and brilliant. "They're going back!" Giles shouted.

"You mean that's it? They're giving up?"

"Apparently. For now."

Incinii stared at the dizzying vortex. She asked Giles a question, which he answered at length. Buffy couldn't understand a word. She didn't like this. Who was the fleeing figure who'd stayed out of the fight altogether? The elusive Lucien? And why would they give up like that? Sure, their fellow assassin had died, but it didn't make sense to come all the way back here and then give up—unless he was planning on coming back at a different time. He was definitely outgunned this time. But they'd made the decision in an instant, and left so quickly. Why not bide their time to kill her in the same visit? It didn't make sense.

Unless, she thought, *unless this is only* one *of his stops.*

"He's going to kill another Slayer," Buffy said, turning to Giles. "We've got to follow him!"

Giles stopped, searching her face in the darkness. Incinii stood silently by, glancing back toward the battle.

"You think they've targeted more than one Slayer?" he asked.

"That's got to be it. They must have more options. They have all of time. They can travel anywhere, to any time period. Right now, another Slayer is about to die. We've got to stop them!"

CHAPTER ELEVEN

As the portal tugged at their hair and clothes, Victor took a final glance around ancient Britain. Once again, he'd lost his best friend. What was the point of Lucien saving him, only to lose him in the next time jump? Lucien and Victor readied themselves for the trip back to 1998. This wasn't the kind of travel Victor preferred. Too nauseating.

"What do we do now?" Victor asked above the roar of wind.

"We kill the next Slayer."

"What about Buffy?" Victor asked, curious about Lucien's reaction. "She knows about this."

"We can't be certain that she knows about the others. My

guess is she stumbled onto our hideout and took the primitive version of the spell for 60 C.E."

"You left that lying around?" Victor asked, incredulous.

"It was a rough draft! It didn't even land us on the island, remember? When we tested it out, it put us on the Welsh mainland. Besides, it's the only spell I left there. She doesn't even know we've targeted more than one Slayer."

"If she knows where the hideout is, she can catch up to us there," Victor pointed out.

"We have no reason to go back. We have the incantations." Lucien patted his jacket. "You've got a copy too, and so does Gorga in case we fail."

"That ought to be rich." Victor thought of the three-hundred-pound slab of meat with the battle-ax.

"We just move on to the next Slayer. There's no sense returning to a time period Buffy has the incantation for. We'd just be fighting her over and over."

"Sounds like fun," Victor growled, eager to fight her again.

The portal gained in intensity, lifting them off their feet. Together the assassins vanished into the future, ready to kill again.

CHAPTER TWELVE

As the vampires' portal faded in the distance, Giles gathered his thoughts, formulating a plan. "Okay. Right now we need to regroup. It's important we not think of time as our enemy. We don't have to rush. We can think this out. No matter when they've targeted another Slayer, we have time to return to 1998 and figure it out."

"But, Giles! They could be killing her right now!"

Giles gripped her shoulder. "No. They are killing her in another time period, just like this one. We will find out when, and arrive at the same time as the assassins, just as we did this time."

"It makes my head hurt, Giles."

He looked at her reassuringly. "Let's go find Willow and Xander and return to 1998."

"Right. Okay. We do a little recon work, find out where they went, and follow them. How will we find Lucien? We only have the one spell."

"Are you sure there were no others in the cavern room?" Giles asked.

"Positive. I collected every scrap of paper in there."

"Then he must be keeping any other incantations on his person," Giles surmised.

"So how do we find him? Wait in that little room? He'll notice that I've been there, or that someone's been there, anyway," she pointed out. "He might move to another location."

"When we return, we can have Angel put surveillance on the room. If they move, we'll know."

Buffy agreed. It made sense.

Giles turned to Incinii, speaking to her urgently. She shook her head, pointing back toward the battle, then launched into a lengthy monologue, which Giles asked her to repeat twice.

Buffy followed as they turned around, heading back toward the beach. Giles explained as they walked. "I believe I understood most of her response. I told her we needed to rejoin our friends, whom we left back by a bonfire. She responded that if her Slayer duties were finished for tonight, then she must rejoin the battle. She will help us find our guide, and he will lead us back."

They walked a little farther in silence, Incinii turning to smile apologetically at Buffy. She saw something in the Celtic Slayer's eyes—a kind of age, wisdom, and deep sadness. Buffy realized she was lucky in comparison. She definitely had issue with living her teenage years dusting vamps in graveyards and slicing the heads off demons. But while Sunnydale was certainly under continuous attacks by the forces of darkness, at least it was not also under attack by marauding invaders. She briefly imagined what Incinii must feel, torn between defending her home against an invading army and simultaneously fighting off the usual vampires, praying mantis women, and mother Bezor demons. Incinii must get close to no time to shop. And Buffy also imagined she rarely felt safe. Even when she'd spent an evening slaying, Incinii contended with the looming threat of Roman invaders. Plus Giles had told her that Incinii had struggled with the night terror demon for years, a creature Buffy herself had faced. The beast repeatedly took over Incinii's body while she slept. She couldn't rest peacefully. For her, it never ended.

As they hurried back toward the battle, Buffy watched Incinii straighten, then check her armor clasps, her short sword and bow. She was a warrior, made for battle. Unlike Buffy, though, she seemed to be eagerly anticipating the conflict. Even now Buffy caught her smiling, awaiting the fight before her. Buffy didn't enjoy fighting, didn't enjoy killing and destroying things, even when they were evil. The day she did enjoy it would be the day she lost something integral to her soul.

The clashing of swords on metal grew louder, and then Buffy could hear the screams of pure agony and terror. When they crested the rise once again, she sucked in her breath in horror. The Romans had lit the Celtic warriors on fire. Everywhere she looked, figures bathed in flame raced to and fro, shrieking in anguish. The Druids who had been gathered in a circle no longer stood there. Buffy couldn't make them out in the chaos. One of the stone creatures had fallen, lifeless, onto the beach, and Roman archers climbed it to fire arrows from higher ground.

The smell of burning hair and flesh hung heavily in the air, and Buffy felt her gorge rise in her throat. Incinii screamed in anger and lifted her sword high. She rushed down onto the warfield, trilling out a battle cry. She struck down one Roman centurion, then another, driving her sword deep into their bellies and throats. As she waded into the combat, she threw down burning warriors and smothered flames with their fallen cloaks. Wheeling, she dragged a Roman cavalryman from his saddle and viciously slit his throat. When Buffy last caught sight of her, Incinii was mounting the stolen horse and riding into the thick of the battle, striking downward with her sword.

This was a different world. Completely foreign. Buffy couldn't imagine killing other humans and was glad she didn't have to defend her homeland like this. As the firelight flickered on the glinting, bloody armor of the Romans, Buffy stood utterly still. The screaming around her grew so intense it almost felt like it came from inside her own head. Men and women on fire shrieked and panicked. Romans stole torches and lit the forest on fire. Another stone giant toppled, and a tree creature ground to a halt. The Druid magick was not holding together. The Romans broke their circle, and now, with flames licking at the trunks of trees, they desecrated the sacred forest.

"We need to leave," Giles said, "now!"

"But, Giles," Buffy argued, shocked at the horrific scene before her. "We can't just go—these people need help!"

Giles grabbed her shoulders, forcing her to look at him. "Buffy," he said firmly, "this happened a long time ago. I know it feels very immediate right now, but all this happened more than two thousand years ago. These events unfolded just as we see them now."

"But, Giles!" she pressed, watching a woman dive into the dirt, desperately trying to quench the flames engulfing her hair.

"We must go. These events have to occur as they did historically. We can't interfere, or we're no better than Lucien. Besides, if we change the sequence of events, we could even make this worse."

"It doesn't feel right!" Buffy insisted.

"I know it doesn't," Giles agreed, looking around him. "But the two of us couldn't do much good here anyway. The Romans are just too powerful, too many in number. It's why they won."

He turned her away from the scene, forcing her to move off the rise, down the slope. "What about Incinii?" she asked.

"She'll be fine," Giles reassured her. "She's one of the longest-lived Slayers. She lives through this night. She lives a long time."

Feeling hollow and haunted, Buffy allowed Giles to lead her into the quiet of the forest. "I don't think we're going to find our guide," he said. He peered into the forest. "And I don't know about you, but I don't think I'd be able to make my way back to the bonfire where we left the others."

Buffy stared in that direction too. She thought of the meandering way the guide had led them. "Not a chance."

"We might be able to retrace our footsteps back to the cabin, though," Giles said. "Then Eyra can lead us to the bonfire."

Buffy thought of the trees, alive and sinuous, and dreaded returning to that crawling forest. She swallowed her fear and followed Giles into the darkness.

CHAPTER THIRTEEN

After only twenty minutes of stumbling lost through the forest, they spotted the flickering candlelight from Eyra's cabin.

"Oh, what a relief!" Giles sighed, unable to help himself. He didn't want to let Buffy know how nervous the willowy trees made him.

He rapped on the door, and in a few moments Eyra opened it hurriedly. Her expression visibly fell when he saw it was only them. "Did you see her?" she asked Giles in Old Welsh.

"Yes," Giles answered.

"And is she . . . ?" the Watcher's voice trailed off.

"She's fighting. And doing quite well the last time we saw her."

"Thank the gods for that," Eyra responded, letting out a sigh of relief. "She is so stubborn. I ordered her not to fight, then I begged her."

"I know how you feel," Giles said sympathetically, with a sidelong glance at Buffy.

Eyra frowned. "But then again, I myself am involved. I just sent word to the other encampment. Now I must just wait here, hoping Incinii is all right."

Eyra then remembered her manners and invited them in. But Giles said, "Actually, could you help us get back to our friends? I'm afraid we lost our guide in the ruckus of battle." At least, that's what he hoped he said. His Old Welsh wasn't exactly spanking accurate.

Eyra nodded. "I can walk you back there. The guide mentioned you'd been at Fendoch's fire."

"Thank you. It's time we left."

"And where exactly did you hail from?" asked Eyra.

Giles paused, unsure of what to say. Then he told Eyra the truth, that they'd come from a land on the other side of the world. As far as current archaeological evidence held, these people had not yet visited North America. Eyra marveled at his explanation. Giles decided not to mention the time bit. "You must tell me about it!" Eyra said curiously, perking up for the first time since they'd met.

Giles agreed, hoping he wouldn't throw off the time

continuum by talking vaguely about California. Eyra closed her cabin door, glancing hopefully one last time down the path that led from the beach. No sign of Incinii.

Then, with Giles describing the wonders of Sunnydale, they started off for Fendoch's fire.

Thirty minutes later Buffy and Giles arrived at the roaring bonfire where they'd left Willow and Xander. Eyra bowed, saying her good-byes, and melted away into the shadows. To Buffy's utter relief, her two friends still sat next to the flickering flames. Color shone on Willow's face. Her cheeks stood out, ruddy and healthy. Her lips were pink instead of blue.

"Buffy!" she cried out as they drew near. She leaped up and hugged her friend.

Xander stood up, squashing Buffy at the same time. "I'm so glad to see you! Can we get out of here now?"

Giles regarded the group hug sadly. "I was in mortal jeopardy as well, you know."

"Oh, Giles," Willow said, breaking away and hugging him, too. Xander just extended his Buffy hug until she pulled away. "So did you find the assassins?" Willow asked, turning back to Buffy.

"Yes. And killed one of them. But the other got away. And there was someone else, too, hiding in the shadows. He ran off too."

Xander raised his eyebrows incredulously. "You're kidding."

"Unfortunately not," Giles said. "And Buffy has a theory that this is only the first of a series of attempts on Slayers' lives."

"We have to get back to 1998 and figure out who the next target is," she explained.

"As long as we get off this creepy island," Xander whispered, glancing surreptitiously around at the nearby stones glistening with blood.

Giles motioned for them to follow. "I suggest we move away from witnesses before opening the portal."

All four took turns bowing and thanking the Celtic warriors for allowing them the use of their fire. They smiled, grasping the visitors' arms in parting, but Buffy clearly saw the grayness beneath the smiles, the worries of the incoming Roman army. Once again she felt the pang of abandoning people who needed help. But Giles was right, she supposed. This wasn't their fight. It had been waged long ago without her help. Tonight would have to be no different.

Following Giles off into the dark of the forest, Buffy forced herself to go.

They gathered together, and Giles spoke the incantation. In moments the portal expanded into view, brilliant and swirling. A wind kicked up, sucking leaves and pine needles into the vortex. Buffy's hair whipped toward the spiraling light and then she felt drawn toward it, feet sliding in the mud. The force grew in strength, and she fought the urge to grab on to something. Her feet lifted off the ground and she careened headfirst into the vortex. Willow's hand found hers, and they screamed as their velocity increased. Just when she thought they would crash headlong into concrete on the other side, the speed cut down. Her stomach lurched. In the next instant the light dimmed and winked out, and they tumbled out onto asphalt. A car honked and swerved around them, its headlights blinding Buffy. She closed her eyes to the night. Willow landed on top of her, then Giles and Xander smacked onto the ground to their left.

As more cars braked and honked, Buffy forced herself to stand and drag Willow out of the street. They'd landed in downtown Sunnydale, she saw with bleary eyes. She staggered into the street again, grabbed Giles's foot and Xander's wrist, and dragged them out of harm as well. Then she collapsed on the sidewalk, nausea rising in her throat. From a club nearby, she could hear the distant strains of "One Week" by the Barenaked Ladies. They were definitely in 1998. Now they just had to find out who the next targeted Slayer was and dive into the dizzying wormhole once again.

She had to find Lucien.

She struggled to stay on her feet and failed. As she fell to her knees, a second blinding flash of light startled her. She closed her eyes against the brightness and felt another body slam into hers. She fell on her side. Whoever it was weighed a ton.

She rolled the person off her and turned to face him. She didn't recognize the man. He was a vampire. She knew that instinctively. His clothing style dated from at least the early eighteen hundreds, but they were new. His long brown hair was pulled back in a ponytail and affixed with a black ribbon. She grabbed him by the back of his neck, forcing him to his feet.

"Lucien, I presume?" she asked him.

The vampire whimpered. "Oh, damn."

Holding him, she looked up to the sky to see a second portal spinning just to the left of their own. Another vampire flew out of their vortex, landing near Giles.

Lucien twisted in Buffy's grip, and she slammed him against the alley wall. "You leave before us, and we still arrive first. Tough luck." He tried to throw her off. She stood her ground. "Don't make me dust you. You might live a whole extra day if you cooperate."

"How generous," he snarled.

Groggy, the second vamp rose to his feet. "Giles!" Buffy shouted. "Get him!"

Giles lay on the ground, shaking his head lightly. "Get whom?" he mumbled.

"The other assassin!" Briefly she thought of dragging Lucien over to Victor, trying to get them both. But she knew Victor was too good a fighter for her to pull it off. Lucien had stayed out of the action on Anglesey, which meant he thought himself too good to get his hands dirty in combat. Even now he only struggled slightly in her grasp. She could even feel him trembling beneath her grip.

"Xander!" she shouted. "Willow! Get him!" Victor chanced a look over his shoulder at the Slayer, taking in his boss's condition.

"Lucien!" he shouted. "Damn it! I can't always cover your sorry ass!"

"Go on without me," Lucien called back. "Just carry out the plan."

"Shut up," Buffy yelled, slapping her hand over his mouth and punching him in the stomach. He licked her hand, and she involuntarily pulled it away in disgust.

"Enlist help. You remember," Lucien reminded Victor.

"Yeah, yeah," Victor said, and darted away down the alley.

"Get him!" Buffy yelled again to her friends. "Or come guard this guy!"

Stumbling, Giles rushed to her side, pinning Lucien against the brick.

Buffy gave chase on unsteady legs, running through the dark alley. Ahead she heard a garbage can overturn, the crash of glass bottles rolling and shattering on asphalt.

He wasn't far ahead.

She picked up speed, her head swimming with the motion. Dizziness claimed her and she tripped, stumbled on a high crack in the cement, and righted herself. She ran on.

A dog barked, and she turned the corner in that direction. Ahead she saw Victor's fleeing figure. His woolen cloak bloomed out behind him as he ran. He, too, staggered, still intoxicated from the vortex's effect.

At an intersection, he headed away from the graveyard, away from the entrance to the underground tunnels. He was trying to mislead her. But it didn't matter. She knew where the hidden room was. In time, Victor would realize that she knew it too.

He darted out of view around a corner, and she reached the spot a few seconds later. The alley was a dead end. She peered up, catching his fleeing shape jumping from rooftop to rooftop above.

Damn. She couldn't catch him now.

She tried anyway, running along the base of the buildings, but ultimately lost him in the maze of the warehouse district.

By now she felt completely putrid, and she stopped to catch her breath.

"Bad trip?" asked a voice behind her.

She spun to see Angel standing there. "Don't do that!" she told him, her heart hammering from the start he'd given her.

"Sorry." He came closer to her, took her in his arms. "You're wet."

"It was raining."

"I think I remember what that is," he said wryly. Buffy was glad she wouldn't experience a drenching like that in Sunnydale.

"Did you get them?" he asked.

She shook her head. "One of them. Caught another."

"That's something."

"Not enough. One got away. The worst one."

He put his arms around her. Kissed her forehead. He brought his hand up under her chin and lifted her head. His lips pressed against her, and Buffy felt the stress and tension of the trip spill out of her, replaced by a pleasant tingling feeling of excitement.

She kissed him back passionately.

Then she pulled away, keeping her arms around him. "How long were we gone?"

"An hour," Angel told her.

An hour? She couldn't believe it.

"I left the others back there with Lucien."

He raised his eyebrows. "He's the one you caught?"

"Yep."

"I'd like to meet the guy."

"I'd like to beat the guy," she retorted. "This way."

She led Angel back to the others, who now stood circled around Lucien, held firmly by Giles.

"Ah, Angel," Giles greeted him. "How long were we gone?"

"An hour," chorused Buffy and Angel.

"Wow, that's all?" Willow asked, amazed.

Xander regarded her knowledgeably. "That's the way it is with time travel. What's an eternity in one time period is a mere blink of an eye in another."

"Yes, Mr. Expert," Giles said blithely as Lucien struggled in his grasp. "Let's get our criminal mastermind here back to the library."

Lucien sneered at them in contempt. "What are you going to do with me?"

"Torture you," Buffy told him, narrowing her eyes at him. "But first . . ." She strode forward and frisked him, immediately finding the folded incantations in his jacket pocket. She opened them, then scanned the page. "Thank you," she said.

"Ooh, may I?" asked Giles, holding his hand out for the pages. She swapped with him, a handful of pages for a stranglehold on Lucien. Together they all marched toward the library.

At the library, Buffy pushed Lucien into the cage and locked it. It mainly held file cabinets, but it doubled as a handy lockup. Over time, they'd captured quite a few people and left them in that same cage, Xander among them. Last year he'd been possessed by a hyena demon, and they'd locked him in there while they figured out how to cure him.

Now Lucien scowled on the other side of the cage door grating. "This stops nothing," he told Buffy.

"Oh, I think it stops a great deal," she said, waving the incantations in front of him.

His frown deepened. "If that's all of them."

Buffy bluffed. "Well, I have a feeling it is. Mainly because you wouldn't reveal to me just now that there were more if there actually were. You'd just bide your time, hoping I wouldn't figure that part out. You wouldn't just give it away. You may not look it, but you must have a modicum of intelligence to have gotten this far."

Lucien blanched at the insult, and Buffy knew immediately that his intellectual ego would be a good weapon to wield against him.

"I'll watch him if you want to talk," Angel offered. He crossed his arms, staring in at Lucien threateningly.

"Thanks." Buffy glanced at the clock.

"You know, we have a little bit of time, and it would be worth it to do things right," Giles told her, noticing her anxiousness. "Whenever we leave for the next jump, we'll still arrive at the same time as the assassins. We can take a little time to eat something and prepare for the next trip."

"Are you serious?" Xander asked, then turned to his friend. "Will. Pizza."

"Definitely," she agreed.

"Great," Giles said. "You two bring us back food, pizza if it has to be," he added distastefully. "Buffy and I will plan."

They nodded and left the library, discussing toppings.

Buffy grew excited at the thought of food. She hadn't eaten in more than twenty hours, and her stomach growled voraciously. She hoped they'd return soon with cheesy goodness.

"Giles," she said, gesturing with her chin at his office.

He nodded, and they entered the office. "Okay. What do we need to do?"

Giles opened his notebook where he'd translated the three spells. "There are three time periods here. A Civil War Slayer named Agatha Primrose, a Sumerian Slayer named Ejuk, and a

Slayer named Marguerite Allard, who lived during the French Revolution."

"Civil War? French Revolution? Why do I have a feeling this is going to be even worse than Anglesey?"

"Because it probably will be," Giles answered. He glanced out of the small window in the door at the cage. "After all, getting caught in the crossfire of a war waged with guns will be far more dangerous. Lucien can survive gunshot wounds. We can't."

"I'd like to give him something pointier than a bullet and see if he survives that." Buffy glared at him.

"We need him alive for now," Giles reminded her.

"I know," Buffy said. "But I just want to stake that smug look off his face." She turned back to the translations. "So which Slayer do we save first?"

Giles leaned back in his chair. "It shouldn't matter, actually. Remember, we'll arrive at the same time as the assassins in all the time periods."

"Ack. I get it. So we just choose whichever one we want?"

"Essentially, though we may want to choose the French Revolution last."

"Why is that?" She sat down on the edge of his desk.

"We'll have to have proper attire for that—long pants, and specifically liberty hats and red, white, and blue cockades."

"Why?"

"So we don't get our heads cut off."

"Good idea. That would put a crimp in the plans."

"Indeed." He stood up. "Let's raid the drama department again."

"Giles! You're such a ruffian!"

He grinned. "I know."

In the costume closet of the drama room, they found some simple shirts, pants, and dresses made of light cotton and polyester. "I'm afraid none of these will do. The styles and material are all wrong," Giles said. He picked up a few headdresses and some earrings from a box of jewelry. "You could wear this, I suppose," he told her, handing her a headdress. Made of cheap, bronze-colored metal, it sported three flowers sprouting from the back of it.

She eyed it dubiously. "Is this authentic?"

"Well, not authentic metal, but the style is pretty accurate. These come from that talent show act last year—the one where the students recited part of the *Epic of Gilgamesh*."

"The epic of who?"

"Gilgamesh. He was a Sumerian king. He happens to be *the* Sumerian king in the era we're traveling back to."

She picked up one of the blue cotton dresses. It was made of old T-shirts, she realized. "And you don't think they'd buy this?"

Giles set down a shirt he was holding and regarded her resolutely. "Well, I suppose they'll more likely 'buy' this, as you say, than suspect we're actually time travelers from the future there to thwart an assassination on a secret Slayer of vampires."

Buffy held up the headdress. It was lined with tinfoil on the inside. “I’m not so sure. Isn’t there some costume shop we can go to?”

Giles looked at his watch. “That’s not a bad idea.” Returning armfuls of the clothing to the closet, Giles chattered excitedly. “This really is quite fascinating,” he told her over a mound of hastily sewn shirts. Buffy thought she spied some gold lamé peeking out coyly. *That* definitely wasn’t authentic.

Back in his office, they thumbed through the phone book and found a costume shop that was still open. Willow and Xander returned with the pizza, which they all devoured with abandon. Even Giles ate a few slices.

Then he left her to brief the others and departed for the costume shop. Buffy dreaded the getup he would rent. Xander stood terrified, convinced his outfit would involve tights.

“They didn’t wear tights in any of these places, Xander,” Willow assured him. “We’re not visiting an eighteenth-century court in Vienna or anything. We’re going to look like farmers. Something subtle.”

“Except that ‘liberty cap’ thing. That doesn’t sound subtle. What is it?”

Buffy shook her head. “He didn’t elaborate. It’s for the best.” She frowned.

“What is it?” Angel asked, sensing her preoccupation.

“Something Victor said back there.” She looked at them, lowering her voice so Lucien couldn’t hear. “He said he’d killed me twice before.”

"What does that mean?" Angel asked.

"That's what I wondered." She frowned. "Unless they've already been back in time and killed me."

"But they didn't. You're here," Angel pointed out.

Xander regarded her thoughtfully. "She's only here in this point in the time line. If they'd traveled back in time and killed her, she would have ceased to exist in the future, and she never would have known the difference."

"So what happened?" she asked Xander.

"It must have failed for some reason. They obviously didn't kill you, because you're here."

"But Victor said he *did* kill me."

"Well, maybe he traveled back in time afterward and unkilled you, restoring the time line," Xander suggested.

"Why would he do that?" Angel asked.

"Maybe killing the Buffster didn't have the effect they were going for. Maybe things got worse."

"Of course things would be worse," Willow agreed. "Sunnydale would be hell on earth."

"Exactly," Xander said. "So they obviously failed, because despite its overly balmy temperatures at times, and its not so stellar nightlife, it is decidedly not hell on earth."

An hour later Giles returned, boxes of costumes in hand. Quickly they rummaged through them, selecting outfits.

Buffy chose a light blue linen dress for the Sumerian trip. Giles said linen would make them appear upper-crusty and educated. They'd have an easier time talking to people that way, he explained. Buffy didn't see how she'd be able to talk to anyone at all in ancient Sumerian. It wasn't exactly a foreign language elective at Sunnydale High.

They'd have to heavily rely on Giles, except during the American Civil War, to communicate their needs. She'd keep careful watch on him during the time jumps. No more hapless knocks on the head for Giles.

He gave them all simple cloth satchels, each filled with a pencil, paper, a bottle of water, and in Buffy's case, stakes. After putting on a brown linen dress with a fancy metalwork belt, Willow sat down at her computer. She downloaded several maps they would need: the Sumerian city of Uruk in 2700 B.C.E., Paris in 1792, and maps of 1862 Tennessee, near Pittsburg Landing, in the vicinity of that Slayer's farmhouse.

Suddenly she grew pale. "Oh, no . . . April sixth, 1862, Pittsburg Landing . . . I thought that name sounded familiar."

"What is it, Will?" Buffy asked.

She looked up. "The Battle of Shiloh. That's the morning of one of the bloodiest battles of the Civil War."

Lucien laughed inside the cage. "Have fun," he told them.

Giles scowled at him. "Be quiet," he ordered. He placed a gentle hand on Willow's shoulder. "Download battle maps. We need to know where the troops are, where the heavy combat occurred. We should be able to avoid the conflict."

"If you could control exactly where you land," Lucien sneered, "which you can't. You'll be instantly cut down by gunfire."

Willow's eyes grew wider.

"Or maybe just have your head blown off by a cannon-ball," he continued.

Buffy walked over to the cage, placing her hands on her hips. "Well, that would kill off your boys, too, wouldn't it?" she asked.

Lucien shut up.

She turned back to her friends, taking in their Sumerian costumes. Xander wore a handsome brown tunic, tied in the front with a gold thread. Giles wore a similar style, in blue linen with a silver tie.

Willow printed out copies of the maps, and they added them to their satchel contents. Giles studied the Watcher journals, then gathered the others close. "This Slayer is named Ejuk. She lives in the city of Uruk."

Angel walked to Buffy and embraced her. "Don't worry about this loser," he said, hooking his thumb at Lucien. "I'll make sure he doesn't go anywhere."

"Thank you, Angel," she told him, pulling back to meet his eyes. "I wish you could come with us."

"Me too."

Buffy thought again of their daylight arrival in Wales and knew Angel was right to stay behind. Besides, now they needed him here to guard Lucien. She stood on her toes, kissing him softly on the mouth. He returned the kiss, and her stomach erupted in pleasant butterflies.

Then she shouldered her satchel and turned to Giles. "Let's go kick some vampire ass."

Giles nodded and unfolded the incantation for ancient Sumeria. He spoke the words loud and clear, though his voice trembled. As the wormhole opened in the air above them, Buffy didn't know what to expect. She only knew her next stop would take her into the heart of the most ancient civilization on Earth.

CHAPTER FOURTEEN

Uruk, 2700 B.C.E.

Buffy braced herself as the wormhole spat her out into a watery trench. Her hands and legs gushed into wet soil, and her nostrils filled with the rich scent of earth and vegetation. She rolled over in time to see Xander hurtling toward her. She tried to leap up on wobbly legs and fell over again. Xander landed with a loud *plop* in a neighboring trench. Then Willow and Giles appeared as silhouettes in the bright vortex.

They tumbled out, crashing into a row of short green plants nearby.

They lay in an irrigated field, Buffy realized. She propped herself up on one elbow and looked out over their surroundings. Squinting, she watched the dazzling light from the portal before it winked out. With her hands sinking into the freshly tilled soil, she stared out in wonder at the scene before her.

In the distance stretched vast fields of crops. Nearby, about a quarter of a mile away, stood an immense wall of clay bricks, elaborately painted and inlaid with images: dragons, creatures that looked to be half goat and half fish, kings and queens before retinues of servants. She'd expected to land in a sweltering desert, but instead they'd arrived in a lush, vegetated area. To her left roared the vast waters of the Euphrates River. Palms lined the shore. Reeds grew thick in the shallows along the banks. With a clear blue sky above them, and a fragrant breeze drifting off the river, it was heavenly. Buffy felt a strange stirring inside, almost of familiarity. *Maybe because the temperature and humidity are similar to Southern California?* she thought.

Giles was the next to sit up. He groaned. "Perhaps we should consider building a small cushioned vehicle of some sort to travel within," he suggested, rubbing his head.

Buffy had to admit, that sounded pretty good. Right now her knee throbbed from hitting a rock in the field.

Willow and Xander struggled up as well. "Wow," Willow said. "This weather! The air feels . . ."

"Fresh," Xander answered. "It's unpolluted." He breathed deeply.

Buffy herself felt a little heady from all the oxygen. She supposed breathing yellow smog every day for the first sixteen years of her life had left her somewhat ill-equipped for fresh air.

The air must have been fresh in Wales, too, but with the thick humidity and pouring rain, she hadn't noticed it. Now, she breathed in the fragrant air and felt the warmth of sunlight on her face.

They stood up, appraising one another in the bright sun. They weren't too muddy, just a splotch here and there. Giles checked his satchel, making sure all the books were still inside. After pulling out a map and studying it for a few minutes, he pointed to the wall and said, "That's the north gate of Uruk. We need to pass through to the city."

Over the wall rose a dazzling array of buildings—immense ziggurats, a tremendous bell tower, and a variety of temples and columned buildings. Nervousness bloomed in Buffy's stomach. While they were nearly three thousand years earlier than their last time jump, this civilization towered before her, monumental and staggeringly real. Their visit to the Druids, mainly spent in forests, could almost have been in any century. With the exception of the people—armored Romans and woad-streaked Celts—the land itself was so untouched that Buffy imagined it might look the same today. But this was not the case with Uruk. Before her stood a vast and ancient city, vibrantly new and fresh. In her own time, this area, now lush and green, was present-day Iraq, a desert full of dust and ruins. Yet here lay the start of civilization itself, the first great cities. She'd read of them in Western Civilization, been bored into daydreaming during her teacher's lectures. But here Uruk was, real and inviting, and Buffy found herself speechless at its gates.

"We must make our way to the city," Giles said.

Buffy dislodged her feet from the mud of the fields and glanced around. Once again, they'd arrived in the day. It was a good thing they hadn't brought Angel with them, though his help would have come in handy on Anglesey.

If the vamps had landed near them, they would be toast. The only way they could have survived would have been to land in the city itself and dodge into a nearby doorway or shadowed house. No heavily clouded sky to protect them now.

Briefly she looked down at the soil, wondering if the vampires would be able to bury themselves in the dirt before they exploded into ash. She didn't know if this was possible—it didn't seem like it would be. Nevertheless, she began to picture them writhing about in the soil beneath her feet, a hideous crop of the undead.

Giles moved forward, walking down a narrow line of growing barley. Buffy did the same, following close behind.

"Will we be able to get in through the gate?" Willow asked. "Will they have guards?" Her voice sounded small and frightened.

Xander stopped. "Guards? Like guards-with-spears guards?"

"No, Xander," Giles told him. "More likely guards-with-arrows guards."

When he saw Xander's expression of horror, he relented. "Actually, during this time, Sumeria was at peace. I expect we'll be able to walk right in through the city gates without any incident whatsoever. Uruk traded extensively with other

Sumerian city states, and I imagine we will look like travelers to them."

Buffy looked down at her blue embroidered robe. At least it was linen, and not scratchy like the wool she'd worn on Anglesey. She hoped Giles was right about their financial stature. If people saw them in linen, they might be treated with greater respect and be able to ask questions without arousing too much suspicion.

As the four drew nearer, the city wall loomed up before them. Soon Buffy saw a great opening, a doorway that she could have slid her entire high school through, if she were in the mood to drag huge buildings around. No bars or metal blocked their way. As they got even closer, Buffy saw that the gates had the ability to close—two massive doors inlaid with copper stood on either side. But right now they hung wide open. On either side, above the doors, rose two matching towers. And pacing in those towers, staring down at them, were frowning guards. Buffy gave a little wave before Giles stilled her hand. "That might not be the best idea," he counseled her.

"I thought you said we'd look just like traders."

"Well, I certainly hope that's how we'll look," he muttered, passing through the massive doors. When no arrows rained down on him, Buffy and the others followed.

On the other side of the doorway, Buffy stopped in her tracks, bending her head back to take it all in. All around her stood tremendous buildings of golden mud bricks, elaborately painted and glistening with copper inlay. In the center of the city, some distance away, loomed a massive ziggurat. Greenery and blossoms draped down the sides of the pyramid-shaped structure, creating one of the most striking scenes she'd laid eyes on.

"Are those the Hanging Gardens?" Xander asked, staring as well.

"No, those were built later. But these are clearly a striking predecessor. Fascinating!"

Entire orchards stretched out between buildings, the city fragrant and green and teeming with inviting fruit.

As they passed under the thick shadow of the gate, Buffy heard a voice calling out to them. She didn't recognize the language, but that didn't surprise her. As long as Giles could talk to the locals and not get them killed, she was cool with that.

Just inside the gate stood a young man, probably not much older than Buffy. He was lean, tanned, and muscular, wearing a linen tunic decorated with silver thread around the cuffs. He was no commoner.

Giles told them, "I'm going to try to have a conversation."

"Good luck," Xander said without much conviction.

The young man spoke to them again, repeating what he'd said before in a practiced tone. He wore a satchel over one shoulder and clutched a wooden stylus in his hand. He spoke the same line again, and Buffy realized he was some sort of vendor, like a guy selling popcorn at a baseball game. Giles smiled, waved, and approached him. Buffy looked out over the vast city, which stretched far to the horizon, a maze of mud-brick houses, temples, lush greenery, and narrow passageways. Maybe the guy was selling a map. They needed one.

Giles exchanged halting words with the young man, then shook his head. Her Watcher returned, grinning.

"Well?" Buffy asked. "What was he selling?"

Giles chuckled, then stopped. "It's really rather ironic," he said, laughing again. "He thought we were illiterates who needed his help in recording any transactions we undertook while trading in the city. He's a scribe for hire."

"And he thought you were illiterate?" Xander asked, now laughing too. "Did you show him how it's done?"

Giles, clearly amused, pursed his lips. "I resisted. He's just gotten out of school, and selling his ability is one way young scribes earn a reputation for themselves. His satchel," Giles went on, pointing politely in the scribe's direction, "is full of wet clay tablets that he can write on with that stylus. Then he fires the tablets and returns to collect his fee before we depart the city."

"Wow!" Willow said, looking at the scribe with new interest. The young man smiled at her, and she blushed in return. Buffy smirked. It figured that her friend would find him more attractive after learning he was a third-millennium-B.C.E. bookworm.

"Did you ask him about the Slayer?" Xander asked.

"I did indeed," Giles said, "though I didn't call her that. I asked about warriors in the city. He regarded me blankly." He turned his eyes to the numerous avenues and houses before them. “The population of this city must be staggering. Locating the Sumerian Slayer will not prove as easy as it was on Anglesey.”

The four friends stepped away from the gate, moving toward the interior of the city.

“I want to go to that huge ziggurat!” Willow said, pointing toward the tremendous step pyramid rising in the center of the city.

“We’re not here to sightsee,” Giles reminded her mirthlessly.

Oh, come on, Giles!” she argued. “After we save the Slayer, we’ve got to walk around here. This place is amazing! Just think—right now, someone is writing the *Epic of Gilgamesh.* Think of the parallel of flood stories. We could see that in action! Right now Gilgamesh himself is somewhere here in this city. Imagine all the amazing archaeological finds housed in the British Museum. We could see them now, in their original condition!”

Giles began to crack. As beautiful as this place was, Buffy would have been happier to lounge in the temple gardens than traipse around seeing museumy things. She remembered the last time she’d gone to a museum, dragging herself along from exhibit to exhibit, reading countless placards that faded out of her memory mere seconds after reading them. Things had picked up after one of the Incan mummies she saw came to life and tried to kill her friends. But the museum itself was utter dullsville. Buffy didn't relish the thought of seeing an endless stream of "fascinating Sumerian artifacts in their original form."

"We really should go find the Slayer," she said. "It may take us longer than we expected. The population of the city is, as Giles just said, staggering." There. She'd cast her vote. Give her some vamps to fight. A few bruises. A knock on the head. Anything was better than museums.

They nodded assent and continued forward, discussing where to begin. "Oh, I hadn't thought of this before," Giles said, "but what if the Sumerians themselves have museums? Ancient, puzzling artifacts that are long lost or destroyed by our time?" He slapped his hand to his forehead, stopping abruptly. "We could finally understand the gap between nomadic culture and civilization. It's always puzzled archaeologists why humanity jumped from living in scattered villages to full-blown avenues, temples, pyramids, and multitiered societies. Perhaps these Sumerian museums would have evidence of cultures that directly preceded the Sumerians."

"We've got to find out!" Willow said enthusiastically, obligingly becoming Giles's confederate. The betrayal stung deeply. So much for having a best friend. Buffy was going to have to stare at mud bricks until her brain dribbled out of her ear.

Buffy gently took Giles's arm and steered him down the wide avenue. He emerged from his reverie. "This must be the main thoroughfare. Sumerian cities usually contained one main street where a bazaar was held and people hawked their wares. This must be it!"

"So what's the plan?" Buffy asked him. "Do we seek out the Slayer or the vamps?"

Giles stuck his chin out slightly in thought. "In a city of warriors, the Slayer may not stand out as easily. And finding the vamps will prove difficult. I imagine they'll take measures to blend in again. Perhaps finding the Watcher is the way to go in this instance."

"The Watcher?" Buffy asked. "Is this just another chance for you to geek out?"

"I will not 'geek out,' as you put it. At times it is useful to confer with another Watcher. Usually I must do this after a Slayer has died, and they aren't as willing to discuss their experiences. The chance to speak with another active Watcher could prove quite helpful, and I'm considerably more well-versed in Sumerian than I am in Old Welsh."

Xander moved alongside them, listening. "Okay. How do we go about finding the Watcher? Ask around for a stuffy, overeducated person who hangs out with a mouthy, smart-ass, butt-kicking girl?"

"Hey!" Giles and Buffy chorused in protest.

Giles added, "Not all Slayers are like Buffy. In fact, most of them have been quite well-behaved."

"Not appreciated!" Buffy said, pulling ahead of them. Willow caught up to her, still staring around in wonder.

"So we're going the Watcher route?" she asked.

"Apparently so."

"At least we'll have a head start on those vamps with the sun still up."

"Let's hope," Buffy said.

They walked the wide avenue for several more blocks and began to hear a gaggle of voices rising in volume as they continued. Buffy saw a cluster of people in bright and earthy tones milling around one another. Awnings and huge umbrellas shielded tables full of wares, from fruit to cloth to musical instruments. People haggled and examined merchandise, and sellers barked out a litany of phrases, enticing buyers to their stands.

"It's the bazaar," Willow said. "This is where most of the socialization goes on."

"Like the Bronze?" Buffy asked. A lyre player on one corner belted out a lively tune. The music wasn't that bad, but it wasn't Dingoes Ate My Baby.

"This would be an excellent place to ask about the Watcher," Giles suggested. As they entered the sea of buyers and sellers, mingling families, young people, and old men walking with canes, they scanned the tables. Buffy couldn't believe how vibrant the whole place was. She imagined much of the ancient world as dusty relics in museums, or as stagnant images in history textbooks. But this place was so *real*. Something about seeing it in the bright daylight hit her more powerfully than Anglesey. On Anglesey they'd arrived on the island in the heart of darkness. Firelight was the only source of illumination, which made it hard to see faces clearly. But here, swarming in the daylight, the Sumerian culture was alive: ruddy faces wreathed in copper and lapis lazuli headdresses, elaborate beaded necklaces hanging from tanned necks—these millennia-old people were living beings. It hit her hard, and she stopped, staring around at the scene before her. In their costumes, they blended in completely, and people took little notice of them. Only the sellers directed attention their way, as they did to everyone who passed by. Buffy watched one woman in a blue linen dress stroll by. Her black hair was pulled back and fixed in place by an elaborate silver headdress with three large metal flowers protruding from the back. She wore makeup. She'd painted her eyelids robin's-egg blue and highlighted her cheekbones subtly with rouge. She was beautiful, Buffy thought. Not some two-dimensional stone carving she'd seen in a textbook photo. Suddenly all the people around her, some hurrying, some strolling, became nearly overwhelming. She stepped off to the side, next to a peddler's cart.

He asked her something she didn't understand.

Giles turned to search for her, spotted her there, and said, "Oh, Buffy! Good show!" He came to her quickly. Turning, she realized she'd stopped at a scribe's cart. Tablets of fresh wet clay, a number of wooden styluses, and baked tablets filled the attractive young man's table.

Giles spoke to him at length, and the young man pointed in the distance to the northeast. He talked further, gesturing with his hands, presumably describing a dwelling.

Willow listened with rapt attention. "If I had anything to

trade, I'd get one of these tablets and a stylus. Can you imagine what a cool souvenir that would be of our trip?" she asked.

Buffy looked around at the neighboring carts full of gold and silver beadwork, elaborate necklaces, and earrings. "Yeah. A clay tablet. What more could you want?"

Buffy realized Xander wasn't with them, and she scanned the nearby crowd for him. At last she found him, engrossed in listening to a gorgeous woman reading from a stone tablet. Somehow, even though he didn't speak the language, Xander found the recitation fascinating.

Giles pulled the girls aside. "The scribe knows a man who is well versed in tales of the gods and history. And he has a young woman as a ward who is an unparalleled warrior."

Buffy nodded her thanks to the scribe. "Sounds like our guy."

"Where in the dickens is Xander?" Giles asked, noticing his absence. Willow pointed dejectedly out into the street, where Xander still listened in rapture.

"Ah," Giles said, catching a few words. "She's a poet."

"Great," Willow murmured, glancing that way. "Looks and talent. Who wants to listen to some crummy poet? She probably has Mesopotamian cooties." She'd had a crush on Xander since time immemorial, but he didn't seem to notice. Willow was too shy to tell him, and Buffy suspected Xander didn't see her like that. In fact, he made more passes at Buffy herself than anyone else, though he occasionally branched out to fall in love with killer praying mantises and homicidal

Incan mummies come to life. The Incan mummy had actually seemed quite sweet, until they realized she looked so pretty due to sucking the life out of hapless victims. That kind of ruined her image.

"Xander!" Giles called. "We need to go."

Willow turned around sulkily.

When Xander didn't pull away, Giles strode to him and tapped him on the shoulder. Now Xander turned away sulkily.

They met up again in the center of the wide avenue. "The Watcher lives in a mud-brick house to the northeast of here. We'll have to take back streets to get there."

As they veered off the main path toward a narrow alleyway, a bell rang loudly four times.

"What does that mean? They're calling for the sacrifices of the day?"

"Xander, you have sacrificing on the brain," Buffy said accusingly.

"Only because I've almost been one more times than I can count."

"Touché," she conceded.

"No, Xander," Giles said. "It's four o'clock."

Relief spread across Xander's face.

Willow spoke up, pointing to the bell tower, which they could see rising above the shorter buildings around them. "The Sumerians were the first ones to chime the bells on the hour and half hour. They divided the hour and minute into sixty segments. We adopted that from them."

"Indeed," Giles said, appraising Willow with a smile. "Their entire math system was based on sixty because it was divisible by so many numbers. Of course, our math system is based on ten, and—"

Buffy zoned out, staring at the buildings around her. Like the walls of the city, many of them sported colored brickwork depicting scenes. Bulls, the strange goat-fish creatures, and what looked like a hybrid of a snake, dragon, and wolf filled the murals, as did kings and hordes of people carrying a vast assortment of bushels, boxes, and plants.

While Giles lectured, they covered more distance. The sun dipped below the horizon. The shadowed light of gloaming filled the alleyways. Now in the residential section, they passed more modest domiciles, though many of them were still two stories and bigger than her house in Sunnydale. All of them opened to courtyards in the back, where fruit trees grew plentifully and provided shade. If she lived in the ancient world, this place might not be so bad.

"Here it is!" Giles said excitedly, pointing up. It was now completely dark. Buffy followed his gaze to a two-story mud-brick house. A painted banner hung down, emblazoned with a bull, two stars, and what looked like a vase full of dried flowers. "It's the seal he described."

Giles walked to the entrance of the house, a graceful archway leading inside. He peered in. No one sat in the front rooms. "I'm quite unsure as to Sumerian etiquette at this point," he admitted.

Willow leaned forward. "Hello?" she called, then realized that the word meant nothing here.

Giles followed suit, calling out in Sumerian. No one answered. Tentatively he stepped inside, glancing around the domicile.

Elaborately furnished, the house was rich with color. Several wooden chairs sat around a table draped with deep red fabric. A reclining couch lay in one corner, clumped with blue and purple pillows. Buffy looked up the stairs. Precipitously narrow, they rose to a loft above, presumably for sleeping. A small light glimmered up there.

"Could he be napping?" Willow asked, voicing Buffy's thoughts.

Giles called out again, but got no response. "Normally I would not be one to enter a house so rudely. But time is of the essence."

"I'll see if anyone's up there," Buffy offered. She climbed the stairs carefully, somewhat worried they'd topple over under her weight. Somehow the word "mud-brick," despite appearing quite sturdy, didn't sound that strong.

At the top of the stairs, she glanced around. A bed stood in the loft, with a small oil lamp burning next to it. And on the bed lay a man in his forties. His open eyes stared up at the ceiling. His jaw hung slack.

He was dead.

CHAPTER FIFTEEN

Giles!" Buffy called. "You need to come up here!"

In a few seconds, all four Scoobies gathered at the top of the stairs. Giles moved to the dead Watcher, taking his pulse. He pulled aside part of the man's garb. Two bloody puncture holes bit deeply into his neck. Vamps had killed him but had not shared their own blood. At least, Buffy hoped they hadn't.

"He hasn't been dead long," Giles told them.

"Is he going to come back?" Xander asked worriedly.

"One way to be sure," Buffy said. Against one wall leaned a gleaming sword. The edge glinted in the light, clearly sharp. She picked it up, strode to the body, and got ready to bring the blade down hard across the neck.

"Wait!" Giles called out, grabbing her arm. "We can't interfere with the time line. If this man ultimately became a vampire, then we must let him become one again."

Buffy didn't like this. "What if he was killed by the assassin vamps?"

Giles paused. "We need to find out for sure before we take any action."

"I don't see signs of a struggle," Xander said. "They must have killed him while he was sleeping." After a pause, he added nervously, "Do you think they could still be here?"

Buffy slowly turned around. Near where she'd grabbed the sword stood a curtain covering the entrance to another room. Deeper darkness gathered beneath the fabric. While the open doors and courtyard still let in the dying rays of dusk, that room clearly had no windows. She crept to it quietly, signaling for the others to keep up the chitchat.

While they bantered on about who could have killed the Watcher, Buffy moved to the curtain and whipped it to the side suddenly. Beyond lay a storeroom containing nuts and fruits. Noticeably cooler than the rest of the house, the storeroom offered little additional space to hide. Disappointed, she replaced the curtain.

"But where is the Slayer?" Willow asked. "If the vamps came here looking for her and killed her Watcher instead . . ."

"We need to search for the vamps!" Buffy said. "They could still be nearby. They could be fighting the Slayer right now!" Quickly she moved to the stairs, but stopped abruptly when she saw that they were no longer alone in the house. They'd been making so much noise talking and searching that they hadn't heard the intruders creep in.

A dozen soldiers lined the steps. The lead one, a shrewd-looking man with a scar on his left cheek, glanced toward the bed. He took in the dead man, then his eyes traveled to the sword in Buffy's hand. His eyes narrowed accusingly. Buffy shook her head in protest, but the men poured onto the upper loft, surrounding them.

The lead soldier shouted at her in Sumerian, and Giles answered him pleadingly. Whatever he said didn't wash. With spears pointed at their backs, they were forced from the house, then marched toward the monstrous palace in the center of the city.

"They're accusing us of murder," Giles explained unnecessarily.

"Where are they taking us?" Buffy asked.

"To be sacrificed," Xander put in.

"Now look," Giles said, being nudged forward by one of the guards. "There's nothing to be afraid of. The Sumerians had a complex legal system, with the rights of civilians very highly honored."

"But we're not civilians," Xander muttered pathetically.

"The Sumerians weren't into sacrifice," Willow told him encouragingly.

"Well, that's something," he muttered.

As they marched toward an uncertain future, Buffy gazed

out into the darkness of the city streets. Somewhere out there, the Slayer could be fighting the assassins. Her Watcher was dead. She was probably filled with grief and rage. It might cause her to make mistakes. Buffy needed to break away, to find her and help. But right now, she knew that would only get her killed.

For now, all she could do was wait for a chance to escape, and hope the Sumerian Slayer could hold on a little longer.

CHAPTER SIXTEEN

"Where are they taking us, Giles?" Buffy asked, glancing once again at the armored guards. How could she catch them unawares?

"Presumably before the king," he answered. "Most grievances are heard by a king and a council of people who come to a decision together."

"Like a judge and jury?" Willow asked.

"And executioner?" Xander added.

Giles nodded.

"You're not supposed to nod, man!" Xander cried, regarding Giles with exasperation.

"Who is the king right now?" Buffy asked.

Giles thought a minute. Counted something out on his right hand. Dust motes billowed up around his feet as he plodded along. "Gilgamesh."

At the mention of this name, three of the armored guards turned around, two with upraised eyebrows and the third with a scowl. Of course they would have recognized this one word in a sea of unfamiliar ones. Since English wouldn't be spoken for nearly three thousand years, Buffy guessed the men had no idea what they were talking about. She realized the advantage.

"I'm thinking of breaking away to go find the Slayer," she said.

Xander sucked in a breath and then released it. "Hey!" he said, catching on. "I think these guards are a bunch of big, smelly, nose-flute-playing funkyduddies."

Willow laughed. "And I think they wouldn't know algebra if it bit them on the patootie."

Xander stifled a laugh. "Good one. Way to be brutal, Will."

Giles regarded Buffy over his shoulder. "I wouldn't advise it, Buffy. They'd search everywhere for you, and you can't exactly dust them. You'd be putting yourself and this mission in grave danger."

"And you don't think that rotting in a prison or being put to death would jeopardize this mission?" she retorted.

Giles thought.

One guard spoke to him brusquely, then pushed him slightly on the shoulder.

"He doesn't want us talking," Giles explained.

"I'm going to take my chances, then," Buffy said. "I've got to find the Slayer. We don't have time for this."

"What about us?" Willow asked.

"No offense, but I'll be faster without you. Go on and hear what King Gorgonzola-Mess has to say. I'll join up with you at the palace."

"I don't like this," Giles said.

"Neither do I. But we can't take the chance that we'll get locked up while the assassins run free."

"Okay," Giles said. "You're sure you can find the palace?"

Buffy sighed, rolled her eyes. "You mean big, pointy building in the middle of town?"

Giles looked in the direction of the tremendous step pyramid. "Ah, yes. Right."

"Okay, guys," she said. "See you later."

And with that, Buffy fell out of line. The two guards behind her turned to stop her with their staffs, which they brought together to block her. With a leap she kicked them aside. Momentarily the guards stood stunned, and then they cried out for help. She kicked one in the head, punched the other one in the stomach, then ran into an alley.

Reluctant to leave the rest of the prisoners unguarded, only three guards pursued her into the narrow corridor.

Quickly outpacing them, she turned one corner, then another. The men separated, covering more ground. In one particularly narrow alleyway, Buffy chimney-crawled up twenty feet, then planted both boots firmly on opposite walls.

One of the guards passed beneath her, then a second one. If they were vamps, she'd have pivoted down and staked them. But now she let the men run beneath her and remained silent.

Their shouts echoed up and down the streets around her. The first guard passed beneath her again, going back the way he came.

She waited patiently.

The other guard ran beneath her.

The soldiers waiting in the main corridor called out to their comrades. Five minutes passed. Then ten. Buffy's legs began to ache, and she eyed a balcony just a few feet above her.

But then the main retinue called out once more. Below, the three soldiers met up again and walked out to the main street.

A minute later, she saw the group of soldiers pass by her alleyway, Willow, Xander, and Giles marching along with them.

She'd escaped. For now.

Now she just had to find the Slayer, and then rescue the Scoobies from a Sumerian prison. She didn't know what the Slayer looked like, had no idea where the assassin vamps were hiding, and couldn't imagine what awaited her in a Sumerian jail break.

Better odds than usual.

CHAPTER SEVENTEEN

Giles watched Buffy disappear down a darkened alley and hoped for the best. His Slayer was not the most patient girl in the world. In fact, she was downright impetuous. Of course, he himself had been rather impetuous when he was younger, in his Ripper days, but that scarcely bore thinking about. At least Buffy didn't resort to the black arts and inadvertently kill one of her friends, as he had done.

He trudged on in the dust, sneaking surreptitious looks at the guards. At any inattentive moment, perhaps the rest of them could slip away as well.

But as the palace loomed nearer and nearer, Giles abandoned this thought. The guards ushered them through the main entrance. Two more soldiers guarded the doorway with spears. They scowled at the prisoners as they passed.

Giles hoped Gilgamesh would be a little more friendly than these fellows were turning out to be. Downright surly they were, and clearly of a mind to think one guilty before proven innocent.

The guards led them down a wide, high-ceilinged corridor lit by wall-mounted torches. The smell of burning oil crept into Giles's nostrils, and he stifled a cough. Thin, acrid smoke hung in a layer near the ceiling of the corridor.

Giles expected to be locked up for the night, but instead the guards marched them to the center of the palace.

They paused at a pair of double doors embedded with detailed copper, lapis lazuli, and gold and adorned with scenes of rams, sheep, goat-fish, kings, chariots, and barley.

Guards posted on both sides of the entryway narrowed their eyes at the new arrivals. One bowed to the commander of the retinue, and then reached up high over his head to grab the door handle. He heaved it outward, revealing the opulent throne room. A long, narrow strip of cloth led up to a throne made of gold and copper. Sitting on the throne was a man, presumably the king, with an impressive beard hanging down to his navel. He wore a large crown, akin to a pope hat but made of precious metals hammered into delicate designs.

In front of him three women, a child, and a lone man were

speaking. He listened patiently, then conferred with a group of people Giles couldn't quite see past the doorway.

Then the king turned back to the group of people, smiled, and waved his hand amicably. They bowed and thanked him, backing out of the chamber. Giles could catch only a few words. They spoke far too fast for him to understand everything. But he heard enough to understand that the king had listened to their case—something about them buying their freedom.

Giles had read of this; people could sell themselves into slavery in Sumeria. They could also buy their freedom. Slaves could own land and run businesses. These people had probably sold themselves into slavery, then saved up enough money to buy back their freedom, with the king's blessing.

Giles waited expectantly. Should they enter? Plead their case before King Gilgamesh? He looked anxiously at the guards around him. They did not motion for him to proceed through the door, so Giles just stood. He looked to Willow and Xander, who craned their necks to see through the door.

Then a young man was pushed forward into view. He stood before the king, pleading desperately. Giles caught a few remarks—something about theft, and selling an item illegally. The king conferred with the unseen group of people, then pointed a finger accusingly at the young man.

Giles heard "three months' labor" and "until debt is repaid," and then guards grabbed the young man, who protested beseechingly. The king would have none of it. He pointed angrily toward the door, and Giles felt his heart sink. This was one tough monarch. He hoped that the stories he'd read of his fairness were true. If not, they were going to the gallows.

CHAPTER EIGHTEEN

Out in the crowded city street, Buffy blended in with the throng of people walking to and fro. She'd lost the guards. She was certain of it. Within minutes she had retraced her path back to the Watcher's house. Inside, men labored on the second floor by lamplight, throwing their shadows into the courtyard. After a few minutes, they emerged from the front door, bearing the dead body on a stretcher. A thin sheet covered the Watcher. People stopped and stared, murmuring questions. None of them fit the profile of a Slayer. Many were men, and most of the women were old enough to be her mother, too old for a Slayer to have stayed alive. Two little girls watched. Too young.

As the men carried the body away, Buffy watched them go. The Slayer was not here.

Was she already murdered?

Buffy regretted not being able to speak the language. She needed Giles. Maybe she'd been wrong to leave them. But if they'd all been locked up, she could have done nothing to save the Slayer, and the Master would rise.

Slipping into the shadows, Buffy began her search for the assassins.

CHAPTER NINETEEN

The guards pushed Giles and the others before the king. Giles walked uncertainly down the long center rug toward the monarch. King Gilgamesh's dark eyes glittered beneath a furrowed brow. He gripped an intimidating spear in his left hand. Giles wished for the comforting presence of Buffy and hoped that she was out there right now, finding the other Slayer.

The guards spoke quickly to the king, again too fast for Giles to catch every word, but he did hear "murder." Lovely. Oh, what a fantastic place to meet one's end. They'd be put to death, the assassins would kill the Sumerian Slayer, and the Master would open the Hellmouth. Chaos would reign on earth.

Giles took a deep breath and tried to recall all he could about the laws of Gilgamesh's time. He'd read the Code of Hammurabi several times, the famous set of ancient laws translated in the early 1900s. But he knew that came later in history. He struggled to recall what laws would have been different in 2700 B.C.E. He hoped it wasn't laws involving suspected murderers. That they would be torn asunder by lions to prove their innocence, for example. Or that they would be hung above a pit of vipers and slowly lowered down, down to a death by poisonous biting.

No. Giles had watched too many Indiana Jones films. He was getting as bad as Xander. He was thinking doom, and he should be thinking triumph.

The king turned to him and spoke. Giles did his best to translate.

"They say you killed the city's royal scribe."

Royal scribe? Gulp. Giles cleared his throat. "We only discovered the body, Your Majesty," he replied. At least, that's what he hoped he said. It may have also been "I'll gladly wash your socks, given the right incentive." This time jump was his first shot at actually speaking ancient Sumerian in a conversational context, after all. "He was dead when we arrived."

"And who are you?" asked the king.

Here Giles froze. *Time travelers? Watcher, Slayer, and Scoobies? Futuristic vigilantes bent on destroying a team of assassins?* Giles plunged in. They had limited time. He needed to get them out of there fast. "We came on a mission of protection. We learned that the scribe's ward was in grave danger."

"But you didn't see fit to save the scribe himself?"

Gulp. Giles needed a glass of water. "We did not know he was in danger." Here he turned and looked at Xander and Willow. Their eyebrows were raised, faces worried.

Willow whispered, "Ask him where she is!"

"It would greatly help us if you could tell us where the scribe's ward is," Giles said. "She is in terrible danger."

The king's eyes softened a bit. Giles hoped it wasn't his imagination. He turned to the lead guard. "Did you see Ejuk?" he asked. The guard shook his head. "What threatens her?" he asked Giles. This time the king spoke slower, using fewer words. He knew Giles was obviously a foreigner.

"Assassins," Giles answered, opting to leave out the fangs and undead part.

"Vampires?" asked the king.

Giles's mouth fell open. "Yes," he answered, haltingly.

The King nodded, then turned to his guards. "Sounds like something special is going on. Something worse than usual for our Ejuk."

Giles turned around, whispering the translation to Xander and Willow.

"They know about vampires?" Xander said in disbelief.

Giles grinned in spite of himself. "It makes sense. People in the ancient world didn't believe in different things from what we do now, they just believed in *more*."

"Wow," Willow breathed. "So their Slayer gets to fight out in the open? No secret identity?"

"Her identity as the Slayer must still be secret. Otherwise she'd be too much of a target among the undead. But it's likely she's not the *only* known fighter of evil supernatural forces here. The king probably knows that she kills vampires, but not that she's the Slayer."

"Whew," Xander said. "No secret identity would have been a bummer. I've always wanted one myself. Like a secret spy who infiltrates the strongholds of supervillains on small island countries in the Pacific and—"

The king stopped conferring with the guards and spoke. One left the room. Moments later, four young women entered the room. They wore billowing white linen gowns, and wreaths of gold flowers adorned their heads. Strings of lapis lazuli beads hung from their necks and ears. Each held a small bowl of clear water. Giles was terribly thirsty and welcomed the offering.

One of the women, dark haired and in her early twenties, approached Giles, holding out the bowl. He reached one hand out for it, and then she flung the bowl upward, drenching him in the water. He blinked in surprise, wiping water out of his eyes. The other three women threw water on Xander and Willow, then again on him for good measure.

The king laughed. "You look so funny," he told Giles.

Giles turned to him in disbelief. "Glad to oblige," he muttered in English.

The king cleared his throat and resumed his somber composure. "These are the temple priestesses of the water god, Enki. The water they carry is blessed by the god himself. If you were vampires, you would have been badly burned."

"Sumerian holy water," Willow said, wiping water off her face with one sleeve.

To Giles's horror, Xander winked at the nearest temple priestess, casually pulling his dripping hair out of his eyes.

"I am glad to see you are not vampires yourselves," said the king.

Giles felt a little better. Maybe now they could get somewhere. He glanced at his watch, hidden under his heavy sleeve. They'd been separated from Buffy for an hour now. They had no more time to waste.

"What do you propose we do to help?" asked the king.

Help? This was unexpected. Giles felt a little relief and happiness creeping into him. With the king's help, the guards could search for Ejuk, and where she was, the vamps would be. "Can you help us find Ejuk?" he asked.

The king conferred again with the guards. Starting to grin, Giles turned to Willow and Xander. "Do you realize how exciting this is? We are standing in the court of King Gilgamesh himself! The most famous of all Sumerian monarchs! He quested for eternal life and even found the fruit of immortality, which a snake ate, but that's okay. He still found it. He survived the great flood that killed most of humanity. He killed the great giant of the forest, Humbaba. It was during his reign that cuneiform came into regular use to record everything from tales to business receipts."

Willow looked up at the king. "Uh, Giles?"

Giles slowly turned around. The king had overheard him, and with a frown, demanded to know what he'd said about him. Giles obliged, repeating what he'd said in Sumerian.

"You know that much of my deeds?" asked the king.

"Of course!" Giles said excitedly.

The king turned to three of the guards. "Help these three find Ejuk and stop the assassins. Make sure they have plenty to eat and drink and a place to sleep if you do not succeed tonight."

"Looks like you stroked the right ego," Xander said. "Can I have a temple priestess for my room?" He winked again at the nearest one. She turned away in disdain.

"No, you may not have a temple priestess," Giles snapped.

Willow kicked Xander in the back of the leg.

"Hey!" he said in defense. "There could be gorgeous temple priests out there too."

"They're probably bald, forty, and sacrifice virgins to snake pits," she said.

"Wait a minute!" Giles protested. "What's so bad about being forty?"

"It's ancient!" she answered, then caught herself. "But ancient is good. When it comes to you, anyway, Giles."

"Oh, thank you so very much," he muttered, turning away in mock contempt.

The king finished speaking with the guards. "My men will assist you in finding Ejuk. Please report back to me when you have succeeded."

"We will," Giles said. "And thank you."

"Anything for a fan," answered Gilgamesh.

CHAPTER TWENTY

Outside, in the streets to the east of the palace, Buffy hunted vampires. She slunk through the shadows, keeping out of sight. She pulled out her map of Uruk and tried to place herself. To her left rose the immense ziggurat in the center of town. Its vast steps, now silhouetted against the sky, loomed in the darkness. Behind her lay the Temple of Inanna, the goddess of love. The sanctuary around it formed an entire district, called the Eanna district. Giles had gone on and on till her ears bled about how famous it was. Before her stood another sanctuary, with the White Temple, built almost a thousand years before, just visible beyond it. Past these temples, she could make out the dark, low shadow of the city walls, which extended for more than six miles around the perimeter of Uruk.

She closed her eyes, picturing where she stood in relation to the ziggurat, where the Scoobies languished in prison, and where the Watcher had died. If she were the Sumerian Slayer, and vampires had killed her Watcher, where would she go? After royally kicking their asses, she'd go to her friends. Or, depending on the competition, maybe her friends first. She might need some research first. But who were the Sumerian Slayer's friends?

Buffy ducked into the deeper darkness under a balcony as a retinue of soldiers marched by. She was getting pretty sick of hiding from the military. First Wales and now this. She wasn't sure where to go now. Unless the same vamp had been sent again, she didn't know what her prey looked like. And he'd probably brought friends.

Her worried mind turned now to Giles and the others. They could be being tortured. They could be catching gods-knew-what in filthy Sumerian prison cells. She should go to them. Break them out.

Buffy turned in the shadows, waited for the soldiers to pass, then headed for the great ziggurat.

CHAPTER TWENTY-ONE

Inside the ziggurat, Giles was having an excellent time. How thrilling to meet King Gilgamesh! To see the fascinating architecture and cuneiform so vividly detailed and in its original condition! He knew he probably shouldn't be so excited.

They were here to fight vampires, after all, not go on an archaeological holiday. But still, he couldn't help feeling a little tempted now and again to stop at a pillar or stele and read the inscriptions. Consequently, it was taking them nearly five minutes for each step.

The three soldiers Gilgamesh had offered marched ahead of them along the corridor, gaining more and more distance.

As long as they could recognize Ejuk, though, they would be useful.

Willow hooked her arm in his and hurried Giles along. As he craned his neck, trying to take in all he was missing, a young woman rushed past them. Tears streaked her dirty face, and her jaw jutted out in angry defiance.

"That's her!" Willow whispered.

"That's who?" Giles asked.

"The Slayer!"

"How can you possibly know that?"

Willow shrugged, turning to watch her go. "I just know."

Xander retraced his steps back to them. "Looks like she's going in to see the king. Let's go back and listen at the door."

The three soldiers had now reached the main entrance of the ziggurat and turned to look at Giles. He motioned for them to wait.

Together they crept to the door of the throne room and waited. The young woman bowed before the king, then rose. Giles listened in, catching the gist of what she told him. The royal scribe, Sarkassan, had been killed by ruffians. She vowed to bring them to justice. For now, she requested a burial detail. She began to tremble, then straightened, fighting back her emotions.

The king told her that his men had already recovered the body. He spoke to her quietly and soothingly, saddened by her loss.

"Sarkassan was an unparalleled scribe," the king said,

"and generous to all who knew him." He paused, regarding her compassionately. "And you have three strange visitors who have come to help you. They fear for your life." He turned to the soldier nearest him and gave an order Giles couldn't quite make out. "My guard will take you to them." He motioned for them to depart.

At once they turned, heading in Giles's direction. He, Willow, and Xander turned away from the door and hurried to a respectful distance in the great hall. When she emerged, she instantly saw them. Giles recognized now what Willow had seen—the glittering, determined eyes. The age beyond physical age. The sadness, the wisdom, the knowledge that she would never lead a normal life like other girls. The knowledge that she would in all likelihood die prematurely.

As Giles saw her, her tear-streaked face now dry but edged with pain, he knew he would not let that happen.

CHAPTER TWENTY-TWO

Willow rushed to meet her and opened her mouth to say something, but fell silent. She couldn't talk to her at all. She wanted to comfort her; she felt an immediate kinship with her. Then Willow realized why—she imagined Buffy losing Giles, imagined herself losing Giles. How would they survive that? Willow admired Ejuk for searching the city for the killers, and now marching before the king to request a burial detail.

Willow wasn't sure if she'd be able to respond that way. She'd probably curl up, consumed with grief. But then, maybe not. She had discovered more reserves of strength in the last year than she knew she had.

Now she stood before the Sumerian Slayer, unable to speak. Giles quickly joined them, followed by Xander. He introduced them all, speaking with more agility now. Willow was pretty impressed by his amount of knowledge. She hoped one day she'd have as much. Only she wouldn't wear as much tweed. At least, she hoped she wouldn't.

Giles explained that a team of vampires had targeted her, and that it was likely they who had killed her Watcher. Willow saw two tears leak out of the Slayer's right eye, but she did not openly emote. She held it together, her jaw trembling slightly. Only a couple of years older than Willow herself, Ejuk stood almost six feet tall, her skin nearly bronze. Her green eyes glittered with anger, blinking back another tear, and she wore leather armor on her arms, torso, and legs. Over her right shoulder she'd slung a bow, and a quiver of arrows hung on her back. Willow knew the prey she hunted was exceptionally susceptible to wood.

Giles then described Buffy and asked if Ejuk had seen her. The Slayer shook her head. She hadn't seen the vampires who killed Sarkassan, either.

Willow glanced nervously around the hall, expecting to see vampires lurking behind the massive pillars, or creeping up in the shadows.

Now they just needed Buffy. But where was she?

CHAPTER TWENTY-THREE

Outside the ziggurat, Buffy crept to the entrance and saw three guards standing in the doorway. She recognized them from before—they had chased her during her escape. She couldn't risk being seen.

Just past them, down a long, elaborate hallway of pillars and intricate carvings, she saw Giles, Xander, and Willow talking to a young woman.

She sized up the situation. Another guard stood behind the woman. Was she the Slayer? Could Buffy take out the three guards and get them all out?

Leaping out of the darkness, she struck.

The guards, standing around talking, didn't see her approach.

She was on them in two seconds, banging two of their heads together and kicking the third in the chest. He crashed down and she jumped on top of him, ripping off his helmet and clanking his head against the stone floor. He grunted and fell unconscious. Behind her, the other guards lay still but breathing.

She stormed down the hallway, fixing the last guard in her gaze.

"Buffy! Wait! No!" Giles cried, stepping in front of her. "It's all been ironed out. The guards are going to help us!"

She stopped, turning slowly away from them to see the pile of soldiers in the entryway. "Ooops."

When she turned back around, still full of adrenaline, the guard standing behind Ejuk slunk away back into the throne room.

"Has she seen the vamps?" Buffy asked after he left.

Giles shook his head.

She studied the hallway, all the pillars and recesses, places where assassins could easily hide. "This is a bad area. We need to move."

Ejuk spoke, and Giles translated. He explained that they had come to protect her against vampire assassins. She studied them all warily, then relented, grateful for their help. She was exhausted, she explained, from searching the city for her Watcher's killers. She glanced around the room, then told Giles, "We need an open place. The assassins will come to us." Giles translated.

Buffy nodded. "My thoughts exactly." This Slayer was

with it. Strong. Both times now, meeting another Slayer had left her stunned. Here was a woman living the same life as she—dedicated to fighting the forces of darkness, plucked out of the innocence of youth and thrown into a maelstrom of battle tactics, sparring bruises, and ruined dating lives. Great dresses got torn. Dates got killed. Moms got lied to.

But then Buffy realized that this Slayer didn't have a mom to lie to. She'd been orphaned at six, Giles had told her. Raised by her Watcher. Briefly, Buffy missed her parents and then imagined growing up with Giles. He would have dressed her in plaid jumpers. Corduroys. Tweed slacks and sweater-vests. She just knew it.

She smiled at Ejuk, imagining instead what it must be like to grow up in this ancient civilization, with massive stone pyramids and cities filled with fragrant orchards and gardens. When gods and goddesses, monsters and beasts had temples, shrines, and festivals. When magick, divination, and spells were accepted by everyone as a fact of life. In some ways, being a vampire slayer would have been easier at this time. And in other ways, life must have been much harder. Like how often did people take baths here? They had irrigation. Surely they had baths, right? She looked at Ejuk's dirty face, the streaks of tears cutting clean swaths through the filth.

Maybe it was just an off day for her. Buffy had those sometimes. Thinking of the assassins, she hoped today wouldn't be one of them.

• • •

Standing in the grandeur of the long hallway, Xander felt elated. He wandered slightly away from the others, taking it all in. What a cool place this was! What amazing architecture! What delightful temple priestesses. He smiled as one hurried by him, carrying a goblet of dark liquid and a small cake in one hand. She turned away. But he thought she didn't turn away as abruptly as before. Oh, yeah. She was warming up to him. No doubt about it. He glanced around the corridor. There must be something to do here while they yammered on about strategies. As long as he didn't have to do much staking or punching or getting punched or bleeding, he was okay with whatever they decided.

He strolled down the long hallway, taking in the pillars. Some of them depicted everyday scenes of harvesting barley. Others showed glorious battle or the strange beasts with the heads of goats and tails of fish. His feet fell silently on the thick woven carpet. Full of lustrous reds, blues, and golds, the rug extended from the entrance to the throne room. He couldn't believe the craftsmanship that went into all this stuff. Architecture in his time was pretty boring. He didn't pay much attention to it. One mall looked like another, and tracts of houses formed a sea of monotony stretching into the Sunnydale horizon. But this was amazing. Every pillar was different. The walls were etched with symbols, stories, and pictures. Someone had really *thought* about how to make this place awe-inspiring, and they'd succeeded.

He imagined living in a palace like this, lounging on pillows and eating grapes and sipping fruity, refreshing drinks. Manly fruity, refreshing drinks, of course. Another temple priestess walked by, and he winked. She actually smiled back. Not a *hey* smile, but more like a friendly *hey, how's it going* smile. It was nice. And she didn't look like she was a praying mantis at all.

He reached the end of the hall. Lining the wall on that side was a series of immense statues, stretching up forty feet to the ceiling. All of women and men, some figures sat down, while others stood, holding spears or swords or handfuls of grain. At once Xander was struck by their strange eyes. They were huge. Huger than huge. They took up half the statues' heads, bigger than owls' eyes. They stared off into space, looking dazed or spaced out.

Xander stared more closely. They all had mouths on hinges, he saw. Some statues stood with open mouths, others with closed. Some had bits of food hanging out. Willow had told him that the Sumerians fed the statues of their gods and even had huge beds for them to lie down in. But to actually see them was something else.

One statue near the middle had particularly large eyes. In one hand he held what looked like a scythe, and his other hand stretched out, palm up. His lips curled back from stone teeth, and stuck between the front two incisors was a big green glob of what looked like spinach. Xander muffled a laugh. Then he couldn't help it. He burst out into a cackle. As he took in the ridiculous expression on the statue's face, he laughed harder. He listed slightly to one side, and stepped back to regain his balance. The floor shifted under his foot. He stumbled. The stones beneath his feet moved and ground together.

Earthquake! He stepped farther back, looking for a doorway to stand in. And then the shaking stopped. A resonant crack exploded into the hallway. At Xander's eye level, the foot of the statue crumbled and fell away, revealing tremendous, gray, wriggling toes inside. Then the legs of the statue exploded outward, raining stones and dust over Xander. He flung up an arm to shield himself. His eyes followed the statue up, up, to the eyes. With a thunderous peal, the painted stone over the eyes cracked and fell away, revealing two yellow eyes beneath. They swiveled downward, fixing on Xander, an ant at the feet of a god.

The arms shattered. The chest blew apart. And from the crumbling mass of ruined statuary stepped a horrific figure. Forty feet tall, gray, rotted, and clad in maggots and festering sores, the god of the plague rose to his feet, glaring down at Xander. His mouth opened, a dark hole in rotted flesh, and from between the two blistered lips erupted thousands of flies, darkening the air around Xander. They buzzed into Xander's ears, mouth, and eyes. Involuntarily he sucked them in as he tried to get a breath.

Xander went down, crashing to the carpet as a hundred sores opened on his skin, weeping thick yellow liquid. He screamed in agony.

This was not how he wanted to die.

CHAPTER TWENTY-FOUR

One of the priestesses ran by, stopping in horror at the sight. She shouted, and the others ran toward Xander.

"He's awakened Namtar, god of the plague," the priestess told Giles. "And from the looks of it, insulted him somehow."

"Jeez, Xander! We leave you alone for two minutes!" Willow cried out as she ran to him. Then they all saw him lying prone on the floor, his body a mass of roiling insects, no part of his flesh or hair visible beneath the squirming army of flies.

The god stared down at them, anger flaring in his yellow eyes. Buffy gazed up. Namtar recognized them as Xander's friends. And he looked ripe for some anger spillover.

"Namtar will kill you all!" one of the priestesses shouted. Giles was quick on the translation, though with one look at her fallen friend, Buffy didn't need it. "We must submit to his will!" And with that, the priestesses abandoned them, fleeing from the palace.

"Thanks for your help!" Willow shouted after them.

The angry god lifted one foot, bringing it down hard over Buffy. She leaped and rolled away, the sandal barely missing her. The temple shuddered. Buffy hoped this summoning wouldn't forever change the time line. What if the god rampaged through the palace, killing some priest or priestess who figured prominently in history? What if the god unleashed a deadly plague on all of Sumeria, crushing civilization just as it was getting started? They had to take care of this, and fast.

Giles rushed to Xander's side, kneeling down next to him. Immediately the roiling mass of flies transferred onto Giles, swarming over his skin. He cried out in agony, and in an instant Buffy watched festering boils erupt over his face and neck. He doubled over, vomiting, and then the flies covered him completely.

Xander staggered to his feet, his eyes haunted and yellow, jaundiced. He rasped at Buffy through blistered lips ruptured with sores. "Help . . . ," he whispered.

On the ground, Giles writhed in pain, crawling to his knees to vomit again, and then collapsing. Buffy backed up, Willow at her side. The god slammed another foot down, knocking them apart. Willow stumbled and crawled to safety next to a pillar.

"What are we going to do?" she called to Buffy.

Buffy jumped into the air, dodging another blow from the god, who smashed his fist down onto the floor beside her. "Where was that spell book Giles had?"

"He still has it," Willow shouted back, diving out of the way as the other fist screamed down next to her head. It shattered the floor beneath, a spiderweb of cracks spiraling outward from the epicenter.

"We need to get it!" Buffy yelled, leaping over an incoming kick. Namtar's tremendous foot crashed into a pillar, eliciting a yelp of pain from the god. "That was hopeful! At least he can get hurt!"

"Though we aren't doing any of the hurting," Willow pointed out.

Buffy looked to where Giles lay, roiling with flies. She didn't want to fester with boils. If all of them got the plague, there'd be no stopping Namtar, no stopping the assassins, and then the Master would rise. But there was no other option. And she'd need Willow to cast any spells to send this thing back to god oblivion, or god Palm Springs, or whatever hell dimension it had come from.

Sprinting between the god's feet, Ejuk joined Buffy. She made the universal gesture for "What in the world are we going to do?" by raising her hands up next to her head and looking utterly bewildered.

Buffy pointed to Giles, to his satchel, which looked more like a swelling mound of flies than a pouch full of books.

Then she pointed to herself, gesturing that she was going to retrieve the satchel. Then she pointed at Ejuk and then to the god, hoping the Sumerian Slayer would distract him while she got the book. Ejuk nodded and headed off in that direction. A sandaled foot landed where she had been crouching.

With Ejuk distracting Namtar by leaping and jumping around his feet like an espresso-jittered rabbit, Buffy made a break for the book. As soon as she knelt beside Giles and grabbed the satchel, the flies swarmed over her. Darkness filled her vision, and hundreds of squirming insect bodies crawled over her face and into her eyes. She swatted them, trying to shake them off, then rolled as if on fire. Enough buzzed away from her that she was able to get her bearings. Spotting Willow a few yards away, she grabbed the satchel, staggered to her feet, spun around and around, and then let go, launching the bag through the air.

It thumped solidly on the floor next to Willow, and she grabbed it.

Then the flies moved in again. Buffy felt a million points of agony erupt over her body as boils and sores wept open. Bile rose in her throat and she turned to vomit, feeling the aching weight and pain of a high fever sweeping over her body. As she staggered to rise and then fell, coughing and gagging on the roiling mass of flies, she saw that Giles was now insect free.

But seeing his unrecognizable face was almost worse. Infected sores covered his swollen face, spreading painfully down his neck and chest. Maggots crawled on his arms and in his ears. He scraped them away, flinging them to the ground.

Xander looked even worse, his skin yellow and gray, mottled and riddled with lesions.

And then the pain took over her mind. She screamed, squeezing her eyes shut, as her body erupted in sickness, every plague known to humanity sweeping through her simultaneously. She doubled over in agony, then rolled into a fetal position. She could feel her body shutting down, dying.

She couldn't fight like this.

The Master had won.

CHAPTER TWENTY-FIVE

Willow grabbed the satchel. As her Slayer friend fell into unconsciousness, Willow rummaged through its contents. Her fingers found the familiar rough binding of *Lord Echinal's Compendium of Sumerian Oaths, Spells, and Summonses*. It was the most current, comprehensive work on Sumerian magick out there. Of course, it was copyrighted in 1857, but you couldn't have everything. She pulled it out. Giles had placed a worn bookmark near the center denoting the area of special interest to this particular time jump. The bookmark had fallen out.

Willow turned to the table of contents and scanned entries. To her left, Ejuk dodged a blow from a mighty fist, then rolled to the side and kicked Namtar in the little toe. He didn't notice.

And Willow hoped he didn't notice her squeezed against the pillar, flipping through the book.

At last she passed up "Curses Et Cetera Having to Do with Things Borne of Illness" for "Waking Up a Decidedly Unfriendly God." She flipped to that page, glancing up just in time to see a flying chunk of masonry loosed by Namtar's fist. She ducked, clutching the book. The stone hit the pillar above her and crumbled to dust. Ejuk was really working it now, firing arrows into Namtar's toe and jabbing at his Achilles' heel. Too bad he wasn't a Greek god, or that might have worked. Namtar roared and stomped, squatting down sometimes to try to grab her in his fist. He wasn't having any luck. Ejuk grinned, her lightning agility too fast for the god, and Willow liked her more and more.

Balancing the heavy book on her knee, Willow thumbed to the page in question, glad that at least Lord Echinal had written in English, and not a primitive dialect of Coptic script or some other typical Gilesian language.

She studied the spell, read over its words. Luckily, it was an incantation, something she wouldn't need an elaborate list of ingredients to pull off—if she could pull it off.

She pivoted on her heels, facing Namtar, where he clashed with Ejuk in the center of the grand hallway. She cleared her throat, then swallowed, getting ready to speak the incantation to banish the god. Lord Echinal had written the spells themselves out phonetically beneath the cuneiform symbols. She hoped his transcription was accurate.

She spoke the sounds aloud, not sure where to place emphasis, the words unfamiliar to her. She'd dabbled in magick a few times, but mostly with Giles to guide her. Casting something as serious as a god-banishing terrified her. What if she said something incorrectly and sentenced herself and the others to eternal torment in a hell dimension?

At the sound of the words, Namtar stopped fighting, and his eyes fixed on Willow. A puzzled expression swept over his face. As the incantation came to a close, a thundering *boom* resonated through the long hall. The air shimmered to the left of Namtar, quavering like heat rising off a desert floor, then pulsed outward, bathing Willow in a blast of heat. Ejuk dodged away, taking refuge behind a nearby pillar.

Namtar turned to face the shimmering section of air, alarm spreading on his face. *Aha!* thought Willow. *He knows we have him now!*

The god backed away, nearly stepping on Xander, who lay slumped against one wall, struggling to breathe.

As Willow watched expectantly for the shimmering air to overtake the god and make him vanish, she was astonished by what actually happened.

Instead of the disturbed air becoming a vortex to suck the god back to its regular place of dwelling, something dark appeared in its depths.

Willow caught the flash of glittering scales, then a hint of a lashing tail. Another *boom* thundered around her, her chest reverberating with the cacophony. Then a red eye and a mouth full of fangs flashed into sight. The air glimmered, a thousand sparks of light, and exploded outward in a maelstrom of hot wind.

The air pressure changed in the room, and Willow swallowed hard to make her ears pop. The wind dissipated. She peered out through watering eyes.

And she saw a monster wink into view, licking its enormous jaws and fixing her with intelligent, gleaming eyes.

She hadn't gotten rid of the god. She'd summoned a creature from hell itself.

CHAPTER TWENTY-SIX

Ejuk rushed to Willow's side as the creature advanced. She shouted "*Mushussu*!" and pulled Willow out of the way.

Willow didn't know what a *mushussu* was, but with it bearing down on her, snapping its jaws, she wasn't overly eager to find out.

As they dove out of the way, Willow caught a glimpse of Buffy lying prone on the floor, thousands of flies crawling over her body. She had to get to her friend, but she knew that the flies would consume her, too, and then no one would be left to help Ejuk.

Crouching behind a pillar, she showed the book to Ejuk.

Pointing at the incantation, she looked questioningly at the Slayer. Ejuk glanced at the cuneiform, running fingers over the smooth page. Willow pointed to the symbols, then to her own mouth. Ejuk's eyes widened and she nodded. She could read it aloud. Get the words right. But that still didn't solve the problem of the *mushussu*, which was about to mushussu them into stains on the carpet.

Ejuk silently read over the symbols, while Willow turned to the snake-dragon, which winnowed its way toward them through the pillars, weaving and growling as it came.

What did it have against them? They hadn't done anything except summon it into being. What, had Willow called it away from a really great snake-dragon tea party, or lured it from a poker game it was winning? Ruined a *mushussu* date?

Namtar stood against one of the walls, clearly nonplussed at the appearance of the snake-dragon. Perhaps they'd tangled before in some mythological epic, Willow thought.

She pointed again to the god and then to the incantation. Ejuk spoke the first line, and Willow realized just how wrong old Echinal had the pronunciation.

The dragon reached them, rearing its tail up to smash them.

They were so intent on banishing the god and avoiding the lashing tail of the tremendous beast that they didn't see the assassins emerge from the shadows behind them. Willow spun at the last minute as a knife plunged deeply into Ejuk's back. The Slayer slumped forward, bracing herself against a pillar.

The book fell from Willow's hand and crashed to the floor, speckled with blood.

As Ejuk slid to the floor, Willow stood up to face the vampires, a lone would-be witch against two brutal assassins.

CHAPTER TWENTY-SEVEN

Victor sneered at Willow, recognizing her instantly as one of the Scoobies, Buffy's interminably cheery, stalwart companions. Beyond her, the tremendous snake-dragon caught sight of the rampaging god and spun to confront him.

Victor seized this moment of distraction to close in on Willow. He signaled for his latest crony, Justin, to follow him. Justin, a three-hundred-year-old mohawked vampire with as much experience killing for political reasons as for a croquet set, grinned vacantly. Justin was sloppy and impetuous—everything Jason hadn't been. Lucien had really rounded up the worst people for him to work with. And now that Lucien was locked up, his recruits were limited. Maybe before the next jump, he'd take time to find some people himself.

Victor didn't know how this guy had survived for three hundred years, and he suspected that Justin traveled with a pack that did most of his kills for him. Lucien had dug him up in some vampire dive in the bad part of town, and Justin was cheap enough to hire. Most vamps were too lazy to join the fight to resurrect the Master without a little monetary incentive. Of course there were a few diehards, like Lucien, and most of them were just as crazy as the French-Canadian vampire himself. Victor had never had to work with such a motley mix of incompetence and sheer psychopathic reasoning skills since he joined in this whole venture.

As the snake-dragon backed the angry god into a small recess, Victor gripped his favorite knife. The blade dripped with the blood of the Slayer, and he licked along the edge. Now he just had to finish the job.

Willow watched them defiantly, balling her hands into fists. She blinked away tears, and Victor could smell her beautiful terror. Her shoulders and legs trembled, and he relished the thought of bringing her down and drinking that innocent blood.

Ejuk started crawling away, and Victor shoved Willow out of the way, bringing up the knife again. But the young witch surprised him. A violent kick to his hand sent the knife flying. Ejuk continued to crawl, and Victor turned back to Willow. He would deal with her first, killing her where she stood.

CHAPTER TWENTY-EIGHT

Willow made a decision quickly. She needed the book. She needed to protect Ejuk. As the Slayer dragged herself across the carpet, moving away from the assassins, Willow brought the book up suddenly under Victor's chin, snapping his head back painfully.

Ejuk stood up on shaky legs, and Willow could hear her labored breathing. The Slayer coughed, spattering the marble floor with blood. She managed to stagger a short distance away, heading straight for Buffy. Victor looked from Willow to the Slayer and opted to follow Ejuk.

Clutching the book, Willow pursued him, resolving to fight him with everything she was worth.

Ejuk reached Buffy's writhing form. She fell on top of her, the flies instantly swarming over her body. Victor caught up to her, saw the boils and sores on Buffy as the insects cleared away.

Her body teeming with roiling insects, Ejuk had mere seconds. Before the plague could drop her, she ran straight for Victor, throwing her arms around him and embracing him.

Once again the flies transferred to a new home. Nestling inside Victor's ears and eyes, they buzzed and burrowed. The black, wriggling insects covered the assassin's body and he screamed, falling backward. Ejuk released him and crawled away to safety.

Willow caught a movement out of the corner of her eye. The second assassin closed in on Ejuk, producing a long knife from his jacket pocket.

Willow had to act fast. She ran straight for Namtar. The god stood still in one corner, hovering out of view of the *mushussu* in a small recess. The snake-dragon turned now, watching Willow move, its interest rekindled. It slunk low to intercept her. Behind it, the god emerged from his recess, his eyes flashing in anger. The creature moved with more subtlety than the god, who preferred smashing to sneaking. She didn't want to deal with both adversaries at the same time, but had no choice.

Running up to Namtar, she kicked him in the toe. He glared down at her, mouth a grim slit. The snake-dragon was nearly upon them. When she could smell its foul breath close by, she shouted, jumping up and down.

The *mushussu* leaped out from behind a pillar, bringing a clawed hand down on top of her. As the nails crashed into the stone floor, pulverizing it on contact, Willow wriggled out from between two fingers.

The snake-dragon looked up, locked eyes with Namtar.

And then all chaos erupted.

CHAPTER TWENTY-NINE

Namtar stepped out from the recess by the wall as the snake-dragon slammed its tail into his side. He stumbled, knocking over a pillar. The temple shook. That couldn't be good. Which columns were support pillars? Willow didn't know, but she suspected they were all important.

With the god and creature fighting above her, Willow dodged and leaped, avoiding their feet. This was not what she'd had in mind.

"Hey!" she shouted at the god. "You're pathetic! You're the lamest excuse for a plague god I've ever seen!"

Namtar didn't even glance down. He reached out one meaty hand and gripped the snake-dragon around the throat.

The creature whipped its long neck around, flinging off the god's grip and snapping its jaws down hard on his forearm.

Namtar cried out in fury and pounded a fist into the creature's side. The *mushussu* fell over, rolling to a stop in the center of the hall.

Willow looked to Ejuk. She stood, listing, blood pouring from her back and chest, dodging blows from the second assassin.

On the floor, Victor screamed in agony, rolling back and forth frantically in an effort to squash the flies. It wasn't working.

How could Willow piss off Namtar without using words? Her English was about as useless as a wet sock in a fight.

The book weighed heavily in her hands as she watched the supernatural beings clash. The book! Quickly she ducked out of the way, crouching again. She flipped to the table of contents. There was a section on insults! She flipped to it, then scanned through the translations and the transliterated sounds beneath the cuneiform symbols. She hoped Echinal got some of the words right this time.

Peering up at the god, she shouted out, "You extravagant monkey rump!" in ancient Sumerian.

The god stopped. He held one hand out, keeping the *mushussu* at bay, and glared down at her. Then anger and indignation flushed through his face. Heat radiated off him like the sudden ignition of a bonfire.

Behind her, the assassin struck Ejuk to the ground, raising

a knife. The Slayer struggled to kick the blade away, but it descended fast.

Namtar roared. Willow stepped back. It worked. Namtar all but forgot about the snake-dragon and came after her. She ran straight to the assassin, then stopped, jumping up and down and taunting the god. Man, was she destined for a hell dimension now.

He lowered a fist hard, and she jumped away just in time. Unfortunately, so did the vampire.

Ejuk crawled out of range, leaving an alarming trail of blood on the stone floor. She was losing life fast.

Near her, Buffy groaned and came to, blinking open swollen eyes. One had gone white, unseeing. Her muscles had wasted away, leaving a mere skin-covered skeleton. She tried to rise, but immediately fell again, her haunted face gaunt and gray. Willow realized then that the flies had been on her for too long. Her situation was even more precarious than Ejuk's. The Slayer who had been her dear friend for two years was about to die.

A *whoosh* of wind nearly knocked Willow over. Pain erupted in her back as a massive tail crashed into her, sweeping her out of the way. The snake-dragon crawled onto Namtar's back, digging its claws in deeply. Wounds tore open, leaking blood onto the stone below. The powerful tail wrapped around the god's body, crushing the air from his lungs.

Namtar staggered and swayed. Willow ran as he crashed down, the echoing thud raining plaster and tiles down from the ceiling. She covered her head, then saw Buffy lying exposed and vulnerable. Willow ran to the Slayer's side and shielded her with her body.

"Will?" Buffy breathed. "I can't get up."

"I know," Willow said, fighting back tears. Even if she banished the god and the snake-dragon, how would she heal Buffy and the others? She looked to where Xander lay, now unconscious, viscous drool spilling down his chin. Giles lay some distance away, not moving at all. She studied his back for any sign of movement, a hint of a breath. None came.

While she clutched her friend tightly, the tiles striking her in the back and legs, Willow peered out at the fight. Namtar struggled on all fours, shrugging and swaying, attempting to throw off the *mushussu*. But the creature would not relent. It clung tightly to his back, digging the vicious claws in deeper and deeper.

In a minute he would succeed in throwing off the snake-dragon and would crush Buffy and Willow both if she stayed there. Loath to leave her friend, Willow stood up as the rain of masonry slowed. Still clutching the book, she sprinted away. Namtar struggled to his knees, grasping the snake-dragon around the neck and throwing it violently to one side.

The mohawked assassin took advantage of the distraction and moved again toward Ejuk. Willow selected another insult from the page and shouted, "You have all the intelligence of festering pig stool!" in her best Sumerian yet.

Namtar's head snapped down to meet her gaze, fire raging in his eyes. She was so dead.

She ran to where the assassin vamp crouched over Ejuk. Namtar leaped up to stomp on Willow with both feet. She dove to the side. The god landed solidly, crushing one of the vamp's legs, pulverizing the bone instantly. He cried out in agony, and then the snake-dragon lunged for Namtar. It grabbed him around the throat with both forelegs, digging claws into his flesh. The tail swept around to stabilize its balance and connected with the vampire's head.

In one clean swipe, the head was knocked right off. Dust erupted from where the assassin stood. Ejuk glanced over her shoulder at Willow.

With Namtar once again distracted by the snake-dragon, Willow rushed to Ejuk's side, pointing to the inscription. Ejuk read it over once, then spoke it, loudly and clearly. In an instant Namtar vanished and the snake-dragon crashed to the floor, looking rather surprised and confused.

Willow flipped through the book again, found a creature-banishing spell, and pointed it out to Ejuk. She spoke this one aloud. The shimmering air returned, and Willow gave a short little bow to the *mushussu* as it disappeared into the glimmering haze.

Ejuk collapsed, and Willow stood up in the ruined space. A low moan snapped her attention to where Buffy lay. Where moments before the Slayer lay dying, wasted away to nothing but bones, she now knelt, healthy, pink, and boil free. Xander came to, standing up groggily. Giles rolled over, hoisted himself up, and glanced around, confused.

And to Willow's left, Victor groaned and blinked, propping himself up on one elbow. She walked to him, standing over him. Giles joined her, then Xander. Buffy stood and approached purposefully. She placed a boot on Victor's chest and pulled out a stake.

Lightning fast, Victor produced his knife and slashed Buffy across the ankle, biting through her boot. She cried out and staggered backward.

He leaped up, shouting out an incantation and sprinting away from them. Full of adrenaline, Willow gave chase. The portal winked into view, dazzling her, forcing her to shield her eyes. Victor jumped into it and vanished.

Willow had half a mind to leap in, then decided just to curse. But she didn't. Instead she turned, taking in the Sumerian Slayer, now lying unconscious on the ziggurat floor. The plague had been healed miraculously, but her wounds were not supernatural.

She had no Watcher and no family to look after her.

As Willow glanced around the ruins of the ziggurat's great hall, movement caught her eyes. Three temple priestesses and then Gilgamesh himself appeared. He looked sleepy, rubbing his eyes and yawning. Instead of regal robes, he wore a simple sleeping shirt. He'd slept through the battle. She couldn't believe it.

When the priestesses saw Ejuk, they rushed to her side, examining the wound.

Gilgamesh stepped forward, exchanging words with Giles,

who also studied the wound closely. While Willow and the others stood by helplessly, the priestesses fetched a stretcher and carefully placed the Slayer on top.

Ejuk's eyes fluttered as they lifted her. Her gaze found Willow's, and she winked, a faint smile curling her lips. Willow smiled back.

Giles squeezed her shoulder. "She'll be okay. And when we get back, we can check to see how long she lived. And you," he said to her as the others drew near. "I am stunned. We simply could not have pulled that off without you. You showed unparalleled courage and ingenuity."

Willow looked down, bashful. She wasn't used to overt praise. Her mother made a hobby of ignoring her for the most part. The words meant a lot, and she blushed.

Gilgamesh clasped arms with Giles and then left, following the others to attend to Ejuk.

Alone in the crumbling great hall, Buffy said, "Let's go home."

They all nodded. "Remind me not to laugh at any gods in the future," Xander said.

"Count on it," Buffy retorted. "Or if you do, have it be the god of facials or gift cards. No more plague gods. Got it?"

"Got it."

The four drew close together, and Giles spoke the incantation. In a moment the portal returned and they dove into it, bracing themselves for the sickening journey home.

CHAPTER THIRTY

Sunnydale, 1998

Buffy wasn't centered in the portal. She spun wildly, head over hips, feet and arms flailing in the gusting wind. When the velocity slowed and the vortex spat her out, she sailed through the air, arms reaching for something to slow her fall. She opened her eyes, saw the ground rushing up beneath her at a painful angle, and then landed with a soft *splush*. Hesitantly, she lifted her spinning head, hearing a familiar sound sweep into her world. A gentle hush, a sigh, then the hush again. Waves. Her hands wriggled in the ground. Soft sand. For one frightening second she thought Giles had made a mistake, sending them to Anglesey instead. Then she peered out onto the beach. The Sunnydale beach. She knew it well. The sun had long since set, and the horizon over the sea sparkled with stars. Whitecaps glowed as the waves pulsed in and out.

Struggling to sit up in the shifting sand, Buffy squinted up at the portal, which immediately dimmed out. She glanced around her. This time she was the last to arrive. Willow's feet stuck out of a sand dune a few feet away. Giles lay on the beach, the waves washing over him. He struggled to remove an errant strand of kelp from his face. She got to her hands and knees, crawling toward Willow, searching for Xander.

Then she spotted him, hanging from the lifeguard station a dozen yards away. His fingers slipped and he fell into the sand below, giving a soft grunt as he landed. "I hate this mode of travel!" he shouted, lying still on the beach.

"I can't say I disagree," Giles said, spitting out slimy bits of green vegetation. He staggered to Buffy, and together they pulled Willow out of the sandbank. Bits of broken seashells and a dried, washed-up jellyfish clung to her hair.

Xander reached them, unsteady on his feet. A car alarm sounded a few blocks away. They were definitely home.

"What's next?" Buffy asked Giles.

"Sleep," said Xander.

"A bath," chimed Willow.

"English breakfast tea, for the love of Pete," moaned Giles.

Buffy shook her head at them. "You guys are no fun."

On the walk to the library, Buffy stopped to read the date on a newspaper. "It's still Saturday." A wall clock inside a cafe told them it was an hour and a half after they'd left. Buffy felt exhausted. A bath and some sleep did sound good. But she was pretty wound up. Even though she knew they'd arrive at the same time as the assassins on the next time jump, illogically she still felt terrible about taking the time to eat and sleep.

They checked on Angel and Lucien, who cursed when he saw them enter the library. "Killed some more of your boys," Buffy told him.

Lucien's eyes widened. "And Victor?"

"Next time," she assured him, "he'll be dust."

Lucien laughed. "That's unlikely."

Buffy walked closer to the cage. "I seriously doubt it'll be a problem. If he wasn't so concerned with running away all the time, I'd have killed him by now. Where did you dig these guys up? Incompetence 'R' Us?" In truth, she knew at least Victor would be difficult to face down, but she kept that out of her tone and expression.

Lucien scowled, and Buffy turned to hug Angel. Her face pressed against the cool skin of his chest. "Missed you back there," she whispered.

"Missed you back here."

"This guy give you any trouble?" She pulled away.

"No, unfortunately. It would be a real shame to have to rough him up."

Buffy glowered at Lucien over her shoulder. "Yeah. A real shame."

"Well," Giles said, picking up a fresh set of books on the

center table. "It's time we got some rest. These next two jumps may be our most difficult yet."

"I guarantee it," Lucien growled.

They ignored him. Giles looked at his watch. "Let's meet back here tomorrow morning at six a.m."

"Six a.m.!" Xander cried. "I know that's a number on my clock, but I've never actually been awake to personally witness it!"

"Well, this will be a new experience for you, then," Giles retorted. "I want us to leave as early as possible. Every time we return, we do so an hour or more later. If we need sleep again, we draw inexorably toward the school week. And I don't think Principal Snyder would take kindly to having a vampire locked in the library storage cage."

Xander crossed his arms. "Fine."

Giles turned to Angel. "I have some additional research to do here, if you want to go eat."

"Thanks," Angel told him.

Buffy looked up at him. "You going to be okay watching this guy for two more time jumps?"

Angel regarded Lucien menacingly. Their eyes met. "Wouldn't have it any other way." He turned back and touched Buffy's shoulder. "Want me to walk you home?"

She smiled. "That sounds nice." She hefted the satchel off her aching shoulder. "Would you carry my books?"

"Of course."

Xander turned to Willow. "Will. Me. You. Pizza?"

"Sounds good. But after I go home and shower. I still have dried kelp in my hair."

They all said good-bye and parted. Buffy couldn't wait to lie down and shut her eyes. They burned with exhaustion. Having the plague could really tire a person out.

The next morning everyone met in the library on time. Giles laid out plain cotton shirts, woolen pants, vests, and thick brown jackets for them to wear. "We're jumping into the Civil War," he told them. "We're going as farmers. The clothes are neutral. No blue. No gray. Many of these battles were fought in fields that neighbor farms and plantations, so we should quite easily pass as civilians. I thought all of us should dress as men. Fighting in hoop skirts and a corset might prove difficult."

"I'll say," Buffy agreed, glad that her time period afforded her comfortable halter tops, jeans, and short skirts.

"The Slayer we're saving is Agatha Primrose, who lives in Tennessee. Unfortunately, she doesn't live much further into the future. But if she dies even a week before her natural death, a different Slayer could be activated."

Buffy nodded, feeling sad. She wondered how much further into the future her own life would last.

While they changed, Giles checked all of their satchels, making sure they had maps, paper, pencils, and water. To his own satchel, he added another spell book, and a book on the history of Civil War battles and troop movements. He hoped they wouldn't need it.

Buffy rummaged through the satchel contents, pulling out at least three different maps. "Will we really need all this?" she asked, glancing at a map showing the North's and South's battle tactics.

"I hope not," he told her.

Buffy hugged Angel good-bye and gathered with the others while Giles unfolded the incantation. Inside, his stomach gurgled with nervousness. It had been bad enough to jump into the middle of a Roman confrontation. But this would be worse. Over the millennia, warfare had grown more and more efficient. Cannon, gunfire, flying shrapnel. They'd have to tread carefully.

Holding up the incantation, he spoke the words and the portal appeared, its brilliance bathing the library in pulsing light.

Then, holding his breath, he jumped into the vortex, pushing thoughts of errant bullets and the thunder of cannon out of his mind.

CHAPTER THIRTY-ONE

Tennessee, 1862

The blinding light narrowed to a pinpoint, and Buffy braced herself to tumble out into unknown territory. She felt a hand brush her arm and turned, squinting, to see Willow spinning through the air next to her. The velocity ended abruptly as the portal ejected them into a frigid river, where they landed with a loud splash. Instantly her head went underwater. She struggled, trying to get her bearings as she tumbled uncontrollably through swift-moving water.

She found the surface, came up for air, and stretched out her hands to find something solid. Her fingers slipped over a slimy log, then grasped a rough rock. She gripped its jagged edges, pulling her upper body out of the water. Blinking cold wetness from her eyes, she stared out into a dim night. She clung to the rock in the center of the rain-swollen river. A few feet behind her, Willow flailed in the water. As she streaked by, Buffy grabbed her under the arm, hauling her over the rock and to safety. She didn't see Giles or Xander. The rain poured down over her, though she was so thoroughly soaked she couldn't get any wetter. She shivered in the chilly spring air.

The water drained from her ears as she caught her breath, sucking it in deeply. Splashing and a cry of surprise snapped her attention upstream. Giles and Xander bobbed along in the current. Xander was too limp to be swimming. Giles gripped him under the chin, and blood streamed down Xander's face.

A strong swimmer, Giles made it to their rock, and Buffy took Xander from him. "He hit his head on a submerged rock," Giles said. "I don't think he's conscious."

Buffy looked down at her bleeding friend. "We need to get out of the water. We don't want a repeat of Anglesey." She frowned. "I thought we would be arriving in the middle of a battle. I don't hear anything."

"I don't believe it's started yet," Giles whispered. "But when it does, we must all be exceedingly careful. These old rifles weren't always terribly accurate. One stray ball could fell any of us."

While Giles and Willow pulled their unconscious friend from the river, Buffy darted quickly into the trees along the bank. A tiny fire burned in the distance. For now, this particular area looked relatively clear. Of course, skirmishers or scouts could be hiding in the trees, and she wouldn't see them until they gunned her down. Their neutral farmer costumes might help for now, but they would still be targets for robbery or worse. Soldiers, desperate and hungry, who hadn't seen their families in months, pushed to the limit by endlessly firing on fellow countrymen, could be driven to desperate actions.

Buffy scanned their surroundings. Trees lined the riverbank. The countryside beyond was a patchwork of clearings and clusters of trees, with some denser sections of forest here and there. She watched silently for any sign of the assassins. This time they'd landed in the dark. The vampires wouldn't have to waste any time hiding out until night. Even now they could be on their way to the Slayer. The farmhouse where she lived lay somewhere nearby, but Buffy needed Giles's map to pinpoint the direction. Not seeing any sign of the vampires, she crept back to her friends.

On the riverbank Xander groaned, his eyes fluttering open. "You okay?" Buffy asked him when she reached them. He nodded.

Willow's brow creased with concern as she bent over her friend. "That's pretty nasty. How many fingers am I holding up?" She held up two.

"Six," he answered, groaning and rolling over onto his side. "I feel sick." He vomited into the sand, then wiped his mouth on his sleeve. "Can't I have a time jump where I don't vomit? This is two times in a row."

"Yeah, you had it lucky in Anglesey," Willow said.

"Yep. Nothing to worry about but ritual sacrifice," he muttered.

"Sounds like you might have a concussion. We should probably stash you somewhere until we find the Slayer's house," Buffy said.

Xander raised his eyebrows. "*Stash* me somewhere? I'm not a pile of dirty laundry over here."

"Yeah, but you're about as useful with that knock on your head," she retorted.

"Thanks a lot," he groaned. "At least in Sunnydale I'm good for fetching doughnuts."

"I don't think you'll be finding any jelly doughnuts around here," Willow whispered nervously.

"We're okay for now," Giles said quietly. "Most of the fighting will take place during the day. If we can make it to the Slayer's house before dawn, we can skirt around much of the fighting."

"We don't have much time," Buffy said, looking to the sky. A dim light glowed above the eastern horizon.

"What about stashing me?" Xander asked.

"We'll find a place." Buffy stood up, scanning the shore for a good area to hide him. What seemed dark and shadowed now might not be at all come daybreak. The best place to leave him would be in the Slayer's farmhouse, if they could get to it easily. She reached into her satchel and pulled out the maps.

Giles flicked a match, and they studied the lines and

drawings. “Here’s the Tennessee River,” Giles said, pointing to a thin blue squiggle running diagonally across.

Buffy laid a fingertip on a small square. “And here’s the farmhouse.”

“So we just need to figure out where along this squiggle we are,” Willow murmured, scanning the shore.

Few landmarks marked the map. Pittsburg Landing, the spot currently occupied by General Ulysses S. Grant, lay just to the west of the Tennessee River. Shiloh Church stood farther to the west. The farmhouse lay on the eastern side of the river, away from the area of battle. Buffy took the map and walked again to the thick of the trees. Giles followed her.

“Those fires,” he said, pointing to the flames in the darkness on their side of the river, “are likely Union camps. The Confederates wouldn’t risk starting fires if they wanted to surprise the enemy. That means we are clearly on the wrong side of the bank. We need to ford the river.”

Buffy nodded. The farmhouse lay south of the road to Savannah, on a small, unnamed road that wound through the countryside. If they crossed the river now, the house could be to the north or south. They needed to start from a landmark. If they could make it to the Savannah road, they should spot the smaller farmhouse road.

She glanced back at the map, squinting in the darkness. She located where Grant had positioned his men, and where Generals Johnston and Beauregard of the Confederate Army waited. If the fires were Grant’s, they were close to the road, just to the south. A different Union encampment would mean they might have to head north a bit.

"The map was a good idea, Giles," Buffy admitted.

"I thought you'd feel that way once you got here." He grinned. "History still too dusty for you?"

"Right now history's too dark for me," she said, struggling to make out features on the map. She couldn't get her bearings. The road could lie in either direction. If they waited until light, on the first day of one of the bloodiest battles of the Civil War, they'd all be in danger.

Her best chance was to do a little scouting now. The road to Savannah met the river almost directly across from Pittsburg Landing. She just needed to find Grant's encampment at Pittsburg Landing and go from there. Who knew all that orienteering in sixth-grade camp would actually pay off? Maybe one day she'd find a lifesaving reason for making a macrame owl.

She and Giles returned to the others. "You all need to cross the river, and I need to do a little scouting," she told them.

Giles immediately shook his head. "It's not safe."

"None of this is safe, Giles," she argued. "It's better I go out there now than have us all traipsing about with no idea which direction to go." She gripped his arm affectionately. "I'll be careful. They won't even know I'm there."

"Buffy, I don't like this," Willow said, her eyes wide in the dark.

"I know, Will, but I'll be okay. It's the best chance we've got."

"What about me?" Xander said. "I still need to be stashed."

"The others can carry you. Cross the river at this point and wait for me. Stay out of sight if I'm not back before dawn."

"You don't have to tell us that," Xander said. "I'll be burying myself in leaves and dirt, thank you very much."

Buffy watched as her friends lifted Xander and helped him into a shadowed copse. "I'll be back soon," she whispered, and crept away from her friends, toward a nation at war.

CHAPTER THIRTY-TWO

Stealthily Buffy kept to the trees, slinking closer to the flickering fires. She hoped they were Grant's, as his men held the most northern position. If more fires glimmered beyond those, then she would keep heading north until she located Pittsburg Landing.

She scanned the ground for landmarks on the map. She didn't see any. But once she found Pittsburg Landing, she'd swim the river and walk down the opposite bank until she found the others. That way they wouldn't have to cross dangerous ground and risk a bullet.

On the horizon, the glow of dawn grew in intensity. The crack of a rifle sounded to her left, startlingly close. She ducked low beneath the branches, squatting. Peering out, she watched for any hint of movement. Through the trees a hundred yards off emerged two Confederate soldiers, their rifles and pistols gripped tightly in both hands. She sat still, watching them. Fortunately, they hadn't seen her. Quickly they ran across an open space and found shelter again in a nearby copse of trees. They moved furtively, glancing in every direction. Perhaps they were scouts, getting a bead on the Union position.

The rifle sounded again, still from her left, and Buffy watched in horror as one of the men went down, screaming in pain. His friend crouched low beside him, peering backward into the trees. While the wounded soldier cried out, thrashing in the grass, the other held him down and cocked his pistol, aiming it into the nearby forest.

A cloud of smoke billowed up from the edge of the trees as the rifle fired again, much closer. The second soldier cried out, falling dead, sprawling over his companion. From out of the trees stepped a Union soldier, wearing the green uniform of a sharpshooter. Grime streaked his face, and his uniform was torn in a dozen places. He gripped his rifle in one hand and jogged to the two soldiers, his pistol drawn and aimed. When he reached the men, he stood over them for a long minute, checking to see if they were alive. Then he holstered his pistol and wiped sweat from his brow. They all looked about the same age, early twenties, maybe just teenagers. It hit Buffy hard. They were only a bit older than she was. Fighting each other, killing each other. Some states were even split down the middle, with some families fighting for the North and others for the South. Neighbors fighting neighbors. It would be as if she picked up a rifle and gunned down people from her own state or even town, sneaking around in the forests of the United States, shooting other Americans.

She waited for him to go. When he had slunk away across another clearing and entered the trees some distance away, she stood up. Glancing in all directions, she chanced a run across the field.

Up ahead lay another cluster of trees, then a small clearing, then more trees. A gentle hill rose up before her, dotted with oak and hickory trees. Just a few more feet, and she'd be safely undercover.

With a deafening report, a bullet whizzed by her head. She had been spotted.

CHAPTER THIRTY-THREE

Stop!" a man shouted.

Buffy ran.

From the trees behind her emerged a Confederate scout, his pistol drawn. She fled the small clearing, racing up the little hill. Reaching the small grouping of trees, she flung her body flat against one of the trunks and chanced a look back.

The scout charged across the field, heading directly for her.

Her stomach went sour at the thought of being spotted. On top of the shaking fear she felt at being in a war zone, what if this changed the scout's original path? What if he got killed now, when originally he had survived the Civil War? Then all of his descendents would never be born. She had to ditch him.

She left the safety of the trunk and ran farther up the hill, toward a denser part of the forest. The faint dawn light was absent in these thick trees. She stumbled over a fallen log, then turned and looked back at it. It was immense, a centuries-old tree that had toppled years before. Partially hollow, its thick trunk sported dozens of ferns and lush green moss.

"Stop!" the scout yelled again, alarmingly close.

Buffy ran back to the fallen log and lay down next to it. Quickly she wriggled her body inside the hollow cavity, heaping earth onto herself. The smell of dirt crept into her nostrils. With a thud the scout landed on top of the log. He jumped down on the other side, and for a second that lasted far too long, he paused, scanning the trees for her.

"Stop, I say!"

Buffy held her breath. He hadn't seen her hide.

Picking a direction, the soldier rushed away, cocking his pistol and carelessly tripping over fallen branches in his haste.

When she was certain he'd gone, Buffy crawled out of the log, brushing the dirt from her woolen trousers and jacket. She stood up. By now the world was almost light. She could see farther than she'd been able to before. Through the thick trunks, she could make out another clearing, with objects and people moving silently in it.

Hurriedly she crept to the edge of the trees. She stood at the top of the rise. The hill sloped away beneath her, opening out into a vast meadow. A sea of gray uniforms, thousands of soldiers strong, filled the clearing. Lines of cannon brought up the rear. For a second she thought she'd grown deaf, for she couldn't hear them at all. Then one man coughed, and she realized they were poised for an attack, hoping to surprise Grant. She looked out into the distance, hoping to spot the Union camp and therefore Pittsburg Landing.

But instead she saw something else, completely unexpected. A huge river, wending its way through the countryside, vast and swift.

They hadn't landed in the Tennessee River.

For there it was, clearly, a massive, coursing body of water ten times bigger than what they'd tumbled into. They must have landed in some tributary, or in an unconnected stream, which meant she didn't know where she was after all.

Quietly she pulled out the map, gently unfolding it to make as little noise as possible. In the dim light, she tried to make out the squiggles and blocks and arrows. She scanned the brief battle description written down by Giles. With this many soldiers present, this gathering must be the main attack force of Johnston, which surprised Grant by attacking at six a.m.

She wouldn't be able to stick to the shores of the Tennessee River to find the road like she'd thought. For even though she could see it twinkling in the distance, the Tennessee River still lay miles to the northeast. She had to plunge forward, into the heart of the occupied territory. Behind her amassed more and more soldiers from Johnston's stronghold in Corinth, Mississippi. And ahead of her waited Grant's unsuspecting army, thousands strong.

Right now, instead of standing on the edge of the conflict, she was in the center of it.

CHAPTER THIRTY-FOUR

Buffy waited in silence, and light slowly crept into her world. Now about a quarter mile away, she could see a shadowed log building behind a small group of trees. A cross stood on the roof, at the top of a rough-hewn steeple. Shiloh Chapel. She looked at her map. This was the location of one of the most tenacious parts of the attack, where many soldiers lost their lives. It was one of the most dangerous places for her to go. But she couldn't stay where she was, either. If anyone saw her, as the scout had done, they would likely shoot her on sight for fear she'd give away the surprise attack.

Her neutral farmer outfit might not mean much on a day

like this, with soldiers psyched up for battle and everyone tense and terrified.

She studied the map closely. Behind her ran the stream they'd landed in. To her right, she heard the trickling of another small river. If she stood south of Shiloh Church, with the rising sun to her right, that put her somewhere along the Shiloh Branch or Rhea Springs. To get to Pittsburg Landing as quickly as possible, she would have to skirt slightly south, going around the Southern army. When she could no longer see their numbers, she'd head north. Unfortunately, there were no creeks she could follow. She'd have to use the sun. Looking at the scale bar, she calculated about two miles to the farmhouse if she followed that course, and she'd have to cross the Tennessee River along the way.

She scanned the battle description again. For now, the Scoobies were safe where they were. The Confederates would not pass back that way until evening the next day, when they had faced defeat. They'd march along the Corinth Road, which Buffy still had not come across. She had some time.

She looked ahead at the mass of soldiers, which now began to move forward, marching deliberately and silently through the dense sections of trees and open spaces. The battle was about to begin.

Her best bet was to scout ahead, figure out exactly where the Union army waited, and figure out a way around them. Then she'd go back for the others, and together they'd make their way toward the farmhouse.

An eruption of rifle fire ahead of her forced her to clamp her hands over her ears. The deafening shots echoed over the countryside. Birds chattered and flew away, leaving feathers behind. Confederate soldiers whooped and uttered war cries, and another simultaneous boom of a thousand rifles reported and echoed around her.

Screams rose up. Then an answering cry of rifle fire. The boom of a cannon.

Buffy turned and ran, heading south, down the small rise.

She skirted along the side of the battle, choosing her way carefully. Every time she had to run from one thicket of trees to another, her heart pounded heavily in her chest. Soldiers could be anywhere, clustered in any group of trees. But she managed to remain unseen.

Finally she began to head north again. She crossed two meandering streams and placed herself roughly on the map. The crack and report of rifle fire was unending. How many bullets were used? How many soldiers fallen? She tried not to think about that. Instead, she mentally recorded the path she took, so that she could retrace it later with the others.

She ran up another small rise, hid in a cluster of trees, and peered out. Ahead lay some kind of small dirt road, rambling through an orchard. At first she thought snow clung to the branches. She crept closer, moving down from the rise. No soldiers in sight. Now closer, she realized the snow was white peach blossoms. To see such beauty in the middle of a violent battle struck her powerfully.

The fruit trees were thick enough to offer plentiful cover, and she reached them in a few seconds. She studied the road, trying to place it on the map. Over the centuries, so many wagons, horses, soldiers, and carts had passed along this way that the road had actually sunk into the earth. She took in a quick breath. Sunk into the earth. The Sunken Road. She found it on the map.

Here the Union soldiers held back the Confederate advance until the Southern artillery had all but obliterated them and their position. She heard the nearby shot of a rifle. It was already starting—the Union formation of the "Hornet's Nest," a location the South fought to overtake during the entire battle. Though heavy casualties resulted, the maneuver had bought enough time for Union reinforcements to arrive, leading to their victory. But that time was in the future. For now, the Union soldiers fought for their lives, cries of pain echoing up as one after another was picked off by Confederate snipers.

She started to move off the road, then suddenly realized that she was much farther north than she thought. As she ran down one embankment of the road, crossed it, and ran up the opposite, she caught sight of the Union sharpshooters, a hundred feet away. They used the natural sunken contours of the road to their advantage. The riflemen lay on their bellies in the dirt, partially protected from gunfire by the banks of earth on both sides. Scores of uniformed men covered the sunken, deep path meandering through the oak-hickory forest.

The crack of gunfire and the booming of cannon filled her

world. The acrid smell of gunpowder floated low in the air, a layer of smoke visible just above her head. She stood beneath a peach tree, catching her breath, and imagined taking a gun, kissing her mom good-bye, and traveling south to kill Alabamans. Or north to kill Virginians. She shook her head. The idea was crazy.

But it was exactly what these people were doing.

Gunned down by the Hornet's Nest, a Confederate soldier slumped down at the base of an oak, blood blossoming in his chest. She watched, transfixed in horror.

Then she pivoted south, deafened by the roar of gunfire erupting from the Union soldiers. Confederates answered their fire, inviting more, and another thick cloud of smoke rose up through the forest. The acrid stench of gunfire gagged her and made her eyes stream.

Silently she made her way south again, away from the conflict. But as she left the road behind, a solitary shot rang out, a little closer than the others. Buffy ran on. Her leg felt strange and wet, but she didn't stop. She ran farther south but kept getting slower and slower. She didn't understand it. Her leg wouldn't do what she asked it to do. It got sluggish, then locked up. She fell. Forced herself to stand again. Plummeted back to the ground.

Then she looked down at her right leg. Blood soaked her trousers. She'd been hit. Shot. Her body trembled. Her teeth chattered. She forced herself up, gripping the trunk of a tree to steady herself.

Though she needed help, a sudden fear to advance seized her. Breathing in and out, she tried to focus. This was what it had been like. Soldiers scared like this. All the time. They didn't see their families for years at a time, or never again if they fell on the battlefield.

Up ahead, on the far side of a group of trees, she heard a sudden moan of pain, then someone sobbing uncontrollably. She blinked sweat out of her eyes. Tried to think. She was bleeding, and bad. She needed to make a tourniquet. Another crying voice floated by on the wind.

Leaning against the tree, Buffy yanked the belt from around her waist. She wrapped it around her thigh and tightened until it hurt and throbbed. She knew there was a Union field hospital around here, but she had no idea where. And could she go there? She stumbled away from the tree, determined to make it to the farmhouse. She was halfway to it. In either direction, she'd have to walk a mile. Her leg continued to bleed, the tourniquet not yet stanching the flow of blood. Her body began to shake uncontrollably. She wiped her palms, slick with sticky blood, on her pants and staggered forward.

She was thirsty. So thirsty.

Ahead, the moans and cries grew louder. She passed through a clump of trees and fell. Lifting her head, she saw a small pond surrounded by ancient oak trees. Dozens of soldiers, Union and Confederate alike, lay littered around it. Some drank, some bathed their wounds. The water ran red. Groans rose pitifully up from the pond's edges.

The clouds rumbled overhead. A small drizzle began to rain over them, droplets collecting on the branches, glistening in the fallen leaves.

In front of the pond stood one particularly tremendous oak tree, branches the size of its trunk, still bare after the winter. The tree was old, she realized, terribly old. A Union soldier dragged himself over its roots, then propped himself beneath its branches. He breathed his last desperate, ragged breaths in its shelter. Then he slumped over, dead.

The unbearable dryness in Buffy's throat compelled her to drag herself forward. Every muscle trembled and shook, rebelling against the movement. But she forced herself. The crying and suffering soldiers took no notice of her as she pulled herself to the edge of the pond, leaving a trail of blood in her wake.

The water tantalizingly close, but out of reach, her body ached for a drink. A Confederate soldier fell over next to her, his sightless eyes staring up at the gray, roiling sky.

She forced herself to focus on the grand trees and shadowed valleys, golden fields in which the deer gathered at dusk. She tried to imagine what this place must have been like before humans arrived, before scores of soldiers died for causes like securing advantageous locations to fire cannon. She imagined the fields and groves of trees without the thousands of bleeding and broken soldiers, but instead full of foraging deer and black bear.

She pushed past the fallen soldier, trying to reach the

water. She thought of Giles, of how he'd looked out for her, of her mother telling her to do her homework. How she longed to be back there. How welcome doing her homework sounded right now. As her vision swam, Buffy tried hard to hold on to consciousness. She would get a drink and then somehow make it to the field hospital. She had to. If she didn't, she would die and the assassins would kill the other Slayer. The Master would reign, and everything she held dear would perish.

Another soldier fell by her side, then another and another. She became just another body piled before Bloody Pond, fighting for a drink, fighting to stay alive just one more precious moment.

Her vision darkened and tunneled, and Buffy cried out in dismay, flailing in her efforts to force herself to stand. Tears streamed down her face. Then her body stopped shaking, and the world went dark.

CHAPTER THIRTY-FIVE

Buffy's eyes fluttered open, feeling impossibly heavy. She lifted her eyelids, and with considerable effort stared up at the night sky above her. Stars filled the skies, more brilliant than she'd ever seen them before. The Milky Way stretched across the heavens. The sky twinkled with a billion distant suns.

An elbow jarred her shoulder. In her right ear, she heard a slurping noise. Slowly she tilted her heavy head to look in that direction. A dark shape bent over the soldier next to her, dipping its head and licking. Then a horrific face leaped into view, a leering face staring down at her, running a pointed tongue over fangs grown long and sharp.

Her mind fought through a haze of pain as the face loomed closer. It was something she knew, something familiar. And somehow she'd always been able to stop it in the past. But now she couldn't remember. She felt so tired. She tried to lift one arm, but it lay at her side, pinned down by the weight of a fallen Confederate soldier.

Buffy blinked, her worldview filling with the terrifying face, the protruding brow ridges, the yellow, feverish eyes. It bore down on her, grinning, and she felt the cold lips against her neck.

Just as the mouth opened against her flesh and she felt the wet fangs meet her skin, the entire creature erupted into dust. Flecks rained down over her face and eyes, and she squeezed them shut.

When she opened them again, mere moments later, the hideous slurping sound had stopped. Above her swam the face of a young woman. Curls of blond hair escaped from a black riding hat. "You don't look like a typical soldier," she said.

Buffy opened her mouth to answer, but found it so dry that her tongue was rough and her lips cracked open painfully.

"Don't try to talk. I've alerted the field hospital to a number of dying here. They should be here shortly." She gripped Buffy's hand. "I can stay with you for a little while, but then I need to get out there again."

Buffy ran her tongue over chapped lips. "Slayer . . . ," she whispered.

The woman's eyebrows rose in surprise.

"Me . . . too . . . ," Buffy managed, her voice gone. "Danger."

"Don't try to talk." She glanced around, scanning the shadows. "Are you telling me you're a Slayer?" she whispered.

Buffy managed a nod.

"Then I think we need to get you out of here."

She grabbed Buffy's arm to pull her up. When the weight hit her leg, a primal shriek of pain erupted from Buffy's lips. The woman looked down at the gunshot. "You're gravely wounded. I can help you back at my farmhouse. It's not too far from here."

She lifted Buffy up carefully under her knees and shoulders and carried her for an interminable distance. Buffy lost consciousness.

When she awoke, jostling around in the back of a horse-drawn carriage, she reached up and gripped the woman's skirts. "My friends . . . need to save them."

The woman slowed the horse and pivoted in the driver's seat. "Where are they?"

Buffy frowned, trying to fight the haze in her mind to recall the map. "Shiloh Branch . . . or Rhea Spring . . . by the Corinth Road." Pain bloomed suddenly in her leg, and she gritted her teeth, sucking in air.

The woman thought a moment, then wheeled the cart around, riding swiftly back in the direction they'd come. All the jostling hurt Buffy's leg more, but she bit down on the pain, concentrating on the others. At least now they'd found the Slayer, or rather she had found Buffy. All they had to do was wait for the assassin vamps to strike. Of course, Buffy wouldn't be much help when they did.

The carriage bounced along over rolling hills. They forded the two streams Buffy remembered crossing earlier that day. *That day?* she wondered suddenly. How long had she been out? What if days had passed and Giles and the others had moved on, or worse, been killed?

Soon the burble of a larger body of water met her ears. She tried to sit up in the wagon, tried even to lift her head above the side rails, but couldn't. She just lay. "Giles . . . ," she whispered to the other Slayer.

"Giles!" the woman called softly. They rode on. "Giles!" Bouncing along the shores of the Shiloh Branch, she called his name over and over again, careful not to alert any passing scouts.

"Here!" came Xander's voice.

Buffy had never heard such a welcome sound. She tugged on the Slayer's skirts. The wagon slowed, and Xander emerged from the dense foliage near the riverbank, the blood on his head now dried.

He looked first at the woman, then at Buffy lying in the back of the wagon. "Oh my God."

She reached for him, and he took her hand. "Will?" she whispered.

"She's here," he told her. "She just went to get us some water. Giles left hours ago, though, trying to find you."

"I found her at the edge of a pond, among a group of

wounded soldiers," the Slayer told them. "Who are you all? Is she really a Slayer?"

Xander smiled down at her and squeezed her hand. "The best."

"I need to get you to safety, then you can explain. Who is Giles?"

"Her Watcher."

The woman nodded, her mouth suddenly tight. "Then it's vital we find him. But first, she needs medical attention. We must get to my farmhouse."

Xander nodded, releasing Buffy's hand. He jogged back to the river and returned with Willow. "Oh, Buffy," she cried, "am I glad to see you!" As she neared the wagon, her voice trailed off. She stopped in horror, staring at her fallen friend. Then, biting her lower lip, she climbed into the back. When she saw the tourniquet and the blood, she whispered, "Oh, please no." She gripped Buffy's hand.

The crack of a rifle sounded just a few hundred yards away.

"Get in!" the other Slayer ordered Xander. "We need to go now!"

He climbed up hastily, nearly toppling over, and the woman cracked the reins. Whinnying, the horse took off at a solid clip, tearing them away from the gunfire.

Buffy looked at her two friends, thrown around in the small wagon. She felt her eyes sting and swell. So heavy. She had to shut them, just for a little while. As she faded off, she felt Willow checking the tourniquet. And then the blackness swallowed her.

CHAPTER THIRTY-SIX

A violent jostle jarred Buffy awake. Night pressed close. Willow gripped her hand in the back of the wagon, her skin warm. Buffy shook, her body trembling uncontrollably. The wagon tossed them together in the back of the carriage. Xander nearly toppled over, then Willow. Buffy felt sick.

Above them the stars still gleamed, a million jewels in the blackness of the sky. She no longer heard the trickling of the river. Now other sounds filled the night. Moans, sobbing, crying. She tried to lift her head to see over the wagon's edge. Willow pressed a hand to her chest, kept her from rising. "Don't," she whispered. "You don't want this image."

Tears streamed down Willow's dirty face. She pivoted

her head to look over her shoulder, breathing shallowly.

The battlefield. Buffy knew they crossed it now. Thousands of soldiers lay dying in all directions, their pitiful cries like the eerie ululations of ghosts long lost to the living world.

"Look," said Xander to Willow. He pointed.

Willow gasped. "Oh, no . . ."

Buffy tried to swallow, but her dry throat rebelled. "What?" she rasped.

"Vampires," Xander whispered, his voice haunted and hollow.

"Hundreds of them," Willow added. "Feeding off the dying."

Buffy gripped her hand, a monumental effort that took all her strength. "Stop."

Willow shook her head. "You can't fight right now, Buffy," she said, the tears in her voice rising to the surface.

"You may not even—," Xander started.

"Xander, don't," Willow told him forcefully.

Buffy arced her eyes toward the woman driving the wagon. "Slayer . . ."

Xander touched Buffy's shoulder compassionately. "She's stopped, Buffy. More times than we can count. She staked the vamps feeding off soldiers who still have a chance, at least once the doctors from the field hospitals get to them." He paused, glancing in the woman's direction. "She stopped too many times," he said, his mouth now just a gray slit. "It may have cost you your—"

"Don't!" Willow said again, nearly shouting.

Her shout was answered by another, crying out somewhere to the left. The cry was terrified and abandoned, something uttered when there's nothing left to lose, and you are determined to have your last actions on this earth count for something.

It was Giles.

CHAPTER THIRTY-SEVEN

Willow stood up in the carriage, releasing Buffy's hand. "Giles!" she shouted. "Stop the wagon!"

The Slayer slowed the wagon, and Willow jumped out before it came to a halt. She landed hard in the muddy earth. Before her in the dark lay thousands of wounded and dying soldiers, crying out for water, or lost wives, or children.

And somewhere out there was Giles, fighting for his life.

Xander leaped out beside her, then almost fell over with dizziness from his head wound.

"Stay here with Buffy," she told him.

Xander stilled himself on the edge of the wagon. "I can't. The Slayer will protect her."

"I can do this," she told him.

"No, you can't, Will. If he's wounded, it's going to take both of us to carry him back to the wagon."

She looked into his determined gaze and relented. As Giles cried out again, she pinpointed his location, nearly straight ahead, and ran in that direction. As she grew closer, the cries resolved into words. Giles was cursing. And quite the blue streak at that.

Dark shapes slithered and slinked between the dying men in front of them. The littered soldiers of Shiloh were one long smorgasbord for the undead.

The creatures advanced toward a center point. Some of them crawled, drinking from hapless victims along the way. Others crept stealthily forward, bodies braced for a fight. And in the center of those advancing shapes stood Giles. As one reached him, he cried out, thrusting a sharpened stick into the chest of the attacking vampire. The creature exploded into dust. Then Giles pivoted, shouting, driving the stick into the chest of another. Three more came, and he dusted them all.

As Willow drew closer, she heard the rough edges of his accent. Not the genteel Giles she was used to, but guttural, visceral. He cursed again, flipping a vampire over onto its back and driving the stake home. Now only two remained. He egged them on, taunting them, his eyes glittering with hatred. He gripped the first one around the throat, crushing the vampire's larynx, and then drove the stake into his heart.

The last one, now afraid without its brethren, turned and

bolted. Giles didn't let it go. Leaping over wounded soldiers, he ran after it, calling it so many names Willow didn't even recognize half of them.

This was Ripper.

This was the essence of Giles's youth emerging in the heat of mortal battle. In his early twenties, he'd left Oxford University and moved to London. He fell in with a thrill-seeking group of friends who tinkered with the dark arts for fun. One of them died because of it. Giles had gone by the name Ripper, and he'd been violent and ruthless in his actions.

And now their gentle librarian and friend was giving them a glimpse of those days. He caught up with the vampire, swinging out a leg to trip him. The vamp fell hard, sprawling into the grass, and Giles brought the stake down, piercing the heart through the back of the rib cage.

As the vamp blossomed into dust, Giles lifted his head to the skies and gave a primal scream of rage.

Willow ran forward. "Giles!" she shouted.

He spun, tensed, ready to stake her.

She stopped. "Giles!"

He paused, his shoulders relaxing. His grip loosened on the stake, and he said, "Willow." Then, glancing around and seeing no more creeping shadows, he added, "There are so many vampires here. I couldn't find Buffy. And I couldn't just stand by and tolerate . . ." His voice trailed off, and Willow rushed to him.

"You were amazing, Giles," Xander said, hurrying forward to join them. "And no little amount of scary."

And even more amazing was that he had no wounds at all, save the smallest scratch on his arm. His sleeve was torn there, revealing the thin red line. Willow ushered him quickly toward the wagon. "We have Buffy and Agatha. We're all together." They reached the wagon, and Agatha turned around in the driver's seat to watch their approach. "But Buffy's wounded," Willow finished.

She climbed into the back of the wagon, followed by Xander.

"You're her Watcher?" the Slayer asked.

"Yes. And you're Agatha?" he asked.

She nodded, then regarded him curiously. "I can't imagine my Watcher doing what you just did. I didn't even need to step in and help."

"Well, yes," Giles said, climbing up into the bed of the wagon. "Dark past."

"I gathered that." She flicked the reins and the horse moved forward again, taking them ever closer to the farmhouse.

Willow watched anxiously while Giles examined Buffy's wound. "The tourniquet may have saved her life. But she needs a doctor," he said at last.

"Giles," Buffy whispered, then shut her eyes again.

Willow watched while her friend fell into unconsciousness once more. She was glad Agatha had stopped to slay opportunistic vamps on the battlefield. She only prayed that by stopping so many times the Slayer hadn't cost Buffy her life.

CHAPTER THIRTY-EIGHT

Buffy awoke, groggy and disoriented, to someone moving her leg. She grunted in pain, then focused on the person. A strange man met her gaze. He was fairly young, perhaps in his late twenties or early thirties, with a full black beard and shoulder-length black hair. He wore the uniform of the Union army, complete with wide belt and tarnished buttons that had been too long in the field. But his eyes were kind, and she relaxed a little.

"I am Dr. Milton Henderson," he told her, "a surgeon with the Thirty-second Regiment of Pennsylvania."

She raised her head, realizing with great relief that she could. Already she felt stronger.

"I've sewn up your wound. Fortunately, the ball passed through cleanly. Your field tourniquet saved your life. You should heal quickly, but you must take proper precautions to ward off infection."

Giles came into view, peering over the surgeon's shoulder. "Buffy? How are you?"

She nodded, managing a small sigh of relief.

"Agatha convinced Dr. Henderson to come from the field hospital across the river."

The doctor smiled. "I was supposed to be getting some sleep. But Agatha can be insistent."

"We're lucky he was here," Giles added.

She didn't need Giles to tell her how lucky. She'd nearly bled to death, and she had no illusions about that. She swallowed, finding her throat still dry. "Water?" she asked, her voice raspy. She sounded like she'd spent her life chain-smoking.

Dr. Henderson picked up a glass of water from the table and tipped it to her lips. She steadied his hand with her own and drank deeply. How sweet the water was, the finest thing she'd ever drunk. She finished the entire glass, then asked for another.

Encouraged, Giles smiled. "It's good to have you back."

She propped herself up on one elbow and drank the next glass on her own. "What about the"—she looked pointedly at the surgeon—"people we were looking for?"

"No sign of them yet. But with all the people we . . . said

good-bye to on the battlefield out there, we may never meet up with them."

Buffy nodded. She understood. The thousands of dying soldiers out there would attract hundreds of vampires looking for an easy feast. They'd slain countless numbers of them, and there was a chance that the assassins were among their numbers. She frowned then, thinking of Victor. He wasn't stupid, and she doubted he would make himself vulnerable on the field like that, feeding carelessly. He would have stuck to the shadows, his objective to kill Agatha more important than an easy meal.

"Let's stay on our guard," she told Giles. "I have a bad feeling."

Dr. Henderson raised his eyebrows, and Buffy added, "About the cheese. I have a bad feeling about the cheese. It may have gone bad."

"Of course," Giles answered. "When you're up to it, we'll discuss it with Agatha."

Buffy sat up. "I'm up to it now."

Dr. Henderson placed his hands on his hips. "I'm afraid I must differ, Miss Summers. You must rest, at least for one more night. You can't walk on that leg yet. In fact, I advise you not to walk on that leg for several weeks. But I can see you're a determined young woman, so I only advise you not to push yourself. You came very close to death, young lady."

Buffy nodded, then shook his hand. "Thank you."

"My pleasure." He packed up the rest of his kit, gauze,

needles, and thread, and placed everything into a worn black leather satchel. "And now I must return to the field hospital and see to the new arrivals. Miss Summers." He kissed her hand and made a short bow, then turned and shook hands with Giles.

When he exited the room, Giles shut the door behind him. "It's been close, Buffy. I thought we might lose you."

"Well, here I am. And we need to be ready for those vamps." Not for the first time, Buffy felt grateful that vampires couldn't break into houses. They needed an invitation from the people living there. That meant they didn't have to fortify doors or windows. The vamps would have to wait for them to wander outside, and that gave her time to heal and devise a plan with Agatha.

An hour later Buffy wore a clean pair of trousers and a freshly washed shirt. She sat in the kitchen, sipping tea with cream and sugar from a delicate china cup. Of all the time jumps, this had been the most brutal, and it felt strange to be drinking tea from an elegant tea set.

Agatha's farmhouse stood on one hundred and thirty acres of Tennessee oak-hickory forest, with pastures for her cows, horses, and chickens. Most of the animals had been requisitioned by the Union army, but she still had enough for eggs and milk, and they'd left her two horses. Large glass windows overlooked green fields and trees just getting their spring leaves. In the distance, a ridgeline was dotted white with blooming shadbush and dogwood trees. Several redbud trees bloomed purple-pink just outside the yard.

Agatha sat across from her, wearing a plaid day dress complete with hoop skirts. Her long hair, perfectly coiffed, was swept up and held in place by a silver comb. She wore a cameo pin at the neckline of her dress.

Giles and the others had explained to her where they'd come from and why. At first she hadn't believed them, but eventually she'd grown to trust them. Three days had passed since Buffy was shot, and the Battle of Shiloh was over. Grant had won, driving the Confederate soldiers down south, back to Corinth, Mississippi. For now, the field hospital worked around the clock to help the wounded, but more than twenty thousand soldiers had been injured or killed.

The sun, hanging low on the horizon, gleamed in through the windows, giving the illusion of a normal spring day, in which no war was being fought.

Agatha smiled at her over the rim of her teacup.

"Do you live here alone?" Buffy asked her.

"My father lives here too. He's fighting right now. Since he left, my Watcher comes by every day. He bought a little place over that ridge." She pointed to the ridge dotted with white trees. "I haven't seen my father for six months, though his name hasn't been on any of the casualty lists. I check frequently at the field hospital." She sipped her tea, looking out over the yard. "I pray for his return every day."

Buffy wasn't sure what to say, so she continued drinking

the tea, postponing the need to say something. When she'd drunk the entire cup, she said, "I can't imagine what that must be like."

Agatha put her cup down gently, the china rattling against the saucer. "It's hard. I lost my mother when I was a child. Scarlet fever. Sometimes the pain never seems to end."

"I know," Buffy said, thinking of all the killing and death she'd witnessed firsthand, wrought by both the undead and now human warfare.

"We'll never lead normal lives," Agatha said distantly. "You and I. We'll always be different. While some young women are courted and attend balls, you and I will be fighting vampires in the mud and musty, abandoned barns. It's all we have." The sadness in Agatha's voice pressed in on Buffy.

She set her cup down. "It's not all we have," Buffy told her. "We have people who love us. Our parents. Our Watchers. Our friends." She thought of Angel, of how much she missed him, especially now, separated by more than a hundred and thirty years. It occurred to her that he was alive, even now. He'd be in Europe, but the thought that she could cross the Atlantic at that instant and see him hit her powerfully. Then she remembered that he wouldn't be the sweet man she knew, brave and generous. He'd be Angelus, one of the most feared and evil vampires ever to stalk the earth. In 1898 he'd killed the young gypsy girl, and her family had cursed him forever by returning the human soul to his soulless body. Since then, he'd wandered in self-perpetuating torment, grieving the terrible deeds Angelus had wrought on the innocent. But now, in 1862, that redemption of Angel was more than thirty years away, and she never wanted to meet the evil Angelus.

"That may be, but people talk. I haven't been invited to a party or a ball since I started fighting vampires."

Buffy knew what she meant. While she definitely had her share of nights dancing at the Bronze, boys weren't exactly beating down her door to go out with her. There was Owen, who had almost gotten killed on the first date. And Xander, who'd practically torn her throat out while possessed by a hyena demon. And then Angel, who was all doom and gloom, this omen and that omen, and gee, hope you survive tonight because the Master is rising. But it just wasn't the same as good, old-fashioned romance. Whatever happened to seeing a movie? Or eating in a nice restaurant? With Angel it was always fights in garbage-strewn alleys and smoochies in the graveyard. What was wrong with her life?

She smiled at Agatha. This was what she'd missed when meeting the other Slayers: the commiseration. There they'd been, people who really could have understood how she felt about being a Slayer, and she'd been unable to speak with them. "I'm glad you speak English," she told Agatha.

The Slayer smiled, puzzled. "What?"

Just then Giles, Willow, and Xander entered through the kitchen door. They carried pails of milk and eggs. Xander wore overalls, and his cut looked much better.

"Guys," Buffy told them, "the farmer outfits were just a disguise. You don't actually have to be them."

"Very funny," Xander said. "Laugh all you like. But do you know how hard it is to milk a cow? It doesn't just come out like in the movies. You have to work at it. Tease it out. It's hard."

"Sounds like you have another girlfriend," she told him.

"Ha-ha," Xander retorted mirthlessly.

"And, Will, did you have to coax those eggs from the chickens?" Buffy asked.

"Nope. They just laid them and I picked them up."

"Next time you get the cow," Xander told her.

Giles set the pail of milk on the kitchen table and smiled at Buffy. "It's good to see you up and around."

"Any sign of our friends yet?"

Willow spoke up. "Nope. But I thought I caught the shadow of something creeping around outside last night. Could have been one of them."

Buffy looked over her shoulder, toward the west. The sun continued to dip lower. It would be dark in another two hours, and they'd have to be ready then.

After a dinner of fried eggs, biscuits, and gravy, they sat around next to the fire. The sun sank below the horizon. As Buffy sat in a rocking chair, her injured leg propped up on a footstool, she stared into the flames. Already her wound had vastly improved, compliments of supernatural Slayer healing rate.

The back door squeaked open, and everyone but Agatha

spun around in their seats, anticipating an attack. Instead, a brown-haired man in a fancy suit walked through the door and shut it behind himself.

"Evening," he said, his face showing surprise at their presence.

"Niles Hallowell," Agatha said, "I'd like you to meet four extraordinary people." She introduced all of them, saving Buffy for last. "And this," she said, gesturing at Buffy, "is Buffy Summers. She's a Slayer."

"Impossible!" said Niles.

"Niles is my Watcher," Agatha explained.

Buffy raised her eyebrows. "Your Watcher is named Niles? Gee, Giles, you have a lot in common already. Niles. Giles."

"Yes, very amusing," he muttered.

"There cannot be more than two living Slayers," Niles went on, unrelenting.

Giles stood up and shook the man's hand. "We aren't from this time period. We've traveled from the future in order stop a team of assassins from murdering Agatha before her natural death."

"Ooo-weeeee-ooooo," Xander said, then did his best rendition of the *Twilight Zone* theme. Agatha and Niles stared at him blankly, as if he'd gone mad. "Oh, right. 1862."

Niles said nothing.

"I don't think I like the sound of all this," said Agatha. "It's frightening. You all know when I'm allotted to die, and it gives me the creeps."

"Hey, you say 'creeps' back here? Cool! Slang is old."

Agatha raised an eyebrow at him.

"I didn't mean you were old, just that slang dates back further than . . ." Xander trailed off before he made things worse.

"We're here to stop you from dying before your natural time," Buffy told her. "What's worse, knowing that we are aware of the year of your natural death, or dying younger than that?"

Agatha turned away, staring into the fire.

Buffy felt bad. She knew that Agatha didn't die that much further into the future. But if she died in the next few days, a different Slayer would be activated instead of the one who should be. Some powerful Slayers came after Agatha's time, including Lucy Hanover, who roamed the Ghost Roads, helping lost souls. Would that be true of Buffy, too? Would the Slayers after her be powerful and heroic?

She thought of Agatha's wishes to attend balls and meet "a handsome gentleman," as she'd put it. She probably wouldn't have the chance. Would Buffy's life be the same too? Were all Slayers destined for short lives and misery? She gritted her teeth. At least Agatha would have all the time coming to her. No two-bit assassins would rob her of that as long as Buffy was alive.

"Just a moment." Niles cut into her thoughts. "I need some time to assimilate this information. I must have details if we're to trust you."

"Of course," Giles told him.

While Niles listened intently, Buffy and the others told him about Lucien and the time magick. They briefed him on the plot to kill Slayers before their natural deaths in order to disrupt the Slayer time line. Niles asked why they would go to these great lengths, and Buffy explained about the Master and his ascension. Frequently Giles shushed her when she gave away more than he thought was needed. He was quite paranoid about messing up the time line. He warned them repeatedly not to talk of historical events, inventions, or persons of future importance, including those related to the outcome of the Civil War. As if Buffy knew all that, anyway. She knew the North won, but aside from Giles's briefing of the Battle of Shiloh, that was about all she knew.

At last Niles understood. "And we have seen no sign of these devils?"

"No," Agatha told him, "though I killed a lot of vampires on the battlefield. They could have been among them."

"I think we've got at least one more to worry about," Buffy said, thinking of Victor. "Maybe more."

"Perhaps I should stay here for tonight," the Watcher offered.

"That would be wise," Giles said. "If they've been watching the house, then by now I'm sure they've learned you are Agatha's Watcher. If you left now, they could take you hostage, demanding that Agatha give herself up."

"That would be unfortunate," Niles conceded, fixing Giles with an annoyed glance.

And here Buffy had thought they'd get along famously.

"And now, Agatha, I need to have a word with you in private," Niles said.

Agatha nodded, rising from her chair. "If you will excuse me," she said. She looked pointedly at Xander and Giles, who looked back blankly. Then Giles suddenly stood up, pulling Xander up by the arm. Agatha nodded courteously and left the room with her Watcher. The kitchen door swung shut behind them.

"What was that all about?" Xander said after they'd gone. He rubbed his arm and sat down again.

"We're supposed to rise when a lady stands up," Giles told him, taking his seat as well.

"How quaint," Willow said.

Buffy stood up, and on autopilot, so did Giles and Xander. "You don't have to do that," she told them. "I want to go listen at the door."

"Buffy, don't!" Willow told her. "You should respect their privacy."

"This guy is off, somehow. He's seething with anger. Didn't any of you guys feel that?"

Giles tilted his head to the side thoughtfully. "Well, yes, now that you mention it."

With the help of a cane, Buffy crept to the swinging door that separated the kitchen from the living room. She pushed it open just a crack. In the center of the room stood Watcher and Slayer.

"Did you give thought to what I said earlier?" Niles asked Agatha quietly, merely a whisper in the big house.

"Of course, Niles, but I have to do my part," she answered, just as quietly.

"A Slayer does not have time to be a spy."

"But without my help, the Union would have suffered even heavier losses."

Niles pointed vaguely out the window. "That world out there, that fight, is between two political parties. You fight a greater battle for justice between two worlds, evil and good. That's the war that needs you, Agatha. This human war will wage on tirelessly with or without your help."

Agatha turned away from him, her face full of sorrow. "But where do I draw the line between good and evil? Surely humanity causes its share of evil." She turned back to him. "Beyond that window lie thousands of wounded or dead soldiers. If a spy like me had delivered word of the surprise attack, some of those casualties could have been avoided."

Niles crossed his arms over his chest stubbornly. "I won't have it. It's too risky. If you were found out by Confederate scouts, you would be shot or lynched. You're too important to risk by taking part in this god-awful war."

She pointed an accusing finger at his chest. "This war is ravaging my homeland, Niles. It's easier for you to remain distant to it. You are British, and your home is secure. I can't ignore battles taking place in the very fields surrounding my land."

"I don't expect you to ignore it, Agatha. I merely want you to adhere to your duties as the Slayer."

"And I will!" she said, her voice slightly raised. "I will do both." She crossed her arms too, her chin raised defiantly. "Now don't talk to me again of this matter. You are my Watcher, and I listen to your counsel in all things having to do with the slaying of vampires. But I will not turn my back on my country, even if you request it."

Then Agatha spun on her heels and climbed the stairs to her bedroom.

Niles sighed in exasperation, then flung himself down in a nearby chair. He brought one hand to his face, resting his forehead there. Buffy backed slowly into the kitchen, careful not to trip on her injured leg.

"Did you guys hear all that?" she whispered.

"Only some of it," Willow said. "She's a spy?"

Buffy nodded, making her way back to the chair. She sat down with some difficulty and propped her leg up again on the footstool.

A few moments later Agatha returned to the kitchen. She smoothed her skirts and forced a smile. "I apologize for my rudeness as a hostess," she said. "But we had a matter to attend to."

Agatha had just finished her sentence when a Molotov cocktail sailed through a window, shattering it. The flaming bottle of whiskey skittered across the floor. Instantly the window curtains went up in flames. Then another crashed through a different window. Niles cried out in surprise, bursting through the swinging door. The living room was on fire, the windows there shattered.

Three more flaming bottles crashed through the remaining windows, spreading fire in their wake. Buffy and the others leaped up as a wall of flame sealed off the back door. She leaned on the cane, rushing to the front door. A sideboard full of china roared with fire, flames spreading to the door itself.

One cocktail had landed on the stairs leading to the upper floor, and the dry wood erupted instantly, blocking off the route entirely.

They were trapped, and Buffy's world filled with fire.

CHAPTER THIRTY-NINE

Buffy! This way!" Xander's voice cut through the chaos. "There's a basement entrance that's still clear!"

Buffy ran into the front room with the others close behind. Down a narrow hallway stood an open door. Xander waved her forward. She reached him, and he turned and raced down a set of rickety wooden steps into the waiting darkness of the cellar.

Buffy followed closely, the two Watchers, Agatha, and Willow piling up in the doorway above. The smell of dank earth filled Buffy's nose as she hobbled across the dirt floor, following Xander. He reached another, shorter set of steps on the opposite end of the cellar. Flickering light gleamed through the high windows of the basement, shedding some light on the scene. At the top of the short flight of stairs, two double doors tilted at an angle. He went to them and flung them open quickly. The way out was clear. No flames flickered nearby.

As they raced out, Buffy braced herself, ready to fight. She emerged, the heat consuming the house, causing her to turn away from the blaze.

There, standing nearby, were not the two vampires she had expected, but nine.

Victor had found some recruits.

This time, he had to die.

CHAPTER FORTY

Victor watched the Slayer emerge from the cellar doors. They'd just been rounding the house to set fire to those, too. But they'd been too slow. This team he'd assembled left a lot to be desired. All of them had drunk on the battlefield till they were bloated. They moved slowly, and were so overfed that even their coordination was sloppy.

"Set them on fire!" he ordered two vampires closest to the Scoobies. Though they each held two torches, the vamps turned to Victor, blank expressions on their faces.

"Who?" they asked in unison.

"Them!" Victor shouted, pointing at Buffy and the others.

The two moved forward with all the urgency of drunken

sloths racing drowsy snails. By the time they'd reached Buffy's position, Giles and the others had run to safety. Buffy kicked the lead vamp with her good leg, stole his torch, and staked him with it. She set the other one on fire. Both erupted into ashes. Agatha joined her side.

Then Buffy pointed the torch at Victor. "This one's mine," she told Agatha.

As three other vampires moved to attack, Victor crept back. Might as well let the other vamps die and tire out the Slayers as much as possible. He didn't relish the thought of fighting both at the same time.

But Buffy made a beeline for him, the torch upraised threateningly. She limped from an injury, obviously biting back pain, but it wasn't stopping her. A cruel determination gleamed in her eyes, and Victor fought the urge to run.

He did move, though, skirting around her, hoping to join the three more vamps who had not yet attacked.

Behind him, Agatha dusted one, then another vampire. He heard the gasp of their bodies turning to dust. Daring a look over at the struggle, he saw her engaged with the third vampire. Another one of Lucien's lame recruits, the third vampire had been undead for about thirty minutes when Lucien recruited him. Literally. He'd waited for the guy to crawl out of the earth in the cemetery and then gave him his first assignment.

And while he'd been only thirty minutes old—three days and thirty minutes old by now—he had been a black belt aikido instructor while living. And while that sounded really tough, the guy's name was Hiram Gigglesworth. Seriously. Victor had even read the tombstone name twice in disbelief. But the guy could kick some serious ass. Victor had to give that to him. Ever since they'd arrived, he'd been kicking everyone's ass—except, that is, of the people he'd been sent there to defeat.

By now the guy was worn out, cut in a dozen places by bayonets, shot, and even had a hatchet driven into his shoulder blade. Plus, he'd joined the vampire glut on the battlefield. He was like a junkie for the soldiers' blood, and Victor had to pull him off them more times than he could count just so they could reach the farmhouse.

Victor had recruited help along the way. Just telling these new vamps that he was out to dust two Slayers made them join up fast. Well, those that didn't run away screaming joined up pretty fast. And those that did join were generally cocky jerks with something to prove, who were actually stupid enough to think they could take out a Slayer.

But as long as it worked to Victor's advantage, that was fine with him.

Now Buffy moved forward, cutting off his path toward the other three vamps. Xander joined Agatha and together they held Hiram down in an attempt to stake him. They weren't doing too well. He threw both of them off, then leaped and kicked, connecting painfully with Xander's jaw. Agatha got the other boot in her stomach.

Victor continued to back away, seeing out of the corner of

his eye that now even the two Watchers and the young slip of a girl, Willow, were busting out the moves. The vamps were so stupid and slow that the Watchers dusted one with a mulberry tree branch.

The Brits moved on to the next vampire. Now only two lackeys survived, in addition to him and Hiram.

Buffy ran at Victor, favoring her injured leg and thrusting the flaming torch before her. Victor dodged to the side, but she reached his sleeve with the flame. The fire spread up to his shoulder, catching his hair on fire. As it spread over his torso, panic set in. Dammit! He hated fire. Ever since he'd nearly burned to death in the London Fire of 1666, he'd been outright paranoid about it. It was fine as a weapon wielded against his enemy, but when it pointed at him, he nearly lost all self-control. Buffy wasn't supposed to escape from that burning house. She was supposed to die inside.

He made a grab for her, hoping to set her aflame, but she ducked and rolled away. He dropped to the ground, desperate to put the flames out. He rolled in the wet grass, the flames hissing. Most of them went out.

To his left, between rolls, he saw Hiram advancing again on Agatha. Xander lay nearby, unmoving.

He rolled again to crush the last flame, and then Buffy was on top of him, suddenly, her weight landing solidly on his back. He heard his bones crack.

She drove the burning end of the torch deeply into his back. He screamed as the wood connected with his heart.

The heat spread throughout his body, and for the briefest second, he could actually feel his molecules separating as he turned to dust.

His final thought was that he couldn't believe Hiram Gigglesworth had lasted longer than he had.

CHAPTER FORTY-ONE

As Victor turned to ashes beneath her, Buffy reached inside his jacket pocket, pulling out the folded incantations. He vanished beneath her, and she landed with a thump on the ground.

Two vampires came at her sluggishly, a gaunt female and a plump male with long, stringy brown hair. Buffy rose, wincing at the pain in her leg, and whipped the torch around to face them. Flames still licked around the end of the wood, and she rushed forward, impaling and killing the female. When the other vamp grabbed her, she twisted out of his grasp. Niles rushed forward, leaping on the vampire's back. The vampire staggered under the weight and fell. Niles fell clumsily on top of him, so now Buffy couldn't move in for the fatal stake. She waited for the Watcher to get to his feet, then told him to stand back.

Slowly the bloated vampire rose. She spotted a tree behind him with a low-hanging branch, sharp and broken off at the end. With a solid kick, Buffy connected with his head, sending him reeling backward into the tree. The protruding branch pierced his heart. She landed from the kick, sweating from the agony of standing on her injured leg.

Now only one vampire remained, a big brute of a guy fighting Agatha.

Buffy limped to the Slayer. "This one isn't cooperating," said Agatha, leaping high in her skirts and delivering a wicked kick to the giant's neck. His head snapped backward violently, and he stumbled, arms windmilling. Buffy ran up behind him, planted the torch firmly on the ground, and let the beast fall backward onto it.

Dust billowed upward.

Teamwork. It was the best.

Agatha stood gasping over the ash-strewn site, catching her breath.

"We did it!" Buffy exclaimed.

"That was it?" the Slayer asked. "No more?"

Buffy peered into the gloom surrounding the fire. No other vamps loomed on the periphery. Victor had been their leader, and if any had seen this display of dustage, they probably hadn't hung around.

Now Agatha turned toward the fire. Searing heat radiated from it, causing perspiration to spring up on Buffy's brow. "My home," Agatha said. "It's gone." The southern side of the house collapsed as she said it, fiery timbers raining down in the darkness. "I've lived here since I was born."

Niles joined her, placing an arm around her. "You can stay at my house until your father returns."

She stared into the flames, uncertain. "Will he return?" she asked him at last, meeting his gaze.

"Yes," Niles told her emphatically.

Buffy looked to Giles, who stood nearby, hands on his knees, listening. She raised her eyebrows, and her Watcher nodded. *Yes, her father does return.*

Buffy went to her, putting an arm around her as well. "You're safe now, at least from the assassins." Her leg pulsed with pain, as if it were on fire, but she didn't look at it. Blood trickled down her skin under the pants leg.

"Thank you," Agatha said, but her voice was tiny and hollow, small in the face of such a huge loss. Now her mother was gone, her father away, and her childhood home with everything she had was turning to ash.

Buffy felt a hard, painful lump grow in her throat and turned away. She wanted to stay, to help her rebuild, but nothing could make up for this loss. They needed to get back. If more Slayers had been targeted, every moment counted.

She hoped the loss of Victor would prove grave for

Lucien. Victor had been clever and ruthless. But now he was just another demon destroyed.

Buffy and the Scoobies saw Agatha and Niles safely to the Watcher's house, then said their good-byes.

Buffy felt this parting more than the others, perhaps because she had truly bonded with Agatha. Or perhaps because she knew the Slayer didn't live far into the future. Again she questioned her own mortality, but forced those thoughts away quickly.

After they'd all hugged good-bye, Giles ushered her, Willow, and Xander out to the back field.

He performed the incantations. The sickening spiral of light winked into view, pulling at twigs, grass, and fallen leaves. It tugged at her hair, then her body, and all four leaped into the portal, returning once again to their home.

CHAPTER FORTY-TWO

Sunnydale, 1998

With a painful thump, Buffy landed in a pile of garbage behind the Sunnydale health food store. Her hand squished into a moldering pile of wheat germ, and her face plopped down into a discarded tub of garlic hummus. She spat it out, trying to lift her head. Rolling over, she watched Xander, then Willow, surge out of the vortex. Light played over the alley walls. Giles groaned somewhere nearby. Xander tumbled downward, and Buffy shifted to the side just before he crashed down next to her.

Willow landed feetfirst on a garbage bag, which split open on impact. Couscous and part of a vegetarian burger spilled out, oozing over her boots.

Buffy's leg throbbed, and she hoped she didn't get any rotting hummus in the wound. She wiped the garlic concoction off her face. Ack. She wouldn't be kissing Angel anytime soon. Sunlight streamed down into the alley, allowing Buffy to see every bit of festering garbage clinging to her in explicit detail.

"First kelp, now seaweed," Giles muttered. "And we're not even near the ocean." He pulled a long strand of green slime off his face.

Wincing with pain, Buffy used the alley wall to rise and steady herself. Willow rushed to her side and supported her. Xander lay still, unmoving in the heap of trash. "I think I have a banana in my ear," he told them. Rising, Giles offered his hand and shakily helped Xander to his feet. "I can't take much more of this," Xander said. "This is the worst way to travel!" He gestured rudely at the vanished portal.

"Hey, I thought you were all 'I'm the time travel expert,'" Willow told him.

"That was before I knew it involved throwing up, trash heaps, and hanging precariously from lifeguard towers."

As the others brushed themselves off, Buffy pulled out the incantations she'd stolen from Victor. They were a duplicate of the ones they'd gotten from Lucien. "No additional time periods. Do we still need to go to the French Revolution?" Buffy asked Giles as they walked out of the alley.

"What do you mean?"

"I killed Victor. The last recurring assassin. Now neither Lucien nor Victor will be able to get new recruits."

Giles looked thoughtful. "They may have a backup plan—other assassins already chosen in the event Victor doesn't return. I think Lucien's reaction to the news of Victor will be quite telling in this instance." He flicked a piece of granola off his sleeve.

Willow followed his thought. "Right. If he insists that we have no reason to go to Paris, then we can be sure he has someone waiting in the wings. If he encourages us to go, then we'll know he has no one and is just hoping we'll get killed by angry mobs."

"Angry mobs?" Xander asked. "Angry mobs?"

"Yes, Xander," Willow told him. "The French Revolution. Angry mobs. Guillotines."

He swallowed. "Guillotines?" He brought a hand to his neck. "Doesn't this guy ever pick sunny Acapulco or a nice beach in the Bahamas?"

"Tell me about it," Buffy said. "He's evil."

"My Little Pony evil," Xander agreed.

Emerging from the alley, they blinked in the sunlight, getting their bearings. Heading off in different directions, they agreed to all meet at the library in an hour.

Buffy burst through the double doors of the library. "Hah!" she said to Lucien.

The vampire looked up sleepily, then raised his eyebrows.

"Hah?" Angel asked, standing up.

"Consider your master plan officially minus one Victor."

Lucien struggled to hide the dismay in his face. Failed.

He pursed his lips together angrily, his eyes glowering. "Well, then," he said. "You've won."

"Not quite," Giles said, entering the room. He held up the French Revolution incantation. "How many backup assassins do you have?"

Lucien bared his teeth. "None," he hissed. "You've killed them. Victor was my best." But he averted his eyes nervously as he said it.

Buffy looked at her Watcher. "Well, Giles?"

"Right. I'll get the clothes."

Lucien threaded his thin fingers through the cage door. "What are you doing?"

"Getting ready for the next time jump," Buffy told him.

"But there's no reason for you to make the final one," he said. "You've won." He was a little *too* insistent.

"Then you won't care if we just check on the French Slayer, right?"

He cleared his throat nervously. "Why would I care?"

"Exactly. Why would you care?"

After Willow and Xander arrived, they dressed in the clothes Giles laid out—white cotton shirts, black jackets, long black pants, and strange floppy hats, each with a red, white, and blue rosette made of ribbon.

"They're liberty cockades," Giles informed them, pointing to a rosette. "They signify that we support the Revolution. We're jumping to 1792, a time when we don't want to be confused with aristocrats."

Buffy picked up the shirt and pants.

"Again, dressing as a man will give you maximum mobility."

She nodded, then took her outfit to the women's restroom to change.

When they all met back in the library, dressed in eighteenth-century garb, Giles checked their satchels for the obligatory paper and pencil, water, and maps.

"Giles," Buffy said, "I've been carrying that paper and pencil around this whole time. I haven't used it yet."

"Keep it," he told her. Then he lifted the tiny stub of a pencil. "You could use it as a stake."

She rolled her eyes. "Well, if I run into a vampire that's four inches tall, I'll be prepared."

"Okay," Giles said, ready to brief them. "Let's go to my office." Inside, they closed the door. Angel stood close to Buffy, and she welcomed his presence. "This Slayer is Marguerite Allard. She's an aristocrat in a time of great unrest in Paris. This will be dangerous."

Buffy's leg ached, and she hoped this jump wouldn't be worse than Shiloh.

"I've marked her address on your maps. Should we get separated, let's meet at her house."

They all agreed, and Giles took out the incantation for 1792. Angel wished them luck, kissing Buffy good-bye. "Be careful there," he whispered to her. He turned then and left the tiny office.

Giles spoke the incantation, and Buffy braced herself to return to a world at war.

CHAPTER FORTY-THREE

Paris, 1792

Buffy whirled through the portal, landing painfully on one shoulder in a puddle of vile-smelling water. She struggled to her feet, groggy, the shouts from a nearby crowd filling the air.

The darkness of night filled the city streets and dank alleyways. She turned back to the portal to await the others' arrival and saw a second portal, spinning in the air some distance away.

A figure sailed out of it, followed by a second. The assassins! She couldn't believe it! They'd actually arrived in roughly the same place at the same time.

Steadying her legs, she stumbled toward them, nauseous and dizzy from the portal travel. The cobblestones beneath her feet made the going rough. She twisted her ankles more than once in her haste. Finally the grogginess wore off and Buffy quickened her pace, limping on her wounded leg.

One of the vampires had landed in the center of the street. With the shouts and cries of an angry crowd, still out of sight, he didn't hear her approach.

She reached into her jacket pocket, pulling out a fresh stake. The vampire propped himself up, shaking off the ill effects of the transport. She didn't recognize him, but he was huge. A monster of a guy with a bald head and the physique of a school bus. So Lucien did have backups waiting.

Almost upon him, she leaped. The second vampire lay some distance away, trying to rise to his feet. Buffy landed solidly on the bald vampire, straddling him. As he gazed up, surprised and terrified, she thrust the stake into his heart. Dust plumed upward, and she fell to the street beneath.

Now she stood up quickly. The second vampire stood up, staring at her in horror. The shouting of the mob grew closer and closer. The vampire turned and ran. She sprinted after him. As she rounded a corner in pursuit, she ran full-on into an angry mob scene straight out of *Frankenstein*. Torches blazed; swarthy, dirt-clad people shouted. Spittle sprayed. Pitchforks, guns, and swords were lifted above heads angrily.

The vampire dashed into the midst of the roiling mass of people. Buffy followed, immediately slowed by the writhing throng of bodies, and she cursed her bum leg. She clawed her way past a woman in a muddy gown, squeezed by a man who apparently hadn't taken a bath in his entire life, shoved past a guy hawking etchings of a recent hanging, and emerged in a small pocket of space.

She whirled in all directions, searching for the vampire. Twenty feet ahead she saw his brown, frizzy head weaving through the crowd. She pushed on in that direction. A hand grabbed her and shoved her as she moved. People shouted at her, asking her brusque questions in French. She ignored them, couldn't understand them anyway.

Then a mass of shouting sprang up, and simultaneously the crowd roared, "*Vive la nation!*" A rotten cabbage sailed by her head, followed by a stream of decaying tomatoes. She jumped up and down, trying to catch sight of the frizzy head. The crowd was too thick, too vast to see over where she was. She spotted a wooden staircase climbing up the side of a nearby building. Thrusting through the crowd, she reached it, finding it clogged with even more people. Why were they all just standing around like this, shouting?

She pushed by a young boy and his mother and climbed a couple of steps, searching the crowd for the assassin's head.

She saw him nowhere. She scanned the crowd for five minutes, searching for his unkempt brown hair. A sea of hats stretched out before her. She didn't see a single bare-headed person. She'd lost him.

A renewed frenzy from among the crowd brought her gaze up. "*Vive la révolution!*" they shouted in unison.

From this vantage point she saw the reason for the

gathering. She stood at the edge of the Place de la Révolution. In the center loomed a high platform with a guillotine on top. Four soldiers of the Republic stood on the stairs leading to the execution platform.

A wagon had arrived, carrying a young girl no older than twelve and two adults, who could have been her mother and father. Though they were grimy now, their clothes had at one time been very expensive, the height of Paris fashion. Aristocrats, Buffy realized, going to the guillotine.

Her mind traveled to the *Scarlet Pimpernel* miniseries she'd seen once as a little kid, with Anthony Andrews as the gallant English hero saving aristocrats from the guillotine. For a second she expected him to arrive, swinging into view from a grappling hook slung over a nearby building. But as the soldiers dragged the crying and pleading family from the wagon and forced them up the small stairs to the execution platform, Buffy remembered it was just fiction.

She couldn't believe these people were going to be executed. What crime had they committed? Being rich? Being extravagant? The crowd seethed with hatred, throwing more rotted lettuce heads and melons at them. One putrid tomato hit the mother in the face, and she stood shocked for a moment, the seeds and pulp dripping off her cheek.

Then the guards shoved her forward, and the family piled up on the platform. They grabbed the little girl. She screamed in terror as they shoved her toward the guillotine.

Buffy couldn't just stand there and watch. "What's

wrong with you people!" she shouted. "She's just a kid!"

A few people turned to stare at her, but most kept their eyes firmly fixed on the anticipated execution.

Buffy couldn't bear it. She leaped off the stairs, shoving the watching mother and son out of her way, and surged into the crowd. She knew she shouldn't change history. If that little girl lived, she could forever alter the future. But Buffy didn't care. She couldn't just stand by. She pressed forward.

So little space existed between bodies that she'd only pushed forward a few feet before she heard the sickening *snick* of the guillotine blade. The crowd screamed with delight, urging the soldiers to send the next prisoner up.

She continued to fight forward, shoving people, knocking them out of the way, not worried about using her Slayer strength. If they had a few bruises tomorrow, so be it. She shoved a few feet more and heard the second downsweep of the guillotine.

Again the crowd roared with satisfaction, cheering and thrusting their weapons into the air.

Buffy couldn't see the guillotine at all now. She pushed people aside, winnowing her way through the throng. The guillotine blade screamed down for the third time. The crowd jumped and cheered, jostling her violently. An elbow came down on her head, then a knee in her back.

She stopped. The family was dead.

Disgusted and horrified, Buffy pushed her way backward, working toward the alley next to the stairwell she'd used.

Someone bumped into her sore leg, and she sucked in a sharp breath, then pressed on.

After ten minutes of struggling past more elbows, arms, and feet in her path, she emerged from the crowd. Locating the alley, she ran to it, wanting to find the others.

They had a huge advantage this time. She had already staked one of the assassins, and she knew what the other one looked like. They could move quickly this time, perhaps staking the other vampire before even finding the Slayer.

Some of her stress dissipated.

She hurried down the narrow alley back toward their entry point. When she arrived, Willow and Giles spotted her. "How far away did you land?" Willow asked her.

"I got one of them!" she told them. "The vampires landed right next to us! I saw them come out of the portal and everything!"

"I thought I saw a strange glimmer in the sky as I landed," Giles said, "but it vanished almost immediately."

Buffy went on. "I staked one right off the bat. The other one got away, but I know what he looks like."

"Remarkable," Giles said.

"That's fantastic!" Willow agreed.

"Where's Xander?"

"He went off searching for you," Willow told her.

Buffy hooked her thumb in the direction of the guillotine-occupied square. "There's a really angry mob over that way. I don't think it's safe."

Just then a breathless Xander ran out of the shadows. “There’s a really angry mob over there. This place isn’t safe!”

He rested, leaning over, hands on his knees.

“It’s okay,” Giles told him. “We’ve landed during the Reign of Terror.”

“And that’s *okay*?” Xander asked incredulously.

“What’s the Reign of Terror?” Buffy asked.

“One of the bloodiest parts of the French Revolution, when unbelievable numbers of people were sent to the guillotine. Most of them had been fingered by Robespierre, the Revolution’s public accuser. Eventually they even cut his head off,” Willow explained.

“Eeeek,” said Xander.

“I guess they didn’t want to eat cake,” Buffy said.

“It will all be fine,” Giles reassured them. “Just be sure to wear your liberty caps and Republic rosettes.” He pointed to the red, blue, and white ribbon cockades he’d made them all put on before leaving. Buffy’s liberty cap slouched loosely on her head, and the wool itched.

And be sure not to put on any short pants!” he added.

“Excuse me?” asked Xander.

“Short pants. The nobility and bourgeoisie wear them. One of the strongest groups in the revolution, the Sans-Culottes, wear long pants.”

“The French Revolution was fought over knickers?” Xander asked, amazed.

“No, Xander,” Willow told him. “It was more what the

knickers represented. Wealth and the extravagance of the bourgeoisie and the nobility."

"You're going to fit right in, Will," Buffy said.

"Well, the peasants had a point," Willow pressed. "All those rich aristocrats prancing around in their fancy pants, spending money willy-nilly on chocolates and extravagant carriages and clothes that were the latest fashion. The peasants couldn't afford the latest fashions, and their moms weren't exactly pressing to have them fit in and be popular or anything. And then there were the bourgeoisie, pretending to be so fashion-conscious and self-righteous, insulting the peasants every day and putting them down in front of the drinking fountain, when really the aristocrats were just a bunch of shallow cheerleaders who probably couldn't even memorize their own locker combinations."

"Uh, Will?" Xander asked. "We still talking about the French Revolution here?"

"Yes!" she said defiantly, sticking her chin out. "It was exactly like that."

"Well, okay, then. Just checking," he told her.

"Giles, where does the Slayer live?" Buffy asked.

He reached into his satchel, pulling out a small notebook and a map of Revolution-era Paris. "It's near the intersection of Rue Saint Honoré and Rue de Richelieu, near the Place du Carrousel. But we need to be careful. It's a very wealthy part of town, and tensions will be high there."

"Let's go. I say we stick to our habit of finding the Slayer first and waiting for the assassin to come to her," Buffy said. "Meanwhile, I'll keep my eye out for the guy."

Giles nodded his assent, and with Willow and Xander still discussing the finer points of the French Revolution and its cruel football players, they headed in that direction.

Willow looked on in disbelief. "It's burned down."

Buffy stared at the blackened ruins of the house. A light drizzle rained from the sky, hissing on the burned remains. "This happened recently," she said. She scanned the streets, wondering if the Slayer might still be nearby. The garbage-strewn road before them lay empty. Suddenly hooting and shouting pulled their attention to a grimy side alley. A woman and man emerged, raising a bottle of cheap wine, staggering and leaning on each other. They disappeared down a side street.

"It's not the only house that was burned," Willow said, pointing out several other buildings black with fire scars.

"Power to the people," Giles murmured under his breath. "We can still try the Watcher's house." He regarded his map. "It's down this street, a little closer to the library, the *bibliothèque*."

"Now, how did we guess that?" Buffy said ruefully.

"I'm sure it's a complete coincidence," Giles told her.

"I'm sure."

They covered the remaining distance to the Watcher's house, nervously watching any people who passed them.

Shouts resounded. All around, cries pierced the night, and the smell of fires and festering garbage hung heavily in the air.

"This is it," Giles announced when they had reached a rather posh-looking town house, complete with ten chimneys and several balconies.

"And he lives considerably better than you," Xander said.

"She lives, actually," Giles corrected. "She does live considerably better than I."

They walked up the short flight of brick steps to the large wooden double doors and knocked. No one answered. Giles called out to the upper windows, and Buffy tried the doors at the side and in the back of the house. All the windows were dark. No one stirred inside.

"She's out," Willow said at last.

Hastily Giles produced a paper and pencil and scrawled a note in French to the Watcher, warning her of the assassin and stating that he could be recruiting more help. Then he stuck the note between the door frame and the door.

"How will we find the Slayer now?" Willow asked. "She could have fled Paris for all we know, or even the country!"

"We can ask around," Xander offered.

A group of angry-looking ruffians wearing long pants and liberty hats walked by, giving them a nod. Giles nodded back.

Willow gave a little wave, smiling through gritted teeth. "This place makes me nervous. I can feel the tension pressing in on me. It's practically suffocating."

"Yes," Giles agreed. "It is rather like the old cliché about a powder keg."

Buffy could feel it too. She could hear the roar of angry crowds in the distance, and her nostrils filled with the smell of scorched wood. The Slayer and her family had been driven out of their home. Poor people wallowed in the gutter with nothing to eat. Armed soldiers and gangs of thugs roamed the streets. Everyone was looking for someone to blame for their misery. Even the king had been executed.

"I think we need to find the vampire. I know what he looks like, and the sooner we find him, the less time he'll have to get recruits like Victor did."

"Sounds good," Xander said. "I don't like the thought of fighting that many vamps at once again."

Buffy remembered him spending much of that fight slumped in a limp pile on the grass, but she didn't mention it.

"This is an excellent idea," Giles said. "Because you killed his companion, the vampire will almost certainly seek some sort of backup."

"But where do we look?" asked Willow.

"Vampire bars. Eighteenth-century equivalents to Willy's?" Buffy suggested.

How will we find them?" Xander asked. "Hang out in seedy alleyways and wait for vampires to follow?"

"Good idea," Buffy said. "And I think we should split up."

"What?" Xander cried. "Are you crazy? We can't split up! That's exactly what you're not supposed to do in supernatural situations. As soon as you split up, you're picked off one by one. Maniacs spear you with pitchforks. Masked lunatics come after you with chain saws."

"But we don't have that much time, Xander," Buffy insisted. "The more time he has to get help, the more vampires we'll be fighting when we find the Slayer. Paris is a big city, and who knows how many vampire bars there are? We'll break into two groups and search in a circle radiating out from our point of entry."

"Can I be in your group?" Xander asked.

"Agreed," Buffy said. She turned to Giles. "Watch over Willow."

"I will," he said.

"Where will we all meet up?" Willow asked.

"We'll meet in the center square with the guillotine in two hours. There'll still be a huge crowd there, and it'll be easier for us to blend in. And safer."

Xander raised his index finger. "So you're saying it'll be safer for us in the middle of a sea of bloodthirsty people instead of hiding in an alley where the bloodthirsty people can find us?"

Buffy nodded. "Exactly."

"Oh, boy."

Together they returned to the city square where Buffy had lost track of the assassin. Then they parted, agreeing to meet there again in two hours.

Xander walked close to Buffy as they navigated the streets.

They watched for vampires, and Buffy worried about Giles and Willow. More so about Willow, because she knew Giles was tougher than he seemed, as long as he didn't get knocked on the head. At last they spotted two vampires, one with blood clotted in the corner of her mouth. They had already fed for the evening. Perhaps now they'd be looking to socialize.

Buffy and Xander held to the shadows, trailing the pair in ragged clothes. The male vampire walked with a limp but still managed to swagger with that insufferable undead pride.

The pair unwittingly led them down a back alleyway to a grimy little pub teeming with all manner of demons, vampires, and assorted spawn from a variety of hell dimensions.

While the two vampires strolled into the pub, Buffy and Xander crouched down in the shadows next to a reeking pile of garbage. Her leg throbbed from all the walking, and resting it felt heavenly. "How are we going to get in there?" Xander whispered. "We can't just saunter in there and say, 'Gee, anyone seen an assassin?'"

"You're right," Buffy whispered. "They'll immediately sense we're humans." She looked down the alley. A lone vampire approached, staggeringly drunk, weaving in the narrow confines of the alley. "What we need is a distraction."

Xander tensed. "I'm not the distraction, right?"

"No. I won't use you." She pointed behind the teeming stack of garbage. "Quick! Get behind that!"

"Get behind it! I can barely stand the reek from here."

"Then you're volunteering to be the distraction?"

"I'll be behind the garbage." Xander crept over the wet cobblestones, crouching down behind the odoriferous pile of rotting lettuce, coffee grounds, rancid meat scraps, and stained rags reeking of turpentine and urine. "Oh, God." He stifled his gag reflex.

Buffy followed partway, pausing at the edge of the garbage pile, lying in wait for the approaching vamp.

He staggered closer, unaware of them, and just as he turned to step into the pub, she leaped up, grabbing the collar of his shirt. He grunted in surprise as she shoved him into the pub. She ducked back outside as he crashed into a table of horned demons playing cards.

"Hey, what do you think you're doing!" she heard one demon shout in a heavy Scottish accent. "You ruined my hand!"

At the first sound of punching, Buffy ducked her head in the door. The table had erupted into a fight, fists swinging and tails lashing. The next table, jarred by the violence, toppled over. Those patrons, three willowy vampires dressed in elegant clothes, stood up and grabbed the card-playing demons. A horn went through someone's arm, and a table shattered under the weight of a body slam. As a chair sailed overhead, Buffy studied all the faces in the bar. Plenty of vampires, but not the one she was searching for.

She ducked back outside as a bottle shattered against the door frame.

"No luck," she said to the garbage pile. "On to the next bar."

Xander rose, brushing himself off. He sniffed his jacket as he fell in line beside her. “Between this and our last Sunnydale landing, I’m going to smell like a compost heap for a week.”

“And that’s different how?” she teased him.

“Hey!”

They trawled more neighboring alleys, radiating out from the Place de la Révolution. They found two more vampire hangouts, then four, then six. Each time they used a variation of the same method to scan the crowd within, and each time they came up empty.

“You don’t think that guy has already succeeded, do you? Just did it singlehandedly?” Xander warned.

She regarded him gravely. “Let’s hope not.” A group of Sans-Culottes walked by, glaring at them.

“Man! We’re in long pants and they still hate us!” Xander cried.

“It’s seems like everyone hates everyone right now,” Buffy said, knowing it was more complicated than that. But her gut was sick of the hatred in the air, of the tension and the reek of burning buildings and rotted garbage building up in the streets. This was not how she’d envisioned Paris. She always thought she’d be sitting at some cosmopolitan sidewalk cafe, sipping cappuccino with a fiendishly handsome Parisian poet or painter, bags upon bags of designer clothes piled at her feet.

She made a mental note to return sometime when a Reign of Terror wasn’t on.

They worked their way down the next alley, and suddenly

Buffy resisted the urge to cry out in relief. There, in front of her, hurried the assassin vampire, his frizzy hair practically glowing in the light from a nearby window.

"There he is!" she whispered loudly to Xander.

He ducked inside a small door halfway down the alley. Loud laughter and the clicking of glasses emanated from within. "Let's go!"

She slunk to the edge of the door, then peered around it. Inside, a raucous bunch of vampires gathered, their feet up on tables. Women in low-cut dresses sat on men's laps sipping mugs full of red, viscous liquid. The assassin headed directly over to a particular table, as if he already knew someone there.

He stopped at the table, joining a man and a woman. The man had long, dark hair, tied in the back with a black ribbon. His back was to Buffy. The woman, also turned away, wore a very elaborate blue velvet gown trimmed with white lace. She laughed at something her companion said, her blond curls bouncing around her shoulders.

The assassin cleared his throat, and the male vampire turned to face him. Buffy sucked in a sharp breath as she saw his face. Ducking out of the door, she pressed flat to the alley wall.

"What is it?" Xander asked, seeing the alarm on her face.

Buffy tried to catch her breath. The assassin wasn't the only one who knew him. Buffy did too.

It was Angel.

CHAPTER FORTY-FOUR

"Angel!" Xander cried, and Buffy clapped a hand over his mouth. In a harsh whisper he said, "You mean Angelus, right? Like in Giles's Watcher journals? Wasn't this when he was the scourge of Europe? Didn't he personally wage his own Reign of Terror on everyone around him? Didn't he kill his own family?"

Buffy said nothing, only nodded. She needed to think.

After a moment, she dared another peek inside. The assassin now sat at the table with Angelus, talking adamantly with him and his companion. She turned slightly to say something to the hired killer, and Buffy recognized her, too. It was Darla, Angelus's sire. This merciless duo had slaughtered unknown masses of people throughout the centuries.

The assassin continued to talk, and Darla and Angelus nodded. Then he showed them something Buffy couldn't quite see. Angelus's body blocked the way. She strained for a look, but to no avail. Darla looked impressed, and the assassin put it away again.

Then he watched them expectantly. Darla and Angelus rose from the table, entering a room behind the bar. Buffy could no longer see them. She ducked out of the way again, wanting to avoid detection.

"What's going on?" Xander asked her.

"I think he's recruiting Darla and Angelus to help," she told him.

"So what do we do now?"

"We need to lure them out somehow, so we can stake them before they find the Slayer."

"Even Angel?"

Buffy didn't answer that question. It made her sick to think about it. She loved Angel. She thought of him back in the future, guarding Lucien for them. She'd make sure she left here without having to do anything like that. "Hold on a second."

She leaned back in and saw Darla and Angelus return. Between them they held a struggling girl, bound and gagged. She'd been bitten several times, and blood streamed down her neck, staining her once white dress deep scarlet.

The assassin's face lit up with excitement as soon as he saw the girl. He nodded to Darla and Angelus.

What was going on? The girl staggered, weak from loss of blood. The sheer excitement on the assassin's thin face could mean only one thing. This wasn't some snack Darla and Angelus were offering him.

This was the Slayer.

And Buffy was too late.

CHAPTER FORTY-FIVE

Buffy paused outside the pub, getting her thoughts straight. The assassin hadn't arrived at the pub for the first time just now, he'd already struck the bargain with Darla and Angelus sometime earlier.

That probably meant that he knew exactly where to find them from the moment he landed. Which meant it had been the plan all along to enlist two of the deadliest vamps in history.

They'd captured the Slayer for him, and in return . . . in return? How would the duo benefit from such a thing? Why not kill the Slayer themselves? Buffy had to get closer to hear what they were saying over the commotion of the pub. To their right was a small window, only feet away from their table. She signaled for Xander to follow her over there.

They crept silently to a very narrow side alley and waded through piles of putrid garbage. Their feet slid in raw sewage, and Buffy stifled her urge to gag as the stench blossomed up from her feet.

Behind her Xander did gag, and she turned to shush him. Tears streamed down his face. Removing his liberty cap, he pressed it over his nose and mouth.

She reached the small window. Wooden shutters covered it, but they hung slightly open, and the windowpane had long ago been shattered. She pressed her ear against the wooden shutter and listened.

"So where is she, then?" Angelus asked, his Irish brogue thick. Buffy had never heard it before, though she knew he was originally Irish.

"She can't be far away," said a male voice in a American accent, obviously the assassin.

"And you're sure she'll come to us?" Darla asked in her lilting voice.

"Definitely. She's probably been scouring the city for me. But she's sharp, and she'll find us here sooner or later."

"I'm growing bored with this," said Darla. "It was fun drinking the Slayer, but I have other things I'd like to do with my evening."

Buffy heard Angelus give a soft moan, and she struggled to peer through the tiny slits in the shutter. Darla's fingers combed through his hair, then scratched along his back playfully. "Much better things," she added, her voice growing husky.

Buffy felt a tightness in her stomach. She hated seeing this evil vamp flirting with her boyfriend. Even though he wasn't technically her boyfriend. At least, not for another two-hundred-plus years and one soul later. Still. It made her sick.

Darla cooed at him, and he grabbed her harshly behind the neck and brought his mouth to hers, kissing her hungrily and lustily. Buffy looked away. It was too much to bear.

"Who are they talking about?" Xander asked. "I can't quite hear."

"Me," Buffy said.

Darla giggled appreciatively, then said, "You had better produce this second Slayer soon. As I said, I'm starting to lose interest."

"But, Darla," Angelus protested, "think of the power! Drinking two Slayers in one night. It'll be the first time ever that two Slayers were killed at the same time! We'll be infamous!"

"We already are, my darling," she told him, throaty and sensual.

Buffy couldn't take this much longer. Even the garbage didn't make her this nauseous.

A sharp cry brought her attention back to the shutter. She peered through. Darla's teeth clamped down hard on Marguerite's neck, and the young girl swayed in her seat, slumping against the table.

How had she been caught? Buffy couldn't imagine the horror of being the prisoner of ruthless killers. They must have overpowered her, caught her unawares. And now she'd been bitten. But had she drunk their blood as well? Was she forever tainted? Destined to become the very thing she'd dedicated her life to stopping?

Buffy pulled away from the window and looked at Xander in the dark. "The Slayer's weak. I don't think she can last much longer in there. Looks like she's lost a lot of blood."

"What do you suggest?"

"What time is it?"

Xander pushed up his cotton sleeve, reading the Timex hidden beneath. "An hour and ten minutes before we meet the others."

"That's not enough time. They might kill her before that."

"Then what do you suggest? We could start back, look along the route they took—"

"No," Buffy said, holding up her hand. "I've got to face them now."

"But, Buffy! That's not three assassins drunk on soldier blood in there. It's Darla and Angelus! Not to mention the assassin and a whole boatload of drunken vampires just spoiling for a fight!"

"Then I'll have to lure them out here," she said.

"This is a bad idea, Buff. A very bad idea. You can't fight all three."

"I don't have a choice, Xander! That Slayer is about to die, and she's going to continue dying because they're waiting for me. I have to give them what they're waiting for."

She wished now she'd taken a crossbow.

"This is crazy, Buffy. Let's go find the others!" Xander pleaded.

She looked at him gravely, studying his face, the worry there. "Xander, friends are a bonus to a Slayer. We have to do this gig alone. I've been lucky so far to have you all by my side in a crunch, but in a moment like this, I have to stand on my own."

"I'm going in there with you," Xander said, fear making his voice shake.

"No, you're not."

"Then I'm going to find the others," he finished resolutely.

"Good. Do that." Buffy didn't want to worry about him while she was fighting. She had to preserve the Slayer line.

He began to leave, then turned back. "What are you going to do?"

"I don't know," she said honestly, meeting his eyes in the shadows.

"I'll be back soon," he told her, and took off at a run.

She turned back, peering in through the shutter again, and devised a plan for luring them out. Something low-key. Something that wouldn't attract the attention of the other vampires.

She skirted around the edges of the building, trying to find the best place to fight. At last, a block away, she found a wide alley hidden partially from view from the main street, yet open at both ends. It would allow for her to escape with Marguerite if she needed to.

Reaching into her satchel, she pulled out the small pad of paper and pencil that Giles had insisted they all carry. Finally it would see use.

On a sheet of paper, she wrote, "Outside. One block east. The alley. Bring the Slayer." She tore it off, folded it into a paper airplane, and walked around to the open door again. Taking careful aim, she let it fly. It landed expertly in front of Angelus.

Buffy took off for the alley, pulling a stake out of her satchel as she ran. Once there, she climbed a rickety wooden staircase running down the exterior of one building. Her leg felt stiff as she climbed. Even with her Slayer healing abilities, the wound was doing a number on her agility. With some effort, she ducked down out of view behind two large wooden crates. She wanted to gauge the situation first, make sure it was just the three vampires.

She sat and waited, heart thudding, wondering if Angelus was really the evil monstrosity the Watcher journals made him out to be. She breathed slowly to steady her pulse as she waited. Tonight she might have to stake her love in this lonely alley, or it might see her own death instead.

CHAPTER FORTY-SIX

Darla, Angelus, and the assassin filed into the alley, dragging the weakly struggling Slayer behind them. They'd blindfolded her. She stumbled, found her footing, and staggered along behind them. Her skin was as pale as porcelain. She'd lost a lot of blood and was close to losing consciousness. Red poured out of the open wound on her neck.

"Come out, come out, wherever you are," Darla sang.

Marguerite twisted suddenly in Angelus's grasp, trying to break loose. He grabbed her around the back of the neck, pulling her close. "And where do you think you're going? What would a trap be without its bait? You're here to bring us the other Slayer. Don't tell me you mean to disappoint."

She shrugged him off, then swayed and fell to the ground. She delivered a weak kick to his knee, but it was still enough to make him cry out sharply. Angrily he grabbed her hair, wrenching her up to her feet. He pressed his lips close to her ear. "You'd be wise not to do that again."

Buffy watched as the foursome walked farther into the alley. Then Darla turned to the frizzy-haired assassin. "So? Where is she?"

"She'll be here," he assured her.

It angered Buffy to hear him talking as if he knew her. What did he know? But he was right nonetheless. She wouldn't let them just kill Marguerite, even if they were using the girl as bait to catch her.

She knew it was a trap, but she had to descend anyway.

Waiting for her moment, she sized up the situation. She couldn't fight all three. Perhaps if one of the vamps weren't Angelus, she might pull it off. She'd seen Darla fight before, and she could be ruthless. And she had no idea how well the assassin could fight. He was probably blessed with the same martial arts capacity vamps mysteriously achieved upon rising from their graves. But the other assassins, except Victor, hadn't been that tough.

She'd have to grab the Slayer and run. But Marguerite was in no condition to sprint through the streets of Paris right now. Buffy suddenly wished she'd waited for the others. They could have ushered Marguerite to safety while Buffy held off the vampires.

She hadn't thought this through. She was tired, and her leg still ached from the rifle ball that had passed through it. It still wasn't up to par. She was tired—she'd barely slept lately, constantly worried about the next time jump. At least this was the last. Then she could get some decent sleep. And she wasn't even missing any school, because when they returned, it would still be Sunday. That was hardly fair. At least she should be able to get some good, quality no-school days out of all this.

"Show yourself, or we drain this Slayer," Darla shouted, grabbing Marguerite and pulling her close.

The most she could do would be to fight them while the Slayer ran away.

A group of drunken revelers walked by, shouting. The vampires spun suddenly at the noise.

This was her chance. She leaped down silently, landing on top of Darla. Marguerite sprawled to one side, hitting the alley wall. "Run, Marguerite!" Buffy shouted. The French Slayer rubbed her blindfold against the rough brick of the wall, and soon the dirty cloth fell down around her neck. Understanding Buffy's English, she ran.

Sitting on Darla's stomach, Buffy punched her in the face, then stood up and delivered two kicks to her stomach and kidneys. Standing on her hurt leg, Buffy wondered if the kick hurt her or Darla more. But Darla swore, rolling into a fetal position. Quickly Angelus narrowed in on Buffy. She ducked under a kick, then a series of blows. He'd been a vampire for only thirty-nine years but was still deadly, she discovered. She kicked him hard in the face, and as he staggered backward, she swept his feet out from under him. Arms windmilling, he crashed hard onto the cobbles. Buffy looked toward the Slayer. She hadn't made it out of the alley. The assassin blocked her way, dodging back and forth in front of her, leering and laughing.

Marguerite stumbled.

Buffy made a break for the other Slayer and fell flat on her face as a weight crashed into her back and shoulders. She smelled the familiar scent of Angel and was temporarily stunned by the vivid good memories it brought back. Then she elbowed him in the side, flipped on her back, and brought a heel down hard to his groin.

She felt the reassuring weight of the stake in her vest pocket but didn't reach for it. The only vamp she wanted to waste was the assassin. She couldn't mess with the time line, and Darla and Angelus lived far into the future. And she couldn't stake Angelus, anyway. He might be a beast now, but eventually he became her love.

With Angelus groaning and cursing her, Buffy leaped up, reaching the Slayer and the assassin. "Come on!" she shouted to Marguerite, grabbing her by the elbow.

Buffy heard footsteps thundering down the main street, then Willow shouting, "Buffy?"

The assassin turned toward the voices.

"Willow, down here! Get Marguerite to safety!" Buffy

yelled. She tackled the assassin from behind, and he fell hard. She straddled him, punching him harshly in the back of the head. She reached inside his jacket, patting him down for incantations. She found the telltale paper and stuck it in her own pocket. Then she produced the stake, raising it to thrust through the assassin's heart.

A hand grabbed her wrist harshly, yanking her up off the ground. For a second she was airborne, surprised at the brute force of the attack. She landed solidly on her feet, twisting her arm out of the grip.

Angelus stood before her, his head dripping blood from a gash above his eye. He blinked the red liquid away to clear his vision.

"Finish her, Angelus! That's my boy!" Darla shouted from down the alley.

Buffy looked at Angelus, at his dark eyes. When she met him, he never would have listened to Darla. He had staked his sire in the Bronze in 1997 to save Buffy. This time, however, there was no chance of enlisting Angel's help. This time he was the enemy.

CHAPTER FORTY-SEVEN

Buffy readied herself to fight Angelus. She tucked the stake back inside her vest pocket, not wanting to use it. At this action, Angelus raised a puzzled eyebrow.

The assassin jumped to his feet, grabbing Marguerite.

"Take your chance now, Franco!" shouted Darla, keeping safely out of the fray, Buffy noticed. No reason to mess up her pretty dress with all the frills. She had minions to do her bidding.

Angelus stood between Buffy and the Slayer now. Franco, as she now knew he was called, stood near Marguerite. So nice to finally learn his name just as she was about to dust him.

"Run to your left!" she told Marguerite. The French Slayer

must have definitely understood some English, because she took off in that direction, toward the mouth of the alley. Where was Willow? There was still no sign of the Scoobies.

Angelus stood his ground, keeping himself between Buffy and the French Slayer.

"Use your special firearm!" shouted Darla.

The assassin reached into his pocket. Buffy didn't like this. Special firearm?

Franco produced a semiautomatic nine-millimeter from his pocket. This was not good.

He raised the gun toward Marguerite.

"I get to kill the other one," Darla told Franco. "I don't like her."

Buffy charged in the direction of the assassin, and Angelus leaped, cutting her off. He knocked her violently to the ground, and she bucked him off, flipping him to the side.

She had only a fraction of a second and knew that. In the corner of her eye, Franco took aim at Marguerite.

A deafening shot cracked and echoed through the alley. A gray blur streaked into view, knocking Marguerite over. A scream pierced the roaring silence following the shot.

She recognized the voice. It was Giles. He'd been hit.

As Marguerite struggled to her feet again, fighting against her bindings, Xander ran forward with a knife, cutting through the ropes.

"Shoot them! Shoot them!" Darla yelled, running forward.

Buffy jumped to her feet, kicking Angelus in the side before he could rise. Her leg burned with pain.

Darla reached the assassin. She demanded the gun, but Franco held on to it, too caught up in the fight.

Angelus rolled to the side, away from Buffy's reach.

Buffy ran for Franco and the gun. Angelus dashed for Marguerite. They reached their targets at the same time. Angelus shoved Xander away just as Willow ran into the alley. With a wicked backhand, he knocked her sprawling. Giles, shot in the arm, rose unsteadily to his feet and tried to tackle Angelus. Spinning, the vampire grabbed Giles's injured arm, sticking his thumb directly into the wound and twisting. He forced Giles to his knees.

Buffy grabbed at Franco's gun, struggling with him for control. Darla kicked her hard in the kidneys, but Buffy held on, gritting her teeth through the pain. She didn't let go. The gun went off once, twice, discharging harmlessly into the drizzling sky.

Angelus grabbed the weakened French Slayer, spinning her around.

Buffy kicked Darla to the side, then shoved the assassin into Angelus. He staggered back, releasing Marguerite. She ran to Xander and Willow, bending to help them.

"Don't worry about us!" shouted Xander. "Run out of here!"

"I will not leave you," she answered in accented English.

Buffy used the momentum of tackling Angelus to send them

spiraling backward, where she, Franco, and Angelus crashed into the opposite alley wall. She sandwiched Angelus between herself and the assassin. Franco's gun arm was now pinned against the wall, and she could see the very end of the barrel sticking out, shielded almost completely by Angelus's body.

"Shoot! Shoot!" Darla shouted again, recovering and racing toward them.

The assassin angled the gun up toward Marguerite. His finger started to squeeze the trigger.

Buffy hit the gun barrel with her fist, but it moved only a fraction of a centimeter. Angelus's bulk was too heavy for it to move much.

Franco continued to squeeze the trigger. Buffy tried to shove Angelus to the side but, grinning, he wouldn't move. He used his body as a shield. Buffy couldn't reach Franco. Darla grabbed her harshly from behind, choking her. She had only a millisecond before the gun fired, killing the Slayer and possibly Xander and Willow, too.

There was only one thing to do.

Letting Darla continue to choke her, Buffy pulled out the stake. Everything slowed. Franco's finger was almost fully depressed on the trigger.

Buffy thrust the stake into Angelus's heart. He vaporized, leaving only ashes. The stake continued on in its forward thrust, passing through the falling ashes and piercing the heart of the assassin. Dust exploded outward, showering her, and the gun clattered harmlessly to the ground.

"No!" shouted Darla, emitting a piercing scream of rage and grief. Xander rushed forward, grabbed the gun, and pointed it at her.

"That won't kill me," she spat venomously, teeth bared in rage.

"No," said Marguerite, stepping forward. "But I will."

Sizing them up, Darla glared at them with simmering hostility. Then she turned and ran away. Marguerite started after her, her face gray and body trembling from blood loss. She looked on the verge of collapse.

"No," Buffy said, stopping her. "I'll explain this in a minute, but it's not her time to die."

Marguerite stopped, gasping for breath and staring angrily after the receding figure in blue. Then she turned to Buffy. "At least you got the other two," she said in her excellent English. "They grabbed me while I was sleeping in a shelter."

Yes, Buffy thought, *at least I got the other two.* She stared down at the dust, now drifting away in the evening breeze, mingling with the drizzling rain. *It wasn't Angel's time to go either.* She felt numb, unable to move, and sank to her knees. In an instant, Willow was beside her. "Buffy, what did you do?" she whispered.

Buffy looked pleadingly into her friend's eyes. "I didn't have a choice. . . ." She let the stake tumble out of her hands, clattering to the stones of the alley.

She stared at the dust that had been Angelus, her mind

searing with an intense disbelief. "Couldn't you have . . . ," Willow began, but didn't finish.

Buffy sniffed, her eyes welling with tears. "The Slayer would be dead if I'd hesitated even just another second." As she sank lower, Willow grabbed her arm, pulling her to her feet. Buffy wobbled on unsteady legs.

A cry of pain and some rather British cursing brought her back to the immediacy of the situation. Giles stood a few feet away, his arm streaming with blood. Willow tore off part of her jacket to stanch the flow while Xander steadied him.

Buffy rushed to his side. "We need to get you to a doctor." So much blood was leaking out that she couldn't see the wound properly.

"Yes," he said, "but I'd prefer one from the twenty-first century. Fewer leeches."

Willow laughed, then looked at Buffy's expression and stopped.

There was no joy left in Buffy's heart. A silence fell over all of them. Buffy turned back to the drifting dust in the alley, her chin trembling. Willow hugged her.

Marguerite turned to them, confused. "But wasn't it good? To destroy both vampires?" she asked.

After a long pause, when no one else could speak, Giles said quietly, "One of them was different." He placed a hand on Buffy's shoulder and said, "Well, let's at least get Marguerite to an eighteenth-century doctor. We can explain this to her on the way."

"And then let's go home," Xander said, still clutching the gun.

"Are you okay?" Willow asked Buffy gently, squeezing her hand.

Buffy could only shake her head.

With Marguerite leaning on Buffy, and Giles supported by Willow and Xander, they trudged out of the alley, heading for the house of Marguerite's doctor, who lived on Rue Vivienne, on the far side of the Palais Royal.

Fifteen minutes and one painfully jarring hired carriage ride later, they arrived.

They woke up the doctor, who immediately went to work on Marguerite, treating her for blood loss. He laid her in the guest bed. While he cleaned and bandaged Giles's wound, Buffy sat at Marguerite's bedside and explained who she was. Marguerite found it miraculous. Because her English was so good, it made the entire experience simple. In a half hour the doctor appeared at the bedroom door with a rather pale-looking Giles.

"The bullet passed through the meat of his arm," he explained in heavily accented English. "Keep it clean, and it should heal."

"Good to know," Giles said.

"Hey, we match," Buffy told him. "Both of us were shot on the right side."

"Oh, how grand," he responded in a monotone.

"Now we go back?" Xander asked.

"Will Marguerite be okay?" Buffy asked the doctor.

He nodded. "She has lost much blood, but she will recover in no time. I have been her doctor since she was born, and she has always had a remarkable healing rate."

"How about that," said Xander.

"I will be fine now, thanks to all of you."

Buffy exchanged a secret smile with Marguerite and squeezed her hand.

They left, walking out to a back alley behind the doctor's house. Buffy remembered the incantations she'd stolen from Franco and pulled them out. She unfolded them, hoping there wouldn't be more time periods. There weren't. Franco held only the spell for 1792.

"Well, that's a relief," Giles said.

Willow spoke up. "That may be the end of the enchantments, but what about the artifact itself? We still don't know where it is."

Giles grunted in thought. "My guess is that it lies somewhere in the room Buffy discovered. I don't think Lucien would have let it too far out of his reach."

"But, Giles, Angel and I searched that room. It wasn't in there."

"Then it must be hidden."

"Oooh, I sense a trip involving metal detectors!" Xander chimed in.

Buffy glanced over at him. "Knock yourself out."

"That's Giles's job," Xander countered.

Giles shook his head in misery. "Very funny, Xander."

"I thought so." Xander looked at the stone buildings rising around them. "Are we ready? I've seen enough back alleys of Paris to last me a lifetime."

Giles spoke the incantation, and Buffy's heart filled with mixed emotions. She was finally returning to her own time for good. They'd foiled Lucien's plot. But Angel would not be there.

The portal opened, whisking them through dazzling light, dumping them out in 1998 Sunnydale.

But it wasn't the same Sunnydale they'd left.

The portal spat them out into hell itself. The air reeked of guttering fires and rotting flesh. Burned-out cars littered the empty streets. It was night, and vampires roamed in droves, trolling the streets for victims. They closed in when they saw Buffy and the others.

In the sky swooped huge, winged creatures breathing fire. One dropped a half-eaten corpse, which landed with a dull thud next to Buffy. She rose shakily to her feet.

This chaos, this hell, could only mean one thing.

The Master had risen.

And he'd opened the Hellmouth.

CHAPTER FORTY-EIGHT

As the vampires closed in, more than Buffy could possibly count, more than a hundred, maybe more than two hundred, she turned to Giles.

"Speak the incantation!" she shouted to him.

He still lay on the ground, groggy from the portal travel. Slowly he lifted his head, taking in the approaching throngs of hungry vampires. "What?"

"Send us back! Send us back!"

"Oh, gods," he breathed when he saw the red sky, the fires, the creatures jeering and closing in on them.

"Speak it!" shouted Xander.

Willow crawled over to Giles and pulled the incantation out of his pocket.

"What went wrong?" Giles said, his voice small.

"Say it!" Willow told him. She pressed the incantation into his hand.

He lifted the paper and read the incantation. The portal winked into view, sucking them up into the air. Three vampires dove in after them.

They landed with a thud on a cobbled street, with the familiar cries of *"Vive la nation!"* ringing up around them. Buffy struggled to her feet, pulling out the stake. While the vampires stumbled around, unused to the nausea of portal travel, she staked them quickly, one after another.

Then she helped the others to their feet, looking around to get her bearings.

They'd landed on the other side of the Place de la Révolution. In the distance, she saw two other portals opening in the sky, and figures pouring out of them.

Giles gripped her shoulder, steadying himself, wincing against the pain. He saw the other portals too. "That's us," he said.

"What?"

"That's us arriving, the first time. One portal for us, one portal for the assassins."

"This makes my brain hurt," she said.

"What are you going to do?" Willow asked her.

"I know what went wrong. I killed Angelus."

"You changed the time line," Xander said.

"Yes. Angel was the one who discovered Lucien's plot. He was the one who held Lucien prisoner while we stopped the assassins. With him dying here in 1792, he wasn't present for any of those things. The Master rose."

"What are you planning?" Giles asked.

"I've got to save Angel's life." She turned in the direction of the now dissipating portals in the distance. "I have to tell myself not to stake him. You guys wait here, out of sight."

Xander grabbed her arm. "No."

She turned on him, impatient. "What, you're going to try to stop me? I know you're jealous, Xander, but this is the fate of the world we're talking about."

Xander looked stung. "It's not that," he said, hurt in his voice. "It's paradox."

"A pair of what?"

"You shouldn't meet yourself. The entire universe could implode. At least, that's what they always say on *Doctor Who*, even though he frequently met himself. Of course, that was in different incarnations, and—"

She raised an eyebrow. "Xander. Point."

"Right. Don't meet yourself. Avoid yourself. You have to think of another way." He turned to the others. "None of us can run into ourselves. The entire space-time continuum could collapse."

"Been reading Einstein?" Giles asked suspiciously.

"No. But I haven't watched *The Terminator* and *Back to the Future* for nothing."

"Of course." Giles rolled his eyes.

"Hey, don't take it lightly. You guys need to listen to me on this."

"Okay," Buffy said. "Then what?"

"What if you send Angelus a note warning him not to go to the alley?" Willow asked.

Buffy liked the idea.

"You already know what pub he's at," she continued. "It took us hours to find it. You could go now and beat yourself there. If he's not there yet, he will be shortly. You could leave a note for him at the pub."

"I don't like the risk that he might not get it," Buffy said.

"Then wait for him to get there. We'll all stay out of sight, somewhere safe, while you go."

Buffy looked at Giles, at the sweat beading on his brow. He was in no condition to travel. "Okay. You guys stay here and watch over Giles. I'll go straight to that pub and send Angelus a message."

"Glad you have your notebook?" Giles asked.

"Yes, teacher, I'm glad I brought my notebook to class for once."

Giles smiled in self-satisfaction. Then he winced in pain.

"Wait," Buffy realized. "Why don't I just wait at the pub and stake the assassin when he shows up? Then we'll never have that confrontation in the alley with Darla and Angelus."

"No, Buffy," Xander said adamantly. "Then our other selves will never find the assassin, and we'll keep looking and looking. Eventually we might give up, but that wouldn't be for days, and then we'd be altering events again. Imagine if we jumped in here and never found the assassin. Wouldn't you just assume he was lying in wait?"

"Yes," she agreed. "So then we tell ourselves not to chase the assassin, to just go home."

"Now we're back to meeting ourselves again," Xander pointed out.

"Oh. Right. I could give us all a note instead," she offered.

Xander shook his head. "There are too many variables. When dealing with time travel, the best thing to do is make things simple. We know that we already successfully stop the assassins and save Marguerite's life. Now we need to do the simplest thing to ensure that Angel lives." He brought a hand to his forehead and added, "I can't believe I just said that."

Buffy ignored the remark. "Back to the original plan, then."

"Yes."

"Okay, then. I'm off." Around the corner, the crowd roared with malicious glee, and Buffy knew they were executing that family. She fought the urge to help. She'd seen firsthand how bad things could be if the original time line were altered. "I'll be back," she told them, then ran, leaving them behind.

CHAPTER FORTY-NINE

In the alley outside the pub, Buffy snuck a peek through the shuttered window. Angelus sat at a table alone, sipping blood from a glass mug. Perfect. She tore a sheet from her notebook again and wrote:

Angelus. If you value your life, do not go with Darla to any fight in an alley tonight. Make up an excuse. This is serious.

Signed,

A friend

Once again, she folded it into a paper plane and let it sail through the front pub door. It jabbed him in the back, and he turned, scooping it up off the floor. He read it, then immediately spun and scanned the pub. She ducked back outside. He had to take it seriously. *Please take it seriously.*

She hid behind some wooden crates outside the door and waited.

In a few minutes he emerged, glancing up and down the alley. He read the note again. He took out a pocket watch, glanced at the time, and replaced it.

Buffy crouched, tense.

Two minutes later Darla arrived.

She kissed him. “How shall we entertain ourselves tonight, my love?”

He hesitated. “I’m feeling a bit sleepy,” he said in his Irish brogue. “Must have been someone I ate.”

She laughed. “You’re going to bed? This early?”

“If you don’t mind,” he told her.

“Of course I mind,” she said. “You’re supposed to entertain me.”

Ugh. What a brat. Buffy could barely stand listening to her.

“Well, perhaps I’ll bow out just for tonight. But if you want to come by later, I’ll probably be recovered. I can entertain you then.”

He grabbed her, kissing her deeply.

Buffy’s stomach knotted.

Darla moaned with pleasure, then looked up at him coyly. "Until then, my darling."

They parted. Angelus exited the alley, walking past Buffy's hiding place. Darla entered the pub.

Just as Buffy prepared to leave, the assassin showed up. He pulled out a piece of paper, checking the pub name against it. Then, nodding, he folded the paper and entered. So Lucien really *had* planned this from the beginning. He must be having a laugh right now, guarded by the very person who was instrumental in his plot to kill Marguerite.

"Darla, I presume?" she heard him ask.

"Who wants to know?" she murmured in a sultry voice.

Buffy stood up. She ran down to the mouth of the alley and peeked around the corner. Angelus walked some distance away. He passed a different pub, then stopped. It was one of the many Buffy had checked for the assassin. Angelus turned back around. He gave a quick glance toward the alley, then walked inside the bar.

Buffy breathed a sigh of relief. Good. She'd just changed events. If he held true to form, he'd be in this different pub, drinking, for most of the night. If Darla went looking for him at home to join her in Slayer-killing fun, he wouldn't be there.

She'd done it.

She hoped.

Buffy darted out of the alley and ran back to the others.

They waited where she'd left them, Giles now leaning over and groaning in pain.

"He needs to get to a doctor," Willow said. "He needs some painkillers or something."

Buffy studied her Watcher's gray face and furrowed brow. "Well, I think I did it. I think I was successful. We can go."

Shakily Giles stood, and once again produced the incantation to return them to 1998. He spoke it, unhaltingly this time, the spell practically memorized.

The portal emerged, spinning hypnotically. They dove inside, tunneling through space and time, somersaulting and spinning dizzyingly.

The velocity decreased, and Buffy braced for the launching sensation. She shot out, landing this time on soft grass. It was day, and she closed her eyes against the dazzling sun.

She rolled to a stop beneath a merry-go-round. Willow tumbled out, landing beneath a seesaw, and Xander and Giles were thrown into a patch of weeds near the sidewalk.

Buffy got to her hands and knees, peering out into a well-maintained city park. Sunnydale looked as it should. No burned-out cars. No swooping winged creatures. No stench of fire.

And Angel?

She helped the others up, then told Willow and Xander to get Giles to the hospital.

"Where are you going?" Willow asked.

"The library." She didn't need to explain more. Willow understood. Buffy had to see if Angel was alive.

"What if Sunnydale's all *Road Warrior* meets *Blade Runner*?" Xander asked her as she hurried away.

"Run," she called over her shoulder.

She covered the distance to the high school in a matter of minutes, leaping over fences and cutting through backyards. It was still the weekend, she guessed, seeing no cars in the parking lot.

She ran to the side door of the library, opened it, and ran inside.

Lucien paced in the cage. He looked up when she entered.

Angel sat in a shadowed corner, reading a book. His head lifted, and a broad smile spread over his face. "Buffy."

"Angel!" She ran to him, embracing him, kissing him. It had worked. She held him tightly, not letting go.

"Mmmm . . . you should travel back in time more often," he told her, hugging her back. She knew only hours had passed since he'd last seen her. But she had seen him killed and resurrected.

She held him, not letting go, and turned her head toward Lucien.

He'd stopped pacing and stood glaring out at her.

She thought of torturing him, forcing him to reveal the location of the artifact. But she would wait for Xander. Too bad.

Three hours later, with Giles resting at the hospital with Willow, Buffy and Xander returned to the small room. Xander powered up his metal detector, sweeping the floor and walls. Before long it beeped repeatedly, revealing the loose brick and the artifact within. He pulled it out, emitting a long, slow whistle when he took in the gem on top.

"Bring this to Giles," she told him. "He'll know what to do with it."

"Where are you going?"

"I have someone to dust."

"Have fun."

"I intend to."

They parted, and Buffy returned to the library, pushing through the double doors. Lucien looked up nervously as she entered.

"Your plan has failed," she told him. "And I'm afraid there's no reason to keep you alive any longer."

His glare melted away into fear. She walked to Angel and held out her hand to him. He reached into his pocket, produced the key to the cage, and placed it in her palm.

She strode to the cage and unlocked it. Lucien drew farther back inside, pressing against the file cabinets.

"Time for a suntan," she told him, grabbing his arm. He struggled, bringing his hand up to strike her. She blocked the blow, dragging him out. He cleared the door of the cage and she spun him around, using his own weight to wheel him outward. She let go and he stumbled with the momentum, grabbed a desk, and stopped himself, still in the shadows.

"Give my regards to oblivion," she told him, and, leaping up, kicked him in the chest. He shot backward into a blinding patch of sunlight. Instantly his body caught on fire.

Screaming, he flailed helplessly, then exploded into a plume of ashes.

She stood, catching her breath, steadying herself against a table. It was over.

Angel crossed to her in the shadows, pulling her into his arms.

That night at Giles's place, Xander and Willow sat with the wounded Watcher on the couch. Buffy sat next to Angel, balancing on one arm of his chair. He stroked her back.

Her leg gave a twinge, and Giles's arm hung in a sling. In front of him sat a cup of the hard stuff, Earl Grey.

"Next time, let's not get shot," she told him.

"Agreed."

"And next time," Willow said, "let's visit the Galapagos Islands before they've been discovered by humans, or take a nice, relaxing vacation on a virgin beach in Hawaii."

"A virgin beach that gets the Sci-Fi Channel," Xander put in.

"And has ancient ruins to explore," Giles added.

"At night," Angel put in. "You guys had all the fun this time."

"Fun," Xander said. "Last time I checked, fun was riding Space Mountain at Disneyland, not fighting for survival on an American battlefield, or almost getting sacrificed in blood rites."

"You were not almost sacrificed," Giles told him in exasperation.

"How do you know? They could have been working up to that just as we left."

"Yes, I'm sure they were, Xander," he retorted. "After being in your company for several hours."

"Well, I for one caught up on my reading," Angel said.

"Oh?" Giles asked. "Did you read Deserot's *Compendium of Bothersome Demons and Musical Instruments of the Third Century*? I left it for you."

Angel shook his head. "I couldn't get past the nose flute section. That whole bit on cleaning mucus out of—"

"Ew!" Buffy said. "Too much information."

"Yeah. That's what I thought," he said. "So I settled for *Tess of the D'Urbervilles*. You left it at my place."

"That book must be downright cheerful for you, Angel. Enough brooding in it?" she asked.

He gave her a wry smile. "Not quite. I'm reading *Les Misérables* next."

"Perfect," Willow said, grinning.

Buffy leaned back against Angel, who slid his arm around her. They'd done it. Here they all were, a little scratched, but alive. She'd not only met other Slayers, commiserated with them, and protected them, but she realized more than ever how valuable her friends were. Without them, she wouldn't be alive. As Angel stroked her arm affectionately, and she looked across at the others, she realized how much she had to be happy about.

And heck, this year she might even pass history.

About the Authors

John Vornholt has done many things in his life, from being a factory worker to being a stuntman, but writing has always been his first love. He's written for magazines, television, movies, the theater, and computer companies, and he really enjoys writing books and telling a story one reader at a time.

John lives with his wife, two kids, and two dogs in Arizona. Check out his website at www.sff.net/people/vornholt.

Arthur Byron Cover was born in the Dark Ages, a few years before the invention of rock and roll. He is currently old enough to remember a time before *Star Trek* and *Star Wars*, if there is such a thing. He repairs his wheelchair himself.

Today Cover can safely say he's written several novels, a few of which sprang entirely from his own forehead, a handful of comic books, a couple of animation shows, various book reviews, and many drafts of two movie scripts. He has taught writing classes and has been co-host for a radio talk show dealing with science fiction and its sister genres. He manages an SF bookstore in Sherman Oaks, California, and shoots the breeze a lot.

Alice Henderson has been writing since she was six. She holds a master's degree in folklore and mythology, and she has studied the beliefs, traditions, and mythologies of many different cultures, from ancient Sumerian to Celtic and Mayan. In addition to several *Star Wars* video game manuals and strategy guides, she also wrote *Night Terrors*, a Buffy the Vampire Slayer title in the Stake Your Destiny series.

An avid reader, Alice regularly devours books. Her pet rabbit, Captain Nemo, also avidly devours books, but in a different way. She lives in San Francisco, where she is at work on her next novel. Please visit her at www.alicehenderson.com.

THE VAMPIRES LIVE ON. . . .

BUFFY THE VAMPIRE SLAYER 2

HALLOWEEN RAIN
BY CHRISTOPHER GOLDEN AND NANCY HOLDER

BAD BARGAIN
BY DIANA G. GALLAGHER

AFTERIMAGE
BY PIERCE ASKEGREN

Turn the page for a sneak peek . . .

It was getting late. In the dim moonlight, the statues atop the gravestones in the Sunnydale Cemetery cast strange shadow-shapes across the dark mounds under which the town's dead lay. How long they might stay buried was in question, of course, since Sunnydale had another name. Early Spanish settlers called it Boca del Infierno. Buffy Summers didn't need to *habla* to translate: She lived in the Hellmouth.

Literally.

The cemetery provided the clearest indication of the town's true nature. Weeping stone angels became laughing devils. Hands clasped in prayer looked like ripping claws. Crosses hung upside down.

Way boring.

Buffy the Vampire Slayer stood just outside the cemetery and scanned the darkness among the gravestones for trouble. She sighed heavily as she leaned her elbows on the cemetery's granite wall. October 30 was almost over. She'd been out on patrol for hours, and she hadn't seen one vampire, one demon, one witch, one anything.

Well, okay, one witch. In gym. But Cordelia didn't count. She wasn't supernaturally evil. She only acted like a broom rider. Buffy understood. Poor Cordelia was cursed with popularity, great clothes, and, no lie, she was a babe. Naturally she had to take her frustrations out on everybody who didn't have it as good as she did.

Buffy supposed she should count her own blessings. She and Giles, her Watcher, had both expected the Halloween season to be the equivalent of finals for her Slayer diploma. All through October she'd trained hard, kept in shape, and sharpened up some very thick and sturdy pieces of wood. She was psyched for slaughter. She was pumped for pounding.

The little things a teenager gets excited about.

But now, standing outside the graveyard, the only monsters she was fighting were major Godzilla yawns. Buffy was so not thrilled. She hadn't seen any extreme vampire action for three weeks. Or much of anything else. Zip. Zilch. Nada. She'd been so bored she'd actually started to study. But that novelty was so over.

Still, no vamp sightings. Wasn't this cause for putting on a happy face?

Ever since she'd found out she was the Chosen One, all she'd wanted was to be a normal teenage girl. Maybe even a cheerleader. To have a honey of a boyfriend, hang out with her friends, and try to graduate from high school while doing as little actual studying as possible.

Instead, her extracurriculars centered around staking vampires, wasting monsters, and trying to keep her friends breathing long enough for them to graduate from high school. Much joy, what a treat. Smart, cute chick in desperate need of a life. But did she try to get a life? No, she wandered around looking for something undead to re-dead.

Pathetic much?

It isn't bad enough I have to pull the night shift, Buffy thought, *but how much more of a waste of time is it to be the Slayer when all the slayees are out of town or something?*

"Yo, dead guys," she called mournfully. Then she shrugged. What the hell. Her mom would tell her not to look a gift horse in the mouth. Good symbolism: Teeth were a big issue in Buffy's life. If you had long, sharp, pointy ones, she killed you.

Not tonight. She was a soldier without a war. All dressed up and no one to destroy. Time to call it a night, she figured. Maybe Willow would come over for some American history tutoring and they could scarf all the Halloween candy Buffy's mom had bought at the store. Or they could curl up with a good gory horror movie, the way Buffy and her mom used to do before Buffy had to burn down the gym at her old high school to kill a bunch of vampires, and they had to move to Sunnydale.

Out of the frying pan, into the mouth of hell.

From deep within the cemetery, a bloodcurdling scream pierced the night. Without hesitation, Buffy vaulted over the cemetery wall. She scanned left and right as she raced in the direction of the scream, dodging broken headstones, bushes, and tree roots. Just in case, she yanked open her shoulder bag and pulled out a stake. Boy Scouts and vampire slayers should always be prepared.

Another scream, this one louder and more frantic.

She ran faster, wondering what she would be going up against. One vampire? Two? A tribe of them? Or something she had never encountered before, a Halloween treat from hell? For half a second, she wished she had an elsewhere to be, but she brushed the thought away. She'd been looking for trouble. Now it had found her. She was the Chosen One, after all.

Another scream—shriek, more like. Now Buffy could tell it was a girl's voice. Screaming.

"Oh, God, stop!" it went on.

Afraid she might be too late, Buffy charged around the nearest headstone.

A blond-haired girl was struggling and kicking on the long, marble slab top of a tomb. A dark figure held both her wrists in his clutches, and he laughed and lowered his head, aiming for her neck. The girl shrieked even louder.

Buffy put one sneaker on top of a headstone and launched herself through the air. She tore the figure off the girl and they tumbled to the ground beside the tomb together. She threw him on his back, wrapped her hands around the stake, took aim, and—

"Stop!" the girl on the tomb screeched in abject terror. "Leave him alone!"

Buffy glanced up at the shadowed face of the girl's attacker. It was John Bartlett, who sat across from her in trig class. And his "victim" was Aphrodesia Kingsbury, his girlfriend.

"What's your *damage*, Buffy?" Aphrodesia yelled as John scrabbled away from Buffy. Aphrodesia threw her arms around him. "Insane much? Are you, like, asylum bound or what?"

Buffy moved away from John, put the stake in her bag as calmly as she could, and cleared her throat. "Sorry," she muttered. "I, ah, thought you were someone else."

She got to her feet. The two kids stared at her. She tried to smile, her face twisted into a grimace of acute humiliation. "Sorry," she said again. "Ah, happy Halloween."

She turned around and squared her shoulders, walking back the way she had come with as much dignity as she could muster.

"What a psycho," Aphrodesia said, and didn't even bother to whisper.

"Way psycho," John replied. "She's a hottie, though."

"Jo-ohn!" Aphrodesia whined.

Buffy could hear them bickering all the way to the cemetery wall. It was that disgustingly sweet bickering people did when they actually had a someone to bicker with. Buffy the Chosen One, the Slayer, the complete moron, went home to concentrate on eating all the frozen yogurt in the house.

After all, tomorrow was another day. And another night.

Halloween night, actually.

And there had to be something to keep a Slayer busy on Halloween.

wicked

Legacy and Spellbound

Holly Cathers is not the same person she was almost a year and a half ago. After discovering her connection to an ancient legacy of witches, Holly has accepted her destiny as a descendant of the House of Cahors. She is determined to end an intergenerational feud that has plagued her family for centuries.

Holly will have to overcome unworldly obstacles as she battles to protect her loved ones – including Jer, a member of the rival House of Deveraux and her one true love.

A war of magical proportions is being waged,
and Holly is at the centre of it all.

Lives will be lost, and sacrifices will
have to be made . . .